MESSAGE FOR AN OUTSIDER

The withered bushes and low shrubs that reduced Gale's garden into a no-man's-land were now uprooted and thrown in clotted mounds against the cottage wall. Black paint covered the mullioned windows that fronted the study. Gale's computer, which had been on her desk bounded by columns of books and years of research, lay smashed in the corner of the garden. The cracked lip of a dark green crock protruded from its broken screen.

Halford heard a step behind them and then a wretched whisper. "Oh no, oh no, oh no."

The front door was partially opened, its face pointing away from the midmorning sun. Nevertheless, the writing was easy to read. Either someone's a bit shaky with American history, Halford thought bitterly, or he has a grand sense of irony. Directly across the door's wooden middle, in thick red letters, were sprayed the words *Yankee Dixie Bitch*.

Watch for the next Gale Grayson mystery
Coming in November 1996 from Bantam Books

THE GRASS WIDOW

A FAR
AND
DEADLY
CRY

Teri Holbrook

BANTAM BOOKS
New York Toronto
London Sydney Auckland

For
Bill,
who midwifed it,
Chandler,
who inspired it,
 and
Haviland,
who was born during it.

A FAR AND DEADLY CRY

A Bantam Crime Line Book / August 1995

CRIME LINE *and the portrayal of a boxed "cl" are trademarks of Bantam Books, a division of Bantam Doubleday Dell Publishing Group, Inc.*

ISBN 0-553-56859-0

Published simultaneously in the United States and Canada

Bantam Books are published by Bantam Books, a division of Bantam Doubleday Dell Publishing Group, Inc. Its trademark, consisting of the words "Bantam Books" and the portrayal of a rooster, is Registered in U.S. Patent and Trademark Office and in other countries. Marca Registrada. Bantam Books, 1540 Broadway, New York, New York 10036.

PRINTED IN THE UNITED STATES OF AMERICA

OPM   11   10   9   8   7   6   5   4   3   2

ACKNOWLEDGMENTS

I've made no bones about it—Fetherbridge is a concocted town. So I beg the patience of everyone who loves Hampshire, England and ask they excuse my attempt to create in that gorgeous landscape a village where none exists.

Many people helped me in the writing of this book: guides, grave diggers, taxi drivers, policemen on their beats. But several went above and beyond the call of duty in providing this American with the information she requested. They gave of their time and knowledge without restraint. If mistakes were made in the transmission, the fault is mine.

Novelist Guy Bellamy, along with Jean Parritt and Keith Dolly, put aside their toils on the late, great *Surrey & Hants News* to discuss contemporary journalism and the workaday world of the newspaper reporter. Retired Inspector Peter Young of the Hampshire Constabulary answered all my nit-picky questions and helped me with plot issues. The Main General Synod of the Church of England aided in specifics of ceremony and clerical lifestyles, while the Right Reverend Frank Benning of St. James Anglican Church, Sandy Springs, Georgia, provided a historical and architectural perspective. Thanks to Chris Matthews for his cycling expertise, and Debbie Pulley for her medical information. And a very quiet thank you to the stained glass artisan who didn't want his name mentioned but who helped me to understand the technical as well as artistic aspects of his craft.

I am indebted to a special group of writers who are, without hyperbole, my life support system: Deborah

Carlen, Kathleen Crighton, Steve Davidson, Mary Ei-kert, Alan Lind, and D. Scott Schmid. Elaine McClean read a rough draft of the book armed with a knowledge of her native England and was always ready at the phone with answers to my questions. Joyce Holbrook was an enthusiastic supporter who introduced me to my English in-laws, specifically Flo Parrish, Joyce Porter and Tracy Flynn who, in turn, provided hospitality and background to a foreign traveler. I am forever grateful to my agent Nancy Love and my editors Casey Alenson and Kate Miciak for having faith. And it should go without saying, but I'll say it anyway—thank you to my husband Bill for being an artist and agreeing it ain't so bad living amidst the clutter of a writer.

Prologue

In her twenty-six years Gale Grayson had never seen a man buried. The lives of men had always been in the background of her life—her grandmother and aunts would sit at the kitchen table around a pitcher of iced tea and talk about them as they talked about cats and God, shooing one here, cursing one there. But when it came to dying, men simply weren't in the picture. Most of them had either run off, passed on before Gale was born, or over time grown so insubstantial that neither death nor women felt inclined to claim them.

This all dawned on her now as she sat on her cabbage rose love seat and frowned down at the swollen ankles blooming from her tennis shoes. Funerals, she realised, were female, lusty as menstrual blood and filled with the throaty laughs of loose-bellied southern women. As a child in Atlanta, Gale had wondered if men died like the spiders in the backyard shed, crooked legs curled up to clutch hollow chests. On the other hand she knew women died gloriously, ascending into heaven on rivers of light, heralded by a chorus of hungry soprano voices.

She splayed her feet out in front of her. Despite her obstetrician's reassurances, she wasn't convinced that at five months her ankles should be so swollen. She glanced at the ankles of the other woman in the room, the one with the stubby fingers who had tried to place a cup of tea in her lap. The cup had quivered on the saucer for a few seconds before the woman took it away. *She* had really lovely ankles, bony and shaded. Strange for someone with such short fingers.

The truth of the matter was Gale had always enjoyed funerals. She had never come right out and said it, but then neither had any of the other women in her family and she knew they felt the same. A good funeral was the extreme of a family reunion, and since reunions were superfluous among her confined southern clan, death allowed for a catharsis that no picnic in the Georgia mountains could induce. A tiny splinter pierced her chest. She squinted hard at her ankles and the splinter flew away.

"There'll have to be a funeral," she blurted.

A hand gripped her shoulder from behind; breath that smelled like a cough warmed her ear.

"Well, yes, of course, dear, there will have to be a funeral, but don't you worry about it, not now."

If not now, when? If not me, who? It seemed a silly thing to say, and Gale whisked the breath away from her ear as if it were a fly.

She couldn't say how long these people had been here. A woman, she assumed the one with the short fingers, had called early in the morning to say they had some questions, just routine, they would stop by around two. But they had been late, and she was sitting in the dusky light of her study when the woman and the man came to her door apologising—the situation had changed, this wasn't routine.

Soon after that, trailing in like wraiths, came a stream of men, dark and broad and surprisingly graceful. They came in the front door and immediately filtered into the back rooms and up the stairs, leaving her on the love seat. A man sat down on a footstool directly in front of her, the woman in a chair at her right. Should I call someone? the woman had asked, but Gale said no, she was all right, she was fine, there was nothing anyone could do. But the woman had gone to the phone anyway, and in a few minutes Orrin was there standing behind her and his breath made her feel ill and he was saying such silly things.

She glanced at the hands of the man seated in front of her. Unlike the woman, he had long fingers, thick and square-nailed, and they dangled between his knees as he leaned forward. He tried to look into her face but her ankles seemed to balloon in front of her eyes like a born-again morning glory. She wondered if they might keep swelling until they lifted her right off the love seat and carried her, head down and dress bunched under her armpits, out the front door and down the street, past the church, shops, fields, woods, and eventually out to sea.

The image of her bulging body floating over the church brought back the splinter. This afternoon Tom had gone into the church. He had waited until several policemen filled the pews, and then put a gun into his mouth. The man had told her this quietly, one arm under hers, as he guided her down to the love seat she had just told him she didn't need. The man, of course, had known better; he had probably done this dozens of times, come to the doors of pregnant women with news they would not understand and listened to them patiently while they insisted they did not need to sit down.

"Mrs. Grayson, did your husband tell you where he was going today?"

His voice was almost a whisper, as if he too were one of the wraiths moving along the walls. He had shown her his ID and search warrant, placing both beside her on the cushion of the love seat. She picked them up now and ran her finger around the small black leather folder holding the card.

"He was going to the Winchester Library."

Upstairs, something metal clattered to the floor, ringing round and round like a collection plate dropped in a sanctuary.

"They're in my bedroom," she said, referring to the wraiths.

The man took the folded paper from her lap and smoothed it open for her. His voice was helpful, lulling.

"Would you like me to read it to you?"

She didn't. She didn't want to comprehend.

"Mrs. Grayson, did your husband ever mention a Marist Buckner?"

Gale's eyes flickered to the man's face. "He was murdered last week. I saw it in the paper."

"Did you know him?"

"No."

"Had your husband ever mentioned that name to you?"

"No."

"Did your husband ever mention anything about a Queen's Counsel?"

In her belly, the baby darted across in a rolling gurgle. The books said that before too long she would see the baby kick, that it would be able to knock things off her stomach, but so far she was not sure if what she felt was the baby or gas. Last week she had spent an hour crying because she was convinced the baby had no arms or legs, it was just this sad, headed torso tumbling around inside her.

"No."

Her hands were trembling now.

"Constable Ramsden," the man said, "I think we might want to try some tea again."

The woman got up silently on her delicate ankles and headed towards the kitchen. Gale felt Orrin's fingers tighten on her shoulder.

"Surely this can wait," he said. "I mean, good God, you don't really think she knows anything about all this."

The man took his eyes off Gale's face. "I don't know what she knows and I'm sure you don't either, Mr. Ivory. But, yes, a lot of this can wait. I'll be finished directly."

Orrin's fingers drifted away and then immediately returned. Orrin didn't like to be rebuked. That's what Tom said—Ivory was a man horny for propriety.

Constable Ramsden handed the man the tea and returned to her seat. Gently, the man took Gale's hands and settled them around the warm cup, keeping his own tight around them to still their trembling. He led the cup to her mouth. The tea was hot and strong and sweet, the way her grandmother and aunts never made it back home. She took several quick, slurping sips. The baby tumbled in protest.

Two wraiths inched downstairs carrying boxes, their backs to the quartet in the living room.

"Worse luck." The wraith on the stair didn't lower his voice. "To finally twig him for the QC's murder and then give him just enough hints so he kills himself. I think we've done better work."

As Orrin turned on them, his hand wrenched the neck of Gale's dress so violently that it jerked and caught her in the throat.

"Would you shut up!" he snarled. "This is not the place for a goddamn job review!"

The man's hands tightened slightly around Gale's. His voice was quiet but now a sudden tenseness ran through it.

"Your friend is right, Mrs. Grayson. This can wait until tomorrow."

He took the teacup from her but continued to hold her right hand. She looked up at him.

"Church spiders," she said. "We used to sweep them up without a thought."

1

Fetherbridge was not a Darwinian town, evolving higgledy-piggledy across the chalky Hampshire downs as its inhabitants brutally vied for Mother Nature's better spots. Rather, Fetherbridge was concocted, plopped down due east of Winchester in 1762 by Lord James Bannick whose passion for balance compelled him to create his own perfect village: the proper kind of people doing the proper kind of thing behind the proper kind of window.

The village was constructed on a simple grid emanating eastward from the Bannick estate of Tullsgate. The half-mile long High Street contained one of everything necessary for a comfortable and restrained life: one blacksmith, one baker, one publican, one priest. For a century Lord Bannick and his progeny kept the little community gently bound in its rectangular girdle, but by the mid-1800's, capillaries of growth began to curl from the original village. Offspring set up their own homes; newcomers, amused by the prescribed charm, built houses on the periphery. The tendrils coiled out, sly aesthetic infractions. By the late twentieth century an aerial view of Fetherbridge looked like a barrette snatched in haste from a head of tangled hair.

Lisa Stillwell and her family lived in the most recent repudiation of Lord Bannick's dream, a span of modest, semidetached dwellings inexplicably called Heatherwood Beach built on the far end of what had once been the manorial park. For generations Stillwells had lived in one of the first original cottages constructed, a clay-and-flint affair manoeuvred prettily on a patch of land directly behind the family's High Street bakery. By the time Lisa's father came into possession of the property, however, the merry old cottage creaked under a dank and bird-spackled roof, and the clay had become a romantic notion hidden between the rows of newer bricks forced into the frame to keep the structure from crumbling.

Lisa had grown up in that derelict cottage, living there with her parents and brother for fourteen irritating years until the day her mother came home from the bakery and found part of the ceiling on her bed—along with the skeletal remains of several birds, rats, and an indecipherable tree-climbing mammal. The Stillwells contacted an estate agent and within two months the cottage was sold to a pair of fresh-faced London accountants with a yen for weekend tranquility.

Lisa's bicycle skidded on the pebbles in front of the old cottage drive as she braked to a stop. Balancing the bicycle between her legs, she smoothed her black wool gloves along the fingers one by one and studied the cottage objectively. Christmas was little more than two weeks away, but the Londoners had made nothing of it. No wreath hung on the door, no tinseled tree abutted against the sitting room window. In fact, in the eight years they had owned the place, the Londoners had fairly well ignored it. Such a pity, Lisa thought, adjusting her black cloak and mounting her bicycle. Under her care the cottage would be flourishing now. Needlepoint pillows, Staffordshire figurines, yards of heavy damask drapes and upholstery—magazines would send out photography crews and her fellow villagers would murmur with pride about the dramatic domestication of their dear, young Lisa Stillwell.

She pumped her bicycle up Bakers Lane toward the High Street, passing three more cottages, these with red-ribboned wreaths hung and coloured lights flickering through the windows. She smiled. It didn't matter if the village was manufactured and irregularly maintained. To her, Fetherbridge *was* England—the pantiled roofs, the flint facades, the whole bloody primrose-and-privet romance of the place. In the cold morning mist, time blurred, and she could imagine that she was Jane Austen's Emma Woodhouse out for her "tolerably regular exercise." This was, after all, Austen country, and Lisa would have been unduly modest to say that the line of genteel middle-class femininity had found anything less than a suitable descendent in her.

Lisa bumped her bicycle onto the walk that stretched along the High Street and dismounted. From here she could take in the entire length of the street. The names above the shops were the village's own Domesday Book, the current proprietors more often than not, like her own family, descendants of Lord Bannick's chosen few. Her mother once told her that she didn't need a book to learn the history of Fetherbridge, just a shopping list. It was the truest bit of wisdom her mother ever gave her.

The gold-on-black lettering of the sign over her father's bakery perspired with morning dew: *Stillwell's*, then in smaller letters underneath, *est. 1768*. Through the multipaned window Lisa saw her father and the broad back of Editha Forrester as the village matron bent over a table laden with the day's first loaves. Glancing up, Edgar Stillwell saw his daughter and waved. He was still wearing his baking apron, and he wiped his hands across it before pointing towards the rear of the shop. Lisa nodded in understanding. As soon as the baking was done around noon, she needed to drive her nineteen-year-old brother Brian into Winchester to shop for shoes.

She glanced at her watch. It was just gone nine. She had much to do before her sisterly obligation. A tingle of anticipation ran through her.

Slowly, she began pushing the bicycle down the street. The air, the light, and the dulling greys of the buildings made the street into a grisaille of canted roofs and fluid glass. Suddenly, predictably, she was filled with a horrid love for the village. She stopped walking and stood motionless, allowing the air to settle around her.

It didn't happen every time she walked down the High Street, but there were days when she loved the village to the point of despair, when she literally wanted to shovel up the stones along the shop fronts and bury herself in the foundation. It wasn't a poetic impulse—it was hard and real and she found herself torn between needing to flee Fetherbridge entirely and yearning for the joy of dying slowly in its soil. She often wondered if it was herself or the village that insisted on the unnatural bond.

Gripping the handlebars, she started to jog down the street. The aging doors and windows made a diminishing line behind her, and she ran faster, envisioning them collapsing one by one as she passed. The broken pavement occasionally made her stumble; nevertheless, she resolved to go the distance, hoping that when she reached her destination, her eyes would be shining and her voice breathless.

Christian Timbrook was dressed all in grey—hat, coat, trousers, boots—and as he slowly lowered his backside to perch atop a gravestone, he hoped that he'd be taken for a stone seraph, his black hair the trailings of lichen, his ruddy face a reaction to the dead's bawdy mutterings.

Across the cemetery a black-wrapped figure trotted its bicycle past the corner of the church and twisted its head to look around the grounds. Timbrook held his breath. It wasn't that he didn't want to talk to Lisa Stillwell; in fact, he didn't see how he could avoid it, considering he would be joining her and the other members of the planning committee inside the church shortly. The difficulty was he didn't want to see Lisa alone, and as she propped her bicycle against the south wall of St. Martin's Church, Timbrook sat very still.

Timbrook waited until Lisa disappeared through the south door's grand arched overhang before releasing his breath. It was a bit past eleven, for him the worst possible hour for a meeting. The morning light, already frail in December, would be dull soon. It was one thing to be dragged from work for an afternoon of ale and lust, another entirely to waste a morning listening to the babble of do-gooders with the wind up their arses. He had said as much to Jeremy Cart, but the reverend sonorously assured him that it being scarcely two weeks until Christmas, midmorning Friday was the most convenient time for all the *churchgoers* involved.

Timbrook had taken the slight as a compliment. It was enough that he had been born to, reared by, and suffered among the pious; he didn't intend to be mistaken for one as well.

Across the cemetery a bird screamed and wheeled toward Timbrook's perch. Shrugging, Timbrook stood. The cold was beginning to strain his taste for defiance, and besides, as near as he could tell, the only one not yet present was the gracious padre himself.

The smell of paint hit him as soon as he opened the door to the south transept, testimony to a yuletide refurbishment frenzy in the church's meeting rooms. A

chatter of voices—loud, echoing, female—broke from
the building and skittered through the cemetery. Ah,
Timbrook thought, the blithering ninny club. He wondered if Mary Magdalene and her crew had prattled
aimlessly at Jesus and if the Son ever questioned
whether or not having oily toes was worth it.

The jabbering stopped abruptly when he entered
the church nave. Four women, still cloaked and in
shooting gallery formation, took up the whole of the
left front pew. For a moment Timbrook stood awkwardly under the transept arch, trying to judge if their
stares were a natural reaction to his entrance or if he
had invaded the private machinations of a female cult
gathering. Surely it was the latter, and out of deference,
he tipped his hat.

Helen Pane moved first, rising halfway from her
seat. "Oh, God, Timbrook, you're here, finally." Her
voice, usually throaty, rang through the room at an unpleasant pitch. "I was beginning to get worried—afraid
you had overslept or something."

Timbrook moved further into the nave until he
stood a few feet from the women's pew. He looked
down into Helen's face and resisted the urge to brush
away the powder that clung to the fine hairs of her
cheeks. Pretty, he thought—auburn hair, green eyes,
and all that. Pity about her attention to detail.

He slipped off his coat. "I thought my presence was
more ceremonial than functional. I can't imagine what
on earth you need me for. I figured I was simply the
affable figurehead here to suffer your displays of cour-
tesy."

"Oh, you." Helen crossed her legs and settled into
the pew. "You know this congregation has been saving
to replace the stained glass window for over three
years, so a little grace from the artist would be appre-
ciated. We can't very well unveil a work of art without
having its creator here to help us celebrate."

Timbrook smiled down at her. He tossed his coat
across the altar rail. "You, Miss Pane, know nothing of

art. Or artists. Besides, I didn't create the window, I
merely repaired it, although, please, don't let my mod-
esty cause you to underestimate the skill that required.
But, all right. I'm here. I'll be here for thirty minutes.
During that time, ladies, I'm all yours." Without looking behind him, he counted five paces and sat down
on the tiled step that separated the chancel from the
rest of the chamber.

One of the women changed positions and a flurry
of apologies flittered down the line. The lovely Ivory
women, mother and daughter, filled the room with
their coos as they sought to outdo each other in whispered niceties. Timbrook rested his head against one of
the rail banisters. He knew some men in Fetherbridge
who would drop their teeth and a damn sight more to
have a chance with either of that cool duet. He watched
the two blonde heads, hair perfectly parted and
bunned, touch as they bent to speak softly to each
other. It was difficult to think of them as separate be-
ings; Anise Ivory and her daughter Jill were like a per-
fumed figure eight, melding in and out of each other
so efficiently that Timbrook couldn't tell where, or if,
each one had a beginning and end. He closed his eyes.
Bloody phony, that's what they were. The laughter he
had heard when he'd entered had been raucous, even
common. Decorum clearly wasn't so important when
there were only hens in the Master's coop.

He squinted and made a wavy rectangle of the four
women. "So," he said, "are we waiting for our comely
Shepherd Cart out of politeness or concern?"

The women didn't answer. Their legs, now all
neatly crossed, pointed north at the knees, and their
elbows butted against each other like links in a fence.
Dear God, what a bloodless crew, Christian Timbrook
thought. His eyes trailed down the line of heads until
they rested on the one he had been avoiding. He cor-
rected himself. Bloodless wasn't the word for Lisa Stillwell. Whatever else she was, she wasn't that, not by a
long shot.

Several minutes ticked past. The door on the north side of the church slammed shut, and expectantly, the women twisted sideways. The figure who emerged from the north transept was no clergyman, although Timbrook didn't doubt the man considered himself something a bit higher on the human scale. Orrin Ivory, the editor of the local newspaper, was usually a study in grace under pressure. Now, however, Ivory fumbled through genuflection and shifted stupidly from one foot to another, staring at the women who, noticeably disappointed, stared back.

Christ, Timbrook thought. For a guardian of democracy and all that crap, the man could be inept. Timbrook reached over to the altar rail, pulled his woolen hat from his coat pocket, and began tossing it hand to hand. "Excuse our fair lasses, Orrin. They don't always examine us men like we were poor pickings for a blue ribbon. They're just pining away with anticipation of doing the Lord's work."

Ivory cleared his throat. "Well, they'll have to wait a bit longer." He sat behind his wife and daughter, stretching his arms against the length of their pew in an embrace which did not touch them. "I found Cart over at the vicarage still getting dressed. Or dressed again, I should say. He was out walking when he remembered the meeting. Says he can't think what made him forget. He apologised all over the place."

Timbrook yawned and looked at his watch. "Twenty minutes to go."

"Look, Timbrook, you're not the only one who's made concessions to be here." Helen Pane fingered the pricey antique broach at her neck, which matched a gold bracelet she had queerly pinned to her blouse. "I turned my shop over to Beryl Lampson, which was rather trusting of me, and I'm sure Orrin had to leave his earnest little reporters running around untended. But this is important. So please, be polite."

Timbrook wrung his hat between his hands. "Look, perhaps someone could just give me an idea of what will be expected of me at this celebration. Or happening, or occurrence, or whatever you call it."

"The unveiling. We're simply calling it the unveiling, Christian."

Anise Ivory's voice, like her skin, was lemony and, in Timbrook's opinion, too lightly burnished for a woman over forty. Not enough notches on her, that was her problem. No place for a man to hang his soul and grief. As he watched, Anise let her left hand drift to her shoulder. Orrin Ivory lifted his arm wide to avoid mussing his daughter's hair and slid his fingers over the silky glide of his wife's blouse until they rested against her throat. She grasped his hand and tilted her head at Timbrook. "I don't suppose that's too pompous sounding for you, is it?"

Timbrook laughed. "Sounds inviting, Anise. But what are you going to want from me?"

"I think a short dedication speech would be nice, don't you?" Ivory retrieved his hand from his wife's clasp and settled back against the pew. "You know, perhaps something along the lines of the window's imagery and theology. You're quite knowledgeable about ecclesiastical art."

"It's in the middle of a service, Orrin." Helen Pane focused her green eyes on Timbrook. "Hardly a time for an artistic lecture on perspective and skin tones. I think something nice and sweet would be better. Perhaps on stewardship. Or hope. Hope would be good."

"Hope." Timbrook kept his voice level. "Strange topic, given the circumstances, don't you think, Helen?"

Cold fingers of light splayed down Timbrook's back, and he shuddered. From the clerestory windows above him a peal of blue colour, muffled to grey by the clouds, washed over the building's stones and made dusty effigies of the figures in the pews. The transforming qualities of light amazed Timbrook, as always. Lisa rucked the sleeve of her white blouse to her upper arm so that the cuff caught at her elbow and terraced the stiff cotton fabric to her shoulder. Her arm moved under the light, rolling once with the twist of her muscles. Her skin looked like clay. Timbrook could feel in his fingers the coolness, the give her flesh would have if he were to smooth it, sculpt it, beneath his palm.

A sudden flick from Lisa's hand made Timbrook glance at her face. Reddening, he realised she had caught him watching her. The deep azure eyes twinkled, the brow arched in a sardonic pose that mimicked his own well-practiced mien. She kept her eyes trained on him until, her tongue pushing teasingly on her inner cheek, she broke her gaze and looked away.

The south door opened so abruptly that Jeremy Cart was in the church and smiling down at the women before they could completely ruffle and smooth.

"Sorry I'm so late." The vicar shook his head. "Don't know where my brain is these days. All the holiday goings-on, I suppose." He spun around to look at Timbrook. "Don't suppose you'd want to put this off until after the New Year, would you, Christian?"

Helen huffed and flipped the heel of her shoe off one foot. "No, Jeremy, that just won't do. It's all about rejuvenation and rebirth. The Sunday before Christmas is perfect. It must be then."

"I don't know, Helen," said Ivory slowly. "Perhaps Jeremy has a point. New Year's does seem a bit more in keeping with your rejuvenation theme. You know, let's close the door on this tragedy, let the town bury it and go forward. It could be a tidy ritual of passage."

The east wall of the church was a mass of uninspired blocks, thick and unremarkable except for a large disk of amber glass that stoppled the wall's only opening like a giant yellow plug. Hammered in by frightened villagers trying to keep out the night, Timbrook thought. Such an affront to the beauty that had been there before, but, of course, a damn sight better than the horror that had immediately preceded it. Even with his back to it, he could feel the yellow glass—a wreath of cold circled his shoulders.

"What do you think, Timbrook?" Cart asked.

Timbrook shrugged. "It doesn't matter to me. My work is almost finished, except for installation. It'll take a week to arrange it, a day to install. It can be next week, it can be next year. You're the boss man."

"If we did it for Christmas, we could have some sort of program." Jill Ivory turned eagerly to Lisa. "With the children and youth singing. You think it'd be fun, don't you, Lisa?"

Lisa ran both hands through her hair, giving it a little toss. "It's Jeremy's church. It should be entirely his decision. But I think you're all being a bit ghoulish. I mean, has anyone considered how Gale is going to feel about all this?" She trained her eyes on Timbrook. "Well?"

"Don't be ridiculous, Lisa," Helen said firmly. "Gale's spent three years dealing with her grief. All's right in the name of the Lord—or something like that. And by the way, wherever did you get the idea that the church belongs to the vicar? Jeremy, please set the child right."

Cart launched into a soft, self-effacing stammer which Timbrook barely registered. Instead, he focused on the chill yellow beam bearing into his back. It was strange how, when he first came to this village more than a year ago, the people, the history, even this grotty little church had seemed beguiling. Now . . . Timbrook sighed and leaned forward.

"All right," he said. "You good people let me know. I've got to leave." He rose, drew his hat down close to his eyes, and faced the yellow window. The morning light was anemic, its molecules deadened as they smacked against the glass. The plug was getting to him. It had taken a while, but it had happened. He couldn't bear to be in the church a moment longer.

Cart leaned over and retrieved Timbrook's coat. "I'd like to come over sometime either today or tomorrow, Christian, and have a look at the window. I haven't seen what you've done in several weeks."

Timbrook took his coat and grinned. "Don't fret, padre. It's almost back to its original glory. Of course, being an artist, I took a little license. I left in the bullet hole. I liked the way one of the cracks went directly up into the Virgin's breast. Poetic, don't you think?"

Aside from Helen's gasp, the entire building was silent.

Cart spoke evenly. "That was uncalled for, Christian. Tom Grayson's suicide is a sensitive subject around here. If you didn't realise that, I must apologise for not keeping you properly informed."

Timbrook smiled and pulled on his coat. "I'm an artist, Jeremy, not a bloody diplomat. Don't mind me— your window is finished, you can have it in place when you want." He headed for the door. "It takes up a lot of room in my studio. I'm glad to be done with it."

Behind him, Orrin Ivory spoke softly. "We'll all be glad to be done with it, Christian."

Like bloody hell, Timbrook thought as he left the church. Some tragedies are just deep enough to allow people a good wallow.

2

Kathleen Prudence was a bag. She had discovered the value of being a bag yesterday when she pulled the spinning wheel off its spike and sat down hard while it banged her head. The wheel wasn't supposed to hurt her; it was supposed to wobble across the floor like a hoop and crash into the wall. For some reason, that had been lost on her mother, who came sputtering, arms waving, to wrap Kathleen Prudence around her body and sway back and forth. Before her mother could switch from concern to anger, however, Kathleen Prudence had wriggled away and run into the kitchen where, by the time her mother caught up with her, she was a bag, clutching her feet and trying to keep the heavy brown paper that enclosed her from crackling.

Her mother laughed softly. "Katie Pru," she said, "you're a poot."

That made her mad. "I'm not a poot. We don't say 'poot.' You better remember that."

She expected her mother to lift the bag and give her one of those "I mean it" looks that frequently ended with the time-out chair. Instead, she heard her mother's shoes pad across the floor, followed by the whisper of paper being pulled from the cupboard.

"I think," her mother said, "that I'm going to make an ornament for the Christmas tree. With glue. And glitter. And maybe macaroni."

So her mother had won, but that was yesterday. Today Katie Pru had decided she was not coming out from underneath the bag until her mother said she could take all the books from the bookcases and build a castle. And then she was going to climb inside and let Space Lucy, her dinosaur, ram it to bits. It was what she and Space Lucy wanted to do. They were going to do it.

Gale Grayson stepped over her daughter, or what she assumed was her daughter balled up under a sack and waddling around the kitchen floor like a pouting penguin.

"Fine, Kathleen Prudence," she said. "Be a bag." She squatted on the floor and studied the rustling paper solemnly. "I'm not sure what bags do all day—most of the ones I know just fold up. But that might be fun. You let me know."

She rested her knee gently on the exposed tip of a child's pink-and-white bedroom slipper. The bag said something muffled but didn't pull away. Reaching under the paper's serrated edge, Gale walked her fingers over the little slipper and tickled an ankle.

"I don't imagine bags eat breakfast, do they?" she asked. "They don't, for instance, like really big bowls of grits."

The bag tottered a few times. Then, as knees and

arms crossed themselves, the paper bulged and Katie
Pru's bottom plopped defiantly on the cold flagstone
floor.

It didn't surprise Gale, really. The morning had
started out this way when she crept into her daughter's
room before dawn to adjust the blankets. Katie Pru had
been sleeping on her side, a small, hunched form smell-
ing slightly of popcorn. As she did every morning, Gale
slipped her hand into the warm spot between the
child's side and the mattress. She let it rest there under
the pretense of tucking in the covers but actually enjoying the hard little curve of muscles and the rhythmic
pressure of her daughter's breathing. Bending her head
for a light hug, she realised she had been duped. The
small back beneath the covers arched inward and the
child's upper lip curled. Gale waited several seconds,
listening to her daughter's exaggerated snore, before
Katie Pru's eyelids flickered and her mouth spread into
a gap-toothed grin.

It was impossible to know how long the child had
held that pose, but she wouldn't have been surprised
to discover her daughter had lain there playing possum
for ten minutes or more. Stubbornness, after all, was
part of the Alden family's southern code, and Gale was
only vaguely disturbed that at three years of age and
four thousand miles away, Katie Pru had so naturally
fallen into step.

"Okay, ladybug." Gale dragged the bag closer to
the radiator. "Your call. Let me know when you get
hungry."

She dropped a crinkly kiss onto the paper, straightened, and walked to the cupboard. At 7:45 A.M. the
room was dim; the flagstone floor and plaster walls
were lit by a line of white domed lamps suspended a
foot from the ceiling and running the length of the
kitchen. At best the light they emitted was decorative,
and in the darkest winter months Gale had to wedge a
flashlight between two old crocks on her counter to
read recipes.

It was this very intractableness that made the
kitchen Gale's favorite place in the cottage. In the five
years she had lived there, even in the beginning when
she and Tom had lavished the rest of the cottage with
discreet lighting and pastel washes, she had dismissed
suggestions to whitewash the charcoal-sated wall behind the fireplace or install fluorescent bulbs under the
cupboards. The darkness pleased her; then, and even
more so now, the paradox of the room defined her
quiet life. It was like a calcified womb, full-feeding and
warm.

From the cupboard Gale pulled out a box of Martha
White grits her grandmother had sent her, making sure
to give it a loud shake before setting it on the counter.
Gale eyed the bag expectantly. It scooted a millimeter
closer to the radiator.

The container of grits was one of several lining the
top shelf of the kitchen cupboard, the result of Gale's
grandmother's insistence that Katie Pru not lose total
sight of her Georgia heritage. Martha White had always been Ella Alden's grits of choice; she claimed she
could tell by sight which bowl was Martha White and
which was some other brand produced by a northern
company with a Yankee marketing director who
thought he could put grits on every table by teaching
people to put sugar on them. Gale's grandmother
would repeat that statement, word for word, each time
she encountered an alien bowl of grits. It was part
of Ella's southern litany, along with don't-stand-
still-in-front-of-a-kudzu-patch and our-family-used-
to-have-silver-until-the-Yankees-found-the-hole-in-the-
backyard-and-stole-it-all. These were psalms that had
more power than any verse quoted at the Methodist
church, except, of course, when the southernisms
themselves were quoted—during Sunday School, at
covered dish dinners, from the pulpit itself.

Gale sighed. She poured a cup of coffee and glanced
at the old schoolhouse clock ticking on the wall. 7:46.
More and more lately her mornings began like this,

voiceless testimonies to a wavering agnosticism. It wasn't that she despised the South; she simply didn't believe in it anymore, having learned that it, like cold fusion and giants, couldn't bear scrutiny. For a long time she had made as much of a separation as she felt feasible—college, grad school, and finally, blessedly, her marriage to Tom and this fresh, cold world of British reserve and obliqueness. She had sought to be southern in voice only, and for a while she had succeeded. Then Tom died, Katie Pru was born, and the quiet tattoo of her roots seemed to be urging her to reexamine her faithlessness.

She took another healthy swallow of coffee, swigging it back like bourbon. Too damned early for God; too damned late for Dixie.

"Today a work day or a Katie Pru day?" the muffled voice asked.

Gale walked over to the bag. "Sorry, punkin. It's Saturday—one of Mama's work days. But Lisa will be coming over later. You two will have fun."

The bag thought a second. "I'll come out for Lisa."

"Lisa won't be here for a while . . . not until the little hand's on nine. In the meantime, I'll fix you what you want for breakfast."

"I want to build a castle so Space Lucy can bash it."

"Next choice, please, ma'am."

"I want a drink of Coke."

Gale sighed again and took her coffee to the broad harvest table in the middle of the room. She made as much noise as possible as she slid a chair around and sat in it.

"I want a piece of cake," the bag announced.

Gale laughed. Just like Grandmother, she thought. Outside, the silver light flailing at her window was growing brighter. Soon the leaden morning would molt and bring a more palatable slice of chill to the chalky downs. She drew her arms around her shoulders. It was what she loved most about this country, the heavy light that seemed almost no light at all. Its contradiction sharpened her. She tried to imagine her grandmother, sun-shielded and Georgia-proud, turning her face to the Hampshire skies. Impossible.

Katie Pru's dark hair bristled with electricity as she slowly tilted back her head and let the bag fall. She looked at her mother with eyes black and sharp.

"I'd like some grits now, Mama. In a *big* bowl. And I don't need a spoon."

Lisa lowered herself a little further into the hot soapy water, careful not to wet her new hairdo. Relatively speaking, baths were a newly acquired skill for her—she was fourteen before she ever stretched her legs out the full length of a tub. Prior to that, she scrubbed gracelessly in the cramped bath in her family's 220-year-old cottage near the High Street, shivering from inadequately plumbed pipes and tepid water. The move eight years ago to the new house on the outskirts of Fetherbridge had brought her more than her own room and a higher standard of comfort. It had brought her to civilisation.

Her mother had hated the old cottage, acting on her frustration by throwing clods of dirt at passing birds and describing in almost vaudevillian terms the lifestyles of the pestilences that flourished in the muck behind the old cooker. They were reasonable fits, brief rages underlined by a steady discontent that didn't seem particularly odd to anyone bred into a decomposing house in a small town. Madge Stillwell was known around Fetherbridge as a funny lady with a man's easy humor, a characteristic that both delighted and embarrassed her adolescent daughter.

"I swear, Lisa girl," Madge would say, pushing her bottom lip over her top and tugging a red knit cap down so low her hair jabbed her eyes, "I can't take this country life anymore. Some day you're going to come home and I'll have moved to Trafalgar Square where I'll spend my days eating chestnuts and yelling nasties to the pigeons." And she'd shuffle around the kitchen chasing imaginary fowl, cornering one every now and then and grinding it into invisible dust under her foot. Lisa and her brother Brian would collapse on the table, laughter scorching their throats.

Lisa moved her hips slightly against the tub's white porcelain sides and felt the scented water roll across her stomach. Moving to the new house had changed Madge Stillwell. Instead of being comically grumpy, she began a routine that at first puzzled and then alarmed her family. One day she would take all the tins from the cupboard and hurl them at the walls; the next she would lock Lisa in her arms and waltz her wildly around the dining room table. She either adored her children or despised them, ravished her husband or slunk from him. As Lisa watched her father become more and more silent, she attempted to wrap her younger brother in a small, narrow world that recalled the warmer lunacy of their old cottage. *See,* Lisa told Brian after one disturbing scene with a scouring pad, *this is what the suburbs, even the Fetherbridge suburbs, do to you. When we grow up, we'll just move to the Docklands and take on the thugs.* It worked, and Brian slowly turned to Lisa for the reinterpretation of his life. By the time their mother walked out a year later, Brian laughed at everything.

Lisa crawled from the bathtub and slowly towelled herself off. Strange how that hellish year with her mother hadn't tainted the purity of the new house. She soon came to see that time as a brief satanic misstep, as if the Devil himself had mistaken their house for a sinner's and sent up a pet demon to entertain them. They hadn't even needed a Catholic priest to exorcise the place—they simply waited patiently until the demon got up one morning and walked away. Lisa couldn't find any scars, not what she'd call scars, and when they heard eight months later that Madge had died of an aneurysm in a London shelter, she didn't cry. That had been six years ago, and she had maintained beautifully. Lately, however, Lisa had begun to experience her own sudden slams of behaviour, and there were times when the amused look on Brian's face sliced through her stomach like her mother's flying tins.

Lisa slid into her slip, pulled her dress over her head, and looked in the bathroom mirror. Steam had drawn her hair into a black cap around her skull, obliterating the wispy soft do she had gotten in Winchester yesterday. Without the balancing shadow of hair, her face looked broad and doughy. She could see in her features the coarse remnants of her ancestors and the fleshy promise of her old age. At twenty-two, she knew she was as pretty as her genes allowed. By twenty-five she would look thirty, and the aging would proceed arithmetically from there.

She took a jar of make-up brushes from the cupboard and began swiftly applying colour. Quickly, she moved out of the direct glare of the bathroom lights and noticed with satisfaction that the pouches on her cheeks disappeared and her face softened into a smudged prettiness. She took a last whack at her moisture-slain hair with her brush and ran downstairs for breakfast.

"What's gone on here?"

Katie Pru stood with her hands on her hips. Her eyes were serious and concerned, as if she were the one waiting for an explanation to why A) her grits were in the front room and not on the kitchen table, and B) they were dripping from the body cavity of a ballerina doll and not in the bowl which now cradled a plastic, dark-bunned head.

"What's 'gone' on here, indeed." Gale looked slowly around the room, noting that her daughter had chosen the most bizarre sight to which to draw her attention, probably in hopes that she would run from the room in hysterics and not notice the rest of the mess. She glanced at her watch—9:07. Six minutes. She had left Katie Pru alone for six minutes while she finished dressing. In that length of time the child had managed to empty all her toys on the floor, relieve *Madeline's Rescue* of its cover and first three pages, pull all the skeins of spun wool from their baskets, and . . . Gale peered at the wall. A smiley face. Katie Pru had taken face paints and drawn an emerald green, big-nosed smiley face on the wall next to the hearth.

She bit her lip. "Kathleen Prudence, Lisa is going to be here any minute and just look at what she has to walk into!"

Katie Pru lowered her head. Gale didn't have to see the small heart-shaped face to know regret pinched it. For a brief moment, she considered relenting. Then she glanced at the smiley face grinning from the wall. Turning on her heel, she left Katie Pru to her remorse.

The clock in the kitchen read somewhere between ten and fifteen after nine. Lisa was late. On most days, Gale wasn't a clock watcher. Today, however, she had scheduled herself up to five o'clock and was already behind. She scooped up two towels, a sponge, and some liquid soap and went back into the front room.

Katie Pru's sorrow had passed. Now she squatted on the floor, studying the lumps of grits that matted the ballerina's hair.

"This was naughty." Katie Pru pointed to the doll. "Somebody washed the ba'rina's hair."

Gale knelt next to the child, handed her a towel, and began shovelling up the grits now smeared across the floor. "You help me clean this up, please, ma'am."

"Sure will, ma'am." Katie Pru rubbed her towel into the bottom of the bowl and energetically swatted the floor. Grits splattered everywhere.

Gale looked at her watch. 9:20. Where the hell was Lisa?

She was late. She had left her watch on the bathroom sink, but she didn't need a dial to tell her that she had taken too long this morning getting ready, too long mooning and reflecting in the mirror. Gale had

told her today was important. God, she was going to
be narked.

The bicycle gave a metallic purr as she rolled it from
the garage and mounted. Six minutes. Six minutes of
mad pedalling ought to do it.

Gale's house was only a mile away as the crow flies,
but Boundary Road connected Lisa's house to the eastern edge of Fetherbridge in a series of irregular curves.
Lisa had never figured out why the road wasn't
straight; except for the copse of trees that forced it to
protrude into a wide "U" at the midway point, there
didn't seem to be any geographical reason for the design. It swerved past a series of fields, each displaying
vegetation of a different colour and cut, and on cool
clear days such as this, hoarfrost tipped the grass. Usually Lisa enjoyed the ride. Today, however, she
squinted into the chill air and pedalled quickly.

She was making good time, slightly thrilled by the
pace, when she became aware of another rider overtak-
ing her. She glanced over and gave a fast smile, one
she hoped lit up her eyes since she doubted anyone
could see her mouth beneath her long scarf. The rider
came abreast.

A question occurred to her, but she was pedalling
too fast to ask it. Hell, no point in being rude, she
thought, and she stopped pumping her feet, allowing
the bicycle to slow until she was at conversation speed.

She turned to the rider. "Well—"

A stick flicked into the spokes of her front wheel. It
snapped, and the wheel stopped. The bicycle flipped
into the air, carrying Lisa with it.

Instinctively, she put her hands out in front of her.
She hit the pavement hard. For a moment she sat
dazed. Then she started to lift the tangled bicycle from
her legs. Blood filled her mouth—her lip must have
busted. She looked up but could make no sense of the
fist-sized rock that struck her squarely in the forehead.

She fell backwards, feeling nothing. Legs straddled
her body; gloves fumbled with the scarf around her

neck. She looked up into the face bending over hers. The eyes hated her. They actually hated her.

Lights came before the pain. They were tiny and rampant, pecking at her eyes with a numbing violence. The lights reminded Lisa of something she couldn't place. Then she knew. They looked like the pigeons in Trafalgar Square.

3

The party was nearly out of control when Daniel Halford arrived. He parked his blue Ford behind a line of tightly packed, bug-bodied cars, wedged bumper-to-bumper against the kerb like protesters forming the last line of defence against the police. Halford, of course, knew the truth. There was no fear of police here. The cars, the chaos, the theme from *Gilligan's Island* pummelling the quiet London street—this *was* the police.

Without knocking, he entered the house. The cramped room was packed. Either Maura had extended her guest list, or the entire contingent of Scotland Yard CID had decided to show up for one of her famous parties. Knowing his colleagues, however, Halford was fairly confident that he was the only one above the rank of sergeant with the stomach for it.

"Daniel!" A hand with peach-polished nails shoved a glass of cola into his chest. He grabbed the glass and the hand simultaneously in an effort to keep his coat dry, but the fabric darkened as several drops hit their mark. He looked down at the face of Detective Sergeant Maura Ramsden. Or one of her faces. Her left shoulder had been taken over by a Styrofoam wig stand sporting a blonde ponytail and two big felt-and-button eyes.

"I didn't think you would come!"

Maura was shouting, more than was needed, since the stereo had started playing the comparatively restful theme to *Mr. Ed*. Halford grinned at her. People who saw Maura only at work would not believe this was the composed perfectionist tenaciously climbing her way up the ranks. Off duty, his sergeant came across as the daftest thing afloat. Halford hated working with anyone else.

"This one was too good to miss," he told her. "A sixties American sitcom party—so much for yuletide tradition. And who are you supposed to be?"

"*The Patty Duke Show*. I'm Cathy, teenage sophisticate extraordinaire." Maura nodded at her shoulder. The wig stand bobbed. "That's Patty. She is into rock and roll, skinned knees and heavy squinting."

Halford frowned. "Looks more like Zaphod Beeblebrox."

Maura shook her head in mock pity. "Wrong decade, wrong country." She flipped open his overcoat and studied his navy trousers, white shirt, and dark tie. "This is a costume party, Chief Inspector. Who are you supposed to be?"

"Dick Van Dyke."

A snappy rejoinder must have occurred to her for her eyes lit up wickedly, but the comment was forgotten with the arrival of a barefoot man with a rope belt and a shit-eating grin. Halford laughed out loud.

"Let me guess—Jethro Bodine."

The man pulled a piece of straw from his back pocket and chewed on it. "Wee doggies," he said dryly.

Halford held out his hand. "How the hell are you, Jeffrey?"

Out of the classroom, Jeffrey Burke looked as little like a professor at the London School of Economics as his wife looked like a police sergeant. Lanky and knobbed like a newel post, Burke was the university's fair-haired wonder. At thirty-three, he had authored two books on the facilitation of Eastern European market systems and was an advisor to the Prime Minister. Halford glanced down at the hairy feet protruding from a pair of grubby, rolled-up jeans. Without a doubt, Maura Ramsden and Jeffrey Burke were the best couple he knew.

"Not quite into the spirit of things, aye, Chief Inspector?" Jeffrey flicked the straw up and down with his teeth. "Can't see why. Nothing like making fun of the Americans to bring out the vigour in a man." His eyes twinkled. Maura moved her tasteful blue espadrille over his foot and bore down. The straw flipped against his nose. "Of course, there's nothing wrong with the Americans, nothing at all. Especially American mothers-in-law. Love 'em, myself. And I ask you, Daniel, can a country that produced *The Munsters* be a total cultural wasteland? I think not." The shoe lifted and Jeffrey dropped a kiss on his wife's blonde hair. "Of course, it can't be a cultural nirvana, either."

This was a running gag with them, the type of needling banter that was hell in a bad marriage, cement in a good. Halford had met Maura's mother once at a small party in her Kensington flat. Mrs. Ramsden had struck him as an affectionate woman with all of Maura's American enthusiasm uninhibited by British reserve. She had met Maura's father during a London business trip in 1963 and now, after more than thirty years in Britain, she appeared a contained and sensible English lady. Halford, however, had noticed that on an oil seascape in her dining room someone had painted in George Washington and Jesus dancing across the waves. True, it could have been done by Maura, but he preferred to think it was the chignoned elderly woman laughing at him behind her Haviland teacup.

Mr. Ed had given way to *The Addams Family* and the top floor vibrated ominously with sepulchral stomps. Patty's Styrofoam head lurched forward and back as Maura clicked her fingers. An object, shaped of grey foam, darted past.

"I know it's not polite to comment on one's fellow guests, but this is quite a collection of Boschian horrors you have here." Halford waved his drink at a dance line snaking noisily down the stairs. "Police or professors?"

"The *I Dream of Jeannie* contestants," Maura replied. "In a bit we'll have a Barbara Eden look-alike contest. I've seen just a couple of entries, but I think Sergeant Lewis is a shoe-in. It's all that undercover work he does. He even shaved." She rapped her knuckles against Halford's chest. "That's it, Daniel! Get rid of that moustache and you would walk away with the Major Nelson competition!"

Halford protectively stroked his moustache. "Pardon?"

"Jeannie's master! I don't know anyone in the entirety of the Metropolitan Police who better combines boyish good looks with eye-popping exasperation." She wrinkled her nose at him. "Speaking of boyish good looks, I've a friend who wants to meet you. She's here somewhere, dressed as Morticia. Says she's into tall, dark, and sardonic. You came immediately to mind."

He wrinkled his nose back at her. "No, thank you, Maura. The last time you fixed me up, I spent the evening with a very thin young nihilist who recited Allen Ginsberg right through to the pudding. Then she confided that her ultimate fantasy was to make love under the statue of Peter Pan in Hyde Park. You moved off my A-list of matchmakers right then and there."

Over the heads of the other party-goers the grey foam mass bobbed. Halford leaned down to whisper in Patty's ear.

"I'd suss that one out if I were you," he said. "I don't think *Flipper* was technically a sitcom."

He slapped Jeffrey on the back, then began weaving his way through the crowd. A few people he recognised; some, like the Technicolor Endora whacking her wand around like a crazed schoolmistress, he suspected would just as soon he didn't try. He drained his glass. At thirty-seven, he was only ten years older than Maura, but, God, what ten years.

He had decided to survey the scenery upstairs when he noticed Jeffrey holding the telephone receiver over his head in one hand and jabbing his straw into the air with the other. Halford raised his eyebrows. Jeffrey shrugged and smiled.

Great. Halford fought through a circle of guffawing June Cleavers and took the phone.

"Hate to interrupt, Halford." Chief Superintendent Owen Chandler's voice barely beat out that of a burly Granny Clampett shouting for a beer. "I know you don't like missing a minute of Ramsden's soirees. I suppose our more promising junior officers are at this very moment destroying any future they might have with the CID."

"Yes, sir, but they're developing a hell of a future on the game show circuit." Halford paused as Flipper made a grab for the receiver and moved on. "I don't suppose you called to get directions."

"No, we've got a situation. Out Hampshire way."

Jeffrey was evidently trying to explain to the raucously thirsty Granny Clampett that there was no alcohol in the house, which was met by a string of good-natured obscenities that Halford only half recognised. His throat was suddenly tight.

"Hampshire?"

"Fetherbridge, to be exact. The Hampshire Constabulary has asked us to take over a murder investigation. A young woman. She was found Saturday. At first, the local police thought it an accident, but the data suggests otherwise. Three days of lost time, but there you have it."

A roar erupted from the conga line. Halford's voice was cautious. "I'll send someone good."

"Not 'someone,' Daniel," Chandler replied. "You. The girl was Gale Grayson's childminder. You're our resident Grayson expert—you get the job."

The Chief Superintendent broke the connection. Halford glanced around the room, trying to locate his double-headed cohort among the crowd. His height should have given him some advantage, but the cringe in his gut made him no match for the leaping lawmen blocking his view.

When Halford finally found Maura, she was by the front door, waving it back and forth to urge in cool air and usher costumed newcomers inside.

"Lovely party," he said drily. "Get some sleep. I'll pick you up in the morning at seven. Smile pretty— we're going to Fetherbridge."

He kissed Patty on her plastic cheek, patted Cathy's head, and left Maura crestfallen in her doorway.

It took him twenty-five minutes to drive to his flat in Lambeth and twenty seconds to rip off his clothes and throw himself on the divan. Halford closed his eyes to ward off—what was it, again?—eye-popping exasperation. Jesus God.

Gale Grayson. The baby would be about three now, a girl, he remembered. He had seen the infant once, still small enough to be carried in a sling around her mother's chest, in a tearoom not far from the South-ampton Library. He had gone there to find Gale Grayson. He had figured, done some checking, actually, and knew she was doing research for a book. So he had taken his off day and driven to Southampton on the chance . . . No, he was a better detective than that; he damn well knew she would be in that tearoom at that time, feeding the baby.

And she was, hunched over a table in front of the bow window with the infant in her arms, staring into the street. A hundred years ago, he would have sworn she was one of those women who sat looking out at sea day after day, waiting. Of course, women don't do that anymore, do they? But this one gazed at the street as if she knew the ship was lost even though no one had brought her the news. Only someone had. He had.

Even now Halford couldn't quite explain what compelled him to see her. His best guess was guilt, or at least a misplaced sense of duty towards the fetus that had intruded on the inquiry like a corporeal cry. He surely wasn't sentimental when it came to pregnant women. In the early days of his career, in the dirty flats of small-time thieves and vein-streaked drug dealers, he had encountered his share—loud, angry women who arched their backs, cursed him, and wielded their bulging stomachs as shields of defiance. He had learned a firm attentiveness towards them, a form of mutual defence that put them out of harm's way while protecting him from hostile fists or hidden knives.

But this one had been different. During the whole of the inquiry into her husband's crimes, anger never found Mrs. Grayson. Instead, she watched him, dark eyes confused, silently imploring him to erase the damage being done to her life, to repair the wreck they both knew his investigation was making of her.

He hadn't bothered to analyse his motive that morning in Southampton. When he found the tearoom, he went quickly in, rehearsing how he was in the city and noticed her by the window and, oh, is this the baby? But when he walked up to her table, Gale Grayson glared at him with eyes that could have stoned paupers.

Halford mumbled something suitably inane as he sat. On the table in front of her was an empty teacup and a half-finished baby bottle, a white line of residual milk indicating its passing freshness. The fork from his place setting was dull grey and clunky. He nervously turned it as he spoke.

"So, I hope you're getting on all right."

From its pastel nest, the baby mewed. Mrs. Grayson cuddled the infant closer, dipping her head to almost meet the pinked round of the child's face. A white lace cap covered the tiny skull, and Mrs. Grayson pushed it back to gently stroke the wisps of black hair. She drew her finger along the baby's cheek and bent her knuckle into its mouth, urging the infant to suck. It was a simple gesture, a mother's obeisance to a primal need. Only when he glanced at the angry set of her jaw did Halford understand the control behind the tenderness.

He pressed the tines into the tablecloth. "A girl then, is it?" he asked. "My mother had one of each. She always said girls were easier. Not as inclined to bring snakes in the house."

She was silent, watching the baby contentedly gum at her finger. He tried again.

"Look, I know it must be difficult," he said kindly, "but I've been through these things before. People come through it. They move past it. I know you can't imagine it now, but it will get easier."

Slowly she raised her eyes to his. The line of her jaw remained tense, her eyes hard. Then, to his horror, a soundless slide of tears began racing down her cheeks, disappearing beneath the rim of her chin. Her mouth trembled, but she clung to her control as she spoke.

"Please leave," she said. "I don't know why you're here, but there's nothing I want from you. Leave me alone."

He went, embarrassed and depressed. He hadn't seen her since. Only during his most masochistic moods would he admit how often he thought of her. God, he didn't want to see her now.

On the wall above his sofa, in matching gold mats and black frames, hung two Edward Hopper prints: the famous "Nighthawks" nocturnal café scene and the less well-known "Automat" with its solitary woman in a green coat gazing forlornly at her coffee. He stared up at them. Rena had introduced him to Hopper. It had been his wife's way to edge up to an issue, never confronting it head on. A book of paintings open on the coffee table, an afternoon visit to a British Museum exhibit—these were supposed to tell him of her frustrations, of her lonely resentment towards his job and his desperate, sometimes drunken, camaraderie with his fellow coppers. By the time she could articulate her unhappiness, it was too late. Every word became a scream. A year after their divorce, she married a farmer. They now lived in New Zealand with their two children, by all accounts happy and well. He, in turn, had overridden his early days to become respected around the Met for his calm and clear compassion. He had come to see that many dues are paid by foolish young men.

He lifted his hands in front of his face and stared at them. He was a solid man, comprised of strong lines and dark features; he would have fit in well in Hopper's urban world. The prints had been a gift to himself following the Grayson case. The contradiction in trying to pair two Hopper paintings wasn't lost on him. At the time he only had money enough for two. Had he been able, he would have bought ten, cramming them together on his wall, forcing an interconnection that neither the paintings nor his life could declare.

Halford shifted onto his side. Ironically, the Grayson case had made him, which was particularly acrid considering he botched it. Tom Grayson had been one of those intellectuals who couldn't differentiate between ideals and morals. Crime syndicates collect such people and Grayson became a pawn, acting on behalf of a small band of militant British environmentalists as a go-between for a group of wealthy white supremacists in London and two particularly unsavoury weapons suppliers in Yemen. The environmentalists called

themselves In Gaia's Name, and their pledge to create
an ecological balance went beyond recycling cola tins
and drip-drying wet nappies. On paper Gaia's cam-
paign was brutal. Nothing ever came of it, however;
one March evening, a London barrister who worked for
the group informed them he wanted out, and a week
later he was dead, the apparent victim of a robbery
gone wrong.

At first the murder had seemed fairly cut-and-dried.
Halford's name had been in the frame, it was his turn,
so paired with a young DC Ramsden newly promoted
to CID, he had tackled the case routinely and run to
earth Tom Grayson, a noted Hampshire poet with a
five-months-pregnant wife and a misdirected passion
for the ozone layer. Remembering, Halford groaned.
Ran him to earth, all right. Grayson made the passion-
ate gesture when cornered. As Halford and his men
raced past row after row of pews trying to reach him,
the poet-assassin blew his brains out all over the altar
of a quaint village church.

For an idealist, however, Grayson had been smart.
After his suicide, the police found in his home scores
of incriminating letters and lists, presumably saved to
protect himself, that took the case from Halford and the
murder squad's limited hands and into the offices of
MI5. But even when the investigation had passed far
out of Halford's purview, it was still known as his case.
Good job Halford did on that Gaia thing. Fine man.
Remember him when it comes time for a promotion.

Halford rolled off the sofa and went into his bedroom. So Gale Grayson's childminder is found dead
and no one in the Hampshire Constabulary wants to
touch it with a ten-foot pole. Call New Scotland Yard.
It's Halford's case. He fell into bed face first.

4

Maura was waiting on the kerb in front of her house at 6:45 the next morning, a tall, pale figure in camel-coloured clothes. Her hair was starched into a sleek blonde bun, a sure sign that she was at the start of an investigation—by day three, her idea of a coif would degenerate into a pair of combs jabbed into the sides of her head in what she called her "holy-roller do." Halford felt a surge of affection. She was a good partner, a good friend. Pity she had no sisters.

He unlocked the car door. As she slid in, her face moved under the glow of the interior light, and he noticed a delicate violet tint to the skin under her eyes. His professional guess would be three, four hours of sleep at most. He cleared his throat and tossed her a manila envelope.

"Good morning. If I were nice, I'd say finish your beauty sleep. As it is, there's a flask of coffee under your feet."

"Thanks, but after last night, I'm practically spongy." She flipped on the map light and opened the envelope. "Grayson. Good Lord."

"Lisa Stillwell, Mrs. Grayson's twenty-two-year-old childminder, was found dead in a bicycle accident Saturday morning. I don't have any more details. DI Richard Roan was in charge of the inquiry, but the Hampshire Chief Constable called in the Met. No details on that, either."

"Roan. I remember him. Bit of a grouser, wasn't he? As I recall he wasn't very helpful on the Grayson case."

"Yes, well, he wasn't alone." Halford beat his thumb against the steering wheel. "I can't help questioning the wisdom of assigning the two of us this go-round."

Maura shook her head. "I doubt wisdom came into play. The Super looked at the case and said, 'Ho-ho, Halford and Ramsden did such a lovely job on the last Fetherbridge outing, let's give them another shot. They know all the locals, the best sources, the best pubs. Perhaps they'll tidy up the whole business before Fleet Street gets a whiff and we can all sleep peacefully in our beds.' "

Halford pulled the Ford onto Bayswater Road and headed southwest towards the M-3. For a long time, Maura said nothing, her gaze intent on buildings that now shone with an umber wetness. When she turned to him, Halford saw that her eyes had lengthened, the violet tint contracted into crescents.

"Daniel, I know we've discussed the Grayson case until we could vomit details in our sleep, but we've never really talked about its impact—on the two of us, just between the two of us."

"It's not worth discussing. We were police officers doing our job. Period."

Maura toyed with the corner of the manila file. "Well, then, I'll start," she said. "I had difficulty coming to grips with it. For one thing, during the investigation I had the keenest feeling that I honestly liked the man. Had we met at one of Jeffrey's university coffee clatches, I would probably have enjoyed sitting at a table with him, just talking about things." She gave a short laugh. "Of course, he probably would have been boycotting coffee."

Halford was silent a moment. "You've romanticised him, Maura."

"No, I don't think I have. At first I thought so, particularly after he was dead and I was trying to figure out what we could have done to prevent it. But even now he fascinates me. We know from his notes that he despised them—what was the group? In Gaia's Name? God, talk about bad poetry—anyway, we know that he despised them, yet he chose to work for them. Daniel, Tom Grayson was a very complex man with very complex reasons for what he did."

"Oh, Maura." Halford could remember when he thought of terrorism as the irrational outlet for complex and rational men. But a weary impotence had left him almost blindly impassive. He had cared that Grayson died. He didn't care about him or his ilk anymore.

"Grayson was a gunrunner, pure and simple. He took a legitimate concern—ecology, Gaia, or whatever he called it—and used it to justify murder and a whole host of lesser crimes." His voice sharpened as Maura turned, tight-lipped, toward the window. "Maura, what do you expect me to say? The man was no humanist. He was a vessel for other people's ideas. It's a damned pity he had to die, but it was his decision, a decision, need I remind you, that he didn't allow one poor son-of-a-bitch barrister to make. I have only one regret concerning Tom Grayson, and you can damn well guess what that is."

"We shouldn't have stormed the church."

They hadn't discussed it in years, and now the words hung in the air like a contagion. Halford gazed at the dwindling urban sprawl. "No," he said, "we shouldn't have stormed the church. It was bad police work. If we had approached him more carefully, we might have stopped him."

"But perhaps not."

"He was a man with a wife and an unborn child. Surely we could have talked him out of it. . . . "

Maura pushed herself deeper into the seat. She made an effort to sound brighter. "I've forgotten—how did he and his wife meet?"

"At college somewhere in the States—Virginia, I think. In an antigun club, can you believe it? Which shows that the Tom Graysons of this world don't really have any values. They merely have emotions."

The tip of a nail found its demise between Maura's teeth. "What was that book Mrs. Grayson wrote? Something historical, wasn't it?"

"*Shadow Plays*. About the role of the British government in the American War Between the States."

"As I recall, it got fairly good press. A bit surprising under the circumstances, don't you think?"

"Why? That kind of thing's right up their alley. The Grayson name was hot. Publication of the book was bound to send the public into a lather."

"Damned sweet lather," Maura scoffed. "Best-seller, wasn't it?"

"Close to it. Everyone tittered about how horrible it was what her husband did, and then they stormed the bookshops to get a copy. I bet less than one in ten ever bothered to crack the cover."

"Did you?"

Halford shrugged. "It was scholarly, though not overly. Thoughtful. Nicely researched."

"Strange. She struck me as such an insubstantial thing. Grief, I suppose. Still, you were impressed."

"The whole time I was reading I thought, here's a

woman who should have stayed in Stumpwater, Georgia or wherever the hell she's from and become a professor at a quiet little college and spent the rest of her life reading old diaries and slogging through cemeteries. Instead, she ends up in the middle of an international mess, a widowed young mother in a country that can't decide whether to feel outrage or guilt at what her husband has done." The savagery in his own voice made him flinch. He softened his tone. "How can you help but feel irritation towards someone who makes such bad choices?"

Maura murmured something into her lapel. Halford tightened his grip on the wheel and watched the beams of oncoming cars struggle to pierce the thickening morning light.

Detective Inspector Richard Roan of the Winchester Police worked at being a picture of amusement. His cheeks bulged Kewpie-style and his hands pushed at his trouser pockets in a halfhearted effort to hide his happy belly. He rocked, back and forth, figuring that if he kept in motion no one in the room would see just how jolly amused he really was.

He hadn't started the morning in such a good mood—truth was he had been fairly brassed off for the past twelve hours, ever since the Chief Constable had exercised his privilege and called in New Scotland Yard, thereby relieving the local police force of any control over the Stillwell inquiry. Initially, the reason given was Roan's rather embarrassing pronouncement. Well, it had certainly looked like an accident to him. Bicycle accidents do happen. At first he felt humiliated to have a case taken away because of a premature conclusion. Soon, however, he saw the truth. The case wasn't taken away because he'd failed to recognise a murder. It was taken away because of its connection with Tom Grayson. The Chief Constable wanted as little to do with it as possible. He simply wanted it cleared up quickly and

the hullabaloo out of Fetherbridge before the press
went on a nostalgia kick.

So who does the Yard send? Chief Inspector Daniel
Bugger-Your-Mother Halford who was now sitting before him in this godforsaken two-holer of a police station looking ill . . . no, plagued . . . no, bloody well
rotting in the grave. DI Roan kept rocking back and
forth. Even he couldn't rationalise the hate that propelled his heels.

Halford tried to ignore Roan's tick-tocking figure.
Instead he looked sternly at the constable seated across
the desk in the Fetherbridge police station. PC Nate
Baylor was a rawboned young man in his midtwenties,
who had been the lone policeman in Fetherbridge for
two years. Baylor had been assigned after the Grayson
case to help calm the public nerves as the village began
its drift back to normality. His presence was calculated
to be as visible as possible; eschewing an office in the
constable's house which was customary for most villages of Fetherbridge's size, the constabulary had constructed a genuine police station out of what had once
been a fish-and-chips restaurant on the High Street.
Halford imagined he could still detect the odor of burnt
grease on the walls, but otherwise the station was
cheery and serviceable.

A copy of the postmortem report lay open before
Halford on the station's only desk. The girl's murder
had occurred Saturday morning. Death apparently by
strangulation, accompanied by a large contusion on the
forehead, and severe abrasions on hands and legs. He
passed the file to Maura.

"So it was made to look like an accident." He discarded as antagonistic any comment on his part about
it now being Wednesday, four days later, and the in-
herent complications of lost time and cold trails.

Glancing at Roan, who was still rocking impatiently,
Constable Baylor leaned forward and crossed his arms
on the desk. "I believe so, sir," he started, hesitantly.

"One end of her scarf was wound into the front wheel as if it had gotten caught. Of course, if we assume Lisa wore it wrapped around her neck, I suppose it's feasible that one end could get caught and accidentally strangle her. . . . "

"How long is the scarf?" Maura asked.

"Seven feet." Baylor smiled at Maura's surprise. "I've checked it out. It's one of Mrs. Grayson's. Her hobby is weaving and she's forever making scarves and things for folks. She made me one. Ten feet long it is. She said it's because I'm so tall, looks more Dickensian for people to have long, flappy scarves. Americans do like their English looking English." He hesitated. "Mrs. Grayson's going to feel fairly bad about this."

"For more reasons than one," Roan got in.

Halford ignored him, choosing to direct his questions to Baylor. Technically, he knew the village bobby would have only a tangential involvement with the murder inquiry. He wouldn't be a part of the official team. But something about the talkative constable appealed to him. Perhaps it was because he did look so damned Dickensian, like Bob Cratchit with balls.

"So how do you think the scarf got stuck in the front spokes to begin with?" he asked Baylor. "The rear would have been more likely."

Baylor warmed to the detective's attention. "Well, sir, I've given it some thought. It could be the scarf was hanging over the front of the handlebars, as if Lisa didn't tuck it into her coat. It had a series of decorative holes in it—lacy-looking, almost—and the tire's air valve was stuck through one of the holes. At first blush, sir, it looks as if the scarf got caught in the air valve and the bicycle was going fast enough to crank the scarf tight."

"But the abrasions on the neck indicate that the scarf was pulled from both directions," Halford objected. "That puts paid to the idea of one end getting caught in the spokes and causing all the damage."

"That's right, sir," Baylor said. "Which brings up

the question: If it was an accident, why didn't Lisa just reach up and unwind the bloody thing when she felt it choking her? I mean, if the fall didn't break her neck, surely she would have had enough time."

Halford picked up the top photo from a stack on Baylor's desk. "Not necessarily." The photograph focused on the dead girl's neck, with all but the chin and mouth cut from view by the camera's lens. A white scarf had been wound twice around her neck so that only the ends displayed the decorative openings. Halford imagined that under normal circumstances, the wool would have softly buffered the girl's skin, rising above her coat collar to guard her lips and jaw against the wind. As it was, however, the slack hole of her mouth was exposed; the scarf's delicate strands bit into her neck like a noose. Even with a cool head, it might have been difficult to remove the scarf, lethally snared by the bicycle wheel. Nevertheless, Halford knew Baylor was right. This was no accident. A pair of hands had pulled that scarf in two directions.

Roan stopped rocking to fold a piece of chewing gum into his mouth. Halford supposed the grimace on the inspector's face as he dug his teeth into the wad was meant to hide a grin. He didn't know why the man detested him, although he acknowledged the feeling was mutual and equally inexplicable on his part. It was more than professional jealousy, more than two dogs on the same patch. There was animus here.

"So," Maura asked. "Who have you interviewed?"

Nate Baylor pushed a thin folder across the desk. "Well," he said, looking at Roan for direction and receiving none, "the house-to-house team is going out this morning to get background data on the neighbors for the pro formers. Detectives have talked with her father and nineteen-year-old brother—Brian, the brother, he found the body. And Mrs. Grayson. Lisa was evidently on her way to Mrs. Grayson's house when she was killed."

"What does forensics have on the bicycle?"

Roan cut in, answering around the softening wad of chewing gum in such a way that Halford could almost taste the ebbing sweetness. "Final report's not in yet, but they did tell me one thing. Several of the front wheel spokes were bent and they found particles of wood near the axle. Don't know what kind yet, of course, but young Nate here showed a little initiative and went out to take another look at the scene. What do you think he found?"

Halford looked at Roan politely, but Baylor answered.

"Two parts of a stick, sir. Broken at about the three-quarters point, sanded smooth, blunt ends." Baylor looked pleased. "Took a bit of looking. One was about two hundred feet from where the body was, off in a field to the right of the road, the other on the edge of the wood to the left of the road." He added unnecessarily, "I figure they'd been thrown."

Halford carefully closed the file on Lisa Stillwell's contorted features and stood. "Let's just keep that to ourselves for now. Have you told her family it wasn't an accident?"

"No, Chief Inspector." Halford could feel Roan's jubilation. "We haven't told anyone." He smacked once on his gum. "But I hear they've planned the funeral for Friday."

Halford stopped midway through putting on his coat and stared at him. "Hasn't anyone told them the body won't be released until we've made an arrest?"

The scent of spearmint filled Halford's nose as Roan smiled. "We figured we'd let the Yard do their job," the inspector said slyly. "So, please, once again, make yourself at home in Hampshire."

It was a little before eleven when Halford parked his car on the grassy verge on Boundary Road and with Maura walked to where PC Baylor stood with his arms outstretched, indicating roughly the scene of the crime. The dull sun seemed unable to burn off the morning frost: Halford wondered if Saturday morning had been as bleak; if Lisa, ascending, had been able to break through those fortressed clouds. He cleared his throat.

"I'll want to visit the morgue next. Has the inquest been scheduled?"

"Tomorrow at ten," Baylor answered.

Halford looked at the constable, surprised. "A bit soon, isn't it?"

Baylor grimaced. "Quick and quiet is the order, sir. Or so I've heard."

Halford flinched and turned his attention to the lay-out of the crime scene. The victim's body had been found at the apex of the curve. The road disappeared from sight roughly fifty yards on either side. The sound of a car approaching sent the police officers to the verge well before a white Uno rounded the bend. It swerved a little to avoid the parked Ford, then clipped past.

"Well-travelled, this road?" Maura asked.

"Certain times it is. It mainly connects Heather-wood Beach, the estate where Lisa's family lives, with the village. But there are several small feeder lanes that a lot of the farmers use, and some people taking the back roads from Winchester to Alresford use it as a ringway. So there's traffic right along, but I'd say it's heaviest before nine-thirty in the morning and then again between four-thirty and seven."

"How many cars on a Saturday morning?"

Baylor calculated, clicking his teeth. "There's about thirty homes in Heatherwood Beach. Not all use this road to leave Fetherbridge—there's another on the northern side. But my guess, counting coming and go-ing and the odd driver here and there, about fifty, sixty cars a day, maybe a little less on Saturday."

"That's not very many." Maura looked eastward up the road. "If you didn't fumble about much, you could kill someone here and be fairly certain of leaving with-out being seen."

Halford knelt beside the patch of tarmac near Bay-lor's feet. Except for two white scrapes and a single three-centimeter gouge, the asphalt was clean. He recalled the photographs of the corpse. The bicycle, front wheel perpendicular to the ground, had rested at an approximate thirty-degree angle from the edge of the road. From the position of her legs—the left tucked neatly under the seat, the right stretched out over the rear wheel—it appeared that Lisa had made no attempt to move the bicycle from her body. Her torso had rested sideways on the ground.

But it was her head that had made Halford, as seasoned as he felt himself to be, shudder. The photographer had taken a series of shots low to the ground, centred on her face. They were horrific. Unlike the faces of many corpses he had seen, the skin was intact; the only blood was a thick, crooked line where the crimson froth from her gaping mouth merged with the flow from her cut lip. What had caught at his stomach was the effect of the white scarf running tautly from the bicycle wheel to Lisa's neck. The strength of the woven wool forced the head upright so it appeared that she was raising her head to gaze over the upended wheel to the road beyond. Black hair trailed to the pavement like a flange. It must have been a hellish scene—this vacant road and frozen field, the twisted bicycle, and the head of this mere girl, lifted and steady as if she meant to watch her own life seep away. Halford thought of her brother, rounding the road at this copse of trees and slowly comprehending the horror before him.

Halford straightened and stifled an impulse to pull his coat tighter around him. "The report says she left home sometime after nine o'clock Saturday morning and her brother found her body around ten-thirty. So we're not exactly talking about off hours, are we? Even on a Saturday people are up and about by then. I'd say planning a killing for nine-thirty in the morning is taking quite a chance."

"Perhaps it was an impulse killing," the constable

suggested. "Someone spotted her riding by, thought this was as good a chance as any."

"And just happened to be carrying a blunt stick?" Halford shook his head. "Besides, it would take some quick thinking to figure out a way to make it look like an accident on the spur of the moment. Unless it was something the murderer had thought about for a while and he was simply waiting his opportunity. It doesn't seem likely.

"Something else ... The murderer obviously wanted this to appear an accident. Let's say he or she didn't think about traces of wood in the spokes. Nevertheless, why would he pitch the stick—two sticks, as it turned out—so close to the scene? He could have disposed of them anywhere and we'd have had a devil of a time finding them. Or for that matter, he could have burned them. Or whittled them down to nothing. Why throw them away where we are most likely to look?" He stopped abruptly. "You said you found the first several hundred feet from the scene? About here?"

Baylor pointed to the line where the long grasses of the verge met the shorn stalks of a brown field. "About there, sir. Just laying atop the stubble."

Halford frowned. "If the murderer was in a car, he'd be risking Lisa slamming into him as she fell, utterly destroying the accident setup. And again, why throw the stick away if you can hide it in your car? He had to have some form of transportation that would give him the same speed as the bicycle and put him close enough that he could reach out and jab the stick into the spokes."

Maura checked her notes. "The stick was about forty-six centimeters."

"Could have been a motorbike, sir, but the girl's bicycle must have been going fairly slow. It might have been hard to balance the motorbike, steer it, and use the stick at a low speed." Baylor shrugged. "It could have been another bicycle. Or a moped."

"I suppose bicycles and mopeds are as common as flint around here."

"Afraid so, sir. It's the simplest way to get around town. We don't allow cars on the High Street."

"So," Halford said, "what we've got is a cyclist of some sort pedalling away from a dead body with two parts of a stick in his hand. He decides not to take them with him, but rather throws them away several hundred feet from the body. Why?"

"The way this road curves, Daniel, perhaps he heard a car coming and threw the sticks away before it came round the bend."

"So what are we saying? That not only did someone pass the murderer on the road, but also came across the body without notifying anyone?"

Baylor shook his head. "I don't know, sir. Just doesn't seem like Fetherbridge. Now in London, I'd understand it. But here? It just doesn't fly."

•

Bobby Grissom kept a picture of Carl Bernstein taped on the edge of his word processor like a teenage girl keeps photos of her boyfriend on her vanity mirror. He loved him. He big-kissing-lips loved him. He loved him in the way a soccer fanatic loved an idol—passionately, unreservedly, don't-talk-faggot-to-me-I-love-this-bloke loved him. Sure, there were British journalists who had done good work, but in Bobby Grissom's book no one in the Commonwealth world of the press could top Carl Bernstein and his Watergate miracle. Bernstein even had the face of a fighter. It looked ugly, punched, tired. Someday, if he worked really hard, Grissom hoped to look as bad.

Grissom drummed a pencil on his desk. All in all it hadn't been a bad few days. As head reporter for the biweekly *Hampshire Inquisitor*, Grissom had seen his share of misery—hours that ticked by while he listened to old biddies cluck about their latest fund-raising tea, or vacant-eyed birds with too much hair lacquer burble about the unrivaled bliss of being chosen Miss Raw

Milk Curd. His dad was always going on about him having to pay his dues. Well, dues he'd paid aplenty, shilling for the good old *HI*. When he was finally ensconced in front of his own terminal at one of the London papers, he was going to carry a card: "I Paid My Effin' Dues. Now Get Out of My Bleedin' Face."

He turned to his computer and began typing out headlines. "Death By Bicycle." "Death Rides on Two Wheels." "The Wages for Tardiness: Death!" He knew that Orrin had already chosen the bland "Accident Claims Local Girl" as the leader for today's newspaper, but he could dream. Someday, by God, he would be in the position to decide.

The ringing of his desk phone broke into his glee. "*The Hampshire Inquisitor.* Grissom." With a tip of a hat to his hero, Bobby tried to lace his native Islington accent with a hint of New York.

He fell silent, listening to the voice on the other end. His eyes narrowed, then gleamed. "Thank you. Thank you so much."

He hung up the phone as his editor walked into the room.

"They've called in New Scotland Yard."

Orrin Ivory stopped. "What?"

"That was Mitch Yates. He's been watching out the window of the greengrocer's since the car arrived this morning. Man and woman. Went into the police station—that Inspector Roan from Winchester was already there. They came out a little while later with Baylor and drove off." Bobby Grissom swung his chair back and forth and studied his editor's reaction. "I'll wager a fiver there's more to Lisa Stillwell's accident than Baylor's been letting on."

A flicker of pain crossed Ivory's beefy face. He closed his eyes and sighed. "Christ. Get down there and see what you can find. Ring it in. You have twenty minutes."

Grissom shrugged into his coat and scrambled

through the litter of papers on his desk in search of a notepad. He could hardly believe his luck.

"Damn, Orrin, what if it's murder? What if the silly bird went and got herself killed?"

"Bobby." Orrin's voice was weary. "You're living in a community here, not a gangster film. Please remember that whatever happened, there are people around you who are grieving. Lisa was well loved in this village."

Grissom had the decency to let his embarrassment percolate a moment before forging on. "Sorry, Orrin. I know Lisa was a friend of your daughter's."

Ivory reached into his pocket and pulled out a roll of Tums. He flipped at the corners of the photographer's logbook. A slight glimmer, like old tinsel, came to his eyes.

"Twenty years in this business and I thought I had outlived my chance at playing *The Front Page*." As Grissom headed for the stairs, Ivory picked up the phone and fairly shouted into the receiver. "Hold the presses!" Anyone would think he was almost singing.

5

A tall stack of worn notebooks and yellowing newspapers accordioned across Gale's mahogany desk, and sheets of paper cluttered the study floor like shavings, testimony to a preschooler's unfettered exploration. Gale crouched beside the fallen sheets, staring blankly at them. Everything needed to be picked up, put straight. Soon this stunned inaction would have to give way and she would start work again. Her notes needed to be in order. Wearily, she leaned against the desk and closed her eyes. It was all too much of an effort.

At thirty, Gale knew one or two things about death. The first thing she knew, slapped into her brain three years earlier by her husband's suicide, was that her family had lied to her. Death was an anticipated event when she was growing up, surrounded as she was by aging matriarchs and groaning houses. Death brought neither horror nor sorrow—at most there was a momentary confusion as the living waited to redirect their attention.

As a child, Gale spent every summer in her Great-Aunt Nora's yawning sorrel brick house in Statlers Cross, a dust mite of a town in the middle of the Georgia piedmont. She remembered Nora as a red-lipped woman with hair dyed coal black and cottony like a play wig and a voice set between a warble and a squeak. When Gale was thirteen, Nora died suddenly. After the funeral some of the women in the family, still dressed in their girdles and somber garb, retreated to Nora's house to start the slow process of sorting her things.

The mood had been sober at first, the quiet pricking the air like pinpoints. They dumped their coats in the parlour, then looked at one another for a moment, arms raised slightly from their sides in a communal question of what to do next. The house smelled mothy, as if Nora had parted years ago instead of dying suddenly the week before. Gale longed to leave. The idea of all the intimacies in all those closets, the silverfish devouring the books, the dark stains of leaked perfume left unwashed on clothing, the dust built up on the shell figurines of parasoled ladies and fiddle-playing frogs— it was more than she wanted to handle.

Her grandmother finally settled it. She looked at her three daughters and one granddaughter, then eased herself down into an oversized green velvet chair by the window.

"Ya'll take Gale Lynn and go on," she ordered, dismissing them with a wave. "Show her everything. Wake me if you find any dresses I might like to wear."

And then she settled back and closed her eyes. The rest trooped upstairs to Nora's bedroom, opening drawers, hauling boxes from beneath the bed. They started out whispering, but the whispers soon turned

to chatter, the chatter to giggles. They took turns trying
on clothes, each one dipping into the closet and leaping
out with more and more outrageous costumes until
they were doubled over with laughter. They went
through trunks, photograph albums, dresser after
dresser of tattered souvenirs, decaying letters, broken
jewellery. Each piece became a contest—What did it
mean? Where did she get it? Every trinket both told
and withheld stories. By the time they opened the final
closet three days later, Gale knew she was going to
become a historian.

She left that house only half understanding death.
Tragic death lay in her future; mythic death, the death
of old ladies with skin too powdery for the sun and
fingers with nothing left to do but pick at the threads
of their fraying skirts—this was all she knew. It was so
sensible, so perfect, this passage of Nora's life from her
body to her belongings. Nora was no longer the high-
hipped old woman who made Gale count the silver-
ware every night after supper. She was now the
artifacts, the books, the clothes, the torn railway tickets
in the bottom of her desk drawer. It wasn't until thirteen years later when a Scotland Yard detective and his
female sergeant sat in Gale's own house, fingered her
own trinkets, that death finally bit Gale, grabbing her
in its teeth and shaking her until her soul tore.

And now Lisa—Lisa with her jiggling feet crooked
over the rungs of Gale's kitchen chairs, poring over her
charge's baby albums; Lisa with Katie Pru in her arms,
laughing and rolling over the quilts on the living room
floor; Lisa with her consoling eyes, low voice, sympathetic questions, probing all the bruised places . . .

Gale started at the sound of Katie Pru toddling into
the study, her patchwork dinosaur under one arm and
a large silver slotted spoon clutched in her hand.

"Space Lucy's hungry," she announced. "Gotta feed
him."

Gale rose from the floor. "Be careful, ladybug. That
spoon's old."

"Old, old, old." Katie Pru half muttered, half sang the word over and over as she crammed the antique into the dinosaur's wide cotton mouth.

Gale shrugged. The spoon was almost a culinary weapon, heavy, with a baroque entanglement of vines and lilies that ran down its handle, around the rim of the bowl, ending with narrow leaves bending their tips into the points of palmetto cutouts. Gale knew she shouldn't let Katie Pru play with it. The spoon had been in the family for six generations, surviving, the story went, the fiery scorched earth of Sherman's march. Actually, Gale doubted it; as far as she could determine, Sherman's devastating swath missed her family's home by twelve miles, and the silver company named on the spoon's handle hadn't hit its stride until the late 1800's. Nevertheless, the family mythology could be true. Renegade Yankee raiders, like chickweed, spread unchecked through the Civil War South, and her great-great-great-grandmother could have recognized a quality product before the rest of the nation caught on. At any rate, the spoon's tale was what her grandmother had told her—Gale suspected it would be what she herself told Katie Pru.

The phone rang as she heard the crackle of bicycle wheels on her garden walk. By the time Helen Pane stood in the doorway, Gale had picked up the spoon from the floor where Katie Pru had dropped it, and hurled it at the wall.

Gale pulled a hank of wool over the teeth of a wooden card and combed furiously—one, two, three, reverse, one, two, three, reverse. The air around the love seat was gauzy with dander whipped loose from the tangle of fibers. Flecks of dirt danced at her elbow, avoiding its hell-to-be-paid jerks, and finally blew upwards to perch on her hair, safe above the fray.

Across the room Helen watched the melee in silence. Her tea had been cold for nearly an hour, but every now and then she still picked up the cup and tilted it to her lips as if she were the only real person at this tea party.

The clacking of the cards made a mill-sized din in the study's stuffed space. Helen spoke loudly.

"I bet that's saved you a lot of tranquillisers over the years. It's so mesmerizing, so soothing. I understand Gandhi used to meditate by it."

Gale glared at her. "Why are they here? Of all the detectives in Scotland Yard, why *them*?"

Helen rested her teacup on its saucer. One stray mote of dirt whisked from the hive around the love seat and settled on her stockings. Damned expensive stockings, Helen thought, as she pressed the particle into her thumb and flicked it away.

"Want me to ring Orrin again?" she asked. "It's been thirty minutes. Perhaps he's heard something else."

Gale shook her head and jabbed one card into the other until a fluffy roll of wool rose from the metal teeth. Thrusting her fingers into it, she threw the fluff into a basket already overflowing with soft mounds of teased fiber. Helen patted her hair. When she got home, she was definitely going to clean her hairbrushes.

For an hour, while Helen had busied herself settling Katie Pru, making tea, and prodding Orrin over the phone for information, Gale had ripped wool and piled up rolags in a rhythmic fury. The caller on the phone had been DS Maura Ramsden, asking if it would be all right for her and Chief Inspector Daniel Halford to come by around two-thirty. A few questions. Just routine.

"She was very polite," Gale told Helen savagely, for the third time. "I can't get over it. She introduced herself as if I had never heard of her or the monkey-humping Metropolitan Police."

Gale glanced at Katie Pru who was contentedly smashing biscuits under Space Lucy's feet. Her eyes welled. "God, Helen. Do you know that in the three years since Katie Pru was born I have never lost my temper around her? I've gotten angry, I've fussed, I've even stomped, but I've never so much as raised my voice. I can't believe I threw that spoon. How could I have let them do that to me?''

Helen watched the child dip the dinosaur's snout into a half-full teacup. "Well, if it's Katie Pru you're worried about, don't. I think if she were scarred for life, she'd have sent for her solicitor by now.''

Gale twisted her arm to check her watch, a mannerism that in the past hour had taken on the attributes of a tic. "Another fifty minutes," she said. Shivering, she tossed the wool cards into the basket and walked to the fireplace. "I know I'm overreacting." Helen said nothing. "I can't even focus on the fact that Lisa may have been murdered. I just would rather they weren't here. Anyone else but them.''

Helen rose to stand by the window. A haze hung over Gale's pathetic garden. Brown vines curled over wall and grounds like decomposing snakes. Why couldn't Americans make a proper garden, for Chrissakes? Others in the village still clucked their tongues when they talked about Gale's small patch of land. Evidently when Tom's mother had lived here, the front garden had been festooned with clematis, primrose, and hollyhock. Now her dead efforts trailed the ground and bunched at the side of the house like dusty feces. Helen had to agree with the villagers: The grounds lent the whole of Gale's cottage a parched, witchy air. She wondered if there would come a time when children dared each other to run past the cottage at night, and if so, would Gale still be here.

"I'm not sure I understand your reaction, Gale. I mean, you can't think they suspect you of killing Lisa.''

When Gale didn't answer, Helen turned around. Gale had removed the fireguard and appeared to ponder the hearth's black space.

"No," Gale told her levelly. "I'm not worried that they think I killed Lisa. But I do know one thing. Those two are here because of me, because of my connection to Lisa."

"So what of it? They're policemen, for pity's sake. That's their job, to see connections. It's how they earn their pay. Don't take it personally."

Gale's brown eyes narrowed. "I can't believe you said that."

Helen threw up her arms and strode to the love seat. Space Lucy growled and nipped at her ankle as she passed. Frowning, Helen mused briefly about her own inability to truly understand or even enjoy children. They seemed so . . . unlikely. She stepped over Katie Pru's outstretched arm and sat down.

"Listen to yourself, Gale. You sound like one of those damn American conspiracy theorists. 'We're the centre of the world and everyone's out to get us.' The truth is Oswald shot JFK because he was the only one with enough time on his hands to worry about it."

She picked up a fluff of wool from the edge of the cushion and rolled it between her fingers. She felt Gale regarding her carefully.

"So you've decided I'm being paranoid."

"No, sweets, I've decided you're being Gale. But the truth is we don't condone witch hunts these days— they're considered politically incorrect. And policemen don't go around identifying suspects based on tea leaves or tarot cards. Or, for that matter, their dead husband's loopy beliefs. They have laboratories for that sort of thing."

"So I should just let them come and ask their questions."

"Yes. And serve thcm tea." Helen examined the tangled wool in her palm. "It's polite and it gives you something relatively tidy to do with your hands."

The house in Heatherwood Beach was typical middle-class fare: a semidetached with a short drive on one side that had scarce room for the beige minivan the Stillwells had angled onto it. A row of low bushes lined the front of the house to the door, and propped against a holly bush was a black, ten-speed bicycle.

Halford's knock was answered by a man with washed-out brown hair and lips formed too close to the bottom of his nose. Maura had called earlier to arrange an appointment; nevertheless, Edgar Stillwell looked at Halford like a man caught off guard. He gazed wordlessly at Halford's warrant card; his eyes, lost in the folds of bloated lids, roamed vacantly over the detective's photograph. Halford was about to request entry a second time when the man abruptly pushed the door wider and retreated into the front room. He stood by the plate glass window staring at the street.

"This isn't good, is it?" Stillwell's voice was phlegmy. "They don't call in Scotland Yard when a girl falls off her bicycle."

Halford modulated his voice to sound both non-committal and kind. "Mr. Stillwell, I'm afraid Lisa's death wasn't an accident. We have evidence that someone killed her. We need to talk to you."

Stillwell's shoulders sloped further into the sleeves of his mousy brown cardigan. Several small moth holes pocked the cardigan's front; here and there the wool had snagged lint, and dried brown patches, possibly dough, encrusted the rim of the cardigan's ribbed cuffs. When he slumped into an armchair, a button caught in his belt and popped the garment open.

The room, a mean space measuring not more than ten feet by eleven, contained only three pieces of furniture: the blue and white chintz armchair in which Stillwell sat, a long red jacquard sofa, and a Mediterranean-style coffee table which, Halford discovered as he surreptitiously knocked his knuckle against it, was primarily plastic. Neither of the upholstered pieces would stand up to close inspection—the sofa fabric felt slick and cheap as he settled on a crimson cushion. Halford noticed there were no lamps except for the ceiling light, which Stillwell left switched off. Pallid natural light seeped in through the picture window. Halford wondered if the dimness was part of the decorating scheme.

Stillwell sat with his head bent, his eyes closed. Tiny bulbs of flesh hung down among his eyelashes. According to the report he was forty-five. Halford would have guessed sixty.

Halford glanced at Maura, then leaned forward. "Mr. Stillwell, was anybody home when Lisa left Saturday morning?"

Stillwell's eyes opened. "No. Brian, my son—he's upstairs now—he and I were at the bakery."

"What time did you get there?"

"Six. Lisa didn't usually get up until seven. She'd leave around nine to get to work."

"Did she usually ride her bicycle?"

"Every morning it wasn't raining, most when it was. If the weather was bad, I'd either send Brian around for her or Gale Grayson would pick her up herself. She has an old Mini. Black."

The emphasis on the word "black" made Halford change his next question. "Did you like your daughter working for Mrs. Grayson?"

The man barked a laugh. But when he looked at Halford, his eyes had grown moist. "Sure. I sent my daughter to secretarial college so she could go change dirty nappies for Tom Grayson's brat. That's right. That's what I did."

The acid bitterness in Stillwell's answer surprised Halford. He should have guessed there would be some residual ill will toward Tom Grayson, but the Graysons were an old family by Fetherbridge standards, part of the village's original crew. While it might be acceptable to castigate one member of a family, surely it was a trifle odd to extend the disdain to a baby.

"So did you like Lisa working for Mrs. Grayson?"

Stillwell looked out to the foyer. Tears fell. He didn't bother to wipe them away. "No, dammit. She could have done better for herself. Gone to Southampton or London even. I don't know why she wanted to stay here. She said she loved the child. Well, it isn't your child, is it, I tell her. If you want to love a child, get married and raise your own." His sob was ragged.

Maura reached into the pocket of her blazer, pulled out a white linen square and pressed it into Stillwell's palm. He held it flat against his face with both hands like a child playing peek-a-boo. Halford nodded at Maura. She rose silently from her chair and patted the sobbing man's arm.

"I'm going to make some tea, Mr. Stillwell," she said. "Then we can go on."

Stillwell held the handkerchief to his mouth and lowered his head.

"Would you mind, Mr. Stillwell, while Sergeant Ramsden is fixing the tea, if I look around? I particularly want to see your daughter's room."

Stillwell closed his eyes and shook his head once. Except for the hard wrinkle between his eyebrows, one would think he had nodded off to sleep.

Halford hiked the stairs to the upper storey two at a time. Three doors led off a cramped central hall. The first was ajar, leading to what was certainly Stillwell's bedroom. It was a spartan affair with an unmade bed, a chest of drawers, and a bedside table. There were no pictures on the walls, neither photographs nor prints. A single pair of worn brown slippers sat empty next to the bed. Briskly, Halford flipped through the contents in the drawers and the cupboard, noting the musty smell of unwashed pyjamas and the jumbled pile of blue socks. Two rumpled white shirts hung from wire hangers. The report said that Madge Stillwell had left seven years ago—"bolted," as Baylor put it. This was a room almost forlorn in its maleness. It reminded Halford a bit of his own. He left quickly.

The doors to the other rooms were shut. Guessing which was Lisa's, he correctly settled on the one facing the road. When he opened the door, he couldn't decide if he was startled or not. Other than his on-the-job training in the home decor of witnesses and suspects, he was not knowledgeable about interior design; this room, however, showed flair and not a little cost. An iron-and-brass canopy bed dominated the room, hung with swags of white gauze and an intricately knitted white cotton spread. Needlepoint pillows covered the larger bed pillows, and in the center of these sat a porcelain doll, its dirty white dress evidence of childhood play. A lacy blanket—actually too delicate to be what he considered a blanket—was folded at the foot of the bed to display detailed ribbonwork. The chest of drawers and wardrobe were painted white, with elaborate floral designs. Multicoloured perfume bottles topped a matching vanity. The baker's daughter had expensive tastes.

Halford moved to the wardrobe. Several dresses, well cut and cared for, hung neatly from hangers. Seven pairs of shoes sat side by side on the floor. Draped on a rod mounted on the door were three wide woollen stoles and a scarf. He fingered the scarf gently. Like the one in the crime scene photos, it was woven with decorative openings. Unlike the murder weapon, however, this one was a deep red. Irrationally, he found himself grateful Lisa had decided on her last day to wear the white.

In the chest of drawers, silky underwear was folded carefully. Nothing crammed, nothing jumbled. He thought of his sister's dresser, stuffed so tightly during her adolescent years the back threatened to pop its staples. Had Lisa come to this gentility recently or had she been a prim teen inside this cheap, cramped house?

The only books he had thus far seen in the house sat in a two-shelf bookcase under Lisa's window. They consisted mainly of photo-heavy decorating and cookery books, the latter, he thought, an odd inclusion in a bedroom. The novels were by Jane Austen, V.S. Naipaul, Lewis Carroll, and Jackie Collins. He clicked his tongue. Lisa Stillwell was becoming curiouser and curiouser.

Idly, he pulled the Naipaul from the shelf. A set of

folded papers fell to the floor at his knee. They were the standard lined, three-hole notebook fare, the outermost sheet stiff and wrinkled. Halford spread them open. In green ink across the bottom of the first page were written the words "My Dream House." The rest of the page was filled with the ground-floor plan of a massive house, complete with ballroom, conservatory, library. The second sheet was the upper storey, with numerous bedrooms and lavatories, an exercise gym, and a snaking hallway that ended with a slide connected to an indoor pool on the lower level. Drawn without precision, the plans nevertheless included rough room dimensions: ballroom, 60' × 35'; kitchen, 30' × 30', dining room, 40' × 20'. Halford mused on the inaccuracies of youthful perceptions. Fully built, the house would be the size of a cricket field.

The final page, stiff with paste, held samples of fabric and wallpaper, as well as china and silver patterns clipped from store catalogues. Halford ran his finger over a piece of wallpaper, a deep mauve snippet too small to delineate the pattern. Halford remembered his sister having a similar house plan when she was growing up; it seemed to him that all her girlfriends did, kept in little notebooks and shared in the privacy of their bedrooms. But she had been around twelve or thirteen at the time. He peered closely at the papers in his hand. They seemed fairly new. A bit strange for a twenty-two-year-old.

Sliding the papers back into the bookcase, Halford shut Lisa's door behind him. He stood silently a few seconds in front of the last bedroom before rapping softly. Bedsprings creaked and he thought he detected the sound of a lamp being switched on. The door was opened by a spotty young man with an overbite so disfiguring Halford barely kept the shock out of his eyes.

"Brian?" The boy nodded. Halford held out his ID. "I'm Chief Inspector Halford from New Scotland Yard. May I talk to you a minute?"

The young man's swollen lips flexed rapidly. He

looked at Halford with rich blue eyes. When he spoke, his voice was a raspy whisper.

"You don't think it was an accident. I could hear. You think someone did it on purpose."

"Will you let me in?" Halford asked gently. "You can help me, Brian. You can help Lisa."

Brian stood aside and let Halford into the room. Here, as with his father, the sparsity rule prevailed. Bed, dresser, bedside table. The only difference between this and Edgar Stillwell's bedchamber was the presence of a small black-and-white TV on the dresser.

The bed was a mess of crumpled pillows and blankets, but it provided the room's only seating. Brian hugged a pillow to his chest and snuggled against the headboard while Halford sat a nonthreatening distance at the foot.

"I'm sorry about Lisa," Halford began, but when he saw the pillow being forced deeper into the boy's stomach, he changed to a more businesslike tone. "Can you tell me what made you go to Boundary Road Saturday morning?"

When Brian started speaking from behind the pillow, Halford leaned forward and gently pulled the edge away from the teenager's mouth. For a moment Brian managed a self-conscious grin, as if he knew this was not how an adult should act around police but it was the best he could do. Halford smiled back and took out his pen and notebook.

"Do you mind if I take notes? Usually I can remember everything, but you never know when the brain's going to give its last hurrah."

Brian nodded, and Halford hoped the heave of the boy's shoulders signaled relaxation.

"Gale rang the bakery," Brian said. "She wanted to know if Lisa was sick or something because she hadn't shown. That's when I took the van and went looking for her."

"What time was it when Mrs. Grayson rang?"

"Quarter after ten."

"You sure about that?"

"Sure, I'm sure. You hear your sister's not shown, you look to see what time it is."

"Which route did you take?"

Here Brian sucked the pillow deeper. "Not the route I shoulda. I went down Barley Lane to the west entrance to the neighborhood. I thought she might have been at the house hurt."

"That was a reasonable route to select."

"But if I had gone down Boundary Road first, maybe I could have stopped whoever it was. Maybe I could have seen something." His voice sounded raw with despair.

The boy's hair, black like his sister's, was flattened by sweat against his forehead. He never looked in the direction of Halford's face; instead he kept his eyes trained on the bedpost beside the detective's knee. It was hard for Halford to believe the boy was nineteen. His slightly pudgy features, more pronounced because of his teeth, looked babyish. His demeanour, even for one shocked by loss, was that of a scared child. It was that child Halford tried to console.

"I don't think there was anything you could have done, Brian. I think it's natural to want to believe you could have prevented a tragedy, to think that if you had only acted differently . . ." He trailed to silence. He wasn't going to console the boy with lies.

Brian didn't respond anyway. His eyes blinked at the bedpost, his fingers kneaded the pillowcase.

Halford began again. "Tell me, why did you think she might be at home hurt?"

Brian's fingers stopped. "What do you mean?"

"You said you thought she might be hurt. Was there any reason for you to think that? She could have been sick."

The fingers started working again, faster. "I meant sick. I didn't mean hurt, I just said the wrong word."

"What did you do when you saw she wasn't at home?"

"I went down Boundary Road toward Gale's. It's how Lisa always went." The pillow went into the mouth again.

"And you found her?"

Brian nodded.

"Did you see anyone, pass anyone on the side of the road, either before or after you found her?"

"I passed Miss Forrester walking on the High Street as I left the bakery. That was all."

"Miss Forrester?"

"Yeah. Editha Forrester. An old lady, over on Smith Lane."

"Could you tell me how you spent your morning before Mrs. Grayson called?"

Saliva glazed the pillow where it seeped out from the corners of his mouth. He talked around it. "Like I spend every morning, except Sunday. Me and Dad were at the bakery. We got there at six. He made the dough for the bread while I readied the ovens, and then I made the loaves. We were well into selling when Gale called."

"Did either you or your father leave the bakery at any time before you went to look for Lisa?"

"No."

"Tell me, Brian: Who were your sister's friends?"

It was a full minute before the boy brought the pillow down and answered. Then the words were mumbled and dull.

"She had her church friends. They hung out, particularly Jill Ivory. Then there was Helen Pane. And Gale and Katie Pru. She loved Katie Pru."

"Did she ever mention anyone she had problems with? Arguments, maybe? Disagreements?"

Brian's head jerked. "Lisa? There were no problems with Lisa. My God, everyone loved her. You just ask them. You just go ask anyone!"

Halford closed his notebook and pushed himself off the bed. "I will, Brian. Thank you." As he closed the bedroom door behind him, he glanced back at the boy.

He was hunched over, staring at the bedpost, the corner of the pillow even deeper in his mouth.

In the front room, Edgar Stillwell was downing the last drops of Maura's tea. She glanced up from her notes as Halford entered the room.

"Sir," she said. "I've asked Mr. Stillwell the rest of the questions. But we need to discuss something with him."

Halford nodded grimly and returned to his seat on the red sofa.

"Mr. Stillwell," he began. "We're treating Lisa's death as a murder. The coroner's inquest will be tomorrow, but I'm sure he'll simply adjourn it until we close the case." He paused, letting the man absorb the information. "I understand you've made some plans for a funeral. I'm afraid you'll have to delay them."

Stillwell stared at him over the teacup. "What are you talking about?"

Halford took a deep breath. "The funeral, Mr. Stillwell," he said quietly. "I'm afraid we can't release Lisa's body to you yet. We have to keep her until an arrest is made. The defence has to be able to conduct its own postmortem."

Stillwell's face paled, then flamed. The cup clunked onto the thin carpet.

"What do you mean I can't have my daughter?" His facial muscles worked for control. "It's set. She's to be buried with her mum in the church cemetery. I've already spoken with the vicar. It's to be done."

Halford remained calm. "I'm sorry, Mr. Stillwell. Hopefully we'll close the case quickly and you can have the services as soon as possible."

Stillwell leapt from his chair, towering over Halford with his fists clenched. Quickly, Halford rose and stepped sideways, putting several feet between them.

"I'll have my daughter, you bastard. I'll give her a decent burial. You'll not keep her in some bloody bag while you and your men fuck around. You can't do it!"

Maura stood at Halford's elbow. "Let me call someone for you, Mr. Stillwell. Who would you like to come stay with you?"

Stillwell ignored her. His swollen lips and small eyes were engorged with rage. "Tell me you'll give me my daughter!"

"Should I ring the vicar?" Maura murmured to Halford.

"Wait," he said.

Halford spread his legs apart, prepared for Stillwell's anger to turn violent.

"I'm sorry, Mr. Stillwell," he said firmly. "I wish I could do something for you. But this is the procedure. This is the law."

Something in Stillwell suddenly broke. The whole of his body slumped. Shaking, he sagged back into his chair. At first his sobs were inaudible. Then they filled the room with a stream of horrid, steady hacks.

Maura hurried from the room to find a phone. Halford watched the man for a moment, feeling in his own chest the horrible drag of air as Stillwell's shoulders pumped in agony. There was nothing for Halford to do. He left the grieving father to endure alone.

6

It was just past two-thirty when the detectives finally drove away from the Stillwell house. The vicar had been out of reach; instead, Maura rang PC Baylor, who arrived at the house with an assuaging combination of familiarity, authority, and concern. As Maura and Halford slipped out the front door, they had heard the constable's affable voice soothing the elder Stillwell.

"There now, Edgar, these things really do have a rhyme to them. It's nothing you have to worry about. Let us handle it all for you. Now, let me see if Editha can come over. . . ."

Comforting words. Halford wondered if Baylor really believed them.

Halford drove the Ford through the Boundary Road

exit of Heatherwood Beach and into a spattering rain. That morning the skies had looked pregnant with clouds that would sooner fall solid to the ground than break open. Now they had diminished into a weeping curve of bright haze that made his eyes water.

Maura pulled a plastic bag of sliced carrots and a box of raisins from the glove box.

"Interesting household," she said, snapping open the bag and extending it to Halford. "I counted five matching sets of cloth napkins in the pantry. Three lace tablecloths. Very elegant crystal glasses. Not exactly what I expected from a motherless family of three."

Halford took a carrot and crunched it in half. "Perhaps not so odd for a baker's family."

"Right. Dinnertime ambience is important, yet the father can't see his way to keeping his cardigan clean. That wasn't recent dirt on his clothes. You can't chalk it up to grief."

They followed the U-bend around the edge of the copse and glided over the spot where Lisa's body had lain. For several seconds they were silent, letting the fields slide by, shade after shade of diminishing green. Then Halford reached across the seat, grabbed the box of raisins, and dumped some in his mouth.

"Let's go over again what we got from Edgar Stillwell."

Maura rubbed her hands and opened her notebook. "Lisa started working for Mrs. Grayson six months ago. Her father doesn't know how much she was paid, but it was enough to keep her from seeking a secretarial job. She worked four days a week, roughly nine to four, basically looking after the daughter and doing a bit of light housekeeping. She was active in St. Martin's Church, went on regular junkets to the coast and London with friends, although she had no special beaus. Closest friend was Jill Ivory, the eighteen-year-old daughter of the newspaper editor."

"Orrin Ivory. Remember him? Village father type. All seriousness and manners."

"I remember. According to Stillwell, Lisa and Jill spent a lot of time with Helen Pane, a local used-clothes seller. And then there was that sly bit about the stained glass artist."

"Christian Timbrook," Halford mused. "Peculiar name for an artist. Not exactly uninhibiting."

"Perhaps his father wanted a son interested in lions." Maura bit a carrot. "I don't know how seriously I take Stillwell's assertion that Timbrook and Lisa were not romantically involved. He did seem a little too insistent."

"It'll need looking into. What about the mother?"

"Margaret a.k.a. Madge Stillwell left her family about six and a half years ago. Stillwell came home from work before lunch to change his clothes—it wasn't a regular practice only he'd spilled batter on himself—and she was gone. There was a note saying she loved them but wanted more. Most of her clothes were gone, her shoes were gone, her make-up was gone. So were several photographs of the children."

"I wondered about that. There wasn't a photograph to be seen anywhere in the house."

"Gotcha there, guv. I asked him about photos while you were upstairs. He said he has no pictures of his wife. He took one picture of Lisa from a drawer in the kitchen."

She handed it to him. It was a far cry from the face he had viewed earlier in the hospital mortuary. Lisa had a face transformed by animation. The photograph was a head shot, taken outdoors under what looked like the thorned branches of a wild pear tree. She wasn't laughing—the features were controlled and posed with just a tip to the mouth—but the tilt of her head and the shine of her dark hair and eyes turned her into quite a pretty girl.

He thought of the flaccid face under the sheet.

"We need to confirm that the mother died in a shelter. How old was Mrs. Stillwell when she left?"

"Thirty-five. Stillwell was thirty-seven, Lisa fifteen and Brian twelve."

"So we have a motherless adolescent girl who grows into a young woman with decorating and cookery books in her bedroom, a wardrobe of expensive clothes, the adoration of her brother and father, and childminding as her ambition."

Maura reached over and stuck another piece of carrot in Halford's mouth. She missed, clipping the gum, and he jerked in pain. She grimaced in apology. "You're making it sound like she walked the streets."

"Hell, Maura. She wasn't killed because she was Little Miss Homebody. How threatening can budding domesticity be?"

"Do you really need me to answer that one? I'd say domesticity of any kind can be fairly threatening, given the chance. What did you make of the brother?"

A bank of hedgerow suddenly shuttered the view to their right. The windscreen wipers made recurrent scrapes across the glass as they chased down straggling drops, periodically eclipsing visibility. Halford made no move to adjust their pace.

"I don't know," he said finally. "Socially awkward, perhaps a bit slow, although that's pure supposition. The interesting thing is he has a serious overbite—a deformity, actually. If he were my child, I would have looked into corrective surgery."

"Perhaps National Health wouldn't cover it."

"Surely they do. But if not, that would make the goodies in Lisa's bedroom all the more inexplicable. Why pamper one child to the detriment of the other?"

"You're obviously not the father of girls, Daniel. Brian has a job, a future, following in his father's footsteps as the baker of Fetherbridge. Lot of heritage and probably some security in that. What was the need of straight teeth or natural social graces? Lisa, on the other hand, was a female stuck out here in this village, pretty but not unqualifiedly so—I imagine her father consid-

ered the facade of a dowry a reasonable enough investment.''

"A bit backward, don't you think?''

"Of course. But done, nonetheless.''

Halford glanced at her. "You've gained this insight
from your years of daughterhood?''

" 'Knees together, hands folded in lap, there's a
good girl.' And my parents weren't small-town provin-
cials worried about me supporting myself. I was merely
one more of England's young damsels groomed to act
like a lady. I imagine Lisa was, too.''

"Quaint. Only she hadn't a mother to do the groom-
ing.''

"All the more reason for the frills.''

Halford reached for another carrot stick, but Maura
instead dropped the empty, balled-up bag into his
hand. He tossed it into her lap with a mock scowl.

"You'd think properly reared young ladies would
know how to pack suitable refreshments.''

Maura laughed. "Give over, Daniel. I relinquished
all titles to refinement when I learned how to cosh a
head.''

The outside of the cottage was much as Maura remembered it. A three-foot-high stone wall surrounded
the house and garden, buckled together by a white
wooden gate. She followed Halford down the walkway
to the front door. Given the density of the decay
throughout the garden, the dusty foliage along the edge
of the walk had been whacked back with an almost
brutal hospitality. Crawling vines, their ends flayed out
like exploded cable, had been chopped short, and
patches of yellow grass had been whipped into stiff,
spiked mounds. Bushes crouched sporadically along
the walk, restricting access to the grounds beyond.
There is only one acceptable way in and out of Gale
Grayson's home, Maura thought. Step off the path and
beware the somnolent poppies.

Originally the cottage must have been thatched.

Now the lower-maintenance pantile roof that topped it was black and streaked with age. The dwelling was older than the other buildings in Fetherbridge; Maura recalled a gloomy kitchen with bottle glass panes, a feature, Halford had pointed out during the previous investigation, that would have been unfashionable and impractical by the time the village was built in the mid-1700's. Nevertheless, the plump whitewashed facade and black-banded casement windows fit pleasingly with the other, professionally designed flint structures in town.

Not for the first time, she thought of the widowed Gale Grayson alone with an infant in what was surely for her an uncomfortable world, confined in this small cottage with dirty nappies, souring orange juice, and midnight cries. And that didn't include the publicity, the months of newspaper headlines that finally subsided to a two-line mention now and again before finally disappearing altogether. She marvelled at the woman's decision to stay. After all, Gale Grayson had her own country, her own place. Maybe it was the house. Perhaps it didn't give up its dwellers gladly.

A dark blue bicycle, caked around the pedals with mud, rested against the brambles beside the front door. Maura waited beside it, as Halford stepped up to knock. This didn't promise to be an easy interview. The curtness of Mrs. Grayson's answers over the phone were evidence enough of her trenchant hostility. Nevertheless, Maura felt relaxed. If anyone could handle this witness, it was Halford. Empathy was his number one deductive tool. He was a master at making interrogation seem an act of kindness.

He had his work cut out for him. Gale Grayson didn't actually take a swing at Halford when she opened the door; however, her glare would have sent a less formidable man reeling back a step or two.

Halford flicked his warrant card at her. "Chief Inspector Daniel Halford. New Scotland Yard. We'd like to ask you a few questions concerning Lisa Stillwell's death.''

Maura glanced at him. You get more flies with honey than vinegar, Chief Inspector, she thought. Mrs. Grayson shifted her eyes from Halford to Maura.

"Hello, Mrs. Grayson." Urged by an instinct to calm, Maura pushed past her superior. "I know this is difficult for you, as it is for us, but it might be a bit easier if we could come in and sit down."

Gale Grayson stared at Maura, her knuckles hardened like white tumours on the door frame. Then she turned and led them into the house.

The entrance into the cottage was pleasant enough. The whitewashed walls of the foyer were plain, save for a series of colourful child's drawings framed in matching black. The drawings were joyful and benignly surreal—green suns with pink mouths, spindly, prancing animals with no eyes. It wasn't until she entered the cottage's front room that Maura prickled with uneasiness.

Three years ago, the house could have been a magazine layout for English country freshness. Each room had been a conservatory of flowery chintz mixed with the odd stripe and plaid for a cottony trellis effect. Light oak furniture peeped out of the cloth foliage like pale tree trunks. It had been pleasant up to a point but overdone, as if the decorator had to keep reiterating so as not to lose her focus.

Now the front room could well have seconded for a well-scrubbed monastery workroom. Save for a solitary painting of an urban street scene over the fireplace, there were no pictures, and the windows were covered with simple white sheets. The furniture was dark with shellac, relieved by an occasional red-and-brown quilt. A bare green fir, the lone acknowledgement of the impending Christmas season, was pushed into the far corner, its branches thrust forward as if for balance. Along the wall opposite the fireplace stood a large loom, strung with an appealing black-on-white weaving. Col-

lected around it were two spinning wheels—one large,
one small—several baskets filled with coloured yarns
and monochromatic piles of unspun fibers, and a variety of antique textile apparatus that Maura couldn't
begin to identify. The whole effect was cool and stubborn. Maura's gaze settled on a large earthenware jug.
The monastery analogy had been wrong—this place
looked like a seventeenth-century weaver's cottage,
winter-cold without the warmth and stench of a dozen
lowing sheep.

Mrs. Grayson motioned toward a narrow pew, then
selected a ladder-back chair near the hearth and sat.
Halford looked despairingly around for a few seconds
before trying to angle his long, muscular limbs into the
pew's begrudging space. He perched there like a gan-
gly adolescent forced into a toddler-sized chair. Maura
settled with her pen and notepad onto a bench near the
windows and studied Gale Grayson.

Three years of tragedy and motherhood had altered
her. At the time of her husband's suicide, her face had
been soft and rounded, her hair a glossy brown. A pe-
tite woman, she had struck Maura as doll-like with a
child's dimpled hands and diminutive shoes. Despite
her obvious grief, Mrs. Grayson had taken care of her
appearance before each of their several interviews—she
was always conservatively dressed in a woolen skirt
and, as her pregnancy advanced, an increasingly larger
pullover. Maura had joked at the time that it was all so
properly British, strange for an American girl from
Georgia who more than likely only crawled out of her
jeans for Sunday service.

Now Mrs. Grayson looked smaller, sharper. The
face had thinned, shaving small planes from her cheeks
to her mouth. The chin was slightly pointed, the dark
eyes large and thickly lashed. Her hands had lost their
prenatal chubbiness. The only decorations on her short,
slender fingers were an unremarkable engagement ring
and simple wedding band. But the most startling
change was in her hair. It had grown dull and was

sliced with narrow bands of grey. Some women, Maura knew, actually paid money to achieve these day-and-night swatches; she wondered if trauma had given them to Gale Grayson free of charge.

Maura's eyes moved from the face to the clothes: white cotton shirt, cleaned and pressed, faded jeans, no socks. Decidedly American.

Gale Grayson picked up a brown stole that lay in a heap beside her chair and wrapped it around her shoulders. She kept her eyes on Halford's knees.

Halford cleared his throat.

"Mrs. Grayson," he began softly, "I'm sorry if I was abrupt just now. Sergeant Ramsden is right—this is difficult for us as well. Some places are hard to revisit. But I shouldn't have taken it out on you. We're here on an entirely different matter—Lisa Stillwell's death. I'm hoping you can help us."

Without looking at him, Mrs. Grayson nodded briefly.

"So," Halford continued, "perhaps we could start by learning about Lisa's work here."

The dark eyes rose to Halford's face. Maura couldn't tell if anger, despair, or sorrow poured out of them, but whatever the emotion, it was strong and directed. She could almost feel Halford's decision not to flinch at their force.

When Mrs. Grayson answered Halford, her voice was soft, almost whispery, and held a light Southern intonation Maura didn't recall. It was a pleasurable sound—in other circumstances she could enjoy hearing it over a cup of coffee or, strangely, behind a pulpit.

"Lisa pretty much just kept my daughter, four days a week. They varied." The words came fast. "Sometimes she cleaned up, every now and then she cooked. But mostly I needed her for Katie Pru."

Halford glanced around the room. He leaned forward until his hands dangled between his knees. Maura thought she detected a shiver pass through Mrs. Grayson.

"She worked for you how long?"

"Six months."

"Where did you first meet her?"

"At church. St. Martin's. I met her not long after coming here."

"You attend an Anglican church?"

She looked a little startled at the question. "My cousin—my husband's cousin—is vicar there now."

It was an interesting way not to answer a question. Maura waited for Halford to rephrase.

He did so. "So you've adopted the Anglican faith."

"No, not precisely. I'm Methodist, but I believe in the church as part of the community. If the church here were Catholic or even Pentecostal, I would probably still be involved. Is that explanation enough?"

Halford answered with a grim nod. "How exactly did you meet Lisa there?"

"The youth program. The vicar at that time started a small youth group for all the members under twenty. There aren't that many young people in the village. This was about five years ago, so Lisa was around seventeen. I would go with them on outings sometimes—to the movies, retreats. It seemed the thing to do."

"Were there any people she was particularly close to?"

Mrs. Grayson wrapped the woolly stole around her hand and clutched it like a sock puppet. As she spoke, she grasped her free hand in its mouth, absentmindedly letting it gnaw. "Lisa was good with people," she said carefully. "She seemed to make friends easily, but I'm not so sure how good she was at keeping them. I got the feeling she lost interest in people quickly. But I suppose her closest friend was Jill Ivory, Orrin and Anise Ivory's daughter." She paused. "You might remember them."

"What about boyfriends?"

"I never knew her to be involved with anyone seriously." She fingered the stole's fringe. "There was a time when she was quite taken with Christian Timbrook, the village's local artist, but that seemed to pass. Fetherbridge isn't the greatest place for romance."

Halford let a brief silence build, the word "romance" hanging in the air. Maura looked up at the ceiling's timbered beams, the whitewashed walls. The whole bleeding village was fat with romance: old English buildings, old English ways. But what to make of a quiet American in British garb, married to a poet and living in an ancient cottage in a village built on fancy and perfection? For some reason, the idea bothered Maura. Perhaps it was too facile a suggestion that Mrs. Grayson had exchanged one cultural fantasy for another: the hot, moist land of manners and Spanish moss for the wetter clime of white cliffs and precise diction. And what had been Mrs. Grayson's reaction when her God-is-an-Englishman husband, rather than continuing her fiction, put a bloody end to it?

Rip out the draperies, neuter the furniture, slather the walls in white. Maura let her gaze drift over Mrs. Grayson's head to the fireplace mantel. Below the cityscape watercolour sat a solitary bronze figurine of a child. It was of indeterminable sex, its longish locks suggestive of the Victorian period. Seated on a tree stump, the child appeared to be removing a thorn from its foot.

Halford continued. "What about somewhere else? Could she have met someone in another city?"

"I suppose. She did like to go on road trips. I honestly don't know."

Her voice had drifted into a low, flat drawl, so toneless that Maura found it difficult to interpret the unbroken southern lull.

"And what did you do while Lisa was keeping your daughter?" Halford asked.

Mrs. Grayson's fists mashed the stole into her armpits. "I worked. I'm doing research for a book on the C.S.S. *Alabama*—the Confederate battleship that sank in the Channel during our Civil War. I signed a contract to write it about six months ago and that's when I asked Lisa if she would like to work for me."

"Her father says she went to secretarial college. Surely she was qualified to be more than a childminder."

"That's true, although taking care of a child seven hours a day is a special skill, you understand. But I know what you're asking. When I first talked to Lisa about work, I meant eventually as a writing assistant. But she was looking for something immediately and I did need someone for Katie Pru...." Mrs. Grayson took a deep breath. "So while she kept Katie Pru, I spent most of my time at libraries, some of it across the Channel in Cherbourg doing interviews. And I wrote, though not much at this point."

"Cherbourg is more than a day trip. So Lisa kept Katie Pru overnight sometimes?"

"Well, no. If I had to spend the night somewhere, I took the two of them with me." She hesitated. "It was good for Katie Pru to see other places."

Halford ran his thumb over his moustache. "I read your first book. I thought it quite good. I'm not that familiar with the American Civil War. I didn't know England played such a—ah, surreptitious role. You don't intimidate the neophyte. That's unusual for an academician. I appreciate that."

It was the right thing to say. Mrs. Grayson's mouth lifted into a tentative smile.

"I'm not an academician, really." Her tiny hands fluttered through the air. "I never finished my doctorate. I've always had a problem with the scholarly attitude—I know *I* always felt stupid, so I can imagine what others must feel."

"When is the second book to be published?"

"No date's been set, although the deadline for my first draft is in about eight months."

"You'll have to find someone else to help you, with both the book and your daughter. Not an easy combination to come by, I'd guess."

"I haven't thought about it yet." Sourness tinged her voice. She smiled wryly. "I'll think about that tomorrow."

If Halford caught the Scarlett O'Hara reference, he didn't acknowledge it. "Does Katie Pru have a schedule?" he asked. "What would she and Lisa do while you were working?"

Mrs. Grayson scooped the silver and brown bands behind her ears. Her voice was edged with animation.

"No schedule. I usually asked Lisa to get here between nine and nine-thirty if possible, but sometimes it was later. On days when I had interviews, of course, I had to be more definite, but not most times. And as far as Katie Pru goes, I don't believe in schedules. She eats when she's hungry, sleeps when she's tired. She and Lisa go outside when the inside gets boring, come in when Katie Pru needs some quiet time. My daughter regulates herself."

Halford gazed noncommittally at her, but, Maura noted, Mrs. Grayson now looked back with suspicion.

"What about Saturday? How lax was the schedule on Saturday?"

How "lax" was the schedule? Nice move, Chief Inspector, Maura thought. She's now sussed out that you don't know crap about children.

"As a matter of fact, on Saturday I had an interview with an underwater archaeologist down in Portsmouth at one o'clock and several things to do before I left. I told Lisa to get here promptly at nine."

"Mrs. Grayson, could you please tell us exactly what you did Saturday morning between eight-thirty and eleven o'clock?"

Maura had been waiting for the question, hoping Halford would delay asking it for as long as possible. He had chosen not to. Judging from Mrs. Grayson's reaction, perhaps it wouldn't have mattered. Whatever barriers had been gently crumbling were suddenly in place again, the progress of the last several minutes thrown into reverse—the anger and distrust were back, and Mrs. Grayson's eyes were bearing down on Halford with the malice of a lorry driver hell-bent for homicide.

"At 8:30, I fixed my daughter her breakfast, drank a cup of coffee, and washed up a few dishes. At 9:01 I left Katie Pru playing while I finished getting dressed. At 9:07 I came downstairs and found she had made a mess. At 9:10 I went into the kitchen to get some cleaning supplies. At 9:15 I started getting angry that Lisa wasn't here. At 9:20 I called Mrs. Barker down the street and asked if she could keep Katie Pru for a minute while I ran some errands."

Her voice was low, clipped, and loaded with sarcasm. The southern accent was gone.

"At 9:25 I dropped her off. At 9:30 I arrived at the greengrocer's. At 9:40 I returned home to finish cleaning up the mess Katie Pru had made and to call Lisa, but she wasn't home. At 10:15 I called Edgar Stillwell at the bakery. At 10:20 I left to pick up Katie Pru and came back home. Sometime after eleven Edgar called to say Brian had found Lisa." Here she drew a torn breath. "You see, Mr. Halford, I've been practicing."

The sarcasm had evidently drained her. Her face was flushed. Tears had turned her eyes red, but Maura surmised it was more from the will not to shed them than from grief. Mrs. Grayson reached into her jeans pocket and pulled out a folded piece of paper. She tossed it onto the table in front of her.

"Here. I wrote it all down for you. No point in your getting it wrong."

Maura could guess a score of angry retorts Halford had in his head, but his voice was restrained when he framed the next question.

"You didn't think, before you left on your errands, to call Lisa to see why she was late?"

"No. I was in too much of a hurry."

"Weren't you afraid she might be sick?"

"It was so chaotic—I didn't think about it."

"What method of transport did you use Saturday morning?"

"Moped."

"You ride with your daughter on a moped?"

"She has a small seat on the back. It's quite safe. And she wears a helmet."

"Did anyone see you come back to the house after you left the greengrocer's?"

"I'm sure they must have. I didn't take any back roads. I merely went up the High Street."

"You don't remember anyone in particular? Did you wave to anyone, speak to them?"

"I was in a hurry."

Halford was leaning forward. Though his voice was low, the questions were abrasive in their rapidness, a technique he rarely used outside a police station or before a confession was imminent. Maura felt another pang of compassion for Mrs. Grayson. The woman didn't stand a chance.

"In a hurry to do what?" Halford pressed. "To get home and clean something Lisa would normally have cleaned? Or were you in a hurry for some other reason?"

She started to stammer. "You don't understand. I meant I don't know if anyone saw me or not. I didn't have my glasses on."

"Glasses?"

"My eyeglasses."

"I didn't know you wore any."

"I don't often. Just sometimes."

"But you weren't wearing them Saturday morning."

"I forgot. I do that sometimes."

"Do what?"

"Forget my glasses . . ."

"Intentionally?"

"Yes."

"Why?"

"If I don't want to stop to talk . . . if I don't want to see anyone."

Halford drew himself out of the pew and, walking to the oversized spinning wheel, ran his finger up and down one of its wooden spokes.

"What was your relationship with Lisa, Mrs. Grayson?"

She stared at his back. "I don't understand."

"Were you friends?"

"I suppose. I don't know if . . ."

"Was it strictly a business arrangement?"

"Well, no . . ."

"Did you ever do things in town together? Go for a pint? Play darts? Just how intimate, Mrs. Grayson, was your relationship with Lisa Stillwell? Can you tell me that, please, or do you need your bloody glasses to see your way to answer?"

Maura sucked in her breath in disbelief. For three years she had worked with Halford, gratified to have his respect, even more so his friendship. She considered him an innately kind man and consummate at what he did: a deferential manipulator who could question a post-box and get it to talk. But even she could call this one. Daniel Halford had blown an interview. He had lost control, misjudged a witness. Maura stared at her notes and waited.

When it became evident that Mrs. Grayson wasn't going to answer, Halford finally turned to face her. She was pale now, the anger gone, and she seemed slighter and older. She turned sideways in the chair; had it been larger, Maura suspected she would have drawn her knees up to her chest and cried.

Maura rose, uncertain which of the two needed ministrations the most, when from upstairs came a whack of a door hitting a wall, followed by the heavy clump, clump, clump of shoes on wooden stairs. A voice, husky and rambling, followed the footsteps, blaring an atonal song with only one recognisable word: watermelon. A pause on the bottom stair, and then a loud smack sounded on the ground floor.

The legs that walked into the room were sturdy,

bare, and strapped into shiny black patent pumps. An olive green cotton dress covered the rest of the body. The vision boomed one last defiant "Watermelon!" then stood in the doorway making slurping noises. Maura and Halford both stared. Where the head should have been was a wrinkled McDonald's bag, two eye holes punched inexpertly out, a broad blue mouth crayoned on.

Maura fell to her knees and wailed. From the corner of her eye, she saw Mrs. Grayson unfold and look at her in amazement.

"Oh, no, it's the fearsome Big Mac Monster, dreaded far and wide for its big teeth and dirty toes!" Maura put her fists to her temples and rocked back and forth. "Oh, no, what will we do, what will we do?"

The McDonald's bag squealed and ran to Maura.

"I'm gone eat you up," it growled. "Then I'm gone spit you out, flush you down the toilet, and *wash you out to sea!*"

Maura laughed, and the McDonald's bag giggled and dipped out a head. The face was a smooth and pudgy version of Gale's, dark hair, dark eyes, but the eyes were sparked with good humor. Maura reached out and gave the child a hug.

"My name's Maura. You must be Katie Pru."

The child nodded and twisted herself into Maura's lap. She pointed at the dumbfounded figure beside the spinning wheel.

"What's that?" she demanded.

Maura scrutinised Halford's stunned face and decided to play it cool. "That's Mr. Halford. He's a policeman."

Katie Pru studied him uncertainly. "I know all about policemen. When you're in trouble you yell, 'Hey, Mr. Policeman, I need . . . *help!*'"

The "help" was delivered after a loud gulp of air, straight from the diaphragm in a gusty alto peal. Lifting her chin and squinting, the child watched Halford for a reaction. He cleared his throat and stuck his hands in his pockets. Katie Pru scowled. She twisted back to Maura and shook her head.

"That's not a policeman. Policemen have funny hats. He's a postman." And having decided the matter, she settled herself back into Maura's lap and impassively watched the postman fidget.

A second throat cleared in the doorway. A well-dressed woman in a purple belted dress crossed the threshold into the room.

"Sorry," she said. "We were playing along all jolly and content and all of a sudden we had to see Mummy." She looked at Maura. "I'm sorry if we interrupted things. I'm Helen Pane."

The used-clothes seller. A newcomer, too; Helen Pane hadn't lived in Fetherbridge during the Tom Grayson inquiry. Maura wondered if she would be forever breaking people into Tom Grayson and post-Tom Grayson categories.

Either Miss Pane didn't believe in wearing her own goods, or her used clothes were in exceptional condition. The purple dress was crisply pressed and held the soft sheen of well-tended clothing. With her auburn hair cut short and moussed into small waves, Helen Pane would have cut an impressive figure if it were possible to ignore her make-up. Dots and dashes of colour streaked down her cheeks and across her nose. Rubbed mascara made shadows under her eyes. Maura figured that Katie Pru's wasn't the only head to wear the McDonald's bag today.

Halford spoke, his composure returned. "I'm Chief Inspector Halford, and you didn't interrupt us at all, Miss Pane. I believe we've finished here for now. I would like to have a word with you, however. Tomorrow. Sergeant Ramsden will ring to make an appointment."

Maura gently nudged Katie Pru from her lap, then rose to take down Helen Pane's address and number. When she finished she turned to Gale Grayson.

"I wish I could tell you this will be all, but it probably won't be. There are always more questions."

In answer, Mrs. Grayson tightened the stole around her. Resigned, Maura dropped her Biro into her handbag and walked to the hallway.

Halford strode towards the hearth. Reaching the table, he pointedly picked up the folded paper Mrs. Grayson had tossed there, placed it in his breast pocket, and started to leave the room.

At the living room door he stopped. "Is that your bicycle out front, Miss Pane?" She nodded. "I'd like to send someone over to take a sample from the tyres. Any objection?"

"No, not at all."

"Thank you. And you, Mrs. Grayson. We'd like one from your moped, if that's all right."

Gale Grayson looked into his eyes. She lifted her chin. "No, Chief Inspector. I don't believe it is. I'd prefer you get a warrant."

Halford's smile missed his eyes by a good four inches.

He waited until the door shut behind them before imploding. "What the *hell* was that?"

"To what hell are you referring?" Maura asked placidly. "Mrs. Grayson's actions or mine?"

"Hers, although I would like to know what possessed you to roll around the floor like the devil's own monkey. It brought a quick end to questioning, that."

She raised her grey eyes to his. "I would say the questioning had already come to an end, Chief Inspector. Mrs. Grayson had obviously decided on silence. Not much you can do when they get to that point but leave or divert. You taught me that yourself. I was diverting. You chose to leave."

She was treading dangerous ground and Halford knew she had made a conscious decision to do so. The fact that this meant she felt she was irrefutably right did nothing to assuage the irritation he felt. The voice in his brain snapped that subordinates should remember their place. But he said nothing.

His fist was around the car door handle before he glanced back at the house and looked at Maura again. "You think I took the wrong tack."

She waved her arms in exasperation. "Daniel, the woman has every reason to despise us. Whatever we may think of her husband, we know she was completely in the dark about his activities, and yet you go in there treating her as the number one suspect in the first violent crime that comes down the pike after his suicide. You thought she wouldn't react with hostility? God, she's only human. From the way you acted in there, I can't tell if you think she's the devil incarnate or the Blessed Virgin who has suddenly done something to disappoint you very, very badly."

He could tell that she knew she had gone too far. He had no idea what his own face revealed, but the rapid droop of her head reflected the rage she must have observed. When she raised her head again, her words came out in a whisper.

"I'm sorry. I'm sorry, Daniel. That was inexcusable."

"It was, Sergeant. And you don't know what you're talking about worth a damn."

He flung the car door open and threw himself into the driver's seat. Silently, she walked around the car and slid in beside him. From inside the house came the high squeal of childish laughter.

Bobby Grissom let his bicycle coast to a smooth halt directly in front of the blue Ford. He had been watching the detectives for about the length of time it took him to cruise down the small section of Boundary Road that connected Bracken Street, where Gale lived, to the High Street. Of course, he hadn't heard a word; he doubted, in fact, whether he could have heard anything but mumbling had he been right next to them, the police being so adept at obliqueness. Still, one couldn't misinterpret the sentiment. These two were having a regular slanging match.

Now Halford stared at him through the windscreen. Definitely a forbidding man, Grissom thought. And not just physically forbidding. The face was okay—sort of Jeremy Ironsish without the gauntness—but the expression. He'd seen friendlier looks on piranha.

Ah, hell, Grissom thought. The police. What can you do with them? Grissom walked the bicycle to the driver's window.

"Good afternoon, sir. Bobby Grissom, *The Hampshire Inquisitor*. I was wondering if you could answer a few questions."

The female, Ramsden, stared out the windscreen at the cottages across Bracken Street. Pretty, that one, although at the moment she looked like she'd had a tiff with her favourite boy. Grissom dipped his head into the window to give her a smile.

"We're not answering questions at this point, Mr. Grissom. When we feel we have information valuable to the public, we will hold a press conference." Halford switched on the ignition.

"Oh, come on, Chief Inspector. This is *The Hampshire Inquisitor*, not *The Sunday* bloody *Times*. We don't need a press conference. It's just you and me, having a little natter. Come on, just a couple of questions, to stop the gossip mill around here. You know how villages are. Grind, grind, grind."

"You can contact the incidents room tomorrow. Perhaps we'll have some information then."

"The story at the pub is that it was a drifter, a psychopath hitching along the road."

"We're exploring every possibility."

"Really? I would have thought that one'd give you a chuckle." Grissom rested his arm against the open car window and stuck his head further inside. "I mean, it's never actually a roving psychopath, is it? Usually it's the parents or the lover or the kindly old village shopkeeper with the jar of lollies by the front door and a butcher knife in his boot."

"Or a journalist on deadline with nothing to write."

Grissom laughed. "Touché, Chief Inspector. I like that. You're not such a bad sort." He shot the female what he hoped was an engaging grin. "Course, down at the pub I've been getting an earful. Made quite an impression the last time, did your boss here. Sorry I wasn't around. An assassin's suicide. Now *that's* a story I'd like to cover. Not the same as sweet young child-minders dead in the road, is it?"

The smile Halford mustered was as engaging as Grissom's. He slid the car into gear. "Move your head, sunshine. In your profession, you just might need it someday."

7

If the Tullsgate estate were the foot of a cross, the High Street the post, and St. Martin's Church the head, then Orrin Ivory's home and Orrin Ivory's newspaper office made up the far ends of the bar across which latter-day media martyrs could sling their sinewy limbs and wail. Halford glanced at his map of Fetherbridge and gripped the steering wheel tighter. Such an ecclesiastical constellation of real estate. He wouldn't be surprised to discover it was intentional.

Halford let the map slide into the space between the two front seats. He felt like a bear. Maura sat beside him, her face stony with anger. An apology was surely hovering around somewhere, darting between their set jaws and waiting for one of them to lend it breath. Well, hell, she could damn well say she was sorry. Do her a world of good to acknowledge at least once that sometimes her mouth got the upper hand. He settled back in his seat and waited. It was only when they rounded onto the Ivorys' street that he sheepishly realised she already had apologised.

He grimaced at the road. "You were right. I handled that back there badly." For some reason, he found he couldn't give "that back there" a definitive name. He blundered on. "I bloody well screwed up the interview. You were entirely within your province to point this out. I shouldn't have blasted at you and I sure as hell shouldn't have pulled rank the way I did."

He glanced at her. She stared at the glove box. The silence rang in his ears.

The car was barely rolling now. He knew if he looked he would see the Ivory house on his left, but he wasn't ready for it. Finally, still staring ahead, Maura spoke.

"Daniel, you're a damned good detective. You're not condescending, you share credit, and things rarely if ever get past you. You have an ability to read people and to respond to them so they trust and believe in you. It makes you one of the best."

Her voice was pulled along by an urgency that told Halford her point was yet to come. He steeled himself, but suddenly she stopped. When she looked at him, she was smiling.

"That's all, guv."

He stopped the car and turned to study her. "And you, Sergeant, are one of the most unlikely brownnosers I've ever met. You're going to let me off this easy?"

"No." Her eyebrows arched. As she ambled from the car, Halford thought he heard her mutter something about "biding my time," but he wasn't sure.

The Ivory house was unlike any other building Halford had seen in Fetherbridge. The garden was pleasant enough, hugging the house on all four sides with fastidiously rounded hollies and pruned rose bushes.

Someone with a surfeit of leisure time and an eye for
composition had groomed the grounds well. A woman's bicycle, pink and pristine, stood next to the dwelling's brick steps. Blue-and-white delft pots, clean and
emptied of springtime plantings, lined the steps on
both sides. The garden's green grass was trimmed to
carpet perfection. Beneath the line of hollies, the yellow
and shriveled leaves of bulbed flowers lay braided
neatly for their final rest. In contrast, however, the
house was pure architectural dung.

Considerably later than the original planned cottages, the Ivorys' was a Victorian panoply of stunted
brick turrets and skinny spiked gables. Overdesigned
and overbuilt, every square inch was entangled in
twisted, menacing froufrou. The only parts not exces-
sive were the squint-eyed windows winking from the
bulwarks.

Not until he reached the base of the front stairs did
Halford realise the size was misleading. Looking
closely, he doubted it was more than three thousand
square feet. Nothing to sneeze at, to be sure, but not
quite what he would have expected of a house with
such a steadfast commitment to gaudiness. As he
reached for the door's elaborate brass knocker, he
found himself almost buoyantly curious to see the editor operating in this leaden confection.

That Ivory would be home he had no doubt. When
Maura rang earlier to make sure Jill would be available,
Anise Ivory's answer hinted at the level of protection
Ivory extended to his family. Anise informed Maura
she would check with her husband to make sure his
daughter could be questioned. Halford remembered
now that during the Grayson case, Mr. and Mrs. Ivory
had opted for questioning in the fluorescent-lit, plastic-
chaired interview room of the Winchester police station
rather than disturb the sanctity of their home. At the
time, it had irritated him, but then by that point in the
inquiry he was chronically irritated.

The editor himself opened the door. Halford smiled with what he hoped was a fresh friendliness.

"Ah, Mr. Ivory. It's been a long time. Chief Inspector Halford, New Scotland Yard." He brought out his warrant card but was unsurprised when Ivory brushed it away. "This is DS Maura Ramsden. We'd like to ask your daughter Jill some questions about Lisa Stillwell."

"Of course, of course." Ivory ran his fingers through a sparse crop of greying blond hair. He extended his other hand for a firm shake. " 'Good to see you again' isn't quite the proper thing, is it, Inspector? Well, *Chief* Inspector now, isn't it? You two please come in. Anise saw you coming up the lane and ran off to make tea. You could use some, I suppose? Nasty day for a nasty business."

This was Ivory as Halford remembered him, soft-spoken, solicitous, a bit of the nervous chatterer. The incredible ego would emerge later, after the questioning grew personal and Ivory began to feel the narrow chasm between duty and privacy crumble shut. That was how it had been with the Grayson case. For months after the case was closed, Ivory on occasion called Halford's office for a detail or two, but Halford had intuited that he was uncomfortable with his dual role. As a journalist he had wanted the truth told; as Gale Grayson's friend he wanted to throw justice out the door and rock the weeping widow to sleep. Halford looked down at his feet as he wiped microscopic mud onto the doormat. He felt a twinge of bitterness he didn't attempt to excuse.

"The parlour is this way," Ivory said. "It's the one room we try to keep neat for people dropping in."

Ivory was a man who managed to be both tall and paunchy. As he lumbered down the hall, feminine pouches of flesh bunched at his hips. He needs to put his hands in his pockets more, Halford found himself thinking. Stretch the fabric out a touch and he would pass for hard and intimidating.

"I don't believe you've been in the house before.

Quite an interesting history, actually." Ivory turned to
Halford and rolled his eyes. "God. Small talk. Really,
Halford, this has been a bad time for us. We've all
known Lisa since she was a child. Hell, with her mother
gone, she'd more or less become another daughter."

The hall was panelled in mahogany and lined with
glass-fronted bookshelves. Ivory fingered a leaf from a
massive fern that snaked over the top of the cabinet
and spilled fronds past the melee of books inside.

"The girls," he said finally. "Anise and Jill—they've
taken it hard. It was bad enough when we thought Lisa
died in a freak accident. But murder? It's just hard to
fathom, that's all. I know you've got your job to do,
and believe me, we want to help, but if you could just
try to remember . . . Well, Halford, they're just girls."

Behind Halford, Maura coughed. He nodded to
Ivory and the editor turned to direct them through a
pair of French doors into a small parlour.

This room, like Gale Grayson's front room, was all
white. But whereas Mrs. Grayson's was cool with lines
and angles, this parlour strangled the air with an over-
abundance of white lace and flounces. Pleated eyelet
draperies with frilly trim puddled around the base of
the tall windows, forcing even today's dull light
through tiny holes. On sunny days, he imagined the
light dotted the white carpet like sunrise rippling on a
mouldy lake.

Halford fingered one of several lace antimacassars
that dripped along the backs of the white three-piece
living room suite. As if anyone with oiled hair ever set
foot in Orrin Ivory's parlour.

Ivory motioned them into the matching chairs.
"Make yourselves comfortable. I'll tell the girls you're
here."

They dropped their coats on the chair backs and sat
silently until Ivory was well down the hall. " 'The
girls.' " Maura didn't look up as she tugged her notebook from her handbag. "Presumably, one of 'the girls'

is upstairs playing dolls while the other is in the kitchen playing hostess."

"I imagine it's simply a term of endearment. My, my, Sergeant Ramsden, the day's taken a cynical turn, hasn't it? You usually leave the nastiness to me."

"I certainly don't go around referring to Jeffrey as 'the boy.' And if I ever heard him in public referring to me as 'the girl,' he'd be singing Christmas carols mezzo-soprano."

"Or the theme from *The Beverly Hillbillies*."

She barked a short laugh as Anise Ivory wheeled a trolley set with a silver tea service through the French doors. Mrs. Ivory stopped and looked at them with confusion. She's trying to figure out how humour fits in, Halford thought. She's trying to remember if it's all right to laugh so soon after a death. Then the face cleared and she smiled brightly.

"I know you two could use some refreshment. It's already gone three." She pushed the trolley to the sofa and sat down. "Not much variety, I'm afraid—things have been a little out of kilter here. There're only cheese and crackers, but plenty of them."

She said it shyly, sweetly, with a light smile that reached full into her eyes. She was an extraordinarily beautiful woman—close to forty if not past it—and a natural blonde, as evidenced by the strands of silver that leapt at the white in the room. The beautiful hair was pulled back in a loose French knot, some spilling around her shoulders, some tickling her temples and cheeks. Her dress was fittingly old-fashioned—drop-waist denim, lace at the collar and cuffs. Black velvet slippers tipped her feet. She tugged at her skirt to arrange herself on the sofa. Grey eyes, dusky like glass, regarded Halford.

"I suppose you've heard all the typical comments," she said. " 'We're sorry, we're hurt, we're grieving.' We thought we had come to some uneasy peace with her death—when we thought it had been an accident. But now . . . to think someone murdered her . . ." She pressed her hands to her chest and shook her head. "It must all sound so insincere to you."

Her eyes, soft and beseeching, clouded with tears. As Halford stretched forward to take the cup she offered, he noted that she used mascara. It, like so much of her home, was an unnecessary embellishment.

"We hope we eventually learn to discern the sincere from the insincere, Mrs. Ivory. We know this is difficult for your family. I hope you'll find that we're considerate."

Her smile fluttered, perfect teeth calming rose-coloured lips. Three years ago, the fluorescent bulbs of the police station had made her seem dry and drawn. Now the parlour's light-on-white motif smoothed her face into a rich cream. Halford thought of the dim decor of the Stillwells' house and marvelled at the resourcefulness of Fetherbridgians and their possessive use of the Hampshire sun.

"Here we are." Orrin Ivory swung the French doors wide and ushered a stunning young woman into the room. Like her mother, Jill Ivory was statuesque and graceful. Halford rose to shake her hand and immediately found himself warming towards Ivory. These truly were two remarkable women—all beauty, all poise. If they had been his, perhaps he too would be content in this crinoline madhouse.

"You need to know, Halford, that Jill has had a mild sedative." Ivory led his daughter to the sofa and gently guided her down into the cushions next to Anise. "Just for sleep, you know, but I think she's ready to help you if she can."

Halford eased himself into his chair. "Miss Ivory, I'm Chief Inspector Halford and this is Sergeant Ramsden. We've met your parents before, a few years back." She nodded her comprehension. "So, how do you feel?"

Jill took her mother's hand and inhaled deeply. "I'm fine. At any rate, I'll be fine."

The latter sentence was closer to the truth. Despite

her obvious attractiveness, it was easy to see that the past few days had not rested on her lightly. Halford recognised the look—he had interviewed scores of people with the same bed-tossed appearance of the recently bereaved. Jill was dressed in jeans, a worn oxford, and a baggy woolen pullover that, judging from the the the bell-shaped neckline and loose hem, was scavenged from her father's jumble offerings. The requisite thick-soled Reeboks looked both jarringly contemporary and depressingly proper next to her mother's slender velvet slippers.

Ivory dragged a slatted chair across the room and settled himself next to his daughter. "Let's try to do this as quickly as possible, Halford. You can see she's just about all done in."

Halford nodded. He kept his voice friendly. "Let's get the preliminaries out of the way first, Miss Ivory. Can you tell me what you were doing Saturday morning between nine and eleven?"

Whatever sedative she was under, it hadn't diminished her coherency. The girl's words were clear and calm.

"First of all, call me Jill, Chief Inspector. Miss Ivory makes me feel like a schoolteacher. And Saturday morning I was with Daddy. A clamp on the press had broken the day before and we went to Southampton for a replacement. We left around nine-thirty or so. I don't remember exactly when we got back."

"Where were you prior to nine-thirty?"

"At the paper."

"On a Saturday morning?"

Jill nodded. "I'm the newspaper photographer"—she smiled at her father—"at least for the next several months. I'm interning. Anyway, I had several rolls of film to develop, so we went there around seven-thirty or so to work."

"Was anyone else there?"

"Bobby Grissom. He's a reporter. He likes to work on the weekends as well."

"Yes, I can imagine. Sergeant Ramsden and I have already met Mr. Grissom. Quite the diligent young man." Halford turned to Ivory. "Do you have a receipt?"

"For the clamp? Certainly. Or rather, my bookkeeper has it. We didn't return until around eleven, Mr. Halford. We stopped to put petrol in the car."

"Before we leave, please give the locations of both the mechanic and the press repair shop to Sergeant Ramsden. And let me ask you the same question, Mrs. Ivory. Where were you Saturday morning?"

Anise Ivory lifted her shoulders in a different shrug. "Here, I'm afraid. Alone. I was pulling all the boxes of Christmas decorations from the attic."

Halford looked around the room. "I suppose the decorations are still packed up somewhere?"

"Oh, yes. They're stacked in the kitchen. Of course, things have changed, haven't they? I don't know now if we'll even put up a tree this year."

Somehow, Halford felt that by the time Christmas rolled around, this overfed house would be choking on decorations. He returned his attention to Jill. "Tell me, how did you and Lisa get to be friends?"

Jill cleared her throat. Her hand began to knead her thigh above the right knee.

"Lisa was my best friend, my only friend. We met when I was seven, she was eleven. We had just moved here, and she and her mum came to the *Inquisitor* office to buy an advert. She was quite impressive to a seven-year-old. She was wearing this beautiful blue dress— Mummy and Daddy wouldn't let me wear dresses then, felt it curtailed my adventurousness or something—and I thought she looked exactly like my Snow White paper doll." Jill paused. "I decided right then I wanted to be exactly like her. She was nice and friendly and all that, but I wanted to be like her because she was so lovely. For months I told everyone to call me Lisa."

Halford smiled, touched by the child who saw sensuality in what was in all likelihood gawky preadolescence. In a corner curio shelf on the far side of the room sat a framed photograph of the two young women, cheeks pressed together in a sororal hug. The irony was that, all grown up, Lisa Stillwell's average prettiness couldn't have held a torch to Jill Ivory's porcelain beauty.

"And was she a good friend to that seven-year-old?"

Tears filled Jill's eyes. She raised one ankle to rest on her knee and then, as the tears fell, lowered it again and watched her empty hands fumble in her lap.

Ivory started from his chair. "I think that's about enough. . . . "

Halford set his teacup on the trolley, selected a clean one, and held it out to Mrs. Ivory. "I think perhaps Jill could use some tea."

If Anise Ivory was surprised at the usurpation of her role, she hid it. After handing Jill the cup, she slipped her arm around her daughter's shoulder and pulled a hank of thick, shiny hair away from the girl's neck. The combination of tea and comfort worked; Jill's tears dried and she looked at Halford with reddened but intelligent eyes.

Halford began again. "I was in Lisa's room a couple of hours ago. She seemed to have a small but eclectic group of books—Naipaul, Austen, and then some popular best-sellers."

Jill smiled. "I gave her the Naipaul, Gale Grayson the Austen, I think. The others were her choice. Lisa always said she wanted to be well read, but I don't believe she ever put the time into it."

She rotated the cup in her hand. "If you really want to know about Lisa, I can tell you. She was a very empathic person." Halford raised his eyebrows. She shook her head. "I've been thinking a lot about her, you see, and that's what I've sifted it down to—she cared a lot about people and she was able to see things from their point of view. I think it came from losing her mother.

She had to deal with her emotions alone, as well as her father's and Brian's. I think that made her very sensitive. It made her really grand."

Here the tears welled again. Ivory coughed.

"Surely that will do for today," he said.

Halford didn't look at him. "Lisa had many friends?" he asked Jill.

To his surprise, she shook her head. "I've thought about that, too. People think of Lisa as having many friends, but I don't think she really does. She isn't that close to any of the other people her age at church and most of her friends from school have left Fetherbridge. I never knew of her visiting them, except maybe when they came home to see their parents."

"Her brother says she was fairly close to Miss Pane and Mrs. Grayson."

Jill pulled at the fuzzy strands of denim that sprang from a small hole in her jeans. "I don't think they really had a friendship with her. They're so much older, after all—ten years at least—I can't think they would have had all that much in common." She directed her attention to Maura. "This may sound bizarre, but I think they were closer to her than she to them."

Halford had to hand it to Ivory—he at least had cultivated perception in his daughter. "Tell me more about that," he prompted.

"Really, I think—" Ivory began, but his daughter waved him quiet. She leaned back into the sofa and pushed the drooping sleeves of her pullover to her elbows.

"Lisa was a terrific friend. She was supportive and kind and generous. She knew how to listen to people. That's what she told me once—that people needed to be listened to and that's something she could give everybody. Those two ladies . . ." For the first time she hesitated. Halford kept his eyes steady on her face. "They both need someone to listen. Does that make sense?"

"Perfectly. We could all use a sympathetic ear now

and again. So you think they . . . ?" He let the question
dangle.

"Lisa told me once that they are both so lonely.
Well, Gale for obvious reasons, but even Helen. Helen
comes across all funny, but Lisa said she's really unhappy. Man troubles, though she wouldn't elaborate.
She would never betray a confidence. But that's what I
mean about them needing her more. I really can't see
Lisa confiding in them. I mean, they're both at least
thirty, not old, of course, but not young, either."

She might be perceptive, but she was still hopelessly
eighteen years old. "What about boyfriends?"

This question seemed to catch her off guard. The
flush started at her throat and moved rapidly up her
face.

"There weren't any. Lisa didn't date."

Ivory jerked his head toward his daughter, his eyes
perplexed. Anise sat perfectly still, staring at her velvet
slippers. Her hand tightened around Jill's arm.

"I need you to think carefully, Jill," Halford said.
"Lisa was twenty-two years old. It's natural that she
would have dated—or had someone she cared for."

"There was no one."

Halford studied her. She had dropped her eyes and
appeared to concentrate on the hole in her jeans, rotat-
ing her finger around its inner edge until the fabric
widened and curled over to show its whiter underside.
Brusquely, Halford pushed himself to his feet.

"Mr. Ivory, would you come with me into the hall?
I'd like Sergeant Ramsden to talk to Jill for a moment."

He stalked into the hallway, followed by Ivory, who
closed the door behind them.

"She's not being honest with you," Ivory said. "I
don't understand it."

"What do you know about it?"

"Not much. Just what my wife told me. Lisa stayed
over one night a couple of weeks ago. She and Jill were
upstairs in the bedroom when Anise walked in. They
had been giggling, talking, Anise says, about how

good-looking some man was. You know how girls are. When Anise tried to find out who, they wouldn't tell her."

"What makes you think it was someone Lisa might have been dating? It could have been someone on the telly, or a film actor."

Ivory shook his head. "I don't think so. I mean, they are adult women, after all."

Maura would be pleased to hear you say so, Halford thought. "I'm sorry, that's just not very much to go on."

" 'Sweet.' That's it. Anise heard Lisa say how sweet the man was."

Maura turned in her seat and looked at Halford through the French doors. Interpreting her expression to mean they were being distracting, he took Ivory by the arm and led him down the hall.

"Your daughter seems very intelligent, articulate. I'm curious why she's not at university."

"She thinks she wants to be a journalist." Ivory rubbed the back of his neck. "I'm not so sure. She's actually quite bright, I'd even say gifted—I just don't know if she's got the grit. So I agreed to let her intern at the *Inquisitor* to test it out."

"How's it going?"

"All right. It's just—Look, I know I'm old-fashioned, but I'm not sure it's a business for women."

"Really."

"Yeah." Ivory leaned against a bookcase and absently tapped the glass. "I'm afraid I'm a bit of the idealist, Halford. Journalism is very important to me. I believe in it. But it's getting dirtier every day, and it can be hard on the women."

"I can think of several women who would disagree with you."

Ivory snorted. "So can I. And I'm glad I'm not a father to them all." He tore a leaf from the bookcase fern. "By the way, word is you've cancelled the funeral."

"It wasn't me personally, Mr. Ivory. Surely as a journalist you know the procedure. And the reason for it."

"Oh, yes, certainly. But we all thought it was an accident, you see. Everyone was looking to the funeral as the beginning of coming to terms with it. I'm afraid you've thrown this village into a bit of a fit."

Halford glanced up the hallway to the closed parlour doors, silently urging them to open. "I am sorry. I know it will be difficult."

Ivory rubbed the leaf between his fingers until the juice seeped out. "A bit more than difficult, Halford. You know how this village was when you left. Literally ripped apart. All the publicity, the sightseers driving through town, just to see where the famous killer poet lived. It was truly disgusting. It's taken a long time for things to settle down and no one wants to see another flare-up. A funeral would help calm the waters. Is there no way to get this handled differently?"

Halford shook his head. "It's not that I don't understand, Mr. Ivory. I do. But the law's there for a reason. When we arrest someone, he or she will be entitled to a full defence, and that includes a second postmortem. No exceptions. As a journalist, you must appreciate that."

Down the hall, the French doors creaked open and Maura emerged carrying her handbag and both their coats. She glanced at Halford as she pushed past him and went out the front door.

"Thank you, Mr. Ivory," Halford said, following her. "We'll be in touch. And I wouldn't worry. Fetherbridge is a resilient little burg. It will be able to handle this."

When they reached the car, Maura stopped.

She said: "The suitor's name is Mr. E. The letter *E*. That's all she knows."

"What?" Halford was three strides back up the walk, ready to bang on the door again, before Maura could call him back.

"Daniel, I honestly think she told me all she knew."

He returned to the car and stared at the tyre, considering if he was angry enough that a kick would break his toe. He was. "Tell me again."

"Lisa told Jill that he lives in Hampshire, is unmarried, and is, as Jill put it, 'heaps' older. I asked her what that meant, and she said she figured he was at least thirty-five. Lisa never told her his real name. They just referred to him as 'Mr. E.' And she doesn't know if that is actually his last initial or not."

"Great. Did they wear decoder rings as well?" He glared at the trees across the lane. "All I can say is if young women are going to be so bloody clever they ought to make sure they don't bloody well get knocked off. You're only five years older than Lisa Stillwell. Were you that silly at her age? Code names for secret *amores*? Giggling on girlfriends' beds? Shushing each other when Mummy walks into the room?"

Maura shrugged. "I think love at any age makes you silly. But, I admit, twenty-two is a fairly difficult age. People make such a big to-do about adolescence, but for my money those early twenties are the worst. You're wise, invincible, and independent. Disaster-making, if you ask me."

Groaning, he opened the car door and slid into the seat. They were going to have to track down and interview every man in the area over the age of thirty with the first or last initial *E*, married or not. Goddammit, Roan was going to have to cough up some more men. Halford ground the ignition into action. He was beginning to wonder if, by the end of this case, he was going to have any inner cheek left to chew.

8

Helen could think of a hundred places she would rather be than the dark, humming interior of the Stillwell house. She stopped outside the kitchen entrance and peeked inside. A half-dozen tweeded women scrunched against the cabinetry like cereal boxes, ostensibly present to give aid and comfort but, Helen wagered, actually there to savour the entertainment.

The women talked quietly. "She was a sweet child. A dreadful way for a pretty thing to die."

"When I was young, we had no worry of such things. In London, perhaps, but not here."

"Ah, you're living in a fool's world, Mary. Violence is everywhere. Just look at those movies the Americans make. Puts ideas in people's heads."

"Movies! You don't have to go to movies to get ideas, Ruth. Just look at what's happened here in our own backyard. I don't know what's happening. . . . "

Helen stepped inside the doorway and held out a ceramic tureen.

"I've brought soup," she said. "Anywhere in particular I should put it?"

For an appalling half-second, the women stared at her without comprehension. Smiling brightly, Helen extended the tureen further in front of her, feeling like Oliver Twist begging not for food but for recognition.

June Kingston rallied first. "Helen!" Her voice warmed with concern. "It is so thoughtful of you to come. So few people—well, young people, at least—know what's expected of them after a tragedy. And it is such a tragedy, isn't it?"

The postmistress screwed up her features to signal regret. To Helen, June Kingston resembled an ironclad battleship—solid sheets of metal secured by the occasional fastener—so her skewed facial expression gave her the appearance of having undergone a minor maritime accident. Helen looked around at the sympathetic faces of the other women in the room and widened her eyes to match theirs. "Yes, it's hard to imagine such a tragedy. I thought some soup would help. Where should I put it?"

June retrieved a glass from the kitchen sink and began furiously towelling it dry. "You know, none of us was quite sure what to do. I mean, after all, we were just here this weekend, with food and all. It's almost as though there's been a second death."

"You're right, June." Mary Adams's birdlike voice matched her birdlike neck. "If shock's the measure of grief, then I'd say it certainly *feels* like two deaths. An accident, well, that was simply horrible. But to think she was murdered . . ."

"We were just talking, Helen, about how times have changed," June continued. "When we were children in Fetherbridge, nothing like this ever happened."

The tureen, a piece of grey-and-blue reproduction saltware, was never light, and Helen had filled it almost to the rim before leaving her house. She rested it against her hip. The kitchen worktop was blockaded by a sturdy row of wool-covered rumps. Helen peered through the breaks between the women's arms and spied an empty space due east of the sink.

"It's a different world, that's for sure," Helen agreed. She wedged herself next to Mrs. Kingston and slid the tureen across the counter behind the women. "There. I didn't bring any bowls. . . . "

"Now what has me mortified is the way the police have told Edgar there can be no funeral." Ruth Barker crossed her arms. Her wiry red hair sprang in several directions as she bobbed her head. "It was all planned. Editha was going to present the eulogy. Why, Edgar was going today with Ansie Ivory to pick out the casket. I'd already ordered flowers."

"Flowers are the least of it, Ruth," June Kingston said crossly. "That child deserves a decent burial. Who knows how long she suffered, or how long she was out on that road before Brian found her. She was a precious child and she deserves to be laid to rest properly." She selected another glass and recommenced her fierce drying. "It's an abomination, that's what it is. How are Edgar and Brian supposed to put this behind them if they have to wait for the police? It could take months!"

"This didn't use to happen, of course." Mary Adams shook her head. "There were no such things as postmortems or second postmortems. The living were left to bury their dead."

"Yes," said Ruth. "When I was a child—"

"Of course," June interrupted, "when we were all children there weren't as many newcomers then." She moved away from the sink and began wiping crumbs from the dinette table. Helen watched wordlessly as fragments of bread littered the floor. "I think that's what's done it, people with strange ways, strange outlooks. I know it's not a popular thing to say these days, but outsiders do bring change, and that's not always good."

"You're right. Lots of newcomers these days," Ruth huffed. Helen smiled graciously and started moving slowly to the door. "We were just discussing it. Now, I'm not one to say all newcomers are bad—you know I don't feel that way, Helen—but some do tend to bring badness with them. Seems, in fact, to follow them." She looked at June Kingston and raised her eyebrows. "Some of them are flat barmy, if you ask me."

"I suppose you're right, dear. Barmy's a good word." Mrs. Kingston left her tidying and, tossing Helen a smile, lifted the lid from the tureen. She peered inside.

"Wonton!" she sniffed. "What the hell kind of soup is that?"

The Halford who hunched into the Fetherbridge police station like a boulder of solid Burberry was not the Halford who had picked Maura up in front of her house a scant eight hours earlier. His tall, square frame, usually elegant, now resembled a block. He seemed harder and angrier—for reasons she was only on the periphery of understanding.

From inside the car, Maura watched him fling open the station door. Constable Baylor's etched brass bell, hanging from a length of red yarn spanning the door's opaque glass, took the brunt of Halford's displeasure.

She waited for Halford's shadow to move from the door's field of light. "Mr. E." had changed everything. Any hopes of solving the case quickly and quietly could be kissed good-bye. Halford was going to demand a full team, a serious inquiry. That would mean upwards of a hundred people. With a twinge of regret, she wondered if she would be spending Christmas without Jeffrey.

Leaving her superior to do battle alone, she pushed the car into gear and headed east down the High Street. The sullen rain had lifted, leaving the late afternoon sky

unexpectedly clear. Straight ahead St. Martin's Church
sat in its walled plot like a great stone bull, a thick
Roman cross protruding from its Normanesque tower
like a malformed horn. Maura slowed as she neared
the church and followed the street to the right as it split
before the holy ground and circled the cemetery before
connecting with Boundary Road. An uneven wall,
made of brick and flint, lurched past her like a line of
drunks.

Christian Timbrook lived in a converted carriage
house on Tulledge Lane, two blocks from the High
Street. Halford had left the village map crammed between the seats, but Maura didn't need it to tell which
house belonged to the stained glass artisan. To the right
of an uninspired weatherboard sat a small white cottage, tidy under the limbs of a single oak tree. The
south front had been converted to a huge bay of windows, inside of which hung a series of elaborate stained
glass panels. Maura pulled into the small drive and
shut off the ignition. The full damp of the morning had
given way to a sheared gold as dusk neared. Heavy
rays coated the side of Timbrook's house and com-
pacted the panels into tight knots of colour. Maura
made a mental note to drive by the cottage later—at
night, the tinctured light streaming from those lit windows would be positively cathedral.

Maura rang three times before Timbrook answered
the door, intentionally late, she suspected, given the
fact that she had called earlier to tell him she was coming. He didn't merely open the door; he appeared to
wrench it from the frame which he then lounged
against like a person sick. For a moment he regarded
her blackly. His eyes roamed over her face, neck, and
hair. Then he smiled. Her dislike for him was immediate.

"You're not the chief inspector," Timbrook said. "I
would expect something taller in a chief inspector. And
hairier."

"I'm Detective Sergeant Ramsden. Chief Inspector

Halford has other business." She showed him her warrant card. "May I come in?"

"Oh, please do. I've hit a convenient stopping point." He spread both his hands in front of her. The shaft of each finger was mottled with bandages. "See? When I've cut all ten fingers I know it's time to quit for the day."

He folded his fingers across his palm and brought them close to his face. "The pinky is the hardest to cut. I admit that sometimes, when I'm overdue for tea, I intentionally slide it over an edge of glass just to satisfy my rumbling stomach. I treat it as sort of a ritualistic sacrifice—I give the gods blood, they give me colours and light."

Contempt was generally an easy emotion for Maura to conceal, but the physical repulsion she felt towards him overrode her self-control. Timbrook suddenly laughed and stepped aside.

"God, Sergeant. You detest me already. Not very professional of you to let me know, but then I like honesty in a copper. I think we shall be friends. Come inside."

She hunched forward as she walked into the studio then suddenly stopped, aware that if it hadn't been for her gritted teeth, her mouth would have dropped open. The entire expanse of the carriage house was turned over to a workroom with a small kitchen area and a sleeping loft on the far wall. But what held Maura motionless was the colour—spear upon spear of it slashing the studio's white walls and staining the floor. The winter-strong light poured through a series of multicoloured panels suspended from the ceiling, mutating the glass into pikes of cerise, emerald, and sapphire—a numbing aria of sight. The hard white of the walls heightened the effect and slammed the hues against each other with the intensity of a manic fist. The result was stunning. With its jarring juxtaposition of antisepsis and brilliance, the room looked like a morgue suddenly slapped by angelic instruction.

"Amazing, isn't it? It still takes even me aback."
Timbrook's voice was low, his breath stirring an unfettered wisp of her hair. Instinctively, she moved away.
This was not a man to detest or trust casually.

With a pang of recognition, Maura stepped over to
the cottage's long western wall. Tilted upright against
a wood frame was the church's stained glass window.
Truly, this, if nothing else, was testimony to Timbrook's
artistry. The last time she had seen it, the window was
still in St. Martin's, a splintered reminder of the man
who had committed suicide beneath it. The corpse had
lain sprawled in front of the altar, the glitter of glass
covering the chancel floor like lethal confetti. Now the
window was a magnified and perfect icon. The Mother
and Christ Child, once separated by a bullet, gazed beatifically at each other.

She shook her head, amazed. "It's phenomenal,"
she said. "The painting, the colour match . . . I can't tell
the old from the new."

Timbrook clicked his tongue. "Not quite be worth
my upkeep if you could, now, would I?"

Maura gazed around the rest of the room. Shards
of glass covered work tables like dark puzzle pieces. A
light table, switched on, glowed beneath several partly
finished pencil designs. Paintbrushes and supplies
lined shelves mounted on the side of the loft. Elaborate
shelving containing sheets of glass and boxes of lead
came took up most of the east wall. Two small kilns sat
in a corner.

"Your work is quite beautiful," she said, turning
back to the panels. "Do you do several projects at
once?"

Timbrook looked at her with mock horror, a frantic
hand clawing at his chest as if he meant to rip his heart
out before she could do the honor. "Several at once?
My dear Sergeant, do I look like an assembly-line
worker? Do these look like Vauxhalls? These are my
creations, straight from God's head to my eyes to these
hands."

He raised his bandaged hands before his face. For an absurd moment he looked like a West End actor giving his all in a miserably bad play. Lowering his hands, he stared at Maura with such dismay, that she laughed out loud. His face softened; a twinkle split his ice blue eyes. "Ah, Ramsden laughs. Perhaps she sits as well."

He pointed to the only piece of conventional furniture in the room, a massive overstuffed sofa of a plush grey tweed that easily could have seated seven people and possibly slept three. In front of it stretched a thin iron table, just wide enough for the dirty cup and saucer that was its sole ornamentation.

Maura sat on the sofa's edge and brought out her pen and notepad, more relaxed, but wary of the man she was about to question. Timbrook dropped easily down next to her, propped his feet on the table, and began gently tilting it on its attenuated legs.

"So, Sergeant, I suppose you want to know my movements on the morning Lisa was offed."

She flicked open her notepad and pushed a loose wisp of hair behind her ear. "Let's say between eight o'clock and noon."

"Ask me a tough one. I remember precisely what I was doing. I was here, as I am every morning. I do most of my work before two—that's when the sun's the best, and while it's not imperative to work by the sun, it does help to be inspired. So I'm rarely up before eight and I generally start work around nine, which is what I did Saturday. I worked through until about eleven-thirty, then took a break. I had meant to go out not long after that to get some supplies, but Helen Pane rang with the news about Lisa and, well, I didn't go after all."

"What time was her call?"

"Oh, I'd say a little before noon."

"What did she tell you?"

"That Gale Grayson rang her and said that Lisa had been killed in a bicycle accident. A broken neck. Then there was the general commiseration and that was about all."

Maura regarded him calmly. "What kind of general commiseration?"

He brought his feet down and drove his fingers through his hair. "Oh, you know, how she couldn't believe it, she had just seen Lisa on Friday, what were Edgar and Brian going to do—that sort of thing."

"Miss Pane said it was a broken neck?"

"She said Gale had told her it looked like a broken neck. I have no idea how Gale ascertained that. I didn't think to ask. Bicycle accident—broken neck. Made sense to me."

"Other than Miss Pane's phone call, did anyone else see or talk to you here Saturday morning?"

"No. I had no interruptions until Helen's call. That's not unusual. Most people around here know not to call me before two. I can go days without encountering another human being."

I doubt it, thought Maura. Solitude isn't much of a sparring partner. She settled deeper into the sofa and examined her notes. "What method of transport do you have, Mr. Timbrook?"

"You mean like a car? I have a minibus, a 1985 Leyland. Great for hauling."

"You can fit these in a minibus?"

"Well, no, not all. For the windows I have a mate with a larger lorry who helps me."

"What do you use locally?"

"My feet. I don't own a bicycle, if that's what you mean."

"How well did you know Lisa Stillwell?"

"Well enough to know not to have sex with her."

Maura gave him a tired look. "Meaning?"

He crossed his arms in front of him. "There was a time when she wanted to sleep with me. This is a narrow community, Sergeant, and Lisa was a narrow girl. She thought she loved the pilgrim soul in me. We went out a couple of times, once a picnic in Petersfield, once a film in Southampton, but she wanted a 'relationship.' Oh, God, you had to have known her. She was so damn young." He shrugged. "I called a halt to it."

"When did these dates take place?"

"Back in September. I'd say the first and second Saturdays in September. The picnic was first, in a field, I'm not sure I could find it again, and the film was on the evening of the second Saturday. A revival house. *The War of the Roses.*"

"Really."

"Yes, quite my cup of tea, not hers at all. But there you go, she was such a romantic."

"Did anyone know about these dates?"

"Oh, no, I shouldn't think so. She was quite insistent I not mention them to anyone. I don't think 'Duddy' would have approved."

His feet began pushing the table again. Maura reached over and placed the teacup on the floor. "You don't seem particularly saddened by her death, Mr. Timbrook."

His laugh was curt. "That's right, Sergeant. I killed Lisa Stillwell because I'm the one who got away. Sorry, but I'd think you'd have better luck searching for the one who didn't quite make it. Lisa wanted a lover. I'll wager she found a lover and a killer in one tidy package."

His ankle relaxed a little too harshly, and suddenly the iron table toppled over, coming to rest on its side with its black legs straight out like a charred dog. Maura watched him passively. With an angry grunt, he gave the table a savage kick that moved it all of an inch.

"Who would that lover be?" Maura asked finally.

Timbrook was quiet a moment, studying the small clumps of dust and hair that were mashed onto the ends of the table legs. Then his face folded into a smile. He reached across Maura to pick up the teacup she had placed next to her feet.

"I don't know," he said lightly. "Believe it or not, I would help you if I could. I'm certainly not happy Lisa's dead. I'm simply more philosophical about it than grief-stricken. That approach to life seems to work the best for me. So, Sergeant Ramsden, I'm going to fix a nice cup of herbal tea. Would you like to be included?"

Notepad in hand, she followed him back to the kitchen area, which was separated from the rest of the room by a low counter that served as both food preparation and eating space. Maura pulled a stool from beneath the counter and perched on it. She gave a little involuntary gasp as she peered at the worktop surface closely.

It was exquisite. Tiny pieces of tile and glass, some no longer than a sixteenth of an inch, had been laid in a bed of plaster to form a Byzantine-like mosaic of the dying and bloodied Christ. Two women, draped in royal blue robes, lamented in frontal view at the foot of the cross. Their tears were minute slivers of mica.

"My word," she breathed. "And I bet you chop lettuce on it."

"What?" Timbrook looked up as he rummaged through the crockery. "Oh, that. Well, no, actually." He gave the worktop a quick rap with his knuckles. "Plexiglas. Got to protect the creation. Or the crucifixion, as the case may be. Let's see. Today I have lime blossom or fennel. Lady's choice."

"Lime blossom, I suppose."

"Good for headaches. Perhaps I'll give you a bag of it to take back to the station."

Maura dragged her eyes away from the mosaic and watched Timbrook warm the teapot and set the water to boil. He seemed calmed, the earlier burst of emotion spent and forgotten. It was possible that he had been the one to end the relationship with Lisa—nonetheless, that iron table hadn't fallen because of a mere nudge. His hands were steady as he dropped two tablespoons of the dried herbs into a ceramic teapot.

Beneath Maura's hand one of the women sobbed for the fallen prophet. With her finger, Maura carefully followed the outline of her weeping form, down the lined folds, around the limp hem at the woman's feet.

"You know, Mr. Timbrook." She tapped on the mosaic's covering. "This surprises me. The window you were hired to do, but this . . . I wouldn't have taken you as a religious person."

"How imperceptive of you, Sergeant. Two demerits and a whack on the wrist."

"At the very least I would have pegged you for an agnostic."

"Ah, there you're back on track." He located a jar of honey from the cupboard and set it, along with a spoon, in front of her. "Well, if you must know—and I don't know why you'd want to but God forbid I question the ways of the law—my father was a religious art fanatic. Completely obsessed. As a child, I traveled through all the great cathedrals of Europe with him while he slobbered over church artifacts like a dirty little boy with his hands in his trousers. As a result, I can't stand the stuff. They haunt my every waking moment."

Maura levelled her eyes at him, unimpressed and weary of his sardonicism.

"Tough life," she said drily.

Before she could react, his hand was over hers, pinning it lightly to the mosaic. When she tried to jerk away, he tightened his grip. He pushed his face forward until it was so close she could smell his breath.

"It really is, Sergeant," he whispered. "But then I'm sure you know about the unexamined life. Lots of people have them. At least mine is worth living."

Maura twisted her arm and broke his grip. She was perplexed by her own lack of rancour, her utter coolness in the face of what certainly was inappropriate physical contact, if not a threat. She looked at him blandly.

"If you try something like that again, I'll beat you senseless. Now, when did you move to Fetherbridge, Mr. Timbrook?"

Her imperturbability evidently surprised him, and,

more irritatingly, pleased him. He looked at her approvingly and wiped off the counter with a tea cloth. "Ramsden wins," he murmured. He motioned to her closed notepad. "Write this down accurately, Sergeant. I don't want to have to repeat it." When she didn't move, he leaned forward on his elbows and continued. "Let's see. I used to live in London, had a studio with several other artists. But one day about eighteen months ago the good Reverend Cart came knocking at my door looking for someone to repair his church window. I was commissioned. Of course, you know all about that—The Suicide." He wriggled his fingers, summoning spirits. "It's a standard part of village lore now."

"You seem disdainful."

"Well, why not? People wear other folks' tragedy too easily. Take Lisa's death. It'll only truly affect a handful. The communal wailing, however, will last years."

"Is that so bad? It reinforces boundaries, confirms moral limits."

Timbrook rolled his eyes. "Please, Sergeant. Sociologists and priests exit to the rear."

The kettle let out an anemic whistle. Timbrook lifted it from the cooker and carefully poured hot water into the teapot. Maura watched as his face dampened with steam.

"Mr. Timbrook, who is 'Mr. E.'?"

His brow furrowed as he gently set the pot's lid in place. "Hmmmm?"

"Lisa told someone she was seeing a 'Mr. E.' Who would that be?"

He thought a minute, then shook his head. "Can't say that I know any E's. Editha Forrester, but she's older than Methuselah and not nearly so handsome."

"Cute, Mr. Timbrook. Are you being obtuse, or merely uncooperative?"

"No, honestly. I wouldn't be surprised to discover

Lisa was seeing someone, but I have no idea who Mr. E. could be."

"Who wanted her dead?"

Timbrook blotted his moist forehead with a cloth, then shook his head. "No one. I mean, Lisa could be irritating—I certainly found her so, but people don't murder because their nerves get a bit jangled, do they? Lisa was basically a good soul, naive, fanciful perhaps, but decent." He ran a bandaged finger over the teapot's handle. "I know I came on as a bit caustic before, but really, there was no harm in her."

"Who else can give me an idea of what Lisa was like?"

"Oh, I'd certainly talk to Jill Ivory. And Helen Pane. You get around them and they all act like sisters."

"What about Mrs. Grayson? I've been told she and Lisa were close."

"Ah. Well, yes, you could talk to Gale. I'm sure she could help."

"You seem uncertain about that."

"Oh, no. Gale was quite close to Lisa. Lisa told me she . . . she felt Gale treated her like another daughter. You know, solicitous, kind, concerned. Gale's like that. Everything soft, no hard edges. She's a very . . . likable lady."

Maura watched him, fascinated, as his face slid into the same mask of distaste she had worn when their interview started.

9

By six in the evening it was inky black, the night descended, the doors locked. Gale gazed through the bottle glass panes of her kitchen window to where her garden gate stood unseeable in the dark. It, too, was latched, a poor defence against intruders—as if intruders could be bolted out, as if protection were ever possible.

Locks were one of the legacies Tom had left his little village. In her early days as a newlywed in Fetherbridge, Gale, raised in Atlanta with its urban gangs, suburban skinheads and ratcheting destruction, had been the only person in the village to habitually lock her doors. What makes everyone here think they're immune? she had asked Tom. Why does everyone act as if London and all its ills were a million miles away? He had laughed softly, his hand over hers as she turned the lock in the door. My American alarmist, he had called her. But he never stayed her hand or followed her to bed without double-checking her efforts.

At the time she took his acquiescence for concern, or at least loving good humour. In retrospect, she saw it for what it was: a terrorist protecting his turf, a criminal distrusting his cohorts. To hell with her.

Now everyone in Fetherbridge had locks on their doors. Strange, really, for fear to have come to them so suddenly. One March evening they thought they lived apart; the next, latches were thrown in doorjambs, nails hammered into windows, as if every man were a terrorist, every woman a killer in wait.

With nightfall Gale's kitchen appeared to shrink several feet. Shadows cloaked corners and cast grey veils across the floor. Gale glanced down at her notes spread across the harvest table. Her job demanded that she spend the next several months immersed in the story of the C.S.S. *Alabama* and Admiral Semmes's piracy in the name of the Confederacy. It now seemed so smutty. If there was a difference between the slaughter of a lost cause and the dirtiness of a murder, damned if she could see it. She slapped the pencil she was holding onto her notes and hastily began gathering them together. No one could accuse her of not living up to her pedigree, she thought. Born into a region where fire and crosses and swaying ropes were to some tools of honor, she had married an honorable man.

Across the table, Katie Pru had abandoned a bowl of tomato soup for more creative pursuits. She dropped her crayon and held up a piece of paper for Gale to see.

"Look, Mama. I finished."

Gale took the paper from her daughter and angled it to the light. "Wonderful, Katie Pru. Can you tell me about it?"

This was parent-speak for "What is it?" but Katie

Pru was oblivious to her mother's shortcomings. She beamed and stuck out a pudgy finger.

"Mary, Joseph, and baby Jesus. See? That's a donkey."

"Well, so it is, baby. This is very good."

It was, actually: blue, purple, and red crayon in search of the boy King. Each figure was recognisable—Joseph oblong with a crook, the infant Christ a bundle of wiry lines and a smile, Mary kneeling, her belly round, stick fingers splayed out in either delight or supplication.

Gale felt her throat constrict. What a happy trio, blessed by angels, worshipped by kings. Not for Mary the pain of lonely childbirth. No antiseptic delivery room, strangers in plastic gloves, whisking her down the hallway, forcing her bare feet into cold metal stirrups. No nurse telling her over and over: *Push, push, hold my hand now, push, you're doing fine,* and all the while Gale's own voice screaming for Tom, begging him to make it stop, to come back to her, to life, and make the nightmare go away.

Anise had offered to coach her through the childbirth; even her grandmother had called from Georgia, offering as a last olive branch her help. But Gale had refused, determined to see this, as Tom's death, through alone.

Katie Pru had pushed down the birth canal face up. *Your baby's coming sunny side up,* the nurse had told her. *Your baby wants its face to the sky.* But that had been the problem. The foetus couldn't move. For more than an hour the infant was lodged in the birth canal, unable to pass by her mother's bony pelvis. Gale was terrified, in pain, the epidural botched—and no one there but nurses in masks.

"Gimme, Mama," Katie Pru said, taking the drawing from Gale. "I forgot."

Selecting a pink crayon from a basket of coloured bits and peeled paper, Katie Pru bore down hard, making a pink squiggle at the top of the page.

"The star," she announced. "The star of Befam."

"You're right, baby," Gale answered. "That's the star of Befam, no doubt about it."

Katie Pru bent once again over her work. Her hair fell forward, and impatiently she brushed it from her eyes. Dark hair, darker eyes. None of Tom's pale Anglo genes bloomed in his daughter. She was Gale's. Even her temperament—stubborn, playful, intense—if Gale thought back far enough, she could recognise it as her own. The familiar ache started between her breasts. She lifted a strand of Katie Pru's hair and let it fall. *You are me when I was happy. You are me remade whole.*

Gale withdrew her hand and hugged herself tight, a slight shiver undermining the kitchen's warmth. She had been happy that first year in Fetherbridge, relentlessly so. How many times, she asked herself bitterly, had she gone to Tom, arms outstretched, thanking him for bringing her here, for giving her an ideal life? The people of Fetherbridge had been so attentive to her. Tom had laughed that they saw her as a charming enigma, a shy, soft-spoken stranger from an unspecific place. *They know the South has magnolias and Rhett Butler,* he told her. *But when you say Atlanta, they think you mean Atlantic City—boardwalks and gambling casinos. They don't quite know what to make of you.*

When they embraced her as one of their own, it didn't surprise her. It should have. She was a historian, well versed in rural folkways. A foreigner is always a foreigner, an enigma always a threat.

Katie Pru pulled a green crayon from her basket and began making dots over the entire page. "Lightning bugs," she said. "Lightning bugs and angels."

As far as Gale knew, Katie Pru had never seen either one. Gale chuckled and touched her daughter's arm. She had been right to give birth alone. She wasn't sure it made her stronger, but she did know that it consolidated her separateness. It gave her a claim to those door locks.

And now? Would she be able to make it through

Lisa's murder alone? She thought back to the detectives ensconced so arrogantly in her living room. Damn it to hell, she thought. Damn them for ruining everything.

Halford stood in the shadows outside the High Street entrance to The Proper Pale—food, drinks and lodging—and beat his arms against his sides. It was chilly. The afternoon had come close to wrecking the well-tended myth of goodwill between New Scotland Yard and the county constabularies. He had spent a good half-hour on the phone with DI Roan, requesting, then cajoling, and finally berating the man into supplying officers to outfit a new incidents room in the Fetherbridge recreation center. The village police station, with only one desk and three phones, was not going to be adequate for the county-wide search Halford needed for "Mr. E." In the end he went over Roan's head by appealing directly to the Hampshire Chief Constable, further alienating Roan, a man he was going to have to coax into amiability, or at least into a minimal nod of cooperation. He had also made a call to DCS Chandler at the Yard, to fill him in on the preliminary investigation. "Keep a careful eye on the Grayson connection," his superior told him. "Coincidences bear watching."

Through the blackness shone the palpitant beam of a bicycle light. As the rider coasted in and out of the street lamps' foggy halos, Halford recognised PC Baylor. He stepped forward in greeting as the constable slowed to a stop and dismounted.

"Gloomy enough for you, sir?" Not waiting for an answer, the constable chatted on. "I wanted to thank you for the invitation. It's not often I have someone to talk shop with over dinner. It's amazing how many people don't really want to know what your average village constable does during the day." He scanned the area in front of the inn. "I guess DS Ramsden isn't here yet."

"I'm sure she'll be here shortly. I told her eightish.

It's been a hectic day, so I wouldn't be surprised if she was a little late."

Baylor nodded his consent. "Been a hectic day for us all, I imagine. The phone rang constantly at the station. Folks wanting to know if it was safe, wanting to know details. A few even wanted to hire me to drive their kiddies home from school. Glad I'm not in on this inquiry—I wouldn't have the time."

"Actually, I wish you were on the team," Halford said regretfully. "You know this village better than the rest of us. I think your help would be invaluable."

The younger man beamed. "Well, sir, I'm yours for the asking. Never say no to Scotland Yard is my motto."

Halford smiled and watched as Baylor leaned his bicycle against the side of the building and moved towards the pub door. "Don't you lock it up?"

Baylor glanced at his bike and grinned. "Ah, nossir. I guess that doesn't look good for a policeman to leave his property unsecured—especially when you consider how I go on about it to the children—but truth is nothing much gets stolen here. I don't think I've locked my bike once since I've been in Fetherbridge. It's just not that kind of place."

They had started into the pub when Halford heard the quick steps of boots coming up an alley beside the building. Maura broke into the frosted glow of the pub lights with a shiver and a muted exclamation.

"Can you credit this weather? Bleak this morning, sunny this afternoon, freezing tonight. Is this the greenhouse effect or what? I'm going to have to start packing three seasons' worth of clothes just to ensure I don't sweat my way to a slimmer, trimmer me while dying of frostbite."

Halford chuckled at the look of incredulity on Baylor's face. Either the constable wasn't used to women making complete sentences or he was mystified by Maura's television-tuned prattle. If it was a case of both, then Baylor was going to have some slack-jawed days ahead of him. Spreading his arms before him, Halford hustled both of them through the door and into the pub.

The Proper Pale was aptly named—very respectable and spartan to the point of pallid. The pub's dining area was dark, clean, and correct. Through a small alcove came the sound of laughter and brief applause—the drinkers at least had managed to infuse their half of the pub with a little spontaneity. On this side, however, the tables were empty and the mood regimented.

Halford directed them towards a small table by the fireplace. As they passed the alcove, a voice rang out.

"Hullo, Nate. What d'ya hear?"

The police paused at the pub opening and looked in. Fully half of the tables were occupied, mostly with boisterous young men with pints in their fists. Next to the alcove, however, was a group of five people, two women and three men, noticeably withdrawn from the rest of the crowd. It was to this group that the speaker belonged.

"Good evenin', Clive," said Nate. "Everything all right tonight?"

Clive, a middle-aged man with a thick grey beard, lifted his glass. He took a long drink of ale. "Can't say that's the case, Nate."

One of the women, a sixtyish redhead with an arch of puckers around her upper lip, looked vaguely familiar to Halford. Across from her sat a slender, elongated man he was certain he had interviewed during the Grayson inquiry. He could put names to neither of them.

Baylor unzipped his jacket. "I guess you've heard about Lisa. I'm sorry, Ruth. You, too, June. I know you're all close to her family. It's a terrible thing."

Ruth Barker. Halford studied the red-haired woman. He recalled talking to her briefly about Tom Grayson following his death. She had taught him in grade school. And, he recalled from his interview with

Gale Grayson earlier in the day, she sometimes looked after Katie Pru.

An amiable yelling match occupied the interest of the rest of the room. Two men, well padded with track suits and knit hats, commenced what sounded like challenges for darts. The group in the corner ignored them. Ruth Barker laid her hand on the beefy arm of the man seated next to her and looked at Baylor. "Jacob says you think it was murder."

Baylor let his breath out slowly. "Yes, that's right." He pointed to the detectives beside him. "This is Chief Inspector Halford and Detective Sergeant Ramsden from New Scotland Yard. They're here to help."

The group stared at the detectives. "I've met the inspector before," said the slender man. He pointed to the people at the table. "This is June and Clive Kingston, Ruth and Jacob Barker. I'm Ben Hossett. You interviewed me about Tom Grayson."

The bookseller. Halford recognised him now. Tom Grayson had given regular readings of his poems at Hossett's High Street shop, the result of which was that Hossett had become a knowledgeable and expansive critic. He had not only aided the inquiry with details of Grayson's professional life, but had provided a monotone commentary on the dead man's suitability for his chosen occupation. Despite a growing national reputation, the poet had not gotten high marks on the local level. A year before he died, Grayson had published a short volume of poetry which Hossett dutifully stocked. Ten copies sold.

Halford nodded briefly. "Yes, Mr. Hossett. I remember you. We're hoping that our stay in Fetherbridge this time is shorter than the last."

June Kingston drew a beer mat toward her and carefully set her half-empty glass down on it. She directed her attention to the constable.

"Nate, are you thinking it's a stranger? Was it some psychopath? I've got a daughter, you know. What should I do about her?"

A loud hurrah and some applause sounded from the other side of the room as Baylor slipped off his jacket. "Ah, June, we don't know who it was. There's a method to a murder inquiry, you know, and we're following that method. We'll find out soon enough if it was a stranger or not. I suspect it was. As for Lydia, just be careful for a while, until it's cleared up. No need to panic, but use common sense."

Clive Kingston pushed his chair away from the table until he met the wall. He tapped his knee with agitated fingers.

"I'm no bobby, Nate, but I damn well know drifter psychopaths don't do the majority of the murders in this country. You'll be looking at locals. You'll be looking close to home."

When he stood, he towered over Baylor, meeting Halford eye to eye. He looked from Halford to the constable.

"They say that murderers are usually someone the victim knows. Well, just remember, sometimes strangers live in our own pockets. Fetherbridge used to be a safe, quiet community. Now two terrible deaths in three years. It's not right. Lisa Stillwell was a sweet girl. She didn't deserve this."

Halford started to retort that even screaming bitches didn't deserve to be knocked on the head and strangled, but Maura lightly touched his arm.

"Sir," she said. "Our table."

They turned to leave when Clive Kingston grabbed Baylor by the sleeve. "One more thing before you go, Nate. The funeral. We want it to take place."

He said it flatly, a man who would brook no arguments.

Baylor gently disengaged his arm. "I'm sorry, Clive. There's nothing can be done about that."

"That's not acceptable, Nate." His eyes flickered briefly towards the two detectives before settling back on Baylor. "You know what I mean. This village needs to mourn. It needs to bury Lisa and move on."

Baylor stood his ground with impressive diplomacy. "I know exactly what you're talking about, Clive. I've been here over two years. I've watched this village put itself back together piece by piece, and it's done an incredible job. I know this murder is a frightening thing to everyone. It brings back the past, and nobody wants that. But I'm sorry, Clive. We'll have to work through it another way."

One of the game players hit the bull's-eye. The roars were deafening. In the pub's motley shadows, June Kingston's face looked skeletal and harsh.

"How can you do that to a child, Nate? How can you let her just stay there . . . her body all desecrated . . ." She brought her hands to her face, her fingers like bones. "It's too horrible to think about," she said incredulously. "I don't understand how you people can live with yourselves, knowing what you're doing to her, what you're doing to her family."

"Let us bury her, Nate," Jacob Barker echoed. "Do what's right."

"It's out of my hands, Jacob. Just let the police do their job. The quicker it's done, the quicker the funeral can take place."

With a curt good-bye, the police left the villagers in the pub and filed to their table on the far wall of the dining room.

The three were silent as they took their seats. The din from the pub side of the inn receded. Halford slowly opened his cloth napkin and looked at Baylor.

"So. Tell me about those people."

Baylor slowly rubbed his neck. "Well, they're a good sort, actually. June and Clive Kingston, she's the postmistress, he runs the ironmonger's shop. Ruth Barker is a retired schoolteacher, her husband Jacob a lorry driver. And you know Ben Hossett. They're just frightened, sir. This village is so close, Lisa's death is hard on everyone."

Someone shouted from the pub, and the room

erupted in laughter. Halford cocked a questioning eye-brow at Baylor.

"Ah, well, those aren't all villagers, sir. And they're certainly not the original families. The Proper Pale has a reputation around these parts. The Millberrys who own this place, they're quite popular."

As if summoned, Mrs. Millberry entered the dining room. Immediately Halford deduced the inn's popularity. It was run by squirrels. As Halford watched, Mrs. Millberry scampered toward them, froze, turned about, and darted to a sideboard for a cloth and a pen. She started back, got halfway there, and suddenly veered left to retrieve a pad of paper. Then she looked at them again, took a deep breath, and walked forward. Halford sighed. If this had been a road, children would be poking at her with a stick by now.

"So sorry," she said, finally reaching their table. "We don't get much custom this time of year, not for food, anyway—the odd traveller here and there, and of course, Miss Forrester, who doesn't see the purpose in heating up the Aga for just one person—so there you are." She scratched her head with her pen. "I'm afraid I've gotten a bit scattered. But never you mind. My husband is a fearfully good cook. I'm not saying I won't get your plates mixed up, but I am saying that what-ever you end up with I'm sure you'll find it delightful."

With that helpful promise, they all ordered lamb stew. After Mrs. Millberry scurried away, Halford leaned back in his chair and nodded to his sergeant. "All right, Maura, let's give Nate here an update."

Maura produced a sheaf of folded papers from her handbag. "All right," she intoned cheerfully. "This just in from the house-to-house team. They're well into in-terviewing all the residents of Heatherwood Beach where Lisa lived. According to two witnesses, Lisa left her home at around 9:20 Saturday morning. The pro formas are still being completed, but so far, nobody has mentioned seeing anything unusual either in the estate or on Boundary Road."

"Fine. I've put in for an incidents room to be set up in the rec center," Halford said to Baylor. "We should be out of your hair soon."

Here Baylor frowned. "Roan rang after you left and suggested you set up in the Winchester station."

"Did you tell him to bugger off? I want it here in Fetherbridge."

"Well, sir, I didn't exactly say 'bugger off,' but I let your wishes be known. Anyway, the computers, extra phones, and supplies should be in the rec center tomorrow morning in time for the first team."

"Good. Anything else?"

"No, sir."

Halford turned to Maura. "So how was your afternoon?"

"Interesting. I rang the local vicar and got the names of three girls in Lisa's church who he says were fairly chummy with her. When I spoke with them, they basically verified what we've already heard—nice girl, no boyfriend, devoted to church and family. One, however, Bette Seasons, did say that Lisa had been particularly happy the past couple of weeks, says she told her that things were about to change in her life, although Lisa wouldn't say how. Miss Seasons is a very animated young lady of seventeen, so it's hard to tell if that's postdeath hyperbole or not."

Mrs. Millberry scuttered to their table bearing a large tray. With a scattershot of concern, she dropped three steaming plates in front of them, checked the level of their beverages, and scooted away. Halford picked up his fork and gently prodded a chunk of potato.

"What about Timbrook?"

Baylor looked at Maura and broke into a broad grin. Maura tucked a piece of carrot into her mouth and gazed innocently at Halford.

"I take it," Halford continued, "Mr. Timbrook is one of the town characters."

"I think, in Mr. Timbrook's own estimation, he *is* the town character," Maura replied. "I don't want to deprive you of the pleasure of walking into his workshop unprepared, so I'll omit physical descriptions. But the interview itself was extremely interesting."

She passed him her notes. In Maura's cryptic handwriting, only every twelfth word was legible, but it was enough to see her point.

"Well, well. So they dated. Is Timbrook the type a reputedly inexperienced young woman would find attractive?"

"Oh, I dare say he's attractive enough, in a dangerous sort of way. It's an aura he cultivates. The rogue artist with the hidden heart of gold. He started out the interview as a sneering snake and ended it as a concerned citizen. I can see a young girl being attracted to him."

"Doesn't own a bicycle. Hmmm. Of course, Nate, you just demonstrated how easy it would be to procure one for an hour or two. If the village constable doesn't lock his bike, how many other people do?"

Maura jabbed her fork into a sizable chunk of lamb. "Have you heard anything about fingerprints yet, Daniel?"

Halford reached into his coat pocket and pulled out another folded sheaf of papers. "The report came in this afternoon. The only fingerprints on the bicycle were Lisa's, Brian's, and Edgar Stillwell's. Black, brunette, blonde, and red human hairs were found on Lisa's clothing, along with several different fibers that appear to be animal hair—given that she worked at the Grayson cottage, my wager is on fleece. A smudge of dirt on her coat revealed no discernible imprint of shoe or fabric."

"Well, evidently, Christian Timbrook rarely leaves his fingerprints on anything. When he works on his glass, he cuts his fingers—he'd have me believe fairly often. All ten digits are covered with bandages, including the fingertips."

"Sticking plaster or cloth?"

"Plasters."

"Fresh, would you say?"

"He claimed he cuts his fingers 'anew' every day, but I suspect that is an exaggeration. These bandages looked fairly grubby."

"Huh." Halford returned her notes. "What's this about Mrs. Grayson?"

"That was curious. I was asking him about Lisa's friends, and when I mentioned Mrs. Grayson he became very hesitant. When I pressed him, he said rather noncommittal things about her. But his face, Daniel, it looked like he loathed her, couldn't stand talking about her." She wrinkled her nose. "It was terribly strange."

Halford pushed the notes back to her. "Do you think you could get those typed up into something I can read? I'd like to know exactly what he said. About everything. Nate, do you know why Timbrook would feel any particular antipathy towards Mrs. Grayson?"

Baylor took a swig of ale to wash down the bite of lamb he had been labouring over. Between swallows he answered.

"Well, sir, they were sort of involved for a while."

"Involved?"

"Lovers. Leastways, that was the word. A few months back."

Halford studied the brown and green mixture on his plate that was beginning to resemble things people didn't put in their mouths. When he finally glanced at Maura, she was gazing at Baylor with the merest of smiles on her face.

Jeremy Cart felt slightly foolish. The vicar had felt slightly foolish gathering his dirty laundry and placing it in an old bushel basket; he had felt slightly foolish ringing Orrin Ivory and making his peculiar request. And he felt slightly foolish now, hiding in the cover of the vicarage wall with the basket neatly secreted between two dormant, though not declawed, rosebushes. With a quiet yelp, he wrenched his hand from the dry thorns and sent half a dozen feathery canes scattering to the ground. The light from the vicarage porch barely reached the garden corner where he crouched, but he could see three lines of blood sprout across the back of his hand. He brought it to his mouth and licked the blood away.

Headlamps appeared on the street and Ivory's brown minivan slowed to a stop. With a meaty grin, the editor leaned across the seat and popped open the passenger door.

"Operation Gale in effect," he said.

Cart threw the basket of clothes into the backseat and crawled into the front with a warm covered dish cradled to his gut. He smiled weakly.

"Really is good of you to do this."

Ivory shook his head. "I've been worried about Gale myself, but I haven't had much time to check on her. Anise and Jill are in a state. I know they look strapping and all, but they're not nearly as strong as they appear."

Cart glanced at Ivory as the van pulled onto Boundary Road, allowing the irritation he felt to rumble invisible under his kindly young parson's face. Many people aren't nearly as strong as they appear, Editor. One of them he had planned to bury on Friday.

The drive to Gale's cottage took three minutes at most. From the street the house was entirely dark except for one yellow window on the upper storey—Katie Pru's room. It was a little after nine o'clock. Katie Pru would be asleep and her Mickey Mouse night light, plugged into the socket under the window, would be shining with a wide-eyed grin. Once Gale went to bed, Mickey would be the sole light in the house with the exception of the tiny green bulb on the compact disk player in Gale's room. That, Cart knew, stayed on all night, replaying the same CD until morning.

The hand brake on Ivory's van squeaked as he yanked it in place. The two men looked at each other.

"Ready?" Cart asked.

Ivory patted his chest. "Ready, willing, and red-neck." He grinned.

Halford stared at the thin brown pool at the bottom of his coffee cup and tried to remember how much he had drunk. Four, maybe five cups. Mrs. Millberry, with an aborning fascination for follow-through, had appeared at regular intervals to dip the spout into his cup and comment that she was pleased the Chief Inspector didn't share the general consensus that her husband's coffee could make a pig retch. The first time she had said it, he had studied her carefully but judged the pun unintentional. He had gone back to drinking the sub-standard swill, downing one after another as fast as Mrs. Millberry could patter over.

"Daniel."

With reluctance he put the cup down. One of Maura's nails, bitten to the quick, thumped the table.

"You haven't met Timbrook, Daniel. He and Mrs. Grayson—it's damned odd, that's all."

"So you said." Halford picked up his cup again and sipped air. He didn't say what niggled at his brain, that Mrs. Grayson and *anybody* seemed damned odd to him. Impatiently, he twisted around to see if Mrs. Millberry's scuttling heels were heading his way. They weren't. Perhaps she was gathering nuts in the other room for the long cold winter.

"He's so Scarlet Pimpernel and she's so Blanche DuBois." Maura dipped her spoon into an unnaturally pink peach melba and scooped it into her mouth. "It isn't quite right."

Baylor's head bobbed. "That's the feeling around the village, like cats and rabbits mating." He widened his eyes at Halford's scowl. "No, sir, I wasn't being vulgar. That was a quote I heard, from Mr. Millberry, I think it was. 'See what breeds when cats and rabbits mate.' "

Halford pushed his chair back and strode toward the door, empty cup in hand. It breeds squirrels, he thought, pesky, feral squirrels who don't know the first damn thing about coffee. When he reached the threshold, he heard Mrs. Millberry's reedy voice ask the 'boys' to pass her the darts—it was her turn to show them how the bloody game was played. Halford spun on his heels and headed back to the table. Without comment, Maura pushed her half-empty cup of cold coffee toward him. He drank it in two gulps without sitting down.

Maura tapped the tip of her spoon on the table. "Nate, are you certain they were having an affair? Did they ever give you any indication?"

"Nah. Never saw any proof myself. Well, I did see them come in here a couple of times for a pint, but that's for nothing. It was mainly gossip. The thing is, it's been my experience that Fetherbridge gossip is fairly accurate."

"But it's so odd." Maura was emphatic. "I mean, there you have Mrs. Grayson, cocooned and self-protective, having an affair with the village ne'er-do-well. And then you also have Lisa, who evidently not only had a crush on Timbrook, but according to her father, was a bit too attached to the Grayson child."

Halford felt the caffeine in his system trying to suck his hair into his scalp. He had to get out. He put on his coat and then gently pressed both hands on Maura's shoulders.

"Well, mates, you two figure it out. I'm going for a walk. But please, if you're going to play Miss Marple and Lord Peter, don't jump to conclusions. It's early days yet."

Boundary Road at night was a comfortless place. Halford had walked several hundred yards, past the graveyard at St. Martin's church and the bend in the road that extinguished light from the High Street behind him, before he realised how solitary his footsteps sounded. He felt suddenly vulnerable, a lone man in a cloth coat, hatless and cold. A shudder sliced between

his shoulder blades. The tail of a wind lashed his face
and whipped into the darkness.

All afternoon he had avoided thinking about his interview with Mrs. Grayson. Now he cringed. There was
no reason for him to strike out at her, yet he had done
so, and hated himself for it. It had been the look in her
eyes when she opened the door that triggered his hostility. Three years and she still held him responsible.
Three years and he didn't blame her a bit.

He tried to focus his thoughts on the inquiry. Mrs.
Grayson and Christian Timbrook—Lisa and Christian
Timbrook. What could two such seemingly different
women find attractive about one man? This is what
comes of living in a village, Halford thought. Cities afford enough space and variety for people to draw together in common circles, like seeking like. In villages,
the inhabitants are odd bits of fluff gathered into a single ball, interconnected and suffocating because the
laws of human nature tell them it is better to cling un-
wisely than to drift.

The road arched to the Grayson cottage and he
found himself standing next to the shiny white gate
made slick and grey by the night. The ground-floor
windows were all alight, the curtains pushed back, the
rooms empty. At first he thought something was
wrong. The Gale Grayson he knew should have been
swaddled and silent in the dark, particularly after this
afternoon, after what he had done. This seemed too vibrant, and for one wild moment the house looked
tragic, as if its lights were the first impulse of panic,
flung on in fear and forgotten with flight. His throat
swelled as he grabbed the gate latch and fought to jerk
the bolt free.

A movement behind one of the windows caught his
eye and he stopped. Mrs. Grayson, arms out and wrists
dipped like swans' necks, swirled into the illuminated
space of the front room. She spun around once and
stopped, her head turned towards the doorway, the
rich light-and-dark of her hair obscuring her face. Qui-

etly, Halford opened the gate and took a few steps up the walk. The wavy surface of the old glass glazed her like water, making her features difficult to see, but as he watched, her hair fell back to her shoulders, her arms spread wide, and her mouth began to move in fluid shapes.

She was singing. Halford could hear his own breath passing through his nostrils. With exaggerated fineness, Mrs. Grayson let one thin arm trail along the edge of her sweater until her fingernails closed and lifted the hem in a deep curtsy. Something heavy pulled in his chest. She bent forward and brought her tiny hands to her face to stifle a laugh.

Halford stood in the middle of the devastated garden, uncertain what to do. He suspected that part of the reason for his walk had been to see her, to apologise, or perhaps only to check on her, as he had wanted to do in that Southampton tea shop three years earlier.

She was spinning around now, hands clapping over her head. Halford clenched his teeth. A girl was dead, for Chrissakes! There was no gaiety in that. He closed his eyes. He wanted to talk to her. For God's sake, he wanted to understand her.

He was turning to go when Orrin Ivory appeared at the window. Halford groaned. It was too late to scoot out the gate or throw his coat over his head and crouch in the shadows. He had been seen. Feeling chastened and irritated, he straightened his tie, ran his fingers through his hair, and reached the door as Ivory opened it.

"Surely, Halford, even Scotland Yard can call it a night. It's gone ten." Ivory held the door close to his side, his face lit by a slash of light. "Or were you out there on what's commonly called a stakeout?"

"I was walking by and noticed all the lights on," Halford replied easily. "Is everything all right?"

Surprise creased Ivory's forehead. "Well, I wouldn't say exactly 'all right' but nothing's dramatically wrong.

Jeremy Cart—the vicar—he and I had dinner with Gale. She was in the need of some cheering up."

"Ah." Halford's eyes drifted to the doorknob which Ivory continued to grasp. "Well."

Ivory took a deep breath. "Yes. Well, good manners being the salve of civilisation, let me invite you in. It's too damn cold standing out there like the night watchman. Gale has a toasty fire going in the kitchen."

He paused a second, dropping his eyes from Halford's face as if to imply that, under the circumstances, good manners also dictated a refusal and a quick good night. Halford bowed his head slightly as he pushed past Ivory and walked down the hall.

Mrs. Grayson had retreated into the kitchen where she sat at the far end of a long wooden table. Across from her was an annoyingly attractive man. Jeremy Cart rose to his feet when he saw Halford and in three strides was standing in front of him, hand outstretched, his angular face beaming. Had he been a cartoon character, Halford thought, tiny stars would have rotated in his irises. Was it really necessary for men of the cloth to be so damned telegenic these days? In twenty years this man would have iron grey hair and the kind of granite lines that would prompt women to early graves for the fleeting pleasure of having him mist over their caskets.

"I'm Chief Inspector Halford." He grabbed Cart's hand expecting it to jellify in his fingers. Instead the grip tightened and Halford received an impressively strong handshake.

"I guessed as much," Cart said enthusiastically. "I know most people around here, and I generally hear when strangers are about. And besides, Gale's spot on with her physical descriptions."

Halford decided not to glance at Mrs. Grayson, although he heard her chair scrape the floor and felt her move further from him. A cupboard door opened and the clink of porcelain was followed by the chug of liquid spilling into a cup. She was pouring coffee.

"I found the Chief Inspector outside ready to sound the alarm," Ivory said. "He was afraid with all the activity something was wrong."

"Just checking." Halford kept his voice light as he watched Mrs. Grayson wipe up some coffee she had slopped over the side of a cup. On the table was a folded copy of a newspaper. Idly, he turned it around. The June fifteenth edition of *The Hampshire Inquisitor* blasted the government's latest tax restructuring.

"Forgive me for being a bit surprised at your newspaper, Mr. Ivory. I thought most local papers focused mainly on flower shows and church gossip. Don't take that as patronising. Merely showing my ignorance."

Ivory chuckled and ran his hand through his thinning hair. "Well, we do cover our share of pretty puppy contests and school drama productions, but when something affects our readers we try to give the big boys a run for their money. The lads in London can't focus the impact of national news on the local community the way we can. At least, that's what we tell ourselves. As long as we can keep the old village press running and continue to increase our circulation in the cities, we'll be here."

He flicked the paper with his finger. "This edition had a feature on Helen Pane. Gale lost her copy and she's been after me for months to get her another, but I kept forgetting."

"Forgetting or just couldn't find it," Cart said. "If you've never been to the *Inquisitor*'s offices, Mr. Halford, you really must treat yourself. It's a rat's nest. If there ever is a nuclear war, the only survivors will be cockroaches and whoever's working at the *Inquisitor* that day."

Gale Grayson had mopped up the counter no less than seven times in the past minute, her back as straight and hard as a plate. As Halford watched her, she made a decision. The small, sharp shoulders levelled. She picked up the coffee cup and turned to him.

"The cream and sugar are on the table if you would

like them, Chief Inspector. And if you haven't eaten, I believe there's a piece of chicken left. I threatened to make one of my grandmother's award-winning vinegar pies tonight, but knives were brandished. Jeremy's housekeeper, Mrs. Simpson, made a wonderful corn soufflé, but I'm afraid if you want some of that you'll have to lick the bowl. We polished it off."

If she felt awkward, she wasn't showing it. Her smile as she handed him the coffee was utterly relaxed. He bent to get a good look at her eyes—maybe a tranquilliser would explain that languid dance at the window—but they were alert and, he noted uncomfortably, a trifle amused.

Halford surveyed the spread of dirty dishes on the long kitchen table. "Do you think, Mrs. Grayson, that we perhaps could go into another room?" Halford kept his voice controlled and subservient, the polite, uninvited guest. "Perhaps the front room. I noticed you were in there earlier."

A pink flush leapt into her cheeks. Shit. What the hell had made him say that? If he was looking for forgiveness, that was not the way to go about it. She twisted the tip of her shoe into the floor, studying it, before her colour lightened.

"Okay," she said. "Tonight it's policeman's choice."

She led the three men into the living room and Halford, in a mood for self-torture, chose to sit once again in the narrow pew. He found that if he leant against the side of it and stretched his leg half on, half off the white cushions, it wasn't nearly as uncomfortable as he remembered. He settled back and balanced his cup and saucer on his knee.

Glancing around for a chair, Cart addressed the detective.

"I understand you've been getting some bad feedback from the villagers concerning Lisa's funeral. I'm sorry about that."

"I'm sorry about it as well," Halford answered. "I

wish it could be different. I can imagine what people must be going through."

Cart selected one of the ladder-back chairs by the hearth. He regarded Halford speculatively.

"Hm. Perhaps so. At any rate, I'm hoping to talk Edgar into having a memorial service Friday instead. It won't be the same, of course, but hopefully it'll break a little of the tension."

"That's a good idea," Halford said. "Some families don't want that, you know, they prefer to wait. But given the circumstances . . ."

He didn't finish the sentence. The circumstances, of course, were twofold: Lisa's death had initially been thought an easier-to-accept accident, and Tom Grayson's crimes had left this community ripped apart. He would let each person in the room provide their own ending.

Ivory had taken a position beside the giant loom. Gale joined Cart by the fireplace. They all watched silently as Halford examined his coffee.

"Well," he said finally, "I couldn't help noticing that you three were having a little party. I hate to disrupt the fun."

Ivory answered. "I wouldn't say we were exactly having a party, Halford. Just releasing a bit of the strain."

Halford took the smallest sip of coffee possible and looked interested. "How?"

Cart and Mrs. Grayson exchanged glances. Cart squinted his eyes closed and rubbed the bridge of his nose.

"Ah, it was just something silly I decided to do for Gale, Mr. Halford," he said. "She was depressed after this afternoon, so I asked my housekeeper to fix the closest thing to soul food she could and talked Orrin here into dressing up like characters from *Tobacco Road*. It was just a little joke."

Halford looked at the vicar's Calvin Klein jeans and

Nike trainers. "I guess things have changed in the southern backwoods since they made the movie."

Cart glanced down and brushed something from his thigh. "Well, of course we put on other clothes for dinner. I mean, we looked—and I dare say *smelled*—the genuine article. We both pinned our dirty laundry to a clothes line, held it in our mouths, and sort of flapped back and forth on the front stoop. It wasn't a literal rendition of *Tobacco Road*; it was more conceptual."

Halford allowed himself a grin. "And were you cheered, Mrs. Grayson?" he asked genially.

She had picked up a coin from the table and was playing with it, wheeling it along the leg of her jeans. Now she put it down and brought her gaze to his.

"Yes. Some. I admit I was having a hard time after you left. You have to understand that for me you are quite . . . I don't know. It wasn't easy seeing you this afternoon. I apologise for reacting the way I did. I had no business being churlish."

She hesitated and her hands fluttered in front of her. "So, I talked to Jeremy and he and Orrin came over . . . well, in short, yes, I'm cheered. Not about Lisa's death, but about the aftermath. The implications. Does that make sense?"

"Yes, of course." Halford noticed Cart staring at his shoes and Ivory studying the black-and-white weaving in progress on the loom. If this had been one of Maura's 1960's sitcoms, both men would have been standing with their hands in their pockets, looking skyward and whistling.

Mrs. Grayson slapped her hands against her knees and squeezed them hard. "You say that like someone who's quite sure it makes no sense at all. Well, perhaps you're right. Anyway, it was good of them to come over and just let me ramble a bit. It was nice to have a sounding board."

"It's hard for me to imagine you rambling, Mrs. Grayson. What about?"

Cart turned in his seat, the twinkle in his eye gone

and his jaw set. He looked gratingly ministerial. "I'm sorry, Mr. Halford, but really, it's late. If you have any more questions for Gale, wouldn't it be better to conduct this at a more conventional time? Like tomorrow, and perhaps with your sergeant present to take notes so we all know where we stand?"

"Sometimes that's the beauty of meetings like this, Mr. Cart. No one's here to take notes." He kept his eyes on his coffee cup. "Mrs. Grayson?"

She stood and moved towards Ivory, who stopped examining the weaving to watch her. When she spoke, Halford heard the beginning of the edge she had held earlier in her voice.

"Since you're so interested, I rambled about suspicions and the death of privacy and the silliness of alibis and stubbornness and about how some people seem to keep repeating the same pattern over and over."

"You think Lisa's murder has something to do with your husband's death?"

"No, but you do."

Halford said nothing for a moment and then looked at Cart. "Tell me about your silly alibi."

Cart raised his hands in the air and folded them behind his head. "Well, that's what we were discussing tonight. None of us really has an alibi—well, Orrin does, but then a father can get a daughter to say anything. I was alone in the vicarage working on a sermon—Saturday is my housekeeper's day off. Gale was in between places on her moped."

"Actually, Mr. Ivory has a fairly good alibi—a receipt. All we need to do is confirm with the shopkeeper."

Cart blinked. "Yes, well, all right, but what about the rest of us? I've always thought alibis were a curious part of police work. You'd think murderers would know enough by now to be damn sure they had one, and the innocent suspects would be the gormless gits out walking the fields alone collecting berries."

Halford pulled on his moustache. He counted to twenty. "Who is 'Mr. E.'?"

Cart looked at him blankly. Gale Grayson narrowed her eyes. Ivory returned his attention to the loom.

"Who?" she asked.

"Lisa was seeing a man she called 'Mr. E.' We don't know anything about him except that he was older and that she apparently had misgivings about being involved with him—at least, she didn't want anyone to know. I thought perhaps she had mentioned him to you."

"No." Gale Grayson bit her lip. "No, she didn't."

Halford hauled himself to his feet and walked over to her. Lifting her elbow he placed the cup in her hand.

"Thank you for the coffee, Mrs. Grayson. It was just what I needed tonight."

He opened the front door, closed it softly behind him, and strolled down the path. The moon had come from behind the clouds, lighting Boundary Road for his journey back to the inn. He turned up his collar. Two things disturbed him. Why, during all their talk of the murder, had Orrin Ivory not told the other two about the mystery suitor? And why had Gale Grayson lied?

10

Tiny gold stars glistened on the backs of her hands and studded the crimson polish on her toes. Crouched on the floor on aching knees, Helen squinted at a white electric clock, pushed from its place on the counter by waves of fabric and now dangling by its cord in front of the cupboard. Four A.M. Despite the cold outside, the back of her neck was sweaty, and when she lifted her hair to cool it, damp ringlets snared her fingers. She let her hair drop. A kitchen floor was a lousy place to be at four in the morning.

She twisted on her haunches and examined the hexagonal imprints the lino made on her shins. She'd been up since midnight working on the children's costumes for the church Christmas pageant—she'd bent Jeremy's ear and finally gotten him to agree that the window needed to be installed before the New Year. Of course, now she wasn't sure there was going to be a pageant at all. She held up a sheath of white calico, hemmed at the neck and bottom and glued with stars and glitter. It was bound to fit some child—they tended to come in a variety of sizes. And if the pageant wasn't a go, Katie Pru would have a complete wardrobe in which to play wizard, witch, and pining princess. Helen flounced the sheath in the air. It drifted to the floor, scattering gold around her.

The phone rang. Fear yanked at her chest as she fumbled for the cordless under a tangle of florist's wire.

"I knew you couldn't sleep."

"Timbrook, you bloody well scared me witless, you stupid toad."

His laugh in her ear was low. "Ah, well, I don't suppose I should expect overly creative epithets in the wee hours of the morning. No, I decided to call because I knew that if my experience was anything to go by, any sleep you were getting wasn't worth a damn."

Helen pulled a chair away from the kitchen table and climbed into it. "I tried to go to bed early, to catch up on the sleep I lost the past few nights, but every time I closed my eyes I saw gashed tarmac or bent bicycle wheels—or worse. I don't remember it being this bad when my mother died."

"Pneumonia, wasn't it? Well, there you have it. Elderly and expected. Not exactly what we're dealing with here."

"No . . ." Helen cradled her head in her arms. "Are you dealing with it any better?"

A sandpaper sound came over the receiver. Timbrook rubbed his face as Helen had seen him do countless times. "Actually, I think I'm doing fairly well. Is that heartless? Well, this whole business is shocking— this kind of thing always is—but I'm not stirred by it as much as I would expect to be." He paused. "The police were by today."

"They were over at Gale's when I was there this afternoon. They want to see me tomorrow. How did it go?"

"Who knows? At any rate, I'm still here. They wanted to know about Lisa's lovers."

"Lisa didn't have any lovers. That's why she always wanted to hear about mine. She used to show up for tea, acting all concerned and confidential, but I'm no idiot. She wanted details, the kind of stuff a big sister or drunken mother would have divulged."

"And did you oblige?"

"Saw no harm. Just top layer stuff, heaving bosoms in the night."

"Did you tell her names?"

Helen bristled and sat up straight. "Christ, Timbrook. I'm not that stupid, and besides, you make it sound like I have sex partners hidden behind every door."

"It happens, luv," Timbrook said softly. "It happens. So if you have been prudent in your liaisons, however did you keep our girl entertained?"

"Stories. Fabrications. Fairy tales. She believed anything."

"I read somewhere that there are two things one should never lie about: one's mental health and one's sex life. So, tell me, darling, are you really an escapee from one of Her Majesty's more upscale asylums?"

Helen's neck was sweating again. She had been up too long. In her bedroom the sheets would be starchy and cold. The thought of Timbrook—the smell, the feel of his skin—suddenly made her ill.

"I've got to go," she said. "I have to at least try for some sleep."

Silence filled the phone. When Timbrook spoke again, his voice was gentle. "I'm sorry, Helen, truly. I really did call to see how you were doing."

"Cold comfort."

"I'll drop in and see you tomorrow. Or rather later today."

"I have work to do in Winchester."

"I'll ring first."

The phone rocked on its back like a dying insect for several seconds after Helen rang off. She watched it intently, straining to catch its final twitch.

The glue on the sheath was nearly dry when she swept it up in her arms and buried her head deep in the scratchy folds. She sobbed, not caring if the stars spackled her face or the costume fell apart in her hands. The room felt hot and dirty, but she leaned hard into the back of her chair, sobbing wretchedly, not wanting to go to bed, wanting instead to scream for dawn.

The "tiggle, tiggle, tiggle" of the little brass bell on the police station door sent coffee skidding onto Maura's coarsening red hands and down the sleek navy wool weave of her skirt. Despite her watch's cheerful assertion that it was half past seven, her brain was arguing that it was definitely still nighttime. The sleep she had lost Tuesday night because of the party had not affected her yesterday, but this morning she felt the lights of the police station wrapping themselves around her eyes like bubble plastic. She peered through the plastic now and saw the coffee leapfrog down her skirt one dribble at a time. Dammit to hell, she thought, aiming her hand in the direction of the spill and trying to flick the liquid away. Dammit to hell if that "tiggle, tiggle" is Daniel wanting to get a move on at this hour.

It wasn't, although given the commanding stomps the mistake was understandable. The creature who galumphed towards her was an ancient cross between a wigged walrus and the type of nanny that Mary Poppins sent billowing skyward on the breeze. It even carried an old carpetbag.

Maura grabbed a napkin from a stack near the coffeepot and quickly wiped her hands before turning and putting on her helpful face.

The woman stopped a good bosom-length in front of and—by virtue of height—below her. "Good morning," said the quiet voice, all Received Standard English, all well modulated, all wrong, Maura decided, for the pulpy face that looked like caramel slowly boiling to the soft ball stage. "Beastly cold out. I've come to see Constable Baylor. Wanted to get here early before he was out and about, otherwise I wouldn't have braved the elements. Is he in?"

"He's not here now, but he'll be back. He went for provisions. I'm Detective Sergeant Ramsden. Could I help?"

"Ah, well, late again." Maura watched as the woman plopped the carpetbag on Baylor's desk and pulled out three loaves of bread, four tins of biscuits, a pot of marmalade, a tin each of coffee and tea, and a small plastic container of sugar. Gathering them to her breast like a bulldozer moving earth, she dumped them onto a fold-out table in the corner of the room, which already held a sputtering coffee maker. She began laying them out as ceremoniously as if she were preparing high tea.

"I'm Editha Forrester." The woman didn't look up from her task. "I went into town yesterday because I knew Edgar wouldn't be baking for several days, although how he can afford to be closed I really don't know. While I was there it occurred to me that Constable Baylor—such a nice, such a clean young man—well, he always outfits the police station with Edgar's goods, so I decided to buy him a few things while I was about it."

She turned and looked at Maura approvingly. "You must be Scotland Yard. I didn't know they had girls."

Maura laughed. "Oh, they've had girls for quite a while now. This was very nice of you, Miss Forrester. We'll be doing a lot of phone work—the food will come in handy."

"Yes, well, I thought it might." Editha Forrester paused and surveyed the classical balance of her work. "I wanted to do something to help. I was quite fond of Lisa. She was a good, sweet girl with no mess about her. I didn't suppose you needed me to go rummaging through the woods looking for torn-off buttons, so I decided to provide the refreshments. At least I can return home feeling that I have done some good."

She unwrapped the grey scarf from around her neck and clasped her hands in front of her. Regarding the detective warmly, Miss Forrester's face melted into one of the most pleasant smiles Maura had ever seen. "Now, dear. Tell me about yourself."

Maura started, both amused and slightly discomfited by Miss Forrester's guileless curiosity. Under the imperious station lights, the elderly woman looked like a hard-shelled walnut in her black wool coat, charcoal trousers, and lace-up shoes. Maura wondered just how much nut there really was to her.

A blast of cold air invaded the station as Halford entered. The morning had turned almost gelid, and in response the Chief Inspector had buttoned his navy blue raincoat tight to the throat. His head was bare and his dark hair wind-brushed into a cap of crescents. Maura didn't quite know what to make of the expression on his face: It was an uneasy amalgamation of energy, optimism and—she looked closer—worry. His mouth was open to release what she guessed would have been a morning jab when he saw Miss Forrester. He smiled.

"Good morning," he said. He stripped off his gloves and coat and dropped them onto Baylor's desk. "Arctic out there. I think we've offended the weather gods."

"Miss Editha Forrester, this is Chief Inspector Halford," Maura said. "Miss Forrester knew Lisa and she wanted to help. She brought food."

Halford eyed the spread appreciatively. "Lovely. Citizens occasionally lavish us with information, Miss Forrester. Few are so gracious as to lavish us with delectables. Thank you."

The Halford charm, absent during the past twenty-four hours, now curled its way home to the formidable

Miss Forrester. She crinkled her faded blue eyes. "Anything else you need, Chief Inspector?"

Halford ran his hands over his hair, patting the peaks in place. "Actually, Miss Forrester, if you've got a minute. . . . I need some background information on the village."

Miss Forrester began unbuttoning her coat. "Oh, well, I don't suppose anyone can help you as well as I, except perhaps Alban Carny and I've never thought he had all his wits about him. I've lived here all my life, born in the very house I live in now."

Halford motioned her into a blue plastic chair in front of Baylor's desk and pulled another one around to face her. "So you're one of the original families," he said. "Quite an interesting village, this."

"Oh, yes." Miss Forrester settled herself in the chair, scooting far enough back that only the tips of her shoes touched the floor. "A bit of a social experiment, you know. Of course, there are other model villages in England—Somerleyton in Suffolk, Old Warden in Bedfordshire—but to my mind Fetherbridge is the most exciting. Lord Bannick didn't want simply to provide picturesque housing for his labourers. He wanted to set up a community with a perfect mix of people to see how they would get along. And two-hundred-some-odd years later, I would say we succeeded admirably."

Maura leaned against Baylor's desk and waited for Halford to signal that she should take notes. As of now, he had elected to let the elderly woman ramble, urging her on evidently in the hope that a nugget would burble forth from the dross.

"It amazes me," Halford said, "that so many of the original families are still here. It speaks well of Bannick's sense of balance."

"Yes, it does. Of course, it's changing now. Young people think we're old-fashioned, so they move away. Newcomers think we're quaint, so they move in. My great-great-great-great-grandfather came here as a chandler back in the early 1770's, and I would never

leave." She lifted her chin and looked at Halford
sternly. "I believe in Fetherbridge, Chief Inspector. It
was Lord Bannick's quest for utopia, and personally I
think he succeeded."

"Things have changed some since I was last here,"
Halford told Miss Forrester. "I've noticed new shops
on the High Street, new faces around the town. Many
of the houses are being refurbished. It seems Fetherbridge is enjoying some prosperity."

Miss Forrester nodded emphatically. "You're quite
right. Life used to be insulated around here, but today,
it's a few minutes to Winchester by bus, a short jaunt
to London by train." A hard line formed between her
eyebrows. "Tom Grayson certainly put a light on us.
But who's to say that's all bad?"

She didn't slow her prattle as Halford stretched forward to help her slip off her square wool coat. It fell
on either side of her chair and brushed the floor. Underneath her coat she wore a surprisingly contemporary teal knit pullover.

"When I was a girl," Editha Forrester continued,
"you could go weeks, sometimes months, without seeing a stranger. Everyone was a friend, everyone was
family. Strangers never passed through the village taking the lives of young girls. Children today simply
don't have the sense of trust and security we had." She
shook her head and her face grew wistful. "I find it
makes them grow up to be cynical and self-important
adults, don't you? That's one of the reasons I'm particularly grieved about Lisa's death. She still had that
sense of trust and security. She would have made a fine
woman some day."

Halford looked at Miss Forrester with deep per-
plexity. "I would have thought, given the fact of her
mother's leaving, that Lisa would have had a particularly insecure adolescence."

Miss Forrester compressed her lips. "Oh, Madge
Stillwell. Poor woman, not happy at all. She wasn't
from Fetherbridge—Brighton, I think. I don't suspect

she understood our ways. No, Chief Inspector, you're wrong. I think Lisa had security even with her mother gone. Some mothers are better off gone, don't you think?"

"Would you care for some coffee or tea, Miss Forrester?" The diversion was smooth. Halford's voice was charming and courteous, the crow's-feet at the tips of his brown eyes creased with bashful goodwill. Maura stifled a smile. In the course of his work, and elsewhere, Maura imagined, Halford used his eyes to control what people thought of him. He wanted Miss Forrester to think him delightful.

He succeeded. Miss Forrester beamed. "Since the coffee's made, I'll have some, lots of sugar and milk if you have it. It's one thing I think the Americans do better than us, coffee, don't you agree? I don't know why that should be—it's not nearly as delicate to brew as tea. Perhaps that's it. Of course, the best cup of coffee to be had in Fetherbridge is in Gale Grayson's curious little cottage. Not that I take coffee there often, but I have a few times, just to be polite and maybe a little kind. I treasure my solitude, you understand."

"Ah, yes, a precious commodity to be sure, Miss Forrester," Halford said. "But about Lisa, tell me a bit more. What about her did you like so much?"

Miss Forrester planted her black leather shoes solidly on the station floor and gave her trousers a tug at the knees. "If you had known Lisa, Chief Inspector, you wouldn't have to ask. She was just such a sweet child, those blue eyes so innocent, so full of kindness and concern. She made it her business to help everybody. Why, she knew Ruth Barker was going to be a grandmother before Ruth did. And she did the loveliest thing. She and that little Katie Pru Grayson went all over the village, collecting what Lisa called 'granny gifts' to surprise Ruth. They had a basket, and when the basket was full, we all marched to Ruth's and presented her with it. Ruth couldn't have blushed any deeper." Here Miss Forrester clasped her hands in her lap. "Of course, it was all very sad when Ruth's daughter lost the baby. It was her fourth miscarriage. Habitual abortion, I think they call it. At any rate, the marriage couldn't take it—she and her husband later divorced. But, still it was a sweet thing for Lisa to have done. I adored that girl." She sighed. "Lisa would come round my cottage at night and listen to all the old stories about Fetherbridge. It was so gratifying. When you get to be my age, Chief Inspector, it's comforting to feel that the little bits of life you know will continue on."

Halford smiled gently and, taking the cup of coffee Maura had prepared, handed it to Miss Forrester. "Who would you say was Lisa's closest friend?"

Miss Forrester blew the steam away from the milky liquid. "Oh, Jill Ivory. Occasionally I would invite them both in for tea. I always found them so amusing. Lisa could be very funny. She was such a bounce of a girl. Jill, on the other hand, is quite different. Nice, but in a different way. Such a sombre, serious thing. Very conscientious."

"You know the Ivorys well?"

"Just the girl, really. The family moved here when she was quite young, I believe from somewhere up north, but I've never actually spent that much time with the parents. Mr. Ivory is so busy with that newspaper of his, and Mrs. Ivory, well, she's such an ephemeral thing—she brings to mind one of James's 'vague aliens,' although while she might be an alien to Fetherbridge one can tell by her deportment she's a properly reared Englishwoman. Nevertheless, they are a fine family, pleasing to look at. Height is something to admire in women, don't you agree? Jill used to help me in my garden when she was younger. Now, of course, it's boys and work and parties, no time for an old woman and her fight against dandelions."

Miss Forrester took a sip of coffee, ignoring the handle and holding the cup by the rim. She considered the flavour and then sat back in her chair, evidently satisfied.

Halford looked at Maura, who picked up her note-book and quietly took a seat behind Baylor's desk.

"Tell me, Miss Forrester," Halford said carefully, "what did you mean by some mothers being better off gone?"

Miss Forrester waved her hand, dismissing the obvious. "Oh, Chief Inspector, you can't tell me, living in London as you do, that you don't know what I'm talking about. Mothers who don't understand children, don't like children, haven't the time for them. Mothers who are so consumed with their own problems that they forget there are young people under their care who need direction. I'm not saying that Madge Stillwell was abusive—that, of course, would never cross my mind—but I do feel she was neglectful. Why, the whole village had to do her child-rearing for her, even before she ran away. So many of us tried to take Lisa under our wing. It's a credit to this village that she turned into such a fine young woman."

Maura glanced from her note-taking to Halford. He was studying a point just north of Miss Forrester's head, a brown splotch on the otherwise piercingly white wall. Halford kept his eyes on the spot as he asked the next question.

"What about Brian, Miss Forrester? Did anyone take him under wing?"

If Miss Forrester understood the accusation beneath the question, she did nothing to register it. She sipped her coffee and shook her head.

"Oh, well, Brian's a different case altogether. Not very social, is he? Always has been a bit of a loner, poor child. Hard to know what to do with him. Besides, Lisa cared for him so completely. Doted on him, really. And he, of course, adored her. Well, why not? She was so pretty, so caring. I'd imagine she was the perfect older sister."

"So does Brian have any friends of his own? Who do you suppose is helping him through Lisa's death now?"

"I'd imagine the Ivorys will do what they can for him." She paused and frowned, balancing the coffee cup in the palm of her hand and slowly running her pinkie around the rim. "It's true, Brian doesn't have many friends his own age. Of course, there was that time everyone thought he was interested in the Simpson girl, the one whose mother works as housekeeper at the vicarage, but it was just gossip. Nothing could possibly have come of it, him being how he is. So graceless, and the Simpson girl is, well, quiet but pretty. But other friends? I doubt it. Brian's never been as involved in the church as Lisa was."

"St. Martin's."

Miss Forrester looked up at Halford in surprise. "Well, of course. There is a Baptist church down off Boundary Road a bit, near the new houses, but it's small and no one I know goes there. No, we are Anglicans here in Fetherbridge, Chief Inspector, led by Father Cart. Now, he is a fine, fine man."

"Yes. I met him last night."

"He's from one of the original families as well, although he didn't grow up in Fetherbridge. Jeremy's great-grandfather moved away in the early part of the century. I'm not sure what powers brought him back to us, but I am thankful to them. He is quite inspirational. He's a Grayson. He and Tom were cousins. But of course, I'm sure you knew that. The Graysons have always been such a fine family, very hardworking and recently very well educated. And that Katie Pru, such a sweet child, a bright little girl. She will do the family proud."

Here Miss Forrester heaved a nasal sigh and took a large gulp of coffee. "Which makes it a pity, Chief Inspector, that her mother is such a bitch."

It was too cold for Katie Pru to be outside, too cold, in fact, for anyone to be outside so early, which was why Gale was irritated with herself for putting off the trip to the post office till damn near the eleventh hour.

She glanced down at the pinched face, nose, and eyebrows sticking out from the small red hood beside her. The hood was so tightly bound that little pleat marks whitened the skin where the drawstring bit and her cheeks pooched forward in an unnatural pout. Katie Pru stumped along in silence. Protectively, Gale gripped the tiny mittened hand tighter and pressed it against her thigh.

Damn that moped, damn the cold, she fumed. And damn whatever frailty of machine mentality that rendered the one useless when confronted with the other. If the thing hadn't refused to start, they would be finished by now and back at home instead of tromping through the morning wind. Gale muttered an encouraging noise to Katie Pru and hoisted her onto the pavement of the High Street. The inquest was scheduled for ten in Winchester. She had arranged to leave Katie Pru with Mrs. Baker while she attended it, but if she hoped to make it in time, they were going to have to hurry.

The overnight drop in temperature had brought a density to the air that made everything seem dimmer than usual. Lights from the various storefronts were blunted in front of their windows like pale, glowing swabs. The street was virtually soundless, the cold having dulled anything that might be sharp or lilting. As they walked, their shoes soundlessly slapping the pavement, Gale was aware only of the muffled hiss of their corduroy pants.

The first store they passed was Hossett's Books. The store had never been much of a bookshop—Ben Hossett blithely stocked only the most raging best-sellers plus all the titles by Jane Austen, and made a comfortable living off the embarrassed tastes of the locals and the geographical uncertainty of tourists. The only time he had taken a chance on an unknown author was when Gale's book was first published, and even that, given the amount of notoriety and free press coverage, had hardly been a risk at all. He had thrown all his effort into the promotion: window posters, ads in the regional papers, even a party which Gale refused to attend. This, for some reason, seemed to endear her to him, for whenever they met he would give her a quick hug and a wag of his finger for being "that elusive Grayson woman." And he would wink, as if she were a commodity he himself had made valuable.

As they passed the bookshop window, Gale saw Ben straightening a pyramid of Judith Krantz's latest book. She raised her arm in a wave, which he must have noticed for he drew his head up and started to grin. She expected him to wave warmly and then to return to his work; instead, as he stared into the cocoon of light in which she and Katie Pru stood, the smile vanished. He turned and walked to the back of the store. Even in the cold, Gale's face grew hot. She glanced down at her daughter, the head inscrutable under the red hood, and pulled her gently away from the window.

A warmth, fragrant with oiled wood, and the sound of two soft voices met Gale when she and Katie Pru entered the store that housed the post office. A series of long, low cabinets divided the room into aisles, each filled with various domestic items ranging from bottles of squash to calendars. Gale quietly walked toward the rear of the store, thankful that Katie Pru was not dragging her free hand along the side of the cabinets or periodically shooting it out to touch an object on the sly.

"Mama, I'm hot," Katie Pru said loudly. Quickly, Gale scooped her up and untied the drawstring. The red hood slid from the back of her head and she looked at her mother with round, black eyes. She grasped Gale tightly around the neck and put her mouth to her ear.

"I've been good," she whispered. "Can I have a sweet?"

"We'll see, baby." Gale shifted the child to her right hip and moved to the back of the store.

The postmistress, June Kingston, stood behind the counter. She was talking to Gloria Seasons, a heavyset woman dressed in a worn turquoise coat. Gale knew

the Seasonses from church; they were an active family
and she had worked with their daughter Bette in the
youth group. Both women fell silent and looked at Gale
as she approached.

"Good morning," Gale said. "I have a parcel to mail
to the States." Neither woman responded. "It's a few
sample pages of the book I'm writing. The organisation
that hired me wants to make sure I've hit the right
tone—you know, we Southerners can't treat our sacred
cause with too much levity."

She waited for a smile. Instead, Gloria Seasons
pushed herself away from the counter and walked out
the front door.

"Let me see it, then." Mrs. Kingston folded her arms
across her chest. Setting Katie Pru down on the floor,
Gale reached into a pouch slung over her left shoulder
and took out the parcel. Mrs. Kingston weighed it and
slapped it on the counter. "Six pounds, thirty-two
pence."

Katie Pru clutched her mother's leg and stuck the
swinging end of her coat's drawstring into her mouth.
Gale rustled through her change purse and pulled out
several loose coins. They clattered around the postmistress's outstretched hand.

"You know, Mrs. Grayson," Mrs. Kingston said,
carefully counting the money, "there's a post office in
Winchester. They could get your parcels to the States
quicker than I can. I think you should take your things
there from now on."

Her voice was flat, as flat as the grey eyes she raised
to Gale's face. Gale lifted up Katie Pru and behind blur-
ring eyes stumbled from the building.

11

Bobby Grissom was in no mood to wait. He stood on the staircase of Castle Yard, an ancient maize-coloured structure at the end of Castle Avenue in Winchester, and fidgeted. Within an hour, the inquest into the death of Lisa Stillwell would convene in the Grand Jury Room inside. Unfortunately, Grissom was outside, the door locked, and no activity was visible within the building's bedimmed windows save for a vacated spider's web strung just inside the sill, wafting to a miscreant current.

Turning, he descended the stairs to the brick-covered ground below. The morning weekday traffic squeaked and growled as the cathedral city, once the upstart jewel in William the Conqueror's crown, toiled away in a more plebeian stage. Which was as it should be. Grissom was enough of a leftist—and a hypocrite—to be grateful that cathedrals were the priority of the past.

The Castle Hill complex, which housed the Hampshire High Courts, was a part of that past. An odd amalgam of buildings, the complex ranged from the turreted manorlike construction of the county estates office to the newer civic-styled courthouse. The oddest component, however, had to be the Great Hall, a gaping churchlike edifice that was all that remained of the thirteenth-century castle itself.

It was also a notable tourist attraction. In front of the flint-and-stone castle, a chattering band of German visitors took turns shooting pictures of the Great Hall's Gothic arch door. Pushing past them, Grissom entered the Great Hall. After the venerable facade, the interior was unimpressive. It was a large, echoing space, saved from emptiness by a tourist kiosk filled with booklets and postcards on one side, and a nightmarish statue of Queen Victoria in a corner. Only one thing interested Grissom, however. He sauntered over to the west wall and gazed upward.

A massive circle of wood, eighteen feet across and weighing more than a ton, covered the wall. King Arthur's Round Table, uncleaved and unnervingly decorative, hung above Grissom like an overly preened dart board. He tilted his head to read the names of the twenty-four knights scripted along the circle's outer edge. Kay, Launcelot—he couldn't make out the rest. Not that it mattered. No one believed it was actually King Arthur's Round Table. It was just an antique representation. But there it was, a city's claim to heritage and to heroic possibility.

Myth and chalk, Grissom thought. That's what this city is about. It's in the ground, in the air, in the cheap little postcards selling at the kiosk. A possible lead for his story forming in his head, Grissom had turned to explore the gardens visible through the Great Hall's rear exit when he noticed a drawn, bent figure shuffle through the door. At first glance he would have mistaken the individual as elderly, but as the figure stumbled closer, Grissom recognised with a shock Brian Stillwell.

The boy was dressed all in brown, an oversized suit coat open and drooping towards the ground, a tie swinging listlessly in the air as its owner trudged around the building's interior. Brian kept close to the wall, head bent, one hand trailing along the stones as if to remind himself of the need to stay upright. He walked the length of one wall, mindful of the statue, then turned the corner for the second. His hand continued to brush the stones, stopping only to avoid the wooden lime green uprights that told the castle's story.

It's as if he's blind, Grissom thought. He's become an old, sightless man in borrowed clothing. He waited until Brian was near the garden exit before approaching.

"Hullo, Brian," he said, extending his hand. "Bobby Grissom. I've been into your father's bakery now and again."

Brian dropped his hands to his side and nervously clinched his fists. He kept his eyes towards the floor.

"I remember." The word came out slurred. "The newspaper."

"That's right." Grissom cast about for something to say. The boy looked terrible. His face was unwashed, his hair limp and oily across his scalp. The brown suit was much too loose to be purchased for its current wearer, and in places shiny spots showed its age. Despite the wintry temperature, Brian had no overcoat.

"Jesus, you must be cold," the reporter said, grateful for words that both showed concern and stayed safely away from the obvious topic. "Don't you have anything heavier to wear?"

Brian mumbled something and turned to continue

his walk along the wall. Grissom, alarmed by the boy's behaviour, put a hand out to stop him.

"What do you think you're doing? Don't you touch him!"

From the other side of the Great Hall, Edgar Stillwell's voice reverberated through the chamber. The band of German tourists, clustered about the kiosk, twisted as one to see the source of the booming voice. The saleswoman, stopped in the middle of collecting a handful of coins for a postcard, stared open-mouthed as Edgar Stillwell strode across the room's expanse and shoved Grissom into the wall.

"What do you think you're doing?" Stillwell repeated. "You leave my son alone."

Grissom's padded anorak absorbed most of the impact, but his head snapped backwards and smacked the wall neatly. He pulled away from Stillwell and felt his head.

"What in the hell made you do that?" he asked, incredulous as well as angry. He examined his hand. It was free of blood. He rubbed his head gently. "I was just trying to talk to him."

"I know what kind of talking you journalists like to do. Mewling little gossips, the lot of you. Ruddy interfering meddlers." Stillwell's face was contorted with animosity, but he had retreated a step or two. "Well, I won't let you turn my daughter into some sort of titillation, I won't. She's not going to sell any papers for dirty little bastards like you!"

Over Stillwell's shoulder, Grissom saw the woman from the kiosk scurry out the door. His own anger had dissipated, the pain in his head now a steady throb. He took a deep breath.

"Look, Mr. Stillwell, I wasn't interviewing your son. I simply think he needs help. For one thing, he needs a coat."

Instantly, Stillwell's hand was again on Grissom, but he didn't push him. Instead, he flexed his fingers and lightly tapped the reporter's chest.

"Needs help. Of course he does." The words were whispers. "His sister's dead, man. His mother's dead. Of course the boy needs help."

Stillwell's eyes welled with tears. Brian, silent through the altercation, took his father's arm.

"Just leave my son alone," Stillwell said. "I'm not going to lose him like I lost the others. I'm not going to let any fucking magpies ruin what's left of my family."

With Brian pulling on his arm, Stillwell turned and together, they walked from the Great Hall just as a security guard poked his head through the doorway.

Halford felt bitterly lighthearted. He could still see the image of Miss Forrester's ample form cheerfully thundering from the station, upholstered in self-congratulations that she had done the patriotic thing and helped the constabulary. He imagined the old woman feeling cleansed, like a parishioner who confides in the village priest about the disgraceful goings-on in the loo next door. Well, two toots for the Miss Forresters of the world. Where would the police and the hate-mongers be without them?

Maura handed him her neatly typed notes, then sat across from him at Constable Baylor's desk. The peach-colored polish that at the party Tuesday night had looked so professionally applied was now pitted and peeling away from ragged nails. Halford smiled gently at the papers in front of him. Ravaged hands were evidently Maura's payment for a job well done.

"Nice work, Maura." He closed the folder on the notes and scooted it away from him. "There are a few things I want checked—confirmation on Timbrook's dates with Lisa, a bit more aggressive questioning of her friends about her relationships with men. Surely someone besides Jill Ivory knows about her personal life. Get some of Roan's DC's to do that, women preferably. I think the girls might be more forthcoming with another female, don't you?"

Halford paused and considered Miss Forrester's empty coffee cup still sitting on the desk, orange lipstick scalloping the rim. "What a sturdy old busybody Miss Forrester is. Reminds me of my aunt. Not a pie in town she didn't have her finger in, and all the while she claimed she was a martyr to her solitude. They say after she died, newspaper subscriptions increased thirty percent. Up till then, nobody needed one."

"I would say that's the story in every village," Maura said. "There has to be someone manning the phones, so to speak. It's a community service, actually."

"Right. And in London our next-door neighbour can die from a heart attack and we won't notice he's missing until there's a smell." Halford pulled a second folder from the wire basket on Baylor's desk and slid it across to Maura. "Here. The final PM report came in. Pretty much as we suspected. Except for one detail—Lisa was a virgin."

Maura arched her brow. "Well, well. So Christian Timbrook was telling the truth, at least about that aspect of their friendship."

"Evidently." He glanced down at his own notes. "I want to find out why Jeremy Cart was given this vicarate. Fetherbridge might be a prize living for an elderly clergyman with retirement on his mind, but I have a hard time believing our dimpled young Reverend Cart is content using his talents here. Check it out. Have you set up the interview with Helen Pane?"

"She'll be in Winchester this morning with a client, so I made an appointment with her for one-thirty. We're to meet her at a tea shop across from the cathedral."

"Good. Maybe she can throw a little more light on Lisa's relationship with Mrs. Grayson." He waited for Maura's reaction, but she merely nodded. He prodded her. "You do admit that seems to be an issue."

"It does appear that Mrs. Grayson's not well liked in the village. However, Chief Inspector, I am reserving judgment until I receive more facts."

Halford grinned. "My, aren't we all hooray today."

"No, just aware you were uncomfortable last night when Nate and I talked about Mrs. Grayson."

He shook his head. "Not all that uncomfortable, Maura. I just think we ought to have more to go on than local chatter. I'm not saying we turn our attention away from her. Let's just not limit our imaginations quite yet, all right?" She saluted him with the tip of her finger. "All right. Ring the incidents room and make sure everything's ready to go. We've got to get to the inquest."

Maura had reached for the phone when the bell on the station door jingled and Nate Baylor entered. He was followed by Orrin Ivory.

"I was hoping to catch you, sir," Baylor said. "Could I get a lift with you to the inquest?"

"You can do better than that, Nate. You can drive us." Halford turned to Ivory. "Sorry, Editor. The Press must provide its own transportation."

"I don't need transportation, Halford. I want to talk to you about something. It'll only take a minute."

Ivory's face looked papery, the skin grey and creased beneath the eyes and down the cheeks. A line of perspiration shone on his upper lip.

"Perhaps this can wait. I don't know how important it is," he said, then added: "The newspaper office was broken into last night."

"Really? What was stolen?"

"I don't know that anything was stolen. None of the equipment, as far as I can tell—the terminals, cameras, typewriters, are all still there."

"Any money gone?"

"No. We don't keep that much, just a small float fund in a drawer. It wasn't touched."

"How do you know the building was broken into?"

Ivory absentmindedly pressed his middle finger against the edge of the desk. It arched and blanched white from the pressure.

"A panel of glass on the front door is broken—the

place never was very secure. Stupid of me, I suppose, considering the presses and computers, but it just didn't strike me as necessary. Anyway, when my receptionist went in this morning, the panel was smashed and the door unlocked. She called me, and when I went upstairs to check everything, well, the door to the newspaper archives was open. Wide open. I always make certain it's closed at night. With all those old papers, I'm a bit afraid of fire. I even had a metal door installed last spring."

"Did you go into the archives room?"

"Yes, but there's no way of telling if anything was disturbed." He sighed. "As Gale will tell you, it's one of my chief failings. There's no system or order to it— just random stacks of newspapers and files of photos."

Halford stood and grabbed his suit coat. "Doesn't seem the most efficient way to run a newspaper, Mr. Ivory."

"That's what Gale says. She's tried a few times to organise some sort of filing system, but she keeps giving up. She gets quite upset about it sometimes. The paper dates back to 1874 and she says it offends her historian's sensibilities to have all that information inaccessible. At any rate, I can't tell you if anything was taken. I don't go in there much myself. The reporters do sometimes, and the photographer, but not often. They might be able to tell. And Gale, of course. She probably knows what's in there better than anyone."

"I suppose your reporters have rummaged through the place this morning?"

"Well, no. Since it's Thursday, and the next edition won't go out until Wednesday, there's really no call for them to be in the building yet, so I locked the door and left the receptionist posted to keep the others out."

Halford smiled. "How sensible, Mr. Ivory." He clamped his hand on the editor's shoulder and walked him to the door. "You go on back and I'll send someone over shortly. Don't let anyone in until we get there."

When the door closed behind Ivory, Halford turned

to Maura. "You go. Nate's got to testify at the inquest in less than an hour and we need to get him there. He and I can interview Miss Pane. I want you to take a look at the building, talk to the reporters, and see if they can tell if anything is missing. Get a crew over to dust for prints. It's probably got nothing to do with this case, but I'd feel better if we considered the possibility. After all, Nate here says nothing ever gets stolen in merry old Fetherbridge."

Halford shrugged his blue raincoat over his shoulders and paused. "When Mrs. Grayson gets back from the inquest, take her over and see if she can offer any assistance. And tell me what you think, Maura. Watch her closely."

The front door to the newspaper office, wooden, heavy and speckled with wormholes, reminded Maura of the entrance to an oversized hobbit hole. A wide strip of trim, painted sky blue and notched with a row of chevrons, arched the top of the rounded door and capped a window comprised of many small mullioned panes. Maura calculated the panes quickly: sixty-four. The lowermost left-hand pane had been knocked out; a single jagged tooth of glass still protruded from the frame. The shard appeared clean, no stray threads or ripped clothing dangling from its point. Maura balled her hand into an elongated fist so that its diameter was as narrow as possible and held it up to the hole. Her knuckles stretched past the opening a good quarter inch on either side.

Ivory stood by the outside wall, his face grim. "I hate what they did to the glass," he told her. "The door is quite old. I don't know how I'm going to replace that pane."

Maura didn't say anything as she opened the door and knelt just within the threshold. Pieces of glass lay sprinkled on the carpeted floor. The carpet looked recently hoovered, a small splotch of mud about two feet from the door frame and a couple of pieces of sere grass

near the receptionist's desk the only signs of sullied
shoes. Maura motioned Ivory inside.

"When was this place cleaned last?"

"Yesterday. The charlady comes in on Wednesday
and Friday evenings around seven."

"How long does it usually take?"

"I really couldn't say."

Maura pointed past the reception area to a narrow
hall. "What's down there?"

"Bookkeeping."

Ivory led her into an unexceptional office with bare
beige walls and a black metal desk. He reached over to
the desk and jerked open the lower right-hand drawer.
Inside was a green pouch containing several pound
coins and some loose change.

"The float fund," he told Maura. "I don't know exactly how much is supposed to be in here, but it's never
very much."

Next to the bookkeeper's office was the more lively
appointed sales department, dominated by an entire
wall plastered with aging headlines and photos cut
from the more tawdry practitioners of the press—Fer-
gie's braless back cavorting in the sands, page three
girls with braless fronts pouting for the camera. Maura
turned to Ivory and raised her eyebrows.

"A commendation board? A tribute to the best and
brightest?"

"My word, no. My sales staff has a peculiar brand
of humour—or perhaps I should concede it's rebellion.
Those types of articles are the antithesis of this paper's
philosophy. I won't let them bring clients back here.
It's all right for us to have a little fun, but I won't allow
my people to go around reinforcing the public's perception of how grimy this business is."

"I see." Maura continued down the hall, through a
spare but extremely clean kitchen and into the cavern-
ous, echoing room which housed the printing press.
Maura nodded towards the machine.

"I've never seen one of these before outside the movies. They're big."

Ivory laughed. "Oh, this one's just a child, and an antiquated one at that, I'm afraid. You should see the new ones, very high-tech." He pointed to a clamp attached to a large cylinder. "This is the piece Jill and I went to fetch the morning Lisa died."

A set of back stairs led to the first floor. Here the relative order of the ground floor gave way to a wreck of paper and machinery. The room was divided equally between news and production. On one side, several work tables lined the wall with rulers, tape, and scissors scattered about. On the other, desks were crammed side by side, word processors and typewriters angled haphazardly to reach the nearest socket. On a nearby desk sat a 35mm Nikon. Maura checked the frame indicator—twelve shots left on a roll of thirty-six. She flipped through a notepad on the desk. The scribble inside was illegible. Her mother had wanted her to be a journalist. Evidently God felt she hadn't sinned enough.

"How many people work here?" she asked.

"Upstairs? Not many. We're not a big paper, just an ambitious one. We have four full-time production workers and four full-time reporters. Three part-timers come in during the week."

She walked over to the left wall where a metal door gaped open.

"The archives?" she asked.

Ivory nodded. Gently, Maura pushed it further open and flicked the light on with the tip of her pen. She gawked a second before turning to Ivory.

"You mean it looks like this all the time?"

Ivory flinched. "None of us seems to have time. I've gotten to the point where I just tell the reporters to keep up with their own clips and hope someone's still alive who can answer their background questions. A paper this size doesn't have all that much need for historical perspective anyway. As I was telling Chief Inspector

Halford last night, we're mostly puppy contests and gardening tips. Still, I know, it's no excuse."

Maura gazed around at the fallen stacks of papers and the dusty file cabinets, wondering why Halford hadn't told her about his conversation with Ivory. Her attention was redirected to an ironstone plate on the floor by her feet, the tulips on its face obscured by yellow smears. Not far away, a fork, handle bent, displayed in its tines a shriveled grey morsel that could have been anything from an oyster to dried ectoplasm. She pushed it with her toe. Where was some people's self-respect?

"What about that?" She pointed to a file cabinet, tilted over and resting on a crooked stack of papers.

"Oh, that used to be the photo file. Someone once pulled a drawer out too far and over it went. We never bothered to right it. Anyway, it's been that way for a while." He pointed to a pen and a pair of scissors lying atop a pile of clipped articles to the right of the door. "Gale's efforts. I suppose you can see why she gave up."

Maura tapped her teeth with the pen. "Well, if you can't tell if anything was taken, I'm not sure I can. Who has a key to the building?"

Ivory ran his hand through his hair and sighed. "Oh, there are plenty of keys to the place. I have one, Joe Clark, the pressman does, Bobby Grissom, Deb the receptionist, since she opens up most mornings. And Nate has one down at the station in case there's an emergency. That's five. Yes, I think that's all."

Maura switched the light off and stepped out of the room. "There could be more? You're not sure?"

"No, five. Yes, I'm fairly sure five is it."

Maura put away her notebook. "Well, thank you. I'll send a crew to go over the place. In the meantime, if you could keep the building locked. We'll talk again later."

They walked down the stairs. At the door Maura

stopped. "I'm surprised you're not covering the inquest."

Ivory positioned himself carefully to avoid stepping on the glass. "Grissom's down there. He's my best. He'll be at one of the London papers before too long. Good eye for detail."

"So I suppose we'll be treated to the blow-by-blow high drama of the inquest. When does the next paper come out?"

Ivory folded his arms across his chest. "Wednesday. But that's six days from now, Sergeant. I expect to be printing the blow-by-blow high drama of an arrest by then."

12

Helen Pane wasn't religious. Sitting before the Winchester Cathedral high altar didn't fill her with any more veneration than eating a bag of crisps in her own parlour. This wasn't the first time she had made the observation. She had said so to Jeremy many times. She had even said it to him as a joke after the first and only time they ever made love, in one of the cathedral chapels, curled like snails on the dusty bottom of a cupboard that held a score of choir robes and a couple of faded cassocks.

The robes had been swinging over their heads. Helen had looked at Jeremy, his face still moist and swollen from exertion, and made some funny remark like the Winchester Cathedral high altar couldn't make her see the light of the heavenly hosts but something about this cupboard . . . His whole face had immediately changed. His features, which had been soft and pulpy, became hard. He didn't say a word, just knelt over her, straightened his clothes and hair, and crept from the cabinet, leaving her rumpled, speechless, and tucked sideways into the narrow width of floor like an old towel shoved against the door to keep out the draft. Neither one of them had ever mentioned the incident, and they quickly fell out of love, if they had ever been in it.

She whipped a tissue from her small clasp handbag and sneezed loudly. A band of sightseers stopped their gawking to turn to her and smile sympathetically. She wiped her nose and smiled back, wanting one of them to say, "Bless you." No one did.

The cold had been coming on for the past two days; Lisa's death must have suppressed her immune system because, in addition to the sniffles, a couple of mouth ulcers had broken open on her inner cheek. She touched her tongue to one and winced. Instantly, she was filled with self-pity. Her mouth hurt, her nose was running, and she couldn't stop this pain that kept burning her throat and making her chest ache.

She blew her nose and fought for control. According to her watch it had just gone one. Nate Baylor had called her earlier, while she was fitting that dreadful Collins girl, to confirm that he and the chief inspector would meet her at Millicent's Tea Shop at half one. He also said that the coroner had adjourned the inquest; the police were free to pursue the homicide. The news upset her more than she had expected. She returned to the Collins's drawing room and tried, with shaking hands, to finish pinning and measuring Suzannah Collins's wedding gown, but she kept jerking the tape. At one point she even tore a tiny rip in the delicate lace skirt. Suzannah and her mother hadn't noticed, of course. They had been too busy yammering about the skimpy rehearsal dinner the groom's parents were planning. Helen had always thought fat girls, by virtue of empathy, would be more tolerant than others, but she was wrong. Suzannah Collins and her tubby mother were snakes.

Above her the cathedral bosses—crowns, crosses, nails, hands—rose with the vaulted line of the ceiling to look like the jeweled interior of a pricey Easter egg. God's own Fabergé, Helen thought. She studied her favourite, a pair of dice which she supposed alluded to life's great gamble. She didn't know for sure. Jeremy had tried to explain their significance once, something about a bishop and his ego, but Helen hadn't been listening. With a sudden shrinking in her chest, she realised that despite all the time she had spent staring at those poetic carvings, she didn't know a damn thing about them.

With tremulous hands, she straightened the worn, green needlework cushion beneath her. That may well be why Lisa's death was bothering her so—the intense examination and a thousand unanswered questions. A person dies in an accident, and everyone wonders about God's grand design. A person is murdered, and the survivors pick apart every breath, every movement of the dead, trying to foretell the inevitability. She squinted her eyes shut and felt the tears waver on the small ledge of flesh beneath the lids. If she were honest, she'd admit that not all her memories of Lisa were comforting. Last summer, at Lisa's urging, Gale had constructed a back strap loom and taught Lisa and Jill Ivory how to make simple belts with synthetic yarns. It was to be a money-raising project for the church— the girls would make them, Helen would sell them in her shop. For several days Lisa and Jill met in the workroom of Helen's shop, The Transitional Woman, and took turns slipping the loom apparatus over their backs and weaving the loose, fringed belts.

One afternoon, Helen left the girls in the workroom while she dressed a mannequin in an antique wedding gown she had purchased in Scotland. The gown was gorgeous, heavily beaded with a heart-shaped bodice and a satin train overlaid with rich *point de gaze* lace. The veil was made of the same lace, and on a whim, Helen had lifted it above her head and smoothed it over her face.

She had spent several seconds gazing around the shop through the intricate lace, enjoying the slicing curves of light and gauze. When she looked at herself in the mirror, she saw Lisa behind her in the workroom doorway. The younger woman's smile had been almost patronising.

"Practicing, I gather. Well, I'm sure it'll happen for you one day."

Helen let it pass. She carefully removed the veil from her head and draped it over the mannequin's neck.

"It's just a pretty piece of lace, that's all," she answered. "Needle lace. Nineteenth century, probably Brussels. It's difficult not to admire such workmanship."

"Don't worry, Helen. I'm not judging you."

"I didn't suspect you were. I wouldn't know what there is about me for you to judge."

"That's what I meant." Lisa tilted her head and her voice dropped to a near whisper. "You know, you can talk to me if you ever have a problem. I'm a good listener."

"No doubt you are." Helen began fastening the line of hooks that ran the length of the gown's bodice. "I'm not in need of a listener right now."

Lisa let her gaze trail around the room, past the mannequins, the standing racks of clothes, the walls. Finally, she let it rest on the wedding gown's skirt.

"I know you are lonely. I was talking to Jeremy the other day. He said that you were in need of a good friend. I'm just letting you know that I'm available if you need one."

She had turned and gone back into the workroom, leaving Helen embarrassed and angry. Later, she had discussed the incident with Jeremy. He couldn't remember talking with Lisa about her, but then, he wouldn't deny it, either.

Helen idly picked up the green hymnal from its holder on the chair in front of her and rustled through the pages. Water under the bridge, she thought. And after all, Lisa was just a child. Children can be so thoughtless.

Wiping the last of her mascara from her lower lashes, Helen stuffed the tissue back into her bag. It was nearly half one. She had taken care dressing this morning—a dark gold silk-wool suit and matching blouse, black jewellery, her auburn hair swept back in a loose French braid that was designed to make her look both professional and romantic. Below her hem the pale gold of silk stockings shimmered. Again her eyes started burning. She felt so mature and sophisticated dressed like this, whiling away a few minutes before meeting two gentlemen for tea. She felt like every family's elder daughter, the big sister who makes good and knows how to act tough and dress smart.

She stood up quickly and moved towards the south transept exit. Her heels clicked hollow, and suddenly she felt cheap, her shoes, arms, legs, face transformed to plastic. Someone could pick her up and toss her in this stone vault and she would skitter across the floor, hit the wall, and crack. Timbrook would bounce, Gale would shatter, Jeremy would land with a dull thud, but she would break neatly in half.

And Lisa? How would Lisa have broken? Helen fought a shiver. Lisa wouldn't have broken. She would have died slowly, her eyes never wavering, a slight curve to her lips.

According to the newspaper article—yellowed, taped, and hung by the tea shop's badly shellacked front door—Millicent Webster died in 1773 at the age of eighty-two, and while her shop had been relocated, two hundred years later, from its original site on Friars-

gate to this current structure south of the Cathedral
Close, the proprietors hoped Miss Webster's robust
merriment and dedication to good tea and dainties sur-
vived. Halford looked up at the waitress and doubted
it. Not that he considered himself a male chauvinist,
but he really would have preferred a cap and curls to
the glittery spikes and micromini that adorned the
aqua-eyed creature glaring at him. She had placed his
ploughman's lunch in front of him and waited, as if she
expected him to object so she could yell for somè hoo-
ligans in the back to come out and break his nose. He
put his napkin in his lap and winked at her. She shot
him an Elvis Presley sneer and propelled herself to the
kitchen on churning hips.

He and Baylor ate in silence—there wasn't much to
discuss about the Stillwell inquest; everything had gone
as they expected. The forensics evidence, while not un-
equivocal, had strongly supported their case. Tiny pin-
point hemorrhages spackled the whites of Lisa's eyes,
and while the fragile hyoid bone of her throat had es-
caped damage, rough abrasions and bruises indicative
of a ligature circled her neck. It was possible, though
unlikely, that Lisa's scarf got caught in the bicycle gears
by accident; possible, but even less likely, that her head
injury left her unable to react. She had been a healthy,
active twenty-two-year-old woman, *virgo intacta*, who,
freshly bathed with lavender-scented water and di-
gesting a lean breakfast of dry toast and grapefruit, had
somehow between 9:20 and 10:25 Saturday morning
met with a stick, which, through no force of its own,
had ended up in two pieces, one approximately two
hundred feet from the scene of the crime, the other over
the road another fifty feet further. The coroner adjourned with the case open, pending further investigation by the police.

Halford slathered bright yellow oleo on his bread.
The inquest had invited no dramatics. Everything was
ordered and contained. As he listened to the evidence
and watched the people sitting rapt and grey in the

benches, he was reminded more of a court martial than any aspect of the civilian judicial system. Spontaneity was out, even the spontaneity of grief.

The only incongruities to the regimented tenor were the coroner and his secretary. Seated in the traditional places of the judge and court recorder, they appeared more like retail buyers than participants in a ritual of law. The coroner, a genial-looking man in his fifties with lines of brown hair slicked over his balding pate, wore a bright blue suit coat and a blue-and-green tie. His secretary resembled a springtime robin, outfitted in a red frock with a matching headband in her dark hair. She hunched over her stenographer's pad, studiously scribbling down the course of the procedure.

Despite those colourful injections, however, the tone of the inquest remained fettered. There were rather more people present than Halford had expected. Some he had known would come: the Stillwells, Gale Grayson, the pathologist's representative, as well as the requisite police. But a spattering of spectators occupied the benches, presumably residents of Fetherbridge. Most of them were unfamiliar to him, although he recognised Jacob Barker, Clive Kingston, and Bobby Grissom from his encounters the day before. Also present were the two Ivory women, their shoulders squared, faces intent. They all sat warily, listening closely to the evidence presented.

Gale Grayson's evidence was succinct and terse. Lisa was due at her house at nine. She didn't arrive. Brian Stillwell, too stunned to testify, sat mutely while the coroner read his brief statement for him. PC Baylor, his tones clear and measured, described rounding Boundary Road on his bicycle on a routine patrol at 10:25 and finding the weeping boy bent over his sister's body.

"Mrs. Grayson looked nice."

Halford looked up from his plate. "What?"

Baylor finished his scones and pressed his finger into the remaining crumbs. He scraped it with his teeth a couple of times before speaking. "Mrs. Grayson." He took a swig of lemon squash. "She looked nice. She doesn't always, you know. Sometimes I've seen her on her moped skimming through town with Katie Pru on the back and they look like two witches. And sometimes I've seen her walking around, no make-up, clothes too big, and you want to give her a piece of bread and a blanket. You always hear how American women are such better dressers than English, but not her, I can tell you. But today, she looked nice. Not like Brian Stillwell, that's for sure. Didn't look as if his face had been washed, did it? Wonder if he's going to be able to take care of himself now Lisa's gone. That girl did seem to be the glue that held him together. His shoelaces were untied, did you notice that, sir? It was peculiar. Mr. Cart had to lean down and tie them for him. Imagine, a big boy like that. Not that it's likely he'll get any help from his father anytime soon. I've never seen Edgar Stillwell look so ragged, and that's saying something."

Halford stared at him, trying to decide if Baylor was merely being an observant copper or angling for a job as commentator on the Beeb. He decided to let the younger man lead for a while.

"What did you make of Cart being there? He certainly didn't have any testimony to give."

Baylor shrugged. "Vicar's duties, I suppose. Giving comfort to the grieving family. And he was probably there for his cousin. He held Mrs. Grayson's hand most of the time. Or he could have just been there for Lisa. I've never been a good one for figuring out the thinking of the clergy."

Halford didn't say so, but he, too, was having a hard time with the thinking of the clergy. It wasn't accurate to say that Cart had held Mrs. Grayson's hand through most of the proceedings. He had stroked it. Once the vicar had played with her rings, twirling them between his fingers, and every few seconds straying up to massage her knuckle. Mrs. Grayson's face had remained impassive, but Halford hadn't needed her face to tell him of her turmoil. Her hands were articulate. The one Cart held had been limp and unresponsive; the other clutched her skirt so tightly that when she stood up to testify, the wrinkles hiked the hem a good half-inch on that side.

Halford focused on the constable's large, bony fingers dwarfing the bottle he held.

"How can you drink that?" he asked.

Baylor laughed. "Ah, now, sir, you're being funny. How can you not drink lemon squash? Reminds me of summers when I was a boy. It's good for you to remember those days every now and then. Don't tell me you're such an adult you don't ever think about them. I bet you had a grand childhood, a big house by the sea, lots of brothers and sisters. Bet you had lemon squash every day."

"Wrong on most accounts, constable. I have one sister and we lived in a cramped little house in Nottingham. There was a pond nearby, no ocean. And my mother thought lemon squash would rot our teeth. But it was a grand childhood, as you say. Any neuroses I've developed originated in adulthood."

The waitress let out a whoop and waved enthusiastically as Helen Pane entered the tea shop and surveyed her surroundings coolly. Rather, she attempted coolness, which with someone else might have been enough. She stood with one leg slightly in front of the other, both hands clutching a tiny handbag to her pelvis. With a smile she nodded to the waitress, who understood some implied message and slipped into the kitchen.

Halford walked toward her with his hand outstretched "Miss Pane. Thank you for meeting us here. It seems we've caught you in the middle of work."

She patted the top of her hair. "No, a busy morning, that's all. I'm refurbishing a gown for a Christmas wedding and I was doing the final measurements on it. You would think I would enjoy doing weddings but I don't think I have the interpersonal skills." She gripped the handbag nervously. "You know how trying brides can be. Have you ever been married, Mr. Halford?"

Halford crinkled his eyes. "Many, many years ago. It was so brief, I think both of us have dropped it from our résumés."

"I didn't mean . . . I just meant if you've ever been married, then you know what brides are like." The handbag hit the floor. Halford stooped and picked it up. "Skittish, I mean. Jittery. Not much fun at all."

"I can imagine." He left the smile on his face and, returning the handbag, placed his hand in the small of her back to lead to the table. The waitress was setting a cup of tea and a plate of stuffed dried figs in front of the empty chair. When she finished, she winked at Helen, who blushed. Halford had to admit it was an attractive blush, made all the more interesting because Helen clicked her tongue in answer.

"You know her well?" Halford asked, when the waitress had departed.

"I come here quite a bit. Once or twice a week, I'd say."

Halford looked around at the uninspired furnishings and glitter-lidded help. The waitress had retreated to a far corner, ostensibly to count receipts, but Halford deduced it more likely was to get a better look at their table. "If I were seeking a comfortable place to relax with a cuppa, I don't know that I would choose here."

"You wouldn't?" Helen looked surprised, but Halford suspected that nobody widened their eyes that innocently without being amused. At a distance, Helen Pane was a striking woman. Seeing her up close, however, Halford felt uncomfortable. Her features were too fine, her cheekbones too conventionally carved. Her green eyes were watery and dim, with lashes so sparse he could see the empty follicles where hairs had fallen out and not grown back. Halford fought the urge to glance away.

"I understand you and Lisa Stillwell were good friends," he said.

She speared a fig with a miniature fork and tucked it into her mouth. "Yes. Well, I don't know. Not like school chums, you understand. She was more like a little sister. I was thinking about that before I came over just now. I guess I felt like her older sibling. She didn't have a mother, you know."

"Did she ever discuss boys with you, dating, relationships, that sort of thing?"

The fine lips puckered for just an instant and then were smooth. "A bit. Lisa really wasn't into 'that sort of thing.' Some young people aren't, you know. They get a lot of bad press, but they're not all sex-crazed and apolitical." She lifted her chin, and although she waved her hand through the air to demonstrate her breeziness, her skin turned a dusty pink. "Lisa wasn't that sort. I can tell you she just wasn't."

"Ever hear her mention Mr. E.?"

She wrinkled her forehead. "I don't know what that means."

"How long had you known Lisa?"

"A couple of years."

"Two, three? When did you first meet?"

She paused. "I suppose the first time we met was not long after I moved here two years ago. I had gone to a church jumble and Lisa was working there and we just started talking. She helped me pick out some of the more interesting clothes—she had a good eye for pretty lace, unusual buttons, things like that. I do a lot of renovation work on old clothes, and those little extras are very important. That's the first time I remember talking to her, although I had seen her in the village a couple of times before that."

"And you became friends."

Helen's second attempt at spearing failed. The fig flipped across to Baylor's notebook. Gingerly, the constable picked it up and replaced it on her plate.

"No, not then. We didn't become friends until about

a year ago. When I first met her I thought she was just a child. She was twenty, but she always looked so much younger. I started attending church regularly last year and that's when I got to know her better."

"You say she looked younger than her years. Would you say she acted younger?"

She lifted a red nail to her mouth. Her hands, Halford noted with surprise, were beautiful, the nails perfect. Not what he would have expected from a seamstress, but then, what did he know?

"I suppose she did act young for her age. She always had a sense of innocence about her. In many ways, she wasn't very sophisticated, or rather I should say she was growing into her sophistication late. She was, after all, a baker's daughter in a provincial little village. She'd only lately started going to restaurants now and then, some pubs, trips to London for shopping. I'd go with her sometimes. She had a sense of style but it all seemed to come from books and generally didn't suit her. Well, she hadn't a mother for so long. I expect that kept her young."

"Some might expect being motherless would make her older than her years."

"Well, she was in some ways. She had a perception of things . . . an understanding. It was just very mature. I can't explain it."

A girl listening to a lonely woman with man problems—that had been Jill Ivory's assessment of Lisa's relationship with Helen Pane. Halford pressed his finger into a pebble of cheese and examined the mark it left on his skin.

"What about you, Miss Pane? Did you ever confide in Lisa? Did you ever use her understanding for your own comfort?"

Her reaction was more pronounced than Halford had expected. She blushed deeply, but this time it wasn't attractive at all. Halford cut his eyes to Baylor, who made a show of opening his notebook and uncapping his pen. Helen watched him. When she returned her attention to Halford, the thin green of her eyes had taken on a sheen.

"So you've been talking to the neighbours, have you?" An edge crept into her voice. "Well, there's nothing for me to get upset about, really, is there? I talked to Lisa about my personal life. Relationships, mainly. I suppose I've been through quite a few, not all of them happily." She rotated her teacup once in its saucer. "Fornication isn't against the law, is it?"

Halford shook his head. "So you talked to her about your relationships, to see what insight she could bring to them."

"Was there anything wrong in that? It's not as if she was a minor or some schoolgirl who had never heard of the birds and bees. She was twenty-two, for God's sake."

"But she was a virgin."

Helen's nose gleamed red. "So what? Are you trying to tell me a woman's brain is in her hymen?"

"No. I'm merely suggesting that perhaps a young woman with limited sexual experience didn't quite have the depth of understanding that you supposed."

She turned her head away from Halford and stared towards the tea shop's look-through window. Her breathing grew shallow.

"Maybe I liked it that way," she said finally, looking squarely at Halford. "Maybe it wasn't understanding I wanted so much as solace. Maybe that's what Lisa was good at providing."

"Maybe?"

With her fork, Helen stabbed the last fig on the plate. She left the fork standing upright, ballasted by the fig like a stake taken root.

"No, definitely. Lisa had a long way to go before she could claim understanding. But she was a wonderful listener. She used to tell me so herself."

Baylor stopped writing and poised his pen over his open notebook. Halford noted irrelevantly that the constable wrote in capital letters, neat and perfectly spaced. From where he sat, they looked like blocks of type.

"A self-confessed listener," Halford said thoughtfully. "Not a reader—we've seen her bookshelf. Not a writer—we've been through her papers. But she did appear to love stories. And people appear to have loved telling them to her."

13

All Gale wanted was sleep. The longing hit her about halfway through the inquest, after she had been dismissed, her testimony of Saturday's events finished and recorded by the coroner's earnest secretary. While returning to her seat, she stumbled, the heel of her left shoe clipping her right foot, ripping her stocking and leaving a white scrape that stung the skin. She winced and grabbed the side of a bench for support.

If this had been back home, someone would have helped her, someone officious and unwanted who would drawl assurances in her ear and guide her to her seat with the spraddle-legged gait of the southern old. Someone would have risen from the bench and made a gesture of comfort, if nothing more than a sympathetic nod. As it was, everyone was still.

She swung herself into her seat. Jeremy came out of the communal stupor and fussed with her coat until it formed a bulky nest around her backside. But all she really wanted was to find a pillow and bury herself in it face first.

In the end, it was Jeremy who facilitated it. She was silent on the drive home. Jeremy kept glancing at her until finally she turned away from him and studied the flickering trees. When they reached Fetherbridge he drove straight to the vicarage, shaking his head when she reminded him they needed to get Katie Pru. He led her into the fragrant cleanliness of his house, through the vestibule with its incongruent claret-hued roses molting in a blue vase, and upstairs to a bedroom. There he drew closed the curtains and, satisfied that Gale was settled for a nap, left for Ruth Barker's house to pick up the child. So here she was, the midafternoon light reaching past the gaps in the curtains, the white nibs of the bedspread pressing circles into her cheeks, a long, deep hurt pulling at her heart.

She dragged the cool expanse of the spread over her. Her grandmother had heavy cotton spreads like this in every room of her house in Georgia, overlaid by colourful quilts in the winter, lacy beige tablecloths in the summer. It was peculiar how this bedspread, similar in design and made of the same fibers, could smell and feel so different from those back home. Despite that, she found Jeremy's blanket comforting. It consoled in the way things can when they're only vaguely familiar.

No one had risen to help her at the inquest. She scrunched a small portion of the spread between her toes. It was expecting too much, surely, for anyone to have noticed—the pain had been fleeting, she had handled it quickly. It wasn't antipathy that kept them seated. She jabbed her fist under the pillow.

"That's right, Gale Lynn," she muttered. "We have

grief, anxiety, anger. Let's throw in a little paranoia just
to sweeten the pot."

She remembered the pound coins, a flat grey under
June Kingston's ink-stained fingers. Had it happened
in a movie, the director would have made sure those
coins were placed along the post office counter just so,
lining each one up until it reflected the light into a single glint. And Mrs. Kingston would have been wearing
a poncho, perhaps a gaucho hat, and her eyes would
have squinted at Gale over a thin cigar.

Gale threw off the covers. On a small mahogany
dressing table stood a china bowl and pitcher. She was
able to yank the pitcher out and get her face deep into
the bowl before she heaved once and vomited.

A linen towel lay decoratively across the rim of the
bowl, and she blotted her lips with it, afraid to treat it
indelicately. She walked unsteadily back to the bed,
and for several minutes she lay there, her mouth sour
and the spread smothering her. Finally, accepting that
she wasn't going to sleep, she pushed aside the covers,
and crept downstairs on trembling legs to wait for Katie Pru and Jeremy.

Mrs. Simpson met her at the study door. The housekeeper was dressed neatly in a white blouse and
creased blue gabardine trousers. A pink-and-brown
flowered overall showed telltale signs of work—two
black smudges slashed the middle of the smock—and
in her hand she held a dust cloth.

"You look ill," the woman said shortly. Gale moved
back a step, horrified, as Mrs. Simpson sniffed. "You've
been ill. I told Mr. Cart it was foolishness to cook all
that rich food last night. My mother always said that
in times of grief sweet tea and eggs are all anyone
needs. People who go around bringing fancy dishes to
the house and expect them to be eaten, well, fools,
that's all they are. At times like that if you put something heavy in, it's just going to come back out, one
way or another."

She put her arm around Gale's shoulder and led her

into the vicarage study. Gale wasn't used to people touching her. She wanted to take her fear and nausea and be left alone. But as they approached the study's overstuffed chesterfield, Gale let herself lean into the soft arch of Mrs. Simpson's arm. At least a head taller than Gale, Mrs. Simpson was sinewy and easily bore the smaller woman's weight. Suddenly Gale's throat began to burn. She felt a wave of familiar feeling, a mixture of anguish, helplessness, and relief. Her father, with merely a look, had been able to make her feel defeated and resurrected at once; it was an altar-side emotion that only he could induce. Why Mrs. Simpson could elicit it so sharply Gale couldn't say.

Hiccups started deep in Gale's belly; she began to sob. Implacably, Mrs. Simpson directed her down into the soft green velvet of the chesterfield. A red woolen throw covered the sofa's back, and Mrs. Simpson grabbed it and wrapped it around her knees.

A slap would have been better. The concern in the gesture plunged Gale into a fit of self-pity: No one had risen to help her at the inquest, Mrs. Kingston had indeed snubbed her— and Lisa was dead. She sat upright on the chesterfield, her hands limp on the deep red throw, the hiccups so loud they hurt. Mrs. Simpson left the room and returned in less than a minute with a glass of warm Coke. Gale wanted it, knowing it would taste like home, but all she could do was stare hopelessly at the glass in her hand, unable to lift it to her mouth.

"This won't do." Mrs. Simpson stood over her, arms akimbo, voice stern. "Mr. Cart will be back any time now with that child of yours. You can't let her see you sitting here crying all over yourself."

She walked to a side table and pulled a thin packet of pink tissues from the drawer. "Go wash your face if you need to. If you want to come wait with me, I'm working in the dining room."

The housekeeper made to leave, then turned back.

Gale felt a cold, dry hand grasp her chin and lift her wet face.

"And I want you to know something," Mrs. Simpson said. "After all the damage I've seen that Stillwell girl do, I can tell you she wasn't worth the water you'll wash your hands in after you've thrown a clump of dirt on her casket."

Her fingers tightened on Gale's chin, almost making her cry out. Then Mrs. Simpson straightened, smoothed the front of her overall and left the room.

Gale sat alone in the study and wiped her eyes. She leaned over and carefully set her glass on the table. All around her were the signs of God's work—the Bible on the desk, Jeremy's cassock over his chair, a stack of church newsletters ready for delivery. Lisa would never have fit in here. She had been an ungodly thing, a chimeric mixture of naïveté and worldliness. And ungodly things by nature can't be allowed to exist.

From the dining room came the clink of cutlery and then gradual quiet as Mrs. Simpson moved deeper into the vicarage. Sounds, Gale thought, can get caught in a house the way smells do. Among the sounds her own house held was the shrill, tinny edge of Lisa's voice, rising and narrowing to a sharp point of exhilaration. On occasion the point had pricked; once it had drawn blood.

A slow August day, Lisa had brought Katie Pru home from an afternoon drive. The two girls entered the front door laughing, covered from head to toe in bits of leaves and petals. Katie Pru toddled over and gave Gale a fistful of bedraggled wild poppies.

"We been to Daddy. He lives in the ground in a box. We made his house pretty."

Lisa had laughed, unsnarling grass from her hair. "The wildflowers are so gorgeous, Gale, I'm afraid we got carried away. We picked until we couldn't hold anymore, and since we were in Winchester and near the cemetery already, we took them over to Tom's grave. It was so barren, so plain. You've been neglectful. Well, we fixed it. Every color of the rainbow, isn't that right, Katie Pru? Flowers and vines everywhere. It's lovely now.''

It had been innocent. She had never once felt malice in Lisa's words, only the destructive strike of purity.

And there were other times. Gale ticked them off, the tears drying on her face. Sly references to Gale's sex life, subtle questions about Tom's past. Once she had even found the girl in her room, going through a box of Tom's unpublished poems the police had just given back to her.

"Listen to this, Gale: 'In bothered blessings our new love thrives.' " Lisa had been sitting cross-legged on the floor, the box in front of her. "How romantic. Was he talking about you?"

Gale had been more shocked than angry. "Lisa!" she had said. "Those are private. Please put them back."

Lisa looked up, her blue eyes wide with apology. "I'm sorry, Gale. I would think you'd want to share them. I mean, they're like having Tom with you forever, aren't they?" She had turned back to the poem. " 'Bothered blessings.' What do you suppose he was talking about?"

Gale had nearly ripped the poem from the girl's hands and shoved it back into the box. When Tom had first written it, she, too had wondered what exactly he meant. Now she had no doubt.

The door of the rectory creaked open and the soles of two tiny sneakers squeaked in wild abandon on the foyer floor. Katie Pru was back. Gale felt a familiar sweep of relief that was both warm and confusing— the mother's paradox. Briskly she made one last swipe at her nose with the tissue and stood.

She crept to the doorway and peeked out. Katie Pru kicked aside the edge of the foyer rug and engaged in a dance step that was part manic swivel and part wind-up for a baseball pitch. As she twisted, the oversized double tongues of her coat zipper jangled against each other like reindeer bells. To her delight the ancient floor screeched and whined under her feet and the red hot-house roses on the vestibule table quivered meekly and bowed. Katie Pru clapped her hands. When she saw her mother she stopped, threw back her head and laughed with such glee that her small white teeth bounced against each other. God, Gale thought as she knelt and waited for the small, perfect body to slam into hers, I can't ever love as much as I do now. No life will ever come as close to giving me peace as hers.

She stood, still embracing Katie Pru who, despite the padded bulk of her jacket, managed to clasp her mother tightly with all four limbs and bury her head in her shoulder. Gale rocked her. "Did you have a good time at Mrs. Barker's?"

Katie Pru nodded without lifting her head. "We made cookies."

"Really?"

"Yes, but Miz Barker says they're biscuits. They're not biscuits, they're cookies and she wouldn't let me take any home."

"Well, Mrs. Barker probably needed them for company."

Katie Pru jerked her head up and glared at Gale. "No, she said they were biscuits and I said they're not. She got mad."

Gale looked past Katie Pru. Jeremy stood by the front door, still dressed in his coat and scarf. He shrugged, his face humourless and tight.

"Do you need a ride to your cottage?" he asked. "If so, we need to go soon. What with this morning, I'm behind in my work."

Gale put Katie Pru down and pointed to the study. "I think I left my pocketbook in there, baby. Could you run go get it for me, please, ma'am?"

"Okay."

Gale watched Katie Pru disappear into the study, then turned to Jeremy. "What happened?"

His mouth tightened. He shook his head. "Nothing,

really. Ruth and Katie Pru evidently had an argument on semantics and Katie Pru lost. It's tough being a kiddie. No power except your lungs. Still, she doesn't look any the worse for it. . . . You didn't sleep long."

"I couldn't. Did Ruth say anything to you?"

Jeremy smoothed his scarf into his lapel, avoiding her eyes. "Not really. Just the usual prattle—Katie Pru's such a joy, so bright, no trouble at all. She mentioned the argument, but she was laughing about it. No, nothing for you to worry about."

Gale looked at him calmly. "What the hell does that mean?"

To her surprise, Jeremy erupted. "Oh, come on, Gale. Quit being so defensive. That's all the woman said, all right? Get Katie Pru in here and let's go. I've got a memorial service tomorrow and I'd like to put a little thought into it, if it's all the same to you." He spun around, the edge of his overcoat flapping open, and stalked from the house.

In less than a minute he was back. Gale was kneeling in front of Katie Pru trying to force the bent stem of the jacket's zipper into its metal groove. It must have been an old frame of reference that caused her to recognise Maura Ramsden's legs before she saw her face. The detective stood slightly behind Jeremy, her soft beige coat circling her calves. There was a crooked run in her stocking. Quickly Gale stood and looked past her into the cold air of the vicarage garden. There was no one else there.

"Mrs. Grayson, I'm sorry to bother you here, but I did run round to your cottage first." Maura Ramsden had the irritating ability to look efficient and content even with a run in her hose. "Do you have a minute? I've some questions."

Gale knelt again and directed her attention to Katie Pru's coat. She fitted the two ends of the zipper together, giving it a hard tug. The zipper gruffly chugged up to the child's neck. Katie Pru turned and stood stiffly, her arms floating in the quilted sleeves as she

stared at Maura. The detective must have either met
her eyes or smiled, for Katie Pru tucked her chin into
her jacket and reemerged with the hood string clamped
between her teeth. She flicked her tongue underneath
the string and deposited a neat half-moon of saliva on
her chin, already chapped from the weather. Gale
frowned, unfolded the damp pink tissue she had kept
wadded in the palm of her hand, and wiped the child's
face. Katie Pru looked at her mother and growled.

"Well, actually, Sergeant Ramsden," Gale said, "this
isn't really a good time. Jeremy was getting ready to
take us home."

"Fine. I've managed to procure a car. We can go in
mine."

Oh, how very "City" of you, Gale thought, but she
was silent. She studied Katie Pru's face, judging her
choices. Then she remembered the bowl of vomit upstairs.

"Just a minute," she murmured. "I forgot something."

Mrs. Simpson was already in the bedroom when
Gale dashed in. The air smelled lightly of honey. Beneath the pitcher on the small mahogany dressing table
sat the flower-patterned bowl, cleaned. Gale looked at
Mrs. Simpson and shook her head.

"I'm sorry. I should have taken care of that before
I went downstairs."

"It's quite all right. You've enough on your mind."
Mrs. Simpson bent and deftly adjusted the corner of
the bedspread. "That the detective?"

"One of them. She has more questions. I know I
should be all ready and willing to help, but . . ." She
could complete the sentence with a plethora of phrases.
*But I hate their intrusion, their presumption, their thievery
of my time and solitude. I hate Maura Ramsden's coolness
and the way Daniel Halford watched me at the inquest.*

She left the sentence unfinished. Instead she
shrugged.

"I don't have anything to say that won't sound ridiculous," said Mrs. Simpson. She handed Gale her coat. "As I was telling my Jim last night, I don't know what this town will do having to go through another murder inquiry. We've just barely gotten over the last."

She scooped up Gale's blue scarf from where it had fallen on the floor and held it, sketching with her finger the coarse strain of white yarn woven into it.

"I probably shouldn't be saying this to you," she continued, "but people were changed when your husband died. People thought they had one life, familiar even if it wasn't always happy, and then all that mess came along, and the familiar was gone, just disappeared. That's what I tried to explain to my Jim, although I don't know he ever saw the point. It's a bitter lesson, to know that the things you do every day mean nothing. I suppose most have forgotten. But Lisa's murder will bring it back."

She took a step closer to Gale and wrapped the scarf around her neck, carefully tucking the ends into the coat and turning the edges down so they wouldn't chafe. When she finished, she considered her work a moment, then left without saying another word.

14

The Fetherbridge Recreation Center was an oxblood red building set back from Boundary Road about a quarter mile east of the entrance to Heatherwood Beach. Ten vehicles were scattered through the front car park, just a fraction of the fifty officers Roan had assigned to the case. Inside, Halford knew the building would be thick with the peculiar murmurs and obscenities of police work and choked with the bitter smell of coffee. Some of the officers were conducting the routine business of checking alibis and confirming facts, but the bulk were searching for Mr. E. What a damnable job to hand someone, Halford thought. "Don't know who, don't know where, Constable, just find him." If it is a him. If there really is someone to find.

The possibility that there was no mystery suitor had been bothering Halford ever since Maura's interview with Christian Timbrook. He was nearly convinced that the craftsman was not Lisa's Mr. E.; everyone in town, despite Timbrook's assertions, seemed to know of Lisa's infatuation with him, and Jill Ivory admitted that Lisa had spoken openly with her about their relationship. No secrecy there.

But the idea that Lisa was a fanciful young woman trying to impress friends in the face of her own inexperience—that was a nagging notion Halford was finding increasingly plausible. He thought of his sister Belinda. At the age of thirteen she developed a crush on the actor Alan Bates and convinced several of her classmates that he was a close family friend.

Halford hadn't known about Belinda's Alan Bates lie until a classmate, an older brother of one of Belinda's friends, challenged him on it. He could do nothing but deny it. But then, twenty-five years ago, Belinda had been an adolescent and at thirteen was preboyfriend, preheels, prelipstick. Lisa Stillwell was a young woman in her early twenties in a more sexually cognizant age. Was it even necessary to conjure up fantasies anymore?

Halford trudged over to the recreation center and was about to reach for the door when it swung open and emitted Richard Roan. The DI looked at Halford and breathed deeply. It was a reptilian reaction. His eyelids lowered a fraction and his chin receded into his neck so that in his stiff white collar and Windsor knot he looked like a turtle swallowing.

Halford nodded briefly. "How are things going?"

Roan shrugged. "Progressing. Going through the church roll, interviewing classmates. This Mr. E. business . . . wish we had more to go on."

Contempt clipped Roan's speech. Halford dropped his eyes and examined the pavement. He couldn't comprehend this man. There had been a time, earlier in his career, when he prided himself on his grasp on the human psyche. Nothing was more thrilling to him than laying open to the light every bleak compartment of an adversary's imagination. Then came a suicide in front of a stained glass window and a trembling pair of hands pitifully clutching a china teacup. Halford looked at Roan. He detested the man for making him tired.

"What's turned up from the churchgoers?" Halford asked brusquely.

Again Roan shrugged. "Nothing much. It does seem that Lisa got into a bit of a tussle with one of the girls over the brother, Brian. The girl and Brian were seeing each other—talk of an engagement, actually. Lisa wouldn't have it. There was a row in the middle of Communion. Evidently, Lisa won. Brian and the girl broke it off."

"What's the girl's name?"

Roan looked bored. "Simpson. I've got someone checking it out."

"And Mr. E.?"

"Nothing much there. Been over all her friends at least twice. No one seems to know. Ruled some people out—old men, dead men, a few who sounded offended at the idea of dating a woman. We're concentrating on Hampshire, starting at Winchester and radiating out, but I'll bet we'll not find him here. Don't put a lot of stock into what gossiping girls tell each other. She spent a bit of time going to and from London. My money says he's there."

"Bloody hell," Halford said. It was an overwhelming quest. If he could be sure there was a Mr. E., he wouldn't have the slightest qualm about spending time and resources finding him. As it was, however, he was torn between telling Roan to carry on and ordering him to call in his men until more information could be found.

He was aware of Roan studying him, his turtle eyes hooded.

"I was just thinking, Roan, about the likelihood that

Lisa never mentioned this Mr. E. to anyone but Jill
Ivory. Not good odds, would you say?"

"Lousy."

Halford waited for Roan to elucidate, but the DI
continued to watch his superior impassively. Halford
ground his heel into the gritty surface of the asphalt
and walked away.

Gale stood frowning inside the doorway to the *Inquisitor*'s archives. Something wasn't quite right, but
she was damned if she knew what. Behind her she
heard the rustle of Sergeant Ramsden's pantyhose as
she shifted her weight, but otherwise the detective was
silent, letting her take her time to study the room.
Something was out of place, or maybe missing. Gale
rubbed her temple. She looked at the stacks of newspapers, some forming crooked, perilous columns to the
ceilings, some mushrooming in yellow mounds on the
floor. To her left, stacks fanned out over their own bot-
toms like failed attempts at card shuffling. The evidence of her own work was there—a series of neat little
piles where she had attempted to put the most recent
issues in order, the cuttings she had started to clip and
date. The pen and scissors she had used were still
crossed on top of the cut articles. Still, something was
off.

In the newsroom she heard Ivory's soft mumble, followed by an angry shriek from Katie Pru. Gale tugged
her attention away from the disarray and glanced at
her watch—2:45. The cranky hour. Another ten minutes
and the child would have things leaping off the walls.
She pointed to the dirty ironstone plate and turned to
Maura Ramsden.

"That wasn't there the last time I worked. I think
some of the reporters bring snacks in here when they're
looking for things. Other than that, I'm afraid I can't
help you. If pushed, I would say something is different,
but I can't for the life of me figure out what."

Something heavy smacked the floor in the other

room; Katie Pru let out a wail. Quickly Maura disappeared and was back before Gale could fumble through the door.

"Just a drawing table," she said. "No injuries. Now, Mrs. Grayson, perhaps if you concentrated on the room in quadrants . . ."

Gale turned back to the sagging columns of newsprint. But it was pointless. She shook her head at the detective and with a murmured apology edged out of the room. From the hallway at the back of the newsroom came a blast of angry words.

"I *have* to go potty."

"Well, you can't go 'potty' until your mother gets here. If you'll give me your hand, we'll go back and get her." Ivory's voice was tense.

"I can do it *myself.*"

"Not at my newspaper. Now, Katie Pru, will you come with me nicely or do I have to pick you up and carry you?"

Obviously it was a question backed up by action: Katie Pru's scream didn't quite drown out Ivory's curt expletives. By the time Gale and Maura got to the hall, Ivory had the child grasped to his torso bandolier-wise while Katie Pru's feet pounded his left hip with vicious one-two kicks that made Gale wince.

"What's going on here?" she demanded.

Ivory's face bloomed bright red, and at first Gale wasn't sure if he was going to set the child down or fling her at the belly from whence she came. He shot Gale a grimace, then let Katie Pru slide to the floor. As soon as she was on solid footing, Katie Pru ran into the WC and slammed the door.

"You know, she really can do it herself." Gale tried to keep the amusement out of her voice.

Ivory wiped a bead of sweat from his forehead. "Well, how in the hell am I supposed to know that?" he asked in exasperation. "For all I know she could be crouching in the corner right now. It wouldn't have hurt her to wait just a second for you to get here."

"Oh, Orrin. She's three. You have a daughter. Remember when she was three? A few seconds can seem as long as an hour and besides, adults have a strange way of turning a few seconds into minutes. And three-year-olds *don't* crouch in the corner."

Ivory tilted his head to retort, but instead changed the subject. "So, did you figure out if anything was missing?"

"I just don't know. Maybe."

"Well, they broke in for something."

Behind her, Maura Ramsden replied. "Maybe when they realised that what they wanted couldn't be got at easily, they changed their minds. Decided it wasn't that important, that if they couldn't put their hands on it immediately, no one else could either."

"I guess it's possible," Gale admitted. "But that would be assuming quite a bit on their part. I mean, how would they know there wasn't a filing system in there? The scissors were out, after all. Obviously, someone had been working. Wouldn't it have been worth their while to at least give a cursory look through the place?"

She looked at Maura. The sergeant was chewing on her pen, apparently studying the top of Gale's head.

"But then you said, Mrs. Grayson, that you felt something was different. So maybe someone did give the place a cursory look. Or maybe they didn't need to. Maybe they knew right where to get what they wanted."

Gale hated being led like this. It was almost patronising, as if she was playing the goose-necked crook to Sergeant Ramsden's sharp-as-razors lawman. She kept her voice unruffled. "Then you're talking about someone who knows the paper well."

"Could be. Assuming, of course, that you're right about something being off." Maura looked from Gale to Ivory. "Want to hazard a few guesses?"

Gale didn't give the editor the chance to respond. "Name the names, you mean? I don't think so, Sergeant. You're the professional. Come up with your own list."

Gale grabbed the latch on the WC door and pushed it open. Her daughter was standing on the wastepaper basket, making faces in the smudged mirror.

"Look, Mama. It's my tongue."

Gale scooped her up and without a word, took her back through the newsroom and out of the building.

Halford was lost in thought, his lips pressed against the side of a coffee mug, when Maura opened the door of the police station and flung her handbag the length of the room. He waited without moving until she retrieved the handbag and dropped into a chair.

"Ah, Sergeant Ramsden. Cool as a cucumber and not nearly so green."

"I'm not in the mood for sarcasm, Daniel. It's well and good for you to be smug—you spent the day all nice and toasty at an inquest—"

"I wouldn't exactly call it toasty. . . . "

"—while I had to socialise with a passel of Fleet Street wanna-bes and spend hours with the smell and dust of old newsprint going up my nose. And if that wasn't bad enough, I had to commandeer Mrs. Grayson and cajole her into being cooperative. And on top of that I had to listen to Orrin Ivory argue with a three-year-old about how to use the damn loo." She pulled a handkerchief from her coat pocket. "God, I'm going to have to wash the inside of my nostrils. I'll be sneezing black for a month."

"So, lovely day, was it?"

Maura rolled her eyes. "Know what I've decided? Newsrooms are second only to police stations as the most depressing places to work. Stale air, desks crammed together, nowhere to walk. I bet it's part of the training—you take really intense people and crowd them all in one room where they have to live under each other's mess, and then when they're on the verge of murder, you let them loose on the streets with a pen and a pad.''

"Goodness, Maura, you have had a bad day. By rights, one of Roan's people should have handled the break-in, but crime being so rare in our little village here, I felt better having you do it."

Maura shoved her handkerchief back into her pocket. She walked over to the table where the remainder of Miss Forrester's goodies was spread among a layer of crumbs. She slid the last two coconut biscuits from the tin and bit one in half.

"I did decide one thing," she announced. "I'd rather be a copper than a journalist. At least my work's not dirty. There's a clean imperative to what I do—the law. I rarely go home and wonder about how many innocent people I've hurt. Reporters must do that, and then justify it, all the time. Anyway, the point is I decided it's too agnostic a life for me."

She waited for the usual Halford retort, but he was silent. His eyes were downcast, and for a moment she thought he was angry. Then he flipped shut a folder and his eyes flickered to her face.

"Maura?"

"Yes?"

"Let's talk about the break-in."

"Right. The break-in." She sat, pulled her notebook from her handbag, and leaned back in the chair. "I don't know, Daniel, it seems a bit off to me. For one thing, entry was evidently through the front door. A pane was broken as if someone reached through to unlock it, but the hole is so narrow, it had to be either someone with very small hands or someone with a tool. Yet there were no marks on the knob inside to indicate a tool was used. And Ivory hasn't a clue if anything is missing."

"And Mrs. Grayson?"

"If pressed, she would say something was different in the archives, but she couldn't tell what."

"What about keys?"

"To the building? Five. They seem very easy to procure if someone legitimately needed one."

Halford reopened the folder and started pushing papers back into it. "Well, hand it over to Nate. He can keep at it for a while and see if something turns up missing. Off the top of my head, I see three possible explanations: It was a common burglary committed by persons unconnected with the *Inquisitor*, which seems doubtful; someone connected with the paper broke in either to steal something or to get something without raising suspicions by asking for a key, which seems rather bumbling; or someone connected with the paper wanted to make it look like a break-in, which seems most intriguing. At any rate, let's see what happens. Right now, I need you to help me with a couple of interviews. Ruth Barker's daughter is living in Fetherbridge with her mother at the moment, so I want to talk with her. After that, we need to see the good reverend."

"He won't welcome us, I'll tell you that. He was in a rather strained mood this afternoon when I fetched Mrs. Grayson."

"Oh, I know. I've already talked to him on the phone. He's busy and he has Lisa's prayer service tomorrow. All of which I would be very sympathetic towards if I didn't know the man had been cavorting like a fool over at Mrs. Grayson's last night."

"Last night?" Maura cocked her head. "You mean you weren't tucked in with your hot milk and bickie at The Proper Pale?"

Halford stood, grabbed his coat, and playfully whacked her on the back with a folder. "Look, sister. Do you work for me or the bloody *Inquisitor*?"

"I think I just spent a good portion of your time explaining I work for justice, Chief Inspector."

The woman who opened the door of the snug flint cottage on Tullsgate Lane had Ruth Barker's wiry red hair and long oval face, but there Beryl Lampson's re-

semblance to her mother ended. On the two occasions
Halford had seen her, Mrs. Barker had worn the functional wool and cotton clothes of retired life. This
younger woman, however, had the carefully remote
look of a catalogue model. Her hair was long and artfully unkempt; stray locks curled around her temple
and coiled down the bodice of her indigo print frock.
The dress was vintage Laura Ashley—if not the real
thing, then a like-minded cousin whose intent was to
make the wearer feel young, casually affluent, and
love-weary all at the same time. Above her, as if to
accentuate the point, a sprig of Christmas mistletoe
hung from the doorframe.

"It's a good thing you rang when you did," she told
Halford as he slipped his warrant card back into his
coat. "Mother's gone for the rest of the day. She'd be
mad as hell if she knew you were here." She glanced
next door at the neighbouring cottage, an eighteenth-
century clone of the Barker's home. "Of course, she'll
hear soon enough, I'll wager."

Despite the chill air, and her apparent concern over
the neighbours' prying eyes, she made no move to invite Halford and Maura into the house. Instead, she
flicked her hair over her shoulders, crossed her arms,
and looked at the two detectives expectantly.

"This won't take long, will it?" she asked, slightly
hunched from the cold. "I want to help, but I haven't
much time."

"We'll be brief," Halford assured her. "We're trying
to find out all we can about Lisa Stillwell. Did you
know her well?"

Beryl Lampson shook her head emphatically. "Not
well at all. She was a full four years behind me. I mean,
I knew her some; whenever a group of us would get
together, she might be there, but she generally ran with
a younger crowd."

"Did she ever date anyone in your set?"

Her laugh was curt. "Hardly. To be honest, she was
a bit of a pain. I know that sounds harsh, but when she

did come with us, it was usually because our parents insisted. 'She has no mother, she's lonely, you need to be kind.' You know the kind of thing."

"Did you ever know her to date anyone?"

Again, she shook her head. "No. I can't imagine Lisa dating at all. I don't know how to explain this, but she was too fussy, too fidgety. She reminded me of a little girl who was always having to pull up her socks. I know some of the boys made fun of her—'Lisa Stillborn' they called her. Not a nice thing, but then we were all teenagers."

Nervously, Beryl shifted from one foot to the other, her hazel eyes scanning the road. A gust of wind rushed by, and she rubbed her arms vigorously.

"Look, Mrs. Lampson," Halford began, "I'm trying to be quick about this, but if you'd be more comfortable inside—"

"No," she said sternly. "I'm fine. Mother keeps the house much too musty. Please go ahead."

He glanced at Maura. "When I called to get your address," he continued, "I was surprised to find you living with your parents."

"No more surprised than I am," she said. "Until three months ago, I worked for a brokerage firm in London. I was made redundant. Without work, I couldn't afford my flat. In fact, I was interviewing for a job the morning Lisa died."

"You were interviewing Saturday morning?"

She continued to study the road. "Yes. Starnsby and Lowen, on Haymarket. Mr. Lowen was leaving the country on Monday and wanted to talk with me beforehand." Her face clouded. "I haven't heard anything from them. At any rate, Mr. Lowen can confirm I was with him."

He nodded. "I understand you and your husband are divorced."

Her eyes shifted to Halford's face. "What does that have to do with Lisa?"

"I'm interested in an incident that involved Lisa and

your miscarriage. Do you know what I'm talking about?"

She clinched her teeth. "You mean 'Grandmother's Day' or 'Grandmother's Delight,' or whatever the hell she called it. Yes, I remember it. My fourth pregnancy. Michael, my husband—he and I were being very cautious. Three miscarriages and, well, we wanted to be careful, to give matters a chance before we got too excited."

Abruptly, she turned to Maura, her red hair partially obscuring Halford's view of her face. Her voice was strained. "We really wanted a baby, you see. We were both only children and when we first married, we decided we needed at least two, that we didn't want our children to be onlies like we were. Of course, after the first miscarriage, we prayed for just one, just one healthy baby. By the time we lost the fourth, there didn't seem to be anything left of us."

She kept her body facing Maura, her elbows rigid at her sides. Maura's tone was sympathetic.

"So your mother didn't even know you were pregnant until Lisa told her?"

"No, and God knows how Lisa found out. This place is such a gossip mill and Lisa really knew how to work the gears. I think gossiping made her feel a part of things."

"Can you think of any other particular gossip Lisa was at the heart of?" Maura asked.

"No, not off the top of my head. Just things. I mean, who can dissect the village grapevine? It functions. It works. No secrets allowed in jolly old Fetherbridge." She paused. "I hated having to come back."

"So you and your husband didn't live here," Halford interjected.

"No, but that didn't matter. Once of Fetherbridge, always of Fetherbridge. The village claims you. You can move as far away as you want and you're still the little girl they're all watching." Her voice snapped into a cackle. " 'Is Beryl doing well? Is Beryl making money?

Is Beryl having babies?' They won't let you go." Her
laugh was embittered. "Sometimes I feel like a damned
voodoo doll they made out of wax. They can reshape
my head if they want to, and there's damn all I can do
about it."

She faced Halford again, but her eyes returned to
the road.

"What was your reaction to Lisa notifying your
mother of the pregnancy?" he asked.

Beryl shrugged. "That didn't bother me so much. I
should have told Mother anyway. But the parade
through town, all the presents." She shook her head.
Her voice grew thick. "I just don't understand it. Everyone knew I was having difficulties. Why didn't
someone say, 'Lisa, this isn't appropriate. Give the poor
woman some privacy'? But nobody did. I think Lisa
came along with her little secret and everyone clapped
their hands and went along. They let her get away with
so much."

"Such as?" Halford asked quietly.

Tears brimmed in Beryl's eyes. "Oh, I don't know.
A sort of tactlessness, I guess. I'm not sure Lisa had
much feeling for people. I mean, not to understand
what it must be like to lose baby after baby? Not to
realise how frightened we were with each pregnancy?
Lisa knew how to look concerned and say the right
things, and for all the old biddies around here, that was
enough."

Halford paused. "Does that include your mother?"

The tears spilled down the woman's chapped
cheeks. "Yes, sir," she said, angrily wiping them away.
"That sure as hell includes my mother."

15

Timbrook lifted the hand-painted blue-and-white sign welcoming customers into The Transitional Woman—Renewed Clothes Emporium, and turned it around to read, in exquisitely polite terms, please stay the hell away.

"There, luv. I've fixed it. Pack it in and I'll take you to supper."

Helen stopped pulling mauve tights onto the legs of a mannequin. She glanced at the window where Timbrook was shrugging his regrets to a thickset woman reaching for the door. "Dammit, Timbrook. Let her in. I've a half hour before closing. Quit being a nuisance or I'll send you home."

The thickset woman looked at her watch and

pointed to the shop hours posted on the window. "Stubborn old nanny," Timbrook muttered. He opened the door and popped his head out.

"Sorry, madam, but the shop's closing early. Tragedy in the family, you understand. We'll reopen for custom in a few days. Thank you so much for your consideration."

Behind the plate glass of the closed door, the woman's face played her emotions like a zoetrope. *But I won't take a second. Oh, I'm so sorry. I understand. Of course I'll return. What a nice young man.* She hiked her handbag firmly onto the crook of her arm and, with Timbrook waving, trundled happily away.

"That," Helen said, "was uncalled for. Custom isn't so good that I can afford to dismiss people at the door."

Timbrook waited until the woman disappeared into Hossett's Bookshop next door before retreating behind the counter. Leaning on one elbow, he buried his hand in a tray of bright silk scarves.

"You've got it wrong, darling," he said. "The economy is bad—your shop is booming. The joys of an inflation-proof trade. I, of course, wouldn't know about such things, art being both timeless and cyclical."

He watched Helen select a black velvet dress from a rack against the wall. It was an elegant piece of work, full-skirted with mutton sleeves and an elaborate design in matching braid that covered the bodice and reappeared in small medallions around the hem. She carefully removed it from its hanger and slid it over the mannequin's neck.

"That's a beautiful frock," Timbrook offered.

Helen let the skirt fall into place and adjusted the shoulders. "Yes, well, it wasn't much when I bought it. A thrift shop in London, all balled up in the bottom of a box. After a sound cleaning, it turned out all right." She pulled at the sleeves. "I added the braid. Looks nice, don't you think?"

"Hmmm. Sad, really."

"What?"

"No, I mean the frock. It looks sad. Almost like a mourning dress."

Helen frowned and pressed her hands into the small of her back. "Don't start with that rubbish. I'm displaying it because I worked damned hard on it. You make it sound as though I'm building a shrine."

"The thought never crossed my mind."

Helen laughed sarcastically. Retrieving the hanger from the floor, she stalked through the curtained doorway behind the counter and into her workshop. Timbrook slipped a paisley green rectangle from the pile of silk scarves and followed her.

Not for the first time, Timbrook noticed the similarities between his workroom and Helen's. Granted, his was considerably larger, but both rooms shared a common motif: colour. Several small tables were angled through Helen's room, each mounded with fabric and clothes, sorted either by shade or design—checks on one table, pastels on another, fancy trimming on a third. In the corners of the room, the floor itself had become workspace, with boxes and piles of clothes threatening to invade the centre space.

Helen tossed the hanger into a box and plopped into a chair behind a small metal table.

"I need an assistant," she announced, rummaging through a thick jumble of papers. "I'm weeks behind in my billings, this wedding is taking up too much of my time, I have the church program to worry about, and I have to start concentrating on spring and summer." She rubbed her face. "I *hate* it when people die. God, Timbrook, what am I going to do?"

"Give it a few days rest and tackle it next week."

"That's easy for you to say, Mr. I've-Finished-the-Window-Pick-It-Up-When-You-Need-It."

Timbrook held the green scarf to the light. "Lisa was going to work for you on the weekends, wasn't she?"

"Yes. Jill Ivory helps me sometimes, and I've

thought about asking her to do it regularly, but I don't think the editor-king would approve."

Timbrook removed a sparkling wad of red netting from a chair and sat. He looked around at the buried tables. "A char might be more what you need."

"You clot." Helen penciled a few absentminded crosses on a piece of paper. "Do you know what I do at night?"

"Pine."

She ignored him. "I go person to person through the village, conjuring ways each one could have killed Lisa. Miss Forrester could have poisoned her with a biscuit. Ben Hossett could have broken her neck with a whack of a book. Anise Ivory could have bored her to death."

Timbrook wrapped the scarf in and out around his fingers. "Pretty pastime."

"You, of course, would have slashed her with a piece of glass. Jeremy—well, Jeremy would have choked her with the Bible."

"Ah. Isn't that how we all die in the end? Laid out in our coffins, gagging at the sermon?"

"It's just an interesting thing."

"What?"

"We could have each done it, in our own way. So the question becomes, who would have done it on a bicycle, with a scarf?"

Timbrook tightened the slippery material around his fingers, until the exposed silk looked like an opulent version of his usual dull bandages.

"Bit simplistic," he said.

"If you like. But I really don't think so."

Timbrook traced the outline of a single paisley with his thumb. "And what about you? How would you have killed her?"

Helen stretched her arms over her head. Her eyes narrowed. "Oh, whipped the poor thing into a deadly frenzy with stories of my sordid past."

•   •   •

The Book of Common Prayer lay open on the desk next to a blue glass bowl—the Priest Bowl, Gale called it, because in it Cart kept all the little serviceable bits his parishioners sloughed off and left in the carpet after a consoling visit to the vicarage. Cart stirred the contents with his finger. Coins, buttons, paper clips, a pen top, the back of an earring, even a ball of red thread tumbled round and round the sides of the bowl, made sapphire by the suffused light.

The prayer book was open to the Order for the Burial of the Dead, as it had been from the day he first learned of Lisa's death. He didn't really regret the law's forced delay of the funeral. Even without the grimness of the rite, he loathed this sacrament. He had never been able to find the music in it. The rhythm blocked his tongue, and whenever he stood in front of the sanctuary and read the words, he could hear the dissonance echo from the rear. Cart slammed the book shut and turned back to the Priest Bowl.

When the knock at the door came, it was five past five. The police, it would seem, were more or less punctual. Cart glanced around the room. It appeared heavy, the burnished wood of the bookcases umbra-rich behind the glow of the single desk lamp. The lamp's neat circle of light framed the Book of Common Prayer.

Well, good, he thought. Let them know that the Lord's work is sombre and serious. Let them know that the law and the Word must bide each other's time. Before leaving the room to answer the door, Cart flipped the book open again to the burial service.

He directed the detectives into his study and shut the door. "Honestly, I didn't realise how dark it was in here. Let me get that light for you, Sergeant. Here, please sit."

He pointed Maura Ramsden toward the chesterfield. She was a pretty creature, too wholesome looking to be considered exotic, but her movements were fluid enough to be considered, well, something. He leaned over her to switch on a floor lamp. She wore a spicy

scent, a bit surprising for a copper, but then, she had
applied it with taste. Unintentionally, he knocked the
lamp with his arms. The fringe on the shade, oyster-
coloured from age, bobbed jauntily and sent long
curves of shadow jumping on her face.

Halford found an armchair near the desk and
hauled it over to the chesterfield. Cart bit his lip as he
watched the inspector settle into it. The clawed feet of
the legs and the broad scrolls of the arms made the
chair look sturdy, but the creak of the joints as Halford
leaned back testified to the many broad-bottomed
women who had sought pastoral calm while sitting
there. Halford glanced up and stopped moving.

"You'd prefer I didn't sit here?"

"No, no, it's fine. It's just that some of the furniture
in the vicarage is old and on its last legs, so I'm always
attuned to the little noises it makes. But if it decides to
give way beneath you, I'm sure we'll be treated to all
sorts of screeches and cracks first. You'll be able to get
up in time."

Halford smiled and crossed his foot over his knee.
Cart looked around for a seat and discovered that the
most logical was next to Sergeant Ramsden on the chesterfield, directly under the lamp. Clever, these two, he
thought. They must have planned it.

"You don't mind if I smoke, do you?" Cart opened
the drawer on the side table next to him and took out
an ashtray. "It's a nasty habit and Gale keeps trying to
get me to quit, but I say what for—I'm not American."
He struck a match and lit up.

"Father Cart . . ."

"Mister, please. Or Jeremy will do fine. I don't like
clerical titles. Sets up too much of a barrier."

"Mr. Cart, then." Halford shifted and the chair
creaked. "Once again, let me thank you for agreeing to
see us. I understand you are busy, and we appreciate
your time."

Despite the chief inspector's lyrical timbre, the
words were obviously rote. Cart nodded. He let his

eyes drift to the open copy of the book under its halo of light.

Halford continued. "As you know, we're here about Lisa Stillwell. Just now, we're interviewing the people who would have known her best to get an idea of what kind of person she was."

"Ah. Know the victim and you'll know the crime."

"Pardon?"

"It was something I read once. Agatha Christie, probably—I don't remember. It had something to do with the theory that in the victim lies the motive for his murder. Or is that just one of those things fictional detectives run around saying?"

Halford's small smiles definitely could be irritating, but Cart suspected the chief inspector knew that and might even be the type to practice them in front of a mirror. "Well, I'd say that is frequently true, Mr. Cart, but not necessarily. Take Miss Stillwell, for example. If she knew her murderer, then possibly. If it was a random killing, as many of your parishioners believe, then maybe not."

Cart chuckled. "They've been telling you they think this was a random killing? I'm afraid they're being polite, Chief Inspector."

"Really?"

"Oh, I don't mean to say they think it was any one person or anything like that." Cart blew out a puff of smoke. "Have you ever lived in a village? You, Sergeant? Well, I didn't grow up in one either, so my life as a parish priest has been quite educational. But I don't think villagers especially believe in randomness. Maybe it has something to do with the seasons—Druids, pagans, corn kings, that sort of thing. It's just that . . . oh, I don't know. This little place is a bit paranoid. I think my parishioners feel that when bad things happen it's because they somehow have a special relationship with evil. They didn't ask for it, they don't understand it, but they believe it's there and they accept it." He took another drag on his cigarette and let the smoke spiral upwards. "Of course, I've only been here for a few years. Maybe it wasn't like this before Tom died."

He had wanted to say "before Tom killed himself," but he realised that he, like everyone else in Fetherbridge, found the euphemism more tasteful. And it wasn't a lie. But Tom's suicide had never been the problem, not for him, and he doubted it had been for anyone else in the village with the exception of Gale. The fact that Tom had murdered someone was heinous, and that combined with all the other rumours about the group he was involved in made it difficult for Cart to even think about him. He inhaled again on his cigarette and let the smoke sit in his lungs until it hurt.

"How close were you to your cousin?"

Halford's voice was deliberately low, and Cart wondered just how harsh his last comment had sounded. He reached over to stub out the cigarette in the ashtray.

"Not very, actually. I grew up just outside London, in Gravesend, and our families would get together every couple of years. We visited here a few times, but not many. My father was a clergyman. Tom's father was a teacher. It's not that our life-styles were that different. We just didn't see much of each other. We were rather distantly related at that. His grandfather and my grandmother were siblings. I don't even know exactly what that made us, but no, we weren't very close."

"How did you come by the living in Fetherbridge?"

Cart found himself wishing he hadn't smoked his cigarette so quickly, but decided that to pull out another would make him appear nervous. Instead he played with the crease in his trousers.

"Well, the living was available and my father thought it would be good for me to experience the old village awhile. He pulled some strings." Cart winced. "He hadn't very long strings, but then this isn't much of a living."

"You must be a rather amenable son."

Halford's face had shifted to look just slightly less pleasant than a second ago. Maybe it was the light. Before he knew what he was doing, Cart reached his hand up and thumped the lamp shade in an effort to direct the glow onto someone other than himself. The beam bounced three times before settling back onto his face.

"Amenable. Well, yes, it helps if one is to be a clergyman. But that's not the only reason I agreed. There was the child."

"The child?"

"Katie Pru. Look, I suppose whether you believe any of this or not will depend on your level of cynicism, but one of the reasons was to be here for Katie Pru ... and Gale, of course. It didn't seem to make much sense for me to be out guiding the footsteps of other people's children when my own flesh and blood was fatherless here in Fetherbridge. Once I discovered Gale wasn't planning to return to the States, and that the living was available, well, it just made sense, didn't it?" He fell abruptly silent. Perhaps he had said too much.

Halford looked at him with polite skepticism. "How well did you know Mrs. Grayson before you came here?"

"Well, not very, like I said. I had met Gale only twice before Tom died—once not long after they were married when they swung over to see my father and one other time when Gale and Tom met me in London for dinner."

"Becoming vicar here was quite a commitment in order to give comfort to someone you didn't know very well. She might not have wanted anything to do with her husband's family."

"Well, if that had been the case, I think she would have gone back home," he replied easily. "Don't know why she didn't exactly, but there you are. Truth is no one in my family wanted anything to do with her. I'm the only one who's even seen Katie Pru. My father probably would have gotten around to it, but he died a few months after she was born." Cart picked up his packet of cigarettes and drew one out. "Basically, the family blames Gale for Tom's digressions."

"Really?" For the first time, Sergeant Ramsden broke into the questioning. "Why would that be?"

"I think it's a fairly normal reaction. No one wants to think that they've spawned a bad seed, or that their cozy little family home has somehow caused deviant behaviour. Much easier to blame the outside force."

Halford leaned forward and for a second Cart thought the inspector was going to light his cigarette, but instead he removed the pack from Cart's lap and held it, fingering the cellophane wrapping thoughtfully. Cart took a packet of matches from the side table, struck one, and touched it to the tip of his cigarette. The silence became noticeable, but then, as a vicar, he had long ago learned to wait out a silence.

Halford finally spoke. "Who was Lisa in love with?"

Cart inhaled sharply on his cigarette, then stifled a small cough. "I don't know that she was 'in love' with anyone. Crushes, certainly. Lisa was young, after all. But not really love." He shook his head. "Not that I knew of."

"Is it something you usually know about the young people in your church?"

"If they're both in the church, yes, I'd say usually. Otherwise, sometimes, sometimes not. Unless their parents come to me for advice, but that's rare and usually after there's been some trouble."

"Mr. Stillwell ever come to you about Lisa?"

"Oh, no, never any trouble with Lisa. Gale talked to me once about her, but it turned out to be nothing."

"What was that?"

"Christian Timbrook. But it was nothing, just a harmless girlhood crush."

"Timbrook's rather old for her, wouldn't you say?"

"Well, for a serious relationship, yes, but I'm telling you it wasn't serious. Just the long-haired bohemian artist infatuation that all girls get. It's a prerequisite for womanhood, isn't it?"

"But if she had a crush on one older man, there could have been others."

Cart reached over and took the cigarette pack out of Halford's hands. He put it back on the side table. "I told you last night I have no idea who this Mr. E. is, Mr. Halford. Excuse me, but is this going to take much longer? I have Lisa's memorial service tomorrow and . . ."

"Yes, we know. I'm sure you have a lot you need to do." Halford stood and replaced the chair in front of the desk. He turned back to Cart and pressed his suit coat flat against his stomach.

"If I could get you to think about one thing, Mr. Cart," he said. "Everyone talks about how sweet Lisa was, how kind. But I've been to her house, seen her room, her clothes, her perfume bottles, and it bothers me. Her brother and her father lived like monks next to her. I'm hoping at some point someone will be able to explain that to me."

Cart didn't say anything. He helped Sergeant Ramsden into her coat. Her spicy fragrance didn't strike him as nearly as alluring as he first thought.

That night Halford supped alone. Jeffrey Burke had called Maura from Winchester, surprising her with dinner reservations and an entreaty to take a short break from the inquiry to indulge her husband in a little pre-Christmas cheer. Halford had urged her on her way, dismissing her apologies and assuring her that whatever break there might be on the case, it wasn't likely to happen during the evening hours. Baylor, also, had an engagement, one with a social worker he had met the previous week in Portsmouth. So armed with fresh cream in his coffee and a cold meat sandwich from The Proper Pale's kitchen, Halford trudged past the miniature Christmas tree twinkling on the reception desk and upstairs to take a quiet meal in his room.

Outside, the wind knocked along the High Street

and rattled the hanging pub sign. Halford set his tray on the bed and closed the room's heavy cloth curtains. The stillness was blunt. Halford was grateful for the creaking of the bedsprings as he sat down to dine.

He assumed the food was palatable; the last bite was gone before he remembered he was eating. He was lost in thought, lost in the image of a young girl with a line of crimson blood trickling from her mouth, lost in a crisp morning five days earlier when she had bicycled down a soulless road and found a killer.

Jeremy Cart said the residents of Fetherbridge didn't believe in randomness. Halford didn't either, not in this case.

The problem in discerning who elected to end Lisa's life, of course, was Lisa herself. Halford's interview with Beryl Lampson had painted a portrait of Lisa as a meddler, a wide-eyed conduit in an insulated village's destructive chatter.

If what Beryl Lampson said was true, then little Lisa had wedged a place for herself in the community as something of a genteel gossip, the type who forty years ago carried embroidered handkerchiefs and took tea with her gloves on. She was the virgin spinster with the dirty mind who had somehow gotten locked out of her own time and into one less hospitable to calculated silliness.

Surely the idea was too simplistic and certainly too sexist, but he couldn't shake it. Perhaps he was falling victim to the old stereotype, Lisa as Miss Lonelyhearts, like the woman Jimmy Stewart watched through his rear window perform a solitary mime for a nonexistent lover. But then, that lover ultimately turned out to be real, and, if he remembered correctly, threatening.

He placed his tray on the bureau by the door and fished into the inside pocket of his suit coat hanging on the desk chair. He pulled out a piece of paper and, stretching out on the bed, unfolded it slowly.

Gale Grayson, even enraged, had a neat hand. He

examined her notations: left column, times; right column, locations. She had the times down to the minute, an attention to detail that both contradicted and confirmed his observations of her. She was an historian, after all—details were her craft. But Baylor had noted her unconcern about her clothing, and she herself had admitted to not wearing her glasses, a rather sloppy form of avoidance. Yet, her cottage had been precise in its cleanliness, corners swept, baseboards dusted. A working mother with such strenuous standards was certain to watch the clock.

He looked at the vital minutes, the time between 9:40 and 10:15 when Lisa could conceivably have died and Mrs. Grayson could not account for her movements. Unfortunate coincidence for a woman pursued by things unfortunate.

Tiny hands circling a teacup, cold in his grip despite the heat of the drink. The memory intruded relentlessly. Heavy with child, and only him there to comfort her, a poor substitute for the father blown literally to Kingdom Come.

He turned on his side and shoved his arm beneath his head. She seemed to him so fragile, so needy. She had cloaked herself and retreated inward, taking with her the child. Strange, how during that first meeting, with her in shock on her love seat, he had checked that so human impulse to rest his hand on her stomach and feel the infant inside her. He had felt responsible then. Heaven help him, he felt so now.

He rolled over and held the paper at arm's length. The writing turned grainy as light poured through the paper's fibers. Light and fibers. Stained glass and wool. It was a match he couldn't fathom. What could bruised, bedeviled Gale Grayson find tempting in a man like Christian Timbrook, a man who indulged himself in the fevered attractions of sweet young things? Sheltered, withdrawn, wrapped up as she was in child and heritage—what could have been so compelling about him that would have caused her to lower her defences? And if for him, then who else?

He slid his shirt cuff away from his watch and checked the time. Nearly eight. He reached for the phone. He wondered how impressive stained glass looked at night.

16

The first thing Grissom noticed upon entering the *Inquisitor*'s office was the blaring sound of Robert Goulet singing Christmas songs. The second thing he noticed was plaid. Plaid bows taped to the front desk, plaid ribbon tacked around the few pictures hanging on the walls. Ivy vines held aside a cheery green-and-red plaid drape hung across the back hall doorway, and red-berried holly sprigs adorned the plaid skirt wrapped around the base of the office's spindly Christmas tree like fattened polka dots.

Anise Ivory, thankfully, was dressed in khaki. She looked up from her chore of hanging ornaments on the tree and smiled at Grissom.

"Oh, Bobby, just in time," she exclaimed. "I hate

these cursed little wire hangers." She held up the silver glass ball in her hand and wiggled the hanger back and forth. "I've always fancied the idea of a Velcro Christmas tree where all I'd have to do is throw the box of ornaments at it and they'd all stick."

Grissom fingered a plaid bow. "Quite a job you've done here. I've never seen so much yuletide spirit in one place."

She laughed, sweeping a lock of loosened blond hair from her forehead. "Well, it occurred to me that everyone here could use a lift." She grew serious, the silver ball palmed in her hand. "Death at Christmastime. It's like someone slapping God's face."

Or God slapping ours, Grissom thought, marvelling at an editor's wife who felt a murder could pitch a bunch of journalists into the depths of depression. He crouched down beside the sectioned box of ornaments at Anise's feet, and selected a blue one. Untangling a wire hanger from the clump beside the box, he dangled the ball from it. In its convex glass, his face was unrecognisable. He moved aside the tips of several branches and wedged his ornament into the tree.

Anise sang along with Goulet, her voice a pure little warble like a child's. She eyed Grissom mischievously. "So," she said, "what's Father Christmas bringing you this year?"

"Not a blooming thing," he replied, laughing. "I doubt he'd even waste coal on me this year. I haven't exactly been your classic good boy."

"Nonsense. I know Orrin thinks the world of you. He's quite impressed with your reporting skills, you know. And he's not an easy critic. He has remarkably high standards."

She bent down for another ornament. Her khaki pants were neatly pressed, her white pullover spotless. The black velvet bow that held her hair in a bun had none of the residual lint that came from usage. Grissom knew firsthand of Ivory's standards on the job. He supposed Anise was as good a judge as any of his standards at home.

"I've come to see Orrin," he said. "I suppose he's upstairs."

Anise nodded. "Along with Jill. He wanted to take a look at your inquest article, and she had to finish cleaning the darkroom." She gestured at her handiwork. "I decided to put myself to use. It was really too depressing to stay at home alone."

And why be depressed when you can cram the world with joy, Grissom thought nastily. With a mumbled good-bye, he bounded the stairs two at a time. The predictable muddle of the newsroom was a welcome relief. No elegant angel of mercy forcing goodwill down people's throats up here. Just healthy, pagan chaos.

Ivory sat behind Grissom's desk, hard copy in hand. When he saw the reporter, he clapped his hands once and stretched back in his chair.

"Brilliant, Bobby. Beautiful prose. Poignant atmosphere. Five minutes ago I hadn't been to the inquest. Now I have."

Slowly, Grissom pulled off his coat and dropped it on the desk, trying not to show his delight. Once again, he had successfully pulled off the journalist's sleight-of-hand trick. Truth was, the inquest into Lisa's death had been dull as mustard. It had taken quite a bit of work to make it "poignant." "It was something, I'll say that."

Ivory waved his hand over the article. "This pulling in the Round Table to symbolise a fragile facade—outstanding. And your descriptions—Edgar and Brian as 'shredded remainders fumbling with their coats'; the police as 'cubes of decorum.' Good, good, and good."

Grissom decided to milk the praise. "And the bit about Jill. I worked hard for that one."

"Yes. 'Delicate as a page from an old book.'" Ivory gently rubbed the words. "Well, I don't know, Bobby.

Perhaps a bit beyond the context. Jill was simply a spectator."

"Take it out then," he said, trying not to sound sour. "It's only colour." He nodded towards the archives door, shut tight as always. "So what did the police say about the break-in?"

"What do they ever say?" Ivory replied. " 'We'll look into it. We'll call you if we find anything.' They did say to leave the archives alone for the time being."

"Much ado about nothing, if you ask me," Grissom said. "Goes to show what passes for excitement around this gin joint."

The comment passed unnoted by Ivory, who continued to peruse the article. From the darkroom Grissom could hear the clunk of Jill Ivory's efforts to tidy up. He glanced at his watch. It was getting on eight. With any luck, Ivory might finish soon, leaving his daughter free for dinner and a chat.

Grissom cleared his throat. "Well, if you're satisfied with the story, I was thinking of running it up to London and seeing what they think of it."

Ivory's head jerked. "Why would you want to do that?"

"Because you think it's well written. I've been waiting for a truly well-written piece. And because of the subject. 'Grayson Childminder Murdered.' There ought to be some interest in that. The nationals should want it."

Ivory focused his eyes on the story, now fanned out across the desk like a magician's deck of cards. "Early days, Bobby. The inquiry just got under way. The nationals won't want it until there's something definite to report."

"Fine, then. I show them the inquest story, and when this thing pops they let me string it. You've been saying for months I ought to show them my work in London. This seems perfect."

Ivory ran both hands through his thinning hair. "You're saying that because you're personally involved. I don't know that London will be nearly as interested as you think. When the police have a murderer in tow, yes, surely. But now? I think you'd waste your time and perhaps risk being labelled a nuisance."

Bobby snorted in disbelief. "You're joking."

"No, Bobby, I'm quite serious. I don't want you to make a mistake that could damage your credibility."

"Orrin, the police are investigating a homicide. We're not living in L.A. This is England, remember?"

"So what? Unless the police are digging up a truckload of bodies in a back garden, the nationals don't care. They want sensation."

"And this isn't sensational? The Grayson name isn't exactly unknown. I guarantee that by the weekend, all the nationals will have reporters here, if not before then. I'm a little surprised they're not here already."

"Proves my point. They're not interested."

"Or perhaps our friendly constabulary is trying to play the whole thing down."

The knob on the darkroom door rattled and the door swung open. Jill Ivory stepped into the room, her hands covered with thick rubber gloves. Her blond hair was held back by a plastic tortoiseshell headband that allowed the curls to barely sweep her shoulders. Faint smudges of dirt darkened her chin and left cheek. With a stab of sympathy Grissom noted that her eyelids were puffy, her corneas reddened. She evidently became aware of his gaze because she wrinkled her nose and smiled shyly.

"It smells awful in there. All those chemicals." She pulled off the gloves and tossed them into the darkness of the open door behind her. "But anyway, Daddy, I've finished. If there's nothing else, I'm going to walk home."

Grissom's heart sank, only to be lifted by Ivory's words. "Listen, Jill. I need to talk to Bobby here a bit more, but I'd rather you didn't walk home alone. Why don't you wait for me in my office—or better yet, go down and help your mother. I'll be done shortly."

She regarded her father silently for a moment and then impassively retreated into the editor's office, a mean cubicle set off in one corner of the room. Ivory waited until his daughter closed the door. Then, standing, he drummed his fingers on the desk, apparently searching for a decision.

"Look, Bobby," he began, "you're right. I'm being less than honest with you. It is a big story. The nationals are going to pick it up. And you've written an excellent piece here—you deserve to take it to London. But I want you to think about something first."

He picked up the first page of Grissom's article and, rolling it into a tube, absentmindedly rotated it in his hands.

"You haven't lived in Fetherbridge long. Hell, you're young—you haven't lived anywhere long. You weren't here three years ago, and you won't be here three years from now. But I will be. And I want you to believe me when I say this village can't take it. It will not survive another dissection like the one it went through when Tom Grayson murdered that man and then killed himself. I don't know exactly how it will self-destruct, but I know it will."

Grissom's throat constricted and his face grew warm. Ivory leaned forward and rested his weight fully on the upended paper tube. It pancaked beneath his palm.

"I can't stop the London papers from covering Lisa's murder," Ivory said. "I know it will happen eventually, and in all probability Fetherbridge will turn into a zoo, like it did before. But Bobby, we don't have to invite it. There's more to journalism than the news, son. We have a responsibility to our community—to this village. We are part of it, and as such, we have to respect and support it."

Grissom swallowed. "So what are you telling me?"

"I'm asking you to let this thing follow its own path. There will be other stories where you can be first. You have a tremendous future in this business, Bobby. You can afford to wait. Give this village as much time as you can."

The first page of the story, with its perfect lead and brilliant descriptions, spread underneath Ivory's palm like milk. As quickly as he had warmed, Grissom now grew cold. He retrieved his anorak, slipped it on, and gathered the article's remaining pages.

"I'll think about it," he said.

"That's all I ask," said Ivory. "We journalists are accused of never seeing the big picture. I'm asking you to consider it this one time." He picked up the collapsed sheet of paper and carefully straightened it. "By the way, I want you to cover Lisa's prayer service tomorrow. It's going to be very important to the people here. If you can make the inquest poetry, you can make the service sing. And just leave this article with me. It needs a bit of editing—not much, just a bit."

Grissom handed over the pages and with a brief nod started for the stairs. As he passed Ivory's office, Jill called his name. He found her sitting at her father's desk, a thesaurus open before her.

"God, you must have been bored," Grissom said. "First, cleaning the darkroom, now reading thesauri."

She smiled at him. "I find it interesting, really. It's very much like reading a foreign language, seeing all these phrases lined up one after another."

Ivory had followed Grissom. Now he came up to stand behind him. "I'm ready to go, Jill. Let me get my coat."

Grissom, reading what he thought was regret in Jill's expression, turned to Ivory. "If you don't mind, Orrin, I'd like to take Jill to dinner. Just to Winchester. I'll have her back in a couple of hours."

Ivory's uncertainty employed most of the muscles in his face. "I don't know, Bobby. The memorial service is tomorrow. It's still hard . . ."

"I'd like to go." Jill spoke quietly. "We won't stay long."

Ivory studied them both; then he stepped back into

the newsroom. "All right. It's eight fifteen. Be back by ten."

And then he was gone, leaving Grissom happy against the doorjamb.

Editha Forrester rambled through the Stillwells' kitchen drawers—cutlery, oven gloves, screws, combs, orphaned playing cards, a couple of marbles. No pencil. There was none by the phone, none on the table, none, in fact, in any of the usual places she would expect to find one. She crossed her arms, exasperated. The problem with this death was lack of organisation. Sympathy cards had started arriving that morning, food had been coming in since the weekend, and she needed to make a list of people to receive acknowledgements. To do so, she needed a pencil.

She found Edgar slumped in a chair in the lounge. The lamps were off, the only source of light a diffused glow through the thin curtains. She had to stand nearly on top of him to discern the outline of his face.

"I need a pencil, Edgar, and some paper. Where do you keep them?"

His head didn't move. "I don't know. I have some at the bakery."

Editha kept her voice soft. "I'm not at the bakery, Edgar. I need a pencil and paper here. Now, surely you've some squirrelled away somewhere."

"I don't know," he repeated. "Lisa ran the house. I don't keep up with such things."

"Well, I guess I'll go and ask Brian. He's certain to know. And by the way, the boy hasn't eaten all day. Mary Adams tried to make him a sandwich earlier, but it just turned hard on his plate. He needs his strength, Edgar. Perhaps you should talk to him."

At this, the man's head lifted until his forehead shone faintly in the dark. "Why should I talk to him?" The pitch of his voice rose. "What have I got to say? His sister's dead. You think he needs talking to, you do it. You make it all better."

Editha rammed her knee into the Mediterranean coffee table as she wheeled around to leave the room. The pudgy flesh of her leg was instantly sore. She bent to rub it, angry at the blackness in the room, angry at the father who wouldn't help his grieving son.

Edgar Stillwell was still muttering as she stalked away. She retreated into the kitchen, slamming the door shut behind her. Taking a clean plate and glass from the cupboard, Editha began preparing Brian a light dinner.

Upstairs, the boy's room was locked. She pounded the hollow-core door with her foot.

"Brian. It's Miss Forrester. Open this door. I have a nice slice of ham for you."

"I'm not hungry."

"That's beside the matter. Now open this door before I have to bother your father about it."

With satisfaction, she heard the bedsprings creak and the lock release. By the time she got the dishes juggled and the doorknob turned, Brian was back in his bed, blankets pulled around his neck.

Editha inhaled and wrinkled her nose. "My word! When was the last time this place was aired? A child can't live in a room like this. Here, Brian, you start eating your dinner. I can't imagine what Edgar is thinking!"

Setting the glass of milk on the bedside table, she dropped the plate of ham in the tent formed by the covers over Brian's knees and lumbered to the window. The latch didn't give easily, and when it finally did, the entire window whined in protest as she swung it wide.

A sliver of the cold night slipped into the room. "There," she said, wiping her hands on her dress. "You breathe that in for a while and we'll see your disposition improve. Not to mention your health."

Brian stared at the plate in his lap. Frowning, Editha sat on the bed, cut a bite of the ham and held it out to him.

"Now eat this. Your father is going to need you

strong and able to work in a couple of days. Just a few bites. Just enough to keep your strength up.''

Brian didn't move. Editha reached over to adjust the pillows behind him and then recoiled as her hands sank into the heavy, sodden linens. She ran her fingers along the mattress under the covers. The sheets were wet.

"You wait here, Brian," she said softly. "I'll be back in a jiffy with some fresh linens. Don't you worry. You're with friends here. We're family. We'll take care of you."

She hurried from the room, careful that the door didn't lock behind her. The small linen cupboard in the hallway was jammed with clean sheets. She angrily pulled some out.

There's no sense in this, she thought. Something's got to be done. In Fetherbridge, we don't let children become the victims of their families' vices. And as she scavenged through the cupboard searching for matching pillowcases, she plumed with purpose.

The walk from The Proper Pale to Timbrook's cottage was relatively short—past the Stillwell bakery at Bakers Lane, across Bracken Street, down Tulledge Lane where the diminutive white studio sat unlit under its oak tree. Along the way, Halford noted the occasional twinkle of Christmas tree lights through cottage windows, an almost hesitant attempt at celebration.

In contrast to the yuletide lights in the neighbouring houses, Timbrook's studio was pitch-dark. As he rounded towards the front, Halford could see the glass panels hanging in the windows, but they were diminished to clunky ebony blocks, their glory stolen by the absence of sun and filament.

Halford approached the house feeling both irritated and a little cheated. In her description of Timbrook's work, Maura had been effusive: Halford had come with an art lover's anticipation, expecting his first glimpse of the cottage to be startling. Instead, the cottage looked deserted, and Timbrook, who should have been waiting for his arrival, was nowhere to be seen.

And then, at the far corner of the dwelling's exterior wall, a match flared. Timbrook's features were illumined briefly as he held the flame to the tip of a cigarette. He sucked once and waved the match out. The fire was too near the artist's face to effectively light his visitors, but Halford could tell by their sizes and the restless antics of the smaller one that Timbrook was talking to Gale Grayson and Katie Pru.

Silently, Halford drew up behind the oak tree and watched. After a second, the hushed voices grew clear.

"I just wanted to know if you'd heard anything. Maybe I'm being paranoid."

"You, Gale? Paranoid? What a childish thought." The sarcasm was thick in Timbrook's words.

"It's just strange, that's all," Mrs. Grayson continued defensively. "I mean, June Kingston and I have never been great friends, but—"

Timbrook broke in. "June Kingston's never been anyone's great friend, the witch. Listen, Gale, it's cold. Take Katie Pru and go home. Don't worry about it. This murder has everyone jittery, yourself included. Get some sleep. That's something else this village is short on these days."

Beside her mother, Katie Pru began to jump. "Let's go home, Mama. Space Lucy's hungry. See?" Lifting open her coat, the child rammed the stuffed animal into her mother's thigh.

Gale Grayson ignored her. "It's just bothering me. It's hard enough to deal with everything that's happened without having to worry about . . ." She let the sentence hang. "Never mind. You're right. I'm overreacting."

She placed her arm around Katie Pru and turned to leave. "I suppose you'll attend the memorial service tomorrow."

The tip of the cigarette made a circle in the dark.

"Of course. Not for the world would I miss the opportunity to lament our lovely lady lost."

Gale Grayson was moving away. She stopped.

"Don't," she said. Her voice was controlled, but Halford thought he could hear the pain beneath it. "Don't act like that, for my sake."

The cigarette hit the earth. The glow disappeared beneath the crush of Timbrook's boot. "For your sake, luv? I quit doing things for your sake a long time ago."

Mrs. Grayson took her daughter's hand and walked quickly away. As they drifted towards the hedges at the back of Timbrook's property, Katie Pru's gruff voice rang out.

"Lovely lady lost," she sang. "A lovely lady lost."

Halford waited until the voice trailed to silence and stepped from behind the tree.

Timbrook lit another cigarette. "You should have joined us," he said affably. "I saw you peeking round yonder tree. Damned spook, that's what you are."

Twigs cracked beneath Halford's feet as he walked towards Timbrook. "So your treatment of Mrs. Grayson was for my benefit."

"My treatment of Mrs. Grayson? You make it sound like I slapped her. No, Chief Inspector. My treatment of Gale was for my own benefit. As it's my own business, I might add."

"What exactly was she talking about?"

"Problems in the village. Nothing serious, I assure you." Timbrook flicked ash into the air. "Gale's a talented woman. She simply has a tendency to see monsters in the shadows. Probably comes from marrying one."

Halford motioned at the cottage. "As you said, it's a cold night. No thought of inviting the child inside?"

"Oh, certainly. Plenty of thought. The trouble is Gale has never been inside my studio, and I dare say she wouldn't allow Katie Pru inside, either."

"Really? Why is that?"

The point of the cigarette glowed steady in Timbrook's hand. "Because, sir, inside I have a very big, very ornate remembrance of her past. It's not something she could view easily. I'm surprised you, of all people, had to ask."

The bare branches of the oak tree overhead hissed as the wind whisked through them. Halford repressed a shiver. Of course Mrs. Grayson would never have set foot in the studio. Of course . . .

A question struck him. "But she attends the church."

Timbrook regarded him coolly. "Did she tell you that? She's never been inside the church, not since Tom's death. She works with Jeremy on various things, yes. But she doesn't worship. Not with everyone else, and I doubt even alone. God has a way of running out on some people, you know."

"You and Mrs. Grayson were lovers."

Halford intentionally made the statement abrupt, to check the other man's reflexes. To Timbrook's credit, he sounded unaffected.

"Affirmative." Timbrook brought the cigarette to his mouth and sucked slowly. "Is this a professional question, Chief Inspector, or personal? If it's her phone number you want, I can give it to you."

Halford struggled to keep his words noncombative. "I want to know about you and Mrs. Grayson and Lisa," he said evenly.

Timbrook dropped the cigarette and ground it out. "I see. And what if I tell you there was no me and Gale and Lisa? Me and Gale, yes. Me and Lisa, barely. But a dirty little triangle? There was never such a thing."

"Maybe not dirty, Mr. Timbrook, but certainly a triangle. You've admitted you slept with one of the women; the second, by your own modest admission, wanted to sleep with you. Any way you want to look at it, that's a triangle."

Timbrook leaned against the side of the cottage and rested one foot against the wall. "And my bed as the apex. How very manipulating you are. Well, I will tell you this—I slept with Gale because I cared for her. I can only speculate on her reasons for the affair. As for Lisa, I'm interested in adult women. Overgrown schoolgirls with overly ripe libidos are for other chaps."

"So you and Mrs. Grayson never had difficulties because of Lisa?"

"Difficulties? No. Now, was a significant portion of our time together spent talking about her? I'd have to say more than I liked."

"Meaning?"

"Well, meaning that Gale wasn't always thrilled with the way Lisa took care of Katie Pru. She felt she was a bit pushy sometimes, a bit insensitive." Timbrook took a deep breath and brought his foot to the ground. "You asked me if Gale had been in the church. No, not to my knowledge. But Katie Pru has been. Lisa took her."

Halford tried to focus on Timbrook's face, but the opacity of the night made it impossible to see more than vague features.

"And?" Halford prompted.

"I'm not telling you this for your entertainment. I simply want you to understand. Lisa could be troublesome. Oh, according to Gale she was very offhand about the whole incident—Katie Pru didn't understand, and besides, they'd only gone to hear the children's choir practice. But Gale wasn't so sure. In some ways Lisa could be truly guileless. In others . . . Well, Gale half feared that Lisa did it to be cruel, to show the child where her father killed himself, where the window used to be."

Halford shook his head, unconvinced. "That's a bit past cruel, isn't it? Perhaps this is simply another one of Mrs. Grayson's 'monsters in the shadows.'"

Timbrook reached into his coat pocket and retrieved a pair of gloves. He slapped them against his hand. "You're the expert, Chief Inspector. Whatever you deduce. But if she were to be completely honest with herself, I think Gale would admit that she was afraid of

Lisa. And I think in the depths of my dark little heart,
I was, too."

The Italian meal, serviceably administered in a comfortable wood-and-fern restaurant at the north end of
Winchester, was consumed amid frequent pauses and
less than glittering conversation. Grissom blamed himself. In the year he had worked at the *Inquisitor*, Jill
Ivory had been a distant creature to him, outside his
realm by virtue of age and parentage. Of course, he had
noticed that she was beautiful, but even he had drawn
boundaries on what was acceptable behaviour: vicious,
story-grubbing journalist he might be; despoiler of the
boss's young daughter he was not.

Nevertheless, once Jill began her internship at the
paper, all adherence to basic career survival went out
the window. He wanted her. Not necessarily in the carnal sense—although he wouldn't have stopped such an
event—but more than sex, he wanted her presence. She
had been working at the *Inquisitor* for three months
and, while they had engaged in the odd conversation
here or there, it wasn't until tonight that the right constellation of time, opportunity, and parental mind
frame had converged to make his desire feasible. He
had entered the restaurant with a laundry list of topics
to share with her. She hardly spoke a word. He stut-
tered. They left without dessert. As he silently drove
her home through the night, he grappled with the
knowledge that he was an idiot.

They came upon Fetherbridge from the west. The
sky was tarry, moonless, and the road dark. Under the
soft glow from the fascia panel Jill's face looked oth-
erworldly, as if she were far from him, once more the
distant creature he could neither touch nor approach.

"Bobby." He started, spun out of his glumness by
the suddenness of her voice. "Bobby, it's only half nine.
I'm not ready to go home yet. Is there somewhere we
can park and walk the rest of the way?"

"Of course." He turned the car down Parkland

Road, running parallel to the High Street, and turned right onto Blacksmith Lane, pulling to a stop behind the chemist's shop. Grissom looked around. The gravel car park was empty, the shops having closed hours ago. They were now about a half-mile from the Ivorys' house—with plenty of room to walk slowly.

Grissom scrambled from the car and hurried to help Jill out. They stepped carefully through the lot and down a narrow alley to the High Street. Except for the brightly lit windows of The Proper Pale over the road, the whole of mercantile Fetherbridge appeared deserted.

They walked slowly up the street, past The Transitional Woman, Hossett's Bookshop, and the fabric shop. The pavement was badly cracked in front of the ironmonger's; a triangular slice of cement the size of a tea tray had been lifted out, revealing the chalk foundation below. Jill stopped at the edge of the gouge and tapped the bared earth with the toe of her shoe.

"I wasn't much company tonight," she said. "I'm sorry. There's just so much . . ." Her toe pantomimed circles on the ground. "I can't believe she's gone, you know. Sooner or later it's bound to be real for me, but now . . . I keep expecting to see her, to hear her on the phone."

Grissom murmured what he hoped was a comforting sound, understanding now how complete his idiocy was. He wanted to impress her; she wanted to grieve.

"I know it's hard," he managed.

She turned to face him. "It is. It truly is. And I don't know that Mummy and Daddy understand that. I think they feel that it will pass, that I'm young and I'll get over it. But I don't know that I will. I truly don't."

He heard rather than saw that she was crying. She sniffled and brought her hand to her face. He felt utterly helpless and oafish, a clod commanded to perform a minuet, a tadpole instructed to drink the sea.

"It will get better," he stammered. "You just need some time."

"I know," she said. "I need time. We all need time. I just don't believe we're going to get it."

Neither of them was wearing gloves, and at first her hand was icy as she slid it into his pocket and laid her fingers atop his. He stood still, uncertain what to do. Then he twisted his palm up, creating a bed in which her fingers could rest, and slowly clasped them.

They stepped over the break in the pavement and continued up the street. He knew he couldn't bring back her friend; he knew he couldn't stop her grief. But he could give her time. At least for a while.

17

Katie Pru carried purple flowers. They weren't her first choice. Her first choice had been pink, really bright pink flowers with green dots and little yellow feathers coming out of them, but the lady at the shop said she didn't have any flowers like that; she had, in fact, never *seen* flowers like that. So Katie Pru settled on purple—irises, the lady called them—because purple was close to pink, and they looked rather frightening.

When she chose them, the idea of carrying frightening flowers was okay, since she didn't actually feel frightened. But as she trudged up the green hill with her mother, the irises lapped at her hands like dogs' tongues, and she knew she'd made a mistake.

Her mother had been very quiet all morning. It had

started while she was bathing and Katie Pru was reading books beside the tub. The water had smelled nice—a little like the shop where they bought the flowers—and every now and then, when her mother wasn't looking, Katie Pru had dipped her hand into the water and drawn circles on the tub's cold white side.

"Daddy's in a box."

She didn't know why she said it. Her book was about a little boy with a magic hat, and for some reason it reminded her of a box. It reminded her of something else, too.

"Lisa's sup'ose to be in a box too, but she's not."

Her mother didn't say anything for a very long time. She simply stared at the circles Katie Pru was making on the tub.

"Who told you that, baby?" she finally asked.

Katie Pru dunked her whole fist in the water and began pounding on the circles. She thought they would look like the pictures her mother taught her to make with a carved potato and paint, but they didn't. They just looked like dripping water.

"Miz Barker. She says Lisa's hurt and won't come back. She says Daddy's in a box because he was bad."

Her mother sighed deeply. "Mrs. Barker's right about Lisa. She's dead and we won't see her anymore. That's very sad."

Katie Pru waited, but her mother didn't say anything else.

"The box is in the ground," she prompted.

Her mother sat up in the tub, the water slinking off her arms. "Katie Pru," she said gently, "do you remember going with Lisa to see Daddy's grave?"

She didn't. She turned her head to look at the fogged mirror. Little lines of water slipped down it. She wondered what her fist prints would look like on glass.

She didn't have a chance to find out. Her mother climbed from the tub and grabbed a towel.

"Let's get dressed, ladybug," she said. "We're going out."

They both put on dresses, her mother a dark blue one with a pretty pattern along the hem, Katie Pru a bright red with buttons that looked like moons. They slipped on shiny black shoes, and both combed their hair so that it flipped up a bit on the ends.

Then they got into the car. Katie Pru didn't like the car because she had to sit in a special seat in the back. She could see out the windows better, but she didn't like looking at the back of her mother's head. Sometimes, when they had been driving a long time, she would forget what her mother's face looked like. It scared her, and she would kick the driver's seat until her mother turned around and fussed.

They left the village and drove past field after field, farm after farm. They stopped in the city to buy the purple flowers, and then went up a big hill with a long line of brick houses, and past more fields, more farms.

"Katie Pru," her mother said, "We're going to the Winchester city cemetery. I'm going to show you where your father's buried. I want you to see what it's like. I want you to see it with me."

Katie Pru stared out the window. They passed several large trees, humped and naked. She didn't remember Daddy, although her mother had shown her pictures of him. He had been tall, much taller than her mother, with light-coloured hair and a wide grin. He was always grinning. The pictures were in a flat box, all jumbled together, and Katie Pru had shuffled through them like cards. There he was, smiling, smiling, smiling. She asked once why he was always happy. Her mother said that's what people do in pictures— they smile so they'll remember being happy. But her mother looked very sad when she said it.

Katie Pru started kicking her mother's seat.

They drove through the opening of a big black gate, past a flint house, and up a curving drive. Katie Pru stared out the window. She had seen stones like these before; they were all around the church back home. But she had never seen so many shiny new ones. And she had never seen so many flowers.

The drive widened into a little parking area. Her mother pulled to a stop. Not far away, a big yellow machine with a huge claw dug up the earth. It lowered its claw into a hole, scooped out a load of white soil, and dumped it in a pile.

"That, Katie Pru," said her mother, turning around in her seat, "that's where someone is going to be buried. That is how they make a grave."

She opened the car door, climbed out, and unbuckled Katie Pru from her seat. Outside the car, the noise from the yellow machine was loud. It snarled and grunted as it chewed the hole into the ground.

Katie Pru put her hands over her ears. "I wanna go home," she said.

"In a minute, baby. First let me show you something."

So clutching the purple irises in her hands, Katie Pru followed her mother up the hill through thick green grass.

At the top the ground levelled. The munching sound of the machine grew faint. The morning sun shone through several trees and warmed her shoulders through her coat. Here it was very green; there were only a few graves. They stopped in front of a sparkling black stone with three gold letters on it.

"What does it say?" she asked.

"Those are Daddy's initials, the first letters of his name. T.W.G.—Thomas Winston Grayson."

A vase was hidden at the bottom of the stone. Dried yellow leaves hung out of it. Her mother stooped down, pulled them out, and tossed them into the grass.

"There," she said. "Now put your flowers in."

Uncertainly, Katie Pru dropped the irises, one by one, into the little holes in the top of the vase. After she was finished, she looked at her mother.

"It's not scary," she said.

Her mother crouched beside her and drew her close.

"This is where Daddy is buried, Katie Pru. This is where his 'box' is. It's what we do with people when they die. It's not a bad thing. It's just what happens. But I don't want you to be afraid to think about your daddy, to talk about him. I want you to remember that in many ways he was very, very . . ."

She didn't finish. Tears filled her eyes and she looked away. Down the hill, the yellow machine finished digging. Its iron claw hung in the air.

"Well," her mother said, taking Katie Pru's hand and squeezing it, "when Lisa's buried we'll put flowers on her grave, too. I just wanted to show you that it happens to everybody. It's very sad, but it isn't something terrible."

They started back towards the car. All around them were shiny stones, pretty flowers. Holding her mother's hand, Katie Pru began hopping down the hill.

"In-a-box, in-a-box," she yelled. "Some-day-we'll-be-in-a-box."

The paved pathway from the lych-gate to the south door of St. Martin's Church brimmed with people. Most of them were clad in coats and a few carried umbrellas, the sky having taken on a middling appearance as if couldn't decide what kind of weather to let loose upon the pious. Halford climbed from his car squeezed on the verge of Boundary Road and followed the church's flint wall towards the crowd.

At the lych-gate he met PC Baylor. "Afternoon, sir," the constable said. "Respectable turnout, I'd say. It's been a long while since this church has seen such a gathering."

Halford studied the crowd. June Kingston passed through the portal, followed by her husband. Further back, he could see the frizzy red heads of Ruth Barker and her daughter Beryl Lampson peeping from under matching lace scarves. Behind them a band of teenagers, primarily girls, huddled together. An older man, possibly a father, reached his arms around two of the girls, but the comforting gesture had no apparent effect: the youths only pressed closer together. Halford recognised the drama. He knew from experience that to teenagers the death of one of their own was both too horrible and too incredible to induce any response beyond a kind of inclusive and scripted keening.

Halford turned his attention back to Baylor.

"Listen, Nate," he said. "I wonder if you would do something for me. I won't be able to attend the entire service—I left Maura sifting through the reports on this Mr. E. business and I need to get over to the incidents room—but I would like you to stay, if you can. I'd be interested in knowing exactly what goes on—who's here, who's not, anything you think interesting. You know these people better than I do. You'd be able to judge if something's out of kilter."

The young man was visibly pleased. "Yessir," he said. "Think nothing of it."

They joined the last of the mourners, now strung from the doorway like a tail ready to retract inside the church. By the time Halford and Baylor moved into the nave proper, the rest of the congregation was seated. Slipping into the last pew, Halford looked down the length of the building. A simple arrangement of white roses and carnations sat on a linen cloth draped over the step in front of the altar rail. He was sure it was meant to be an elegant tribute, these pure flowers for this pure girl, but they dwindled to pettiness compared to the arcade's graceful swags and the elegantly carved reredos above the altar.

Halford found his attention drawn to the church's east wall, where the round yellow window looked like a sickly eye watching the proceedings.

He was startled by the voice of Jeremy Cart. The vicar stood in the elaborately carved pulpit, his white surplice in folds around him like marble, his chiselled face glowing in the nave's soft light, like an actor's artfully lit.

" 'I am the resurrection and the life, said the Lord . . .' "

No doubt the Reverend Cart was in his element. He grabbed the sides of the pulpit and leaned forward, the bringer of benevolence, the soother of sorrows. Even the plaintive yellow window seemed to honor him. Halford winced. He wondered how many Trollope novels Cart had read before deciding that this, rather than television serials, was his true calling.

It wasn't really a fair assessment. Everything Cart had told him the previous evening, at least the biographical information, was consistent with the Gravesend police report. Only son of a clergyman becomes a clergyman and at his father's behest accepts the living in the family seat. It seemed such an impossibly mired and fanciful existence to Halford—the mysticism, the music, the intricacy of dogma, doctrine, and ritual—but Cart thrived in it. Halford imagined the reverend with straw in his teeth, aping the Lester family for a despondent Mrs. Grayson. What did it matter to the flock that its shepherd was fundamentally a silly man?

Cart was reading the Psalms. His voice was sonorous.

" 'God is our hope and strength, a very present help in trouble.

" 'Therefore will we not fear, though the earth be moved, and though the hills be carried into the midst of the sea;

" 'Though the waters thereof rage and swell, and though the mountains shake at the tempest of the same.' "

In the first pew, Edgar and Brian Stillwell sat side by side, both hunched over with their heads in their hands. At this distance, they were virtually indistinguishable, father and son bent alike in separate grief. Their alibis were confirmed—the shop had been due to open in ten minutes when Lisa reportedly set out on her bicycle for Gale Grayson's house. Mrs. Millberry had been waiting at the door, eager to buy the day's freshest bread for the lunch crowd at The Proper Pale, and said that she had talked with both of them. And it seemed unlikely that either one of them would have plotted Lisa's death; without her, Brian, at least, appeared to be unravelling. Halford thought of the wet pillow the boy held while he interviewed him. He thought of Brian's inability to speak at the inquest, his frayed appearance, the untied shoe that Cart had so carefully fixed. But he also thought of Editha Forrester and her glib suggestion that Lisa had done the inevitable by stopping her brother's budding romance. Behind the Stillwells sat the band of teenagers. He wondered which one, if any, was the Simpson girl.

Halford glanced back at the vicar, the words of the Psalms echoing through the chamber. He could hear no hushed sobs, no hesitant sniffles, none of the little gasps people make when they try to cry silently. Up the aisle, heads were bent: the Ivorys, the Barkers, the Kingstons, Ben Hossett. Only Christian Timbrook seemed to be studying Cart, his head turned toward the chancel. But then, he just as easily could have been contemplating the yellow window, the one man in the entire congregation who in all likelihood thought about it as much as Halford himself.

" 'The Lord himself is thy keeper; the Lord is thy defence upon thy right hand.

" 'The Lord shall preserve thee from all evil . . .' "

Halford had had enough. Tapping Baylor farewell on the leg, he edged from the pew and left the building.

The sky was overcast as Halford walked toward the lych-gate. Beside the church's long west wall, an ancient yew hovered over the broken headstones at its roots. It was a tremendous tree, a grand, spreading, traditional yew that seemed almost as indigenous to parish church cemeteries as the markers themselves.

He glanced at his watch. Maura expected him at the incidents room by two o'clock. With fifteen minutes to spare, he left the paved pathway and walked towards the yew.

Evidently the parishioners had elected in this older section to let nature take its course. Ivy arched over the markers, here and there the deep green leaves of periwinkle bunched between the marble, brambles laced some of the stone borders that marked the plots. Halford stopped beside one marble headstone, an exquisite trail of holly carved into its face. Idly, Halford pulled aside a strand of ivy clutching the stone's splotched grey surface and read the name. Rebecca Lawson, 1880–1902. No inscription, no words of bereavement, no notation to indicate the dead's role as wife or daughter or mother. Just a name and this insculpted sprig of Christ's thorn made blanched and everlasting in the stone.

Perhaps that's all there was of Rebecca Lawson, Halford thought. A life without marks or achievements. What do the young dead ever leave behind but promise? He glanced at the church where from inside he could hear the first tentative strains of a hymn. When youth dies, what does the community lose besides actions left unfulfilled?

Bending down, he tugged a clump of ragged grass from the base of Rebecca Lawson's headstone. The white roots smelled peppery. He let the blades spiral to the ground before reaching down and ripping out another handful. He had almost determined to rid the entire Lawson plot of its greenery when he glanced up and saw Editha Forrester tromp through the south door and across the cemetery towards him.

Bloody hell, he thought, and he dropped the grass he was holding and brushed off his hands. Christ Almighty. Does the indomitable Miss Forrester stomp even in the face of death?

"Chief Inspector," she began jauntily. "I saw you slip away. I was so happy you could come."

Even though he hadn't received one of her invitations to this little soiree, Halford decided to play the gentleman and smile. Editha Forrester beamed. "Of course, this was no substitution for the actual burial.

I've always thought the burial service—the graveside part—such a delightful bit of Scripture. In my day, they honored pure young women with flower crowns on their coffins, and the pallbearers wore white gloves. Lovely sentiment. Pity they don't do that anymore."

Halford nodded towards the church. "Rather nice turnout, would you say, Miss Forrester?"

"Oh, yes, but I must admit not as large as I would have thought. I guess there's too much telly and football and rock music these days for there to be much entertainment value in a memorial service, even one for a murder victim." She leaned forward and whispered delightedly, "I expected a mob."

She turned and pointed to a newer section of the cemetery. "See that grave over there, the one with the dried rosebush on it? That's Madge Stillwell's grave. That's where Lisa will be buried."

Halford looked at the shiny grey square marker. In spring, perhaps, with the flowers in bloom, the grave might have seemed tranquil, a fitting place of rest for a woman tortured in life. Now, however, Halford was struck by the newer stone's mirrorlike starkness. It didn't evoke the same peacefulness as the older stones, even the ones cracked and lying on their sides with lichen staining their words. Such a pity we're dying in this current era, Halford thought. Our heirs won't write poetry by our graves—instead they'll bring a rag and window cleaner and brighten us up.

"A funeral service is supposed to be the first step towards putting a death behind you," Halford said to Editha Forrester. "I'm afraid that can't be the case here, not yet. With a murder case, perhaps never."

"Oh, I don't know, Chief Inspector." She sounded jolly. "That's true to the people most affected, but look at all those teenagers. They'll snap back in no time. Maybe one or two of the more imaginative ones won't wear scarves for a while, or they'll shiver when they snap a stick in two, and for a longer time they'll feel chills driving down Boundary Road, but the Lord blessed them with resilience and short memories. Fetherbridge will get over this."

Halford looked at her sharply. "What about a stick?"

"You know, Chief Inspector. The stick. The one the murderer jabbed into the spokes of Lisa's bicycle. Quite ingenious, I thought, although June Kingston told me she saw it in a film once. So there you go, Mr. Halford. You should be searching for someone who enjoys the movies."

Halford tilted his head toward the sky. Damn Roan. No, as much as he hated to think it, damn Baylor. Roan, with his experience, no matter what he felt about Halford, would never have made such a mistake. The stick was confidential. Now the information was probably the top titillation at every dinner table in the village.

The south door creaked open, and the first group of mourners trooped out of the church. The service was over. "Well, Miss Forrester," Halford began, "I'm sure you have several obligations today...."

"Actually, I came over here to talk to you about something. I've been thinking about it for a while, trying to decide if it was important. Finally, I thought perhaps you should be the judge."

"All right." He leaned against Rebecca Lawson's gravestone.

"Lisa was trying to get custody of little Katie Pru."

Halford didn't move. "Go on," he said.

"Well, that's it, actually. Lisa told someone that she could get custody of Katie Pru and that she was going to do it. After all, we could see how fond she was of the child—well, who wouldn't be? And she was practically raising her as it was. I do think it's a shame mothers have to work, don't you?"

"Who told you this?"

"I can't tell you."

Halford straightened and drove his hands into his pockets. "Miss Forrester, unless you tell me who gave you this information, it's nothing more than gossip and

I've got better things to do." He started picking his way towards the lych-gate. When he reached it, he turned. "Gossip is abhorrent to me, Miss Forrester. If you want to help the police, then fine, tell me the person's name. If not, then I think you'd be wise to shut up."

He strode towards his car. After a few seconds he heard Miss Forrester tramping behind him. He stopped and waited.

"Chief Inspector." When she reached him, she was out of breath and her eyes had ceased twinkling. "I can't tell you because it was a confidence from someone special to me who I feel is worth protecting. But I promise you this person is most trustworthy. And I believe what I have told you is true." She wheeled around and headed back to the church.

In front of the lych-gate she paused, turning to glare at him with her chin lifted and her eyes blazing. "And, young man, don't you ever talk to me that way again."

18

Anise was still dressed in the black wool frock she had worn to Lisa's memorial service, but her coat had been dumped like groceries onto the table and her shoes lay on their sides by the kitchen door. As she bent over the sink, Ivory paused to watch her. His wife was beautiful, even after all these years of marriage—the long line of her leg remained smooth and he could just discern inside the thin wool casing of the frock her spine's narrow indentation. She delighted him, as she had from the beginning when he first saw her at the party in Preston and decided that this was the girl he wanted, this was the girl he would marry.

It wasn't her beauty that had captivated him. Even as a cub reporter in that industrialised region of the country he had seen many beautiful women, old as well as young: He had sat in the frayed parlors of aging beauties and watched their lipstick bleed into the wrinkles of their mouths, their eyes feign sultriness behind smudged and shaky decoration. He learned beauty wasn't a good investment. Anise, however, was the exception that proved the rule. More than a woman, she was the inference of a woman. He had always treated her like a whisper, opening himself up and drawing close to catch the warmth and sound.

He walked up behind her now and slipped his arms around her waist. She was vigorously scouring a roasting pan. A heavy stream of water pummeled the bottom of the pan, missing the gunk and leaving her fingers spackled with black grease. Ivory pressed his cheek to her hair.

"That would work better with a bit of soap."

She shook her head and he could hear the muffled rasp of her hair as it rubbed against his face. "The soap's in the cupboard and it's too much trouble to get." Her voice was thick. "I hate this sink. I'm not married to you at all, you know—I'm married to this damn faucet and this damn drain and all the little pieces of food that I've cleaned out of this damn trap over the years."

Ivory hugged her tighter. "Forget about it. I'll tidy up later."

The pan banged against the side of the sink as Anise scrubbed harder. "No, I want to clean. It's what I do. For you. For Jill. I just hate it, that's all. I just damn well hate everything."

She coughed, and her shoulders arched over the sink as she began to shake. Ivory grasped her hands and held them under the water for a second. Without letting go, he turned her around and guided them into his trouser pockets.

"I'm sorry, Anise. This has been a hellish week."

She sniffed. "Some people handle death well," she said. "I'm no good at it."

He smoothed a stray lock of hair. "Why don't you rest? Jill's in her bedroom. She said she wanted to take a nap, although I doubt there's much sleeping going on."

"She hasn't slept for the past few nights, not well, anyway. She won't take any more sedatives. I've tried to tell her it's okay, but she won't listen. I hear her downstairs at night, walking around, turning the telly on and off. I can only imagine what she's going through."

"The service is over. At least that's one thing out of the way. Maybe things will be easier from here on."

"Maybe so." She pulled away from him and wiped her nose with the back of her hand. "I'm glad we didn't go over to the Stillwells' afterwards. I don't think I could have taken it. They should have enough people over there without us, shouldn't they? Last time I checked, Editha was organising a phalanx. Do you have to go into work today?"

"No. Grissom covered the service. He can handle things on his own."

"You sent a reporter to a religious ceremony?"

"Well, of course." Ivory didn't like the horrified look on her face. "Darling, it's news. It needs to be covered. Besides, you didn't even know Grissom was there, did you? No obnoxious tape recorder shoved into poor Brian's face, no flashing bulbs. Grissom was quite discreet."

"It just seems indecent."

"There's been only one indecency—Lisa's murder. Everything else is just a series of rather uncomfortable steps to deal with that fact."

She frowned and he pulled her to him again. He knew she wouldn't argue with him, but he also knew she didn't agree. This was the only major rift in their marriage: She simply didn't understand the nature of his work. He supposed that had she been a more volatile person, the issue by now would have either been resolved or broken up their marriage. As it was, their arguments generally ended quietly, with her head on his shoulder and his hand on her hair.

She pressed her damp hands to her cheeks. "I think I'll go check Jill."

"Get yourself a bit more collected first. You know how Jill is—if she thinks you're upset, she'll want to comfort you."

"I'll do my face again, shall I? Am I going to be mortified by the mirror?" She lifted her eyes to his.

"Absolutely not. You always have the face of an angel."

When Halford entered the incidents room, only a handful of people huddled amid the maze of tables, marker boards, and telephones. Several clerks sat in front of computer terminals, typing in data from the search for "Mr. E." Near the entrance, Richard Roan was bent over the chair of a young WPC, pointing to a list of phone numbers and talking to her quietly. He glanced up as the door opened, then turned back to the constable. Halford walked over to the coffee maker, which was cooking a thick brown sludge to the bottom of the pot, and switched it off. A small waste bin next to the machine overflowed with Styrofoam cups.

Roan straightened up and held a file out to Halford. "Preliminary bicycle tests," he said tersely. "You'll be interested."

Halford sat down and studied the papers. "So they speculate that the bicycle was going between ten and fifteen miles per hour when the stick was inserted into the spokes, causing it to flip. Hmmm. Not very helpful in narrowing down what the murderer was riding, now, are they? Could have been a motorcycle, as long as Lisa wasn't going any slower than that. Could have been a moped as well. A bicyclist is a bit more problematic. A skilled cyclist would have had no trouble, but your average Joe might have had some difficulty controlling his bike while getting close enough to use the stick. If he wobbled, he could have crashed. But we didn't find any evidence of another crashed vehicle, did we?"

"No," Roan said indifferently. "And we've checked the records on Fetherbridge. Can't find anyone who owns a motorcycle. There is, of course, a moped in the village—Mrs. Grayson's."

Halford stared at the report, letting the letters blur. "Yes," he said slowly. "Still, can't rule out a bicycle." He was silent a moment before handing the file back to Roan. "Well. This'll give the defence something to slather over. Anything else turn up?"

Roan tipped his head toward the table inhabited by the WPC. "Confirming alibis," he said brusquely. "Combine the PM report with the neighbors who saw Lisa leave that morning, and the murder took place between 9:20 and 10:30 when Brian Stillwell found the body. The greengrocer says Mrs. Grayson came into his shop about 9:30 and wasn't there more than a couple of minutes—bought a copy of the *Times*, nothing else. The reporter Grissom confirms that both Jill and Orrin Ivory left the newspaper office at about 9:30. The witness at the press shop says they came in sometime a little after ten, following their stop at the Eastleigh petrol station. That makes it a bit of a stretch for them. We're still working on some others."

Roan evidently took Halford's nod as a dismissal. He stalked to the coffee maker, flicked it on, and took the dirty pot to the sink. Noisily, he turned on the tap and splashed fresh water into the carafe. The heated base of the appliance sent the smell of baked java through the room. Hell, Halford decided, there are other things to do besides watch Roan complete the ritual of territorialism. Leaning over the table, he dragged the telephone toward him and dialled.

The double burr on the other end sounded three times before Gale Grayson picked up the phone.

"Mrs. Grayson, this is Chief Inspector Halford." From the other end of the line he could hear garbled jungle noises. "Have I caught you at a bad time?"

"Depends. What do you need?"

"I'd like to come over and talk to you. Now, if possible."

"In that case, yes, I'd say your timing is bad. I just got back from an outing with Katie Pru and she's not quite wound down from it yet."

"I see. What about a little later?"

"I guess," she answered. "But is it really important to see me today?"

Halford paused. If he were honest with himself, he would admit it could wait. He peered across the room where the WPC was nervously speaking into the phone, her hand covering her mouth. She caught him watching her and blushed. Roan lounged at the back of the room, eyeing Halford and undoubtedly waiting for him to get the hell out of his way. Maura and Baylor were occupied. He supposed he could ask Roan to call in someone to accompany him on the interrogation, but the truth was he didn't want to deal with the man's conceit. Besides, he wanted to see Mrs. Grayson alone.

"It really can't wait."

She sighed wearily. "My daughter should be going down for a nap in about an hour. If you want to talk without her around, I suggest you wait till then."

"That'll be fine."

She hung up without a reply.

The house should have been hushed, but instead Maura got the impression of a train having recently passed through—not a passenger train, but a long string of puffer-bellies, queued bosom to back, chugging slowly and emitting at regular intervals blasts of rose-fragrant steam. The women of Fetherbridge had descended upon the Stillwells. There were men present, too, of course, a batch of them outside the front door, smoking and discussing football. But they were ornamentation: It was obvious to Maura that if the Stillwell men wanted comfort, they were expected to find it within the matronly circle.

It wasn't difficult to locate Editha Forrester. The old woman was holding court in the kitchen next to a dresser whose narrow top was laden with half-empty plates of traditional postdeath cuisine. The space in the kitchen not taken up by food was absorbed by a brigade of somberly dressed women. Their attention and accompanying conversation seemed to focus on Miss Forrester, who commanded center stage with a waving arm.

"Well, it was quite rude and unacceptable," she pronounced as Maura positioned herself within Miss Forrester's view and adopted her most sympathetic expression. "He really had no call to speak to me in that manner. I was only trying to help."

The women offered general coos of assent. As Miss Forrester turned towards her, Maura raised her hand slightly, wiggled her fingers, and mouthed, "May I talk with you?"

Miss Forrester paused, lifting her chin until the thick roll of fat at her neck stretched flat. As tall as Maura was, she had the perception of being looked down upon. Finally, the elderly woman pursed her lips and nodded her head.

"Very well," she said. "You've been nice enough. We can talk."

She adjusted the lace collar on her taffeta dress, brushed her hands, and, pushing through the crowd, exited the kitchen.

Maura started to follow, but found her arm entrapped by a veined hand poking from a black sleeve. The sleeve led Maura's eyes to a dried-apple face, its watery brown irises disagreeably resembling the midstage of rot.

"So what if she wanted the child?" The dried apple had brown lips and a pale, parched tongue, amazing to Maura considering the number of cola tins and used cups piled next to the sink. "That was no reason to murder her, was it?"

Maura grasped the woman's hand and gently disentangled herself, murmuring words that meant nothing and trying to finesse her way from the room. A voice from the rear of the kitchen broke through the crowd.

"Why are you here? Shouldn't you be out doing your job?"

Maura experienced the uncomfortable sensation of pressing bodies, a primal fear that her early years of police work had taught her to control, though not entirely suppress. The Notting Hill Carnival toughs were plenty frightening, she thought, but at least they're not a coven of goddamn kitchen witches. Briefly thanking God that her height at least kept her head above frock-level, she stretched her arms past the bodices of two women blocking her retreat and wondered how much leeway she should allow before grabbing a rolling pin and whacking her way free.

A voice behind her shot out shrilly. "Have you arrested her yet? When are you going to arrest her? She shouldn't be out, you know, a woman like that. . . . "

"Our men are talking. They're thinking . . ."

"Maybe they ought to do something, since the police don't seem to have the inclination. . . . "

Maura hit her limit. Planting her feet, she counted to three and spun around. The women closest to her swayed backwards, little tippy cups unbalanced by the sudden gust. Maura glared at the women until they fell silent.

"No one has been arrested yet because no one has been charged." She let the words hang in the air, increasing the fidget level. "And no one has been charged because there is no evidence. Surely you have wasted enough hours in front of the telly to be familiar with that one simple part of police procedure. What you have evidently heard today is idle gossip. As long as I'm on this case, gossip is not sufficient to arrest anybody. So unless you have anything specific to tell me, I suggest you turn your attention to the family for whom you are supposedly here."

She let her eyes roam over the faces. The women remained quiet. Maura turned and plowed her way from the room.

She met Miss Forrester, Cheshire Cat-contented, by the stairs.

"Miss Forrester," Maura said, "you know that it is not in my best interest to alienate you at this point, but surely you realise that what you just did was highly inappropriate. First of all, we only have your word that Lisa wanted custody of the child. Secondly, even if she did tell someone that, there is no evidence she acted upon it. And thirdly, even if she acted upon it, it doesn't mean Mrs. Grayson, without benefit of counsel who would certainly have told her that such a gambit on Lisa's part was absurd, got her knickers in a twist one cold December morning and rode out to string her hired help up like a Christmas goose."

It wasn't the most tactful way to handle the situation, but Maura gambled that Miss Forrester was the type who reacted to such indiscretions with glee. She judged correctly.

"Oh, Sergeant Ramsden. What a horrible thing to say in a house of mourning." Miss Forrester's blue eyes twinkled. "Let's go into the lounge and talk."

The front room was empty after Miss Forrester shooed away the three teenagers loitering on the sofa. She plopped into the cushions and motioned Maura into the seat beside her.

"You're right, you know," Miss Forrester said. "I shouldn't have told them. For one thing, my friend asked me not to, and now I've told not only the police but half the village as well." Despite her words, Miss Forrester looked less than distressed. "The chief inspector simply shouldn't have talked to me in that manner. It was uncalled for."

Maura nodded sympathetically, suspecting the woman was probably right. "Nevertheless, Miss Forrester, it would help us all, Lisa included, if you could be more prudent. We need everyone to aid us in this inquiry, but mob rule is something we want to avoid."

"Mob rule?" Miss Forrester appeared genuinely taken aback. She pressed her hand into the pearl buttons on her dress. "You think those ladies in there are capable of mob rule? Oh, my dear, you are mistaken. We are churchwomen."

"Maybe not those particular ladies, Miss Forrester, but that gossip won't stay confined to the kitchen. And who knows what can happen once it reaches the street? I've always found that it's simply not a good idea to be careless with confidences. Don't you agree?"

Miss Forrester fussed a bit, her shiny purple dress puffing slightly as she appeared to wrestle equally with embarrassment and indignation. To her credit, Maura observed, embarrassment won.

"I never considered it, really. Yes, you have a point. I shall be much more careful in the future."

"Now, perhaps, for safety's sake, you ought to tell me who your friend is."

The elderly woman set her jaw. "I can't do that."

"Miss Forrester, listen to me. You just told all those ladies that Lisa wanted custody of Katie Pru. They know someone confided in you, that someone trusted you with a secret. There will be speculation about who that person is, and if that person lives in Fetherbridge, it will eventually get back to them. That person will know you betrayed a trust. They'll hear it either in the back row of the church or in a pub, but believe me, it will get back to them, maybe even in the form of a rude joke or nasty comment. On the other hand, I am trained to handle situations like this. If you tell me, I promise I will go to this person and present the whole question in a very understanding and positive way. It will be better. I promise you that."

During the whole entreaty, Miss Forrester's eyes never left Maura's face, at first centering on the mouth, then the eyes. The elderly woman's lips pursed and then disappeared under the flick of her tongue. She was yielding; Maura had won.

"Jill," Miss Forrester said. "Jill Ivory. But be nice to her. I'm taking you at your word."

19

Gale was suddenly hot. The blue silk dress that had seemed so appropriate for the cemetery now enclosed her like a limp bell glass. Sweat formed on her torso and breasts, and under her makeup her face began to pound.

It had been thirty minutes since Halford called. She had raced through the house in short order, occupying Katie Pru in the kitchen with paper and crayons and scooping up a trail of clutter along the staircase which she deposited in a toy bin in her daughter's room. Like the rest of Fetherbridge her cottage showed the stress of sudden death: empty dishes collected on tables in every room; fledgling swags of dust drooped from corners and the tops of curtains; curls of old spaghetti and dried Play-Doh pebbles mixed with the more mundane dirt on the floors. Well, Gale had thought surveying the disorder, Halford could very well go screw himself if he thought a clean house was his due.

The study was the least messy place, and after picking up several papers scattered in the hallway, she had shut the doors to the other rooms downstairs and headed for her bedroom. Regardless of what the afternoon would bring, she was damned if she was going to face it in pantyhose. Opening her bureau drawer, she reached for a fresh pair of panties. Dipping her hands into them, she pulled out a fistful. Clean, silken, not a stained crotch among them. My, but Gale's a fastidious girl. Like a snapshot came the childhood memory of her grandmother in the antique-filled living room of the old house in Atlanta. She had held up a tattered pair of Gale's panties, frowning.

"What did you use these for, child, a flag of surrender?"

The admonishment hadn't worked. Neither had the classic threats of trains, trucks, and buses cruising over her prepubescent body. Gale had figured her chances of actually being hit were fairly slim. Even into her adulthood, her underwear had remained the most dismal part of her wardrobe.

But now Gale knew that daughters were never told the whole story. The trucks always came eventually, careening out of control. In her case, the trucks had come three years ago, a whole brigade of them, broad and dark, slamming in and out of her closets and drawers, leaving like an eternal imprint the sound of heavy boxes scraping down the stairs. By the time they left, all she felt was the numb certainty that her fingers could never pull close the rips, that she could never shutter her life tight enough to block out their screaming, invading light.

Now none of her underwear, cinnamon-scented and hand-washed, was more than three months old. In the drawer of her bedside table the printed receipts from dozens of trips to Debenhams' lingerie department were fading to white. Gale closed her eyes. So this is what Tom left her: mortification turned to compulsion.

The urge to laugh and cry swelled and ceased within a breath. A young woman slain with a scarf around her throat; another woman deadened in her gated cottage. How many ways there are to extinguish life.

Katie Pru was in the room before Gale heard her.

"See, Mama?" She held up a sheet of paper. "It's a monkey with no tail. He sits on his bottom in the tree."

Gale stared at her daughter, her eyes so bright and happy, her pudgy legs sturdy beneath her dress. This is it, she thought. There's been enough death in this cottage. There have been enough victims.

By the time Halford knocked on the door, Katie Pru was napping on Gale's bed and the downstairs was close to immaculate. Tea steeped in a kettle on the stove. Cups of boiled water and vanilla sat in each room. Gale answered the door bare-legged in her wool crepe suit.

The first thing Halford noticed about the cottage was the quiet. The air held an ordered hush, and as soon as the front door closed behind him he realised how comforting the place was, how palliative she had made it, despite the hardness of the furnishings and the starkness of the colours.

Gale Grayson herself, however, made a curiously gnomish figure as she led him into the study, rather what he imagined Mother Goose would have looked like had she been diminutive, young, and not very particular about getting splinters in her feet. After settling him into a chair in the study, she pattered to the kitchen, returning a couple of minutes later with a tea tray which she set on a wooden trunk in front of the love seat. Eased into the love seat's cushions, she looked at the tray uncertainly until finally Halford leaned forward and took a cup.

"Shall I be mother?" he asked.

She looked at him, startled, then to his surprise burst into laughter. Halford wrinkled his brow as she eyed his legs.

"Mama ought to be more careful shavin' her shins, don't you think? It don't look ladylike to have black curlies peepin' over her socks." Still smiling, Mrs. Grayson took the teacup from his hand. "I'm sorry. That's just such a funny expression to me. No, please, allow me to be mother. I'm sure I have more experience."

As she concentrated on her task of pouring tea, alabaster light from the windows bathed her face and bleached her eyes to the colour of drenched sand. Outside, a thin rain had throttled the wind, and pearls of water hung upside down from the bare limbs and dead growth of the garden.

In his parents' house hung a print of Mary Cassatt's "The Boating Party." It was odd that he thought of it now. There was little similarity between Cassatt's summer-bold colors and the subtle maternity of greys Gale Grayson had chosen for her study. Neither was the bright coolness of Cassatt's water any relation to the gauzy veil of winter that shuddered outside the window. Yet the image was there, vivid and strong.

You git, you're being thick, he told himself crossly. The subject of the painting, a mum working to keep her child safe on her lap, had tweaked his consciousness. It was one of the reasons he was here, to see if he could coax from Mrs. Grayson insight into the depth, and perhaps threat, of Lisa's relationship with Katie Pru. He leaned back, satisfied that his mind hadn't proved inscrutable. But the feeling passed, and he found himself thinking of the darkly clothed figure in the painting's foreground—the man at the oars, his back to the viewer—and the unreadable look the mother was giving him.

A pewter bowl of yellow apples sat on one side of the trunk. Mrs. Grayson reached forward, selected one, and wrapped a paper napkin around it.

"I'd offer you more, Chief Inspector, but there isn't anything. I haven't quite gotten back in the swing of things."

"It's all right," he told her. "I appreciate your agreeing to see me."

She nodded, and absently reached up and scratched the bone under her left brow hard enough to leave a warm slice of pink. She folded the napkin back and, biting into the apple, made two sharp chevrons in the pulp.

"It's funny," she said, twisting the fruit in front of her. "All day long I've wanted nothing more than a big paper plate full of green bean casserole, fried chicken, and yeast rolls. Funeral food, at least it is back home. It's strange how you get conditioned to things. I haven't been to more than a handful of funerals in my entire life, but my salivary glands know precisely what to do to formalise mourning." She paused. "I didn't attend Lisa's memorial service, though. It must just be something in the air."

Her mood seemed strange to him. She seemed almost expansive, or perhaps what passed as expansive in her peculiarly constricted world. Halford gave her an understanding smile.

"When I was growing up," he said, "my mother always fixed roast beef when my uncle came to visit. He's my father's uncle, actually, and none of us much liked him. He had lost his teeth during the war—don't ask me how—and he was forever taking out his dentures and tossing them at my sister and me. Checking our reflexes, he said. Of course, our reflexes were to yell bloody murder and go wash our hands. Mother would make roast beef knowing full well he couldn't eat it. He'd grumble and take himself off to a pub while we sat down at the table and blissfully ate our meal. To this day I enjoy a good rare roast beef, but I can't eat it without checking to see if my hands are wet."

Some of the anxiety cleared from her face and she chuckled politely. In the pulse of silence that followed,

Halford remembered that from what he had observed of Katie Pru, she would be the type of child who slept like a set alarm clock. Time was ebbing away. He put his cup back on the tray.

"What about your family?" he asked. "Did your grandfather fight in the war?"

She seemed a little surprised by the question, but she answered it willingly. "World War Two, you mean. I don't know. . . . I don't think so." She gave a little laugh. "I suppose that sounds odd, not knowing, I mean, but I really don't." She paused a second to think. "Well, come to think of it, maybe he did. Huh, isn't that strange? Imagine not knowing a thing like that."

Particularly strange for a historian, he thought. There were two directions he could take the questioning next, and he wasn't sure which would get him answers the quickest. He decided that, given his past record with her, his best bet was circumnavigation.

"Were you an only child?"

She nodded. "My mother died when I was five. My grandmother raised me in Atlanta, but I had three aunts all scattered throughout Georgia, so I spent most of my childhood going from one to another. Ours is a big, boisterous clan."

"And your father? He was gone as well?"

"No. My father was around, but he pretty much left me to the women. I guess he got lost amongst all the hair spray and female hoo-ha." She paused, and her voice shifted from its low southern drift, tightening into a much harsher American accent. "No, my father's always been there. Surely you would know that, from your files, or somewhere."

He did, of course. He knew of the mother, killed at twenty-six in an automobile accident, and of the father, a painter who never remarried. He even knew something of the grandmother, a former teacher who made a name for herself in the 1980's as the doyenne of southern decorating. But those facts told him next to nothing.

"I think people sometimes believe we know more about them than we actually do." He slid his napkin from under his saucer and rolled up one corner. "Hair spray and female hoo-ha. I take it the American South is a bit of a matriarchy."

"A bit."

She paused. "That's not exactly true," she said. "I know sociologists and historians who claim it's still a patriarchy, that the idea of the omnipresent steel magnolia being the backbone of the South is a myth. But I've seen pockets . . . streams. . . . My family is one of those streams. I guess you'd say we verify the myth."

"How so?"

She studied the place on her wrist where her muscles rounded and disappeared as she squeezed the apple. "Well, it's similar to what went on here after World War One. During the war, women went to work because it was their duty, they were needed. But afterwards, when the soldiers returned, they were forced back out, into marriage, into jobs as domestics, back into a low-paying women's sphere. But some refused to go. They refused to give up the little gains in power they had achieved during the war years. That happened in the South after the Civil War, as well, but I think it was more pronounced. It wasn't just money and power women didn't want to let loose of—it was freedom. Literally. Slaves weren't the only people liberated by the Civil War. Hierarchies of oppression have many victims."

The peach colour of the napkin deepened where the juice seeped. She scraped her thumbnail across the stain, tearing the napkin. Hastily, she smoothed it back. "White men came back from the war disillusioned and depressed. In many families, in many areas, women came to the fore. You know, it's curious, but you can see it even today. In Statlers Cross, the little town in Georgia where my grandmother now lives, you can find among a certain generation women with master's degrees married to moonshiners. Not your wealthy, post-Dixie Mafia moonshiners, either, just your garden-variety, dull-eyed type with half his leg shot off." Her voice grew edged. "In my own family, my father is the only exception. All the other men make up one continuous line of derelicts, drunks, syphilitics, and manic-depressives. It's the women who matter. The men just dissipate into nothing."

Halford spoke quietly. "Did Tom dissipate into nothing?"

She unwrapped the apple and rubbed the wet napkin against her palm. "Yes," she said, raising her eyes. "For me he did. Eventually."

He didn't believe her and he knew that it wasn't important to her that he should. He paused for a few seconds before asking his next question.

"How could you have let someone like Lisa take care of your daughter?"

"What do you mean, someone like Lisa?"

"Well, she was immature . . . possessive . . . manipulative. Not exactly characteristics I would look for in a childminder."

She eyed him warily. "Who told you those things?"

"Beryl Lampson's fourth miscarriage was a highly personal and profoundly emotional experience for her. Lisa seemed unaware of her need for privacy."

Mrs. Grayson placed the apple back on the tray. "Lisa wasn't very good at putting herself in other people's shoes. But Beryl is just one person. So many people thought Lisa was wonderful."

Halford studied her expression. The anxiety had left, replaced by a budding anger. "But you perhaps have a more rounded view of her," he suggested.

"And you think I'll tell you about it."

He pulled on his moustache, considering her. "I think part of you wants to. You believe that what you know, what you intuited about Lisa, would help me very much. I'm not asking for facts just now. I want your observations. And your theories."

She took a deep breath and tucked her legs beneath

her frock. "Look. You had to be generous with Lisa. After all, her mother—"

"Oh, come on. I realise that being deserted by your mother can do a lot of damage, but that doesn't explain—"

"What doesn't it explain? It explains a lot, maybe everything."

"Have you been in her house, Mrs. Grayson? Have you seen her room, her clothes? What were you paying her?"

"Sixty-five pounds a week."

"That's not enough to afford what she had. How do you explain that?"

She swung her legs to the floor, exasperated and clearly struggling with herself. When her eyes darted back to his face, they were grim and sharp.

"People gave her things, Mr. Halford. They did things for her. Lisa couldn't cope on her own—I don't know, it was as if she wasn't wholly formed. Whatever core she should have developed, it cooled too soon, perhaps when her mother left, and she never made it to true adulthood. People responded to that. She was like a child you could pamper, nurture, pour your heart out to, because you knew she could never completely understand." She raked her fingers through her hair. "I know that doesn't make sense. I'm just trying to figure it all out now myself."

"Can you give me some specifics of people doing things for her, giving her things?"

"No, I won't do that for you. It's presuming too much. It's too close to implying guilt."

Halford changed tactics. "And you? What did you do for her? Was she someone you felt inclined to pamper and nurture?"

Her voice became hard and she leaned into it as if it were a wind. "No. In fact, if I could have I would've stayed as far away from her as possible."

"Why?"

She shook her head, agitated. "She was . . . she was

a nervous breakdown waiting to happen. If I had had any other choice, or a job where I couldn't have been here in the house with her and Katie Pru most of the time, I would have found someone else, somewhere. I don't know. I just didn't seem to have many options."

"You tried?"

"Yes. But how many people do you think would relish a job working for a woman with terrorist connections? How many mamas would let their teenagers come here after school to tend a bad seed?"

She had tears in her eyes, but she brushed them away impatiently and stood up. The fire in the hearth wasn't lit; she pressed her temple against the mantel's edge.

Her frustration was tangible. He could read it in the set of her mouth, the curve of her back, the flex of her fingers. Suddenly, he wanted to hold her. He wanted to soothe her, to place in those tiny hands her life, his life, both made whole again.

He approached her with caution. "You had options," he said gently. "You could have gone home."

Tears magnified her irises; her face was all eyes, all pain. Her voice barely clung to sound. "Another southern woman, smothered in the bosom of iron and strength. I don't think you know very much, Mr. Halford."

They stood a good three feet apart; Halford towered over her, her head barely cresting the middle of his chest.

" 'I wak'd, she fled, and day brought back my night.' "

Milton's shining summation of grief. Halford didn't know why he said it—it was the type of comment that should have been censored before it left his mouth, no matter how much it applied to Gale Grayson, or how much it seemed to explain.

The effect on her, however, was illuminating. Bringing a clenched fist to the wall, she propelled herself away from him. She picked up the tea tray and had swung away as if to make for the kitchen when she turned back and dropped it clanging to the trunk. The cup that had been his tilted, and the tea he had left undrunk streamed across the silver tray and spread through the bank of napkins.

She whirled around on him. "It's not day that brings back my night, goddamnit. Has that ever once occurred to you? You're such a bastard. You did it, and you don't even have the decency to see it."

He didn't know where to look, at her or at the teacup lolling on its side. They were equally accusing. Her face was twisted, ready to cry. He raised his hands helplessly.

"Of course it has occurred to me, of course I see it." He was beseeching her, and even as he hated himself for it he couldn't take control of his voice. "Do you think I haven't paid also? Do you have any idea what my bloody life has been for the past three years? Southampton—do you honestly believe that I just happened upon you while I was out for a stroll? For God's sake, Gale, I wanted to talk to you, I wanted to apologise. I wanted you to understand."

He stopped, horrified by the look of incomprehension on her features. The air in the room, which several minutes ago had seemed so clean and cool, was now hot and thick. A drop of sweat rolled into his eye and he squinted his lids shut to stop the sting and to slam her out of his vision.

She didn't remember the tea shop. Dear God, she didn't remember Southampton.

He started to move towards the door, but she shook her head.

"Don't go," she mumbled. "Not yet." She picked up the tray. "I'm going to the kitchen. I'll be right back. Please don't go."

She disappeared into the hall, but he could tell by the screech of the kitchen tap and the clink of dishes that she wasn't coming back immediately. He walked to the window, grateful. Outside, the rain had quickened. He rested his head against the mullioned panes and let the glass be a cool cloth on his brow.

Her desk, cluttered in true writer's fashion, sat under the stretch of windows. Halford glanced at the perilous construction of papers and books that climbed beside the computer. Idly, he ran his finger down the edge of the pile, letting paper pop against his nail. He was halfway to the bottom when he stopped, his chest constricting.

When she finally came back into the room, carrying two tumblers filled with brown liquid, he was grimly sitting in her desk chair. In one hand he held a black-and-white photograph. In the other was a copy of the *Inquisitor*, its pages dusty and edges yellowed.

"I didn't know research for the C.S.S. *Alabama* covered such recent history."

She gave a cry and lunged for the photo. Whipping it out of her reach, he dropped the photo and newspaper to the desk. He caught her hand and grabbed the glass just as it left her grasp.

"Where did that come from?" she gasped. "Jesus Christ, where did you get it?"

Halford managed to force the second glass from her hand. Taking her by both wrists, he pushed her back to the love seat. Even under the steadying strength of his hold, her hands were shaking. She sat stiffly against the back of the cushions, her neck stretched into an ugly stand of muscles as she peered past him at the evidence he had left face up on the desk.

Did the Widow Know? the headline read. And lying beside the paper was the photo of Gale Grayson—young, pretty, smiling—surrounded by a cache of guns.

20

If she had suddenly sprouted wings, Jill Ivory couldn't have felt lighter. She lay in her bed, as the gathering blush of afternoon wrapped her room in a rich calm, and dozed intermittently. She had removed her clothes after the service and now lay under the blankets dressed only in a camisole. In her half-sleep, she had the impression of jumping, bouncing high off the bed and skimming the ceiling with her fingertips. Her feet sank deep into the mattress with each leap, further and further down until the mattress thinned to a cotton sheet and her toes tipped the floor before she soared to the ceiling. Again and again she jumped, pushing through the roof of the house, bounding over hedgerows, trees. She felt glorious. It was when her father opened her bedroom door that her last anchor to the earth finally broke. As she heard the hinges creak, her toes curled inward, and her body was wracked with the sensation of both legs shrivelling up and disappearing under the camisole's hem.

She heard her father's whisper. "She's still asleep. I'm not going to wake her."

She struggled to full consciousness and sat up in bed. Her father stood inside her room, talking into the cordless phone.

"Who is it, Daddy? I'm okay. I'll talk."

Frowning, her father passed her the phone. Sergeant Ramsden's voice spattered over the static.

"Can . . . talk? I need . . . questions." The connection was bad. Jill strained to listen.

"You don't have to see her today, darling." Her father sat down beside her on the bed. "I told her you weren't available, but she was very persistent. Nevertheless, you tell her you'll see her tomorrow."

The lightness that had filled her chest while she slept slowly diffused, and Jill's body felt leaded and tired. The back of her head burned where the pillow had heated and flattened like a board beneath her. She rubbed the warm spot and brushed her fringe away from her eyes.

"I can see you today." She spoke into the receiver loudly. "Can you hear me? I can see you in about an hour."

Her father clamped his hands to his knees. Sergeant Ramsden crackled something about the house.

"No," Jill answered. "Not here. I need to go for a walk. At the newspaper. Meet me upstairs."

The dial tone filled her ear, and she handed the phone to her father. His eyes stayed on her face as she slipped on a dressing gown and walked to her clothes cupboard.

"This is ridiculous," he said. "The service was barely three hours ago. It wouldn't be outside the bounds of propriety for you to tell them to bugger off until tomorrow."

She pulled a brown sweater and a pair of jeans from the cupboard. "I need a break, Daddy. It's too much. I need to get out of the house."

"It *has* been too much. That's why you need some rest. You can't just brush something like this off, Jill."

She selected a pair of brown socks from her chest of drawers. They were a birthday present from Lisa three months back, along with a matching velvet headband. She slapped the socks across her hand and closed her fist over them.

"Lisa was my friend, Daddy, not yours. I know how to grieve for her."

"Fine." He heaved himself from the bed. "Do you want me to go with you?"

"No, Daddy. I can answer a few questions on my own. Besides, I rather like Sergeant Ramsden. She's easy to talk with."

Her father managed to sound soft and sharp at the same time. "Ramsden's no friend of yours, Jill. She's the police. No matter how kindly she acts, how concerned, she wants information, not your companionship. Don't fool yourself into thinking she cares about you." He headed for the door and paused. "It's the same with journalists. If you're going to be one, you better be aware of that."

He pulled the door shut behind him. Sighing, Jill dressed quickly, dabbing on a light lip gloss and pinning her hair back with a couple of grips.

She was surprised how liberating it felt to step onto the front stoop. She hopped down the steps and, digging her hands into her coat pocket, trudged through a misting rain towards the *Inquisitor* offices.

For the first time she was able to reflect on the service. It had seemed so sterile, so pointless. Perhaps when it was time for the funeral, and a casket actually stood in front of the altar, perhaps then she would feel something. She wasn't convinced she would. She couldn't get past the idea of Lisa in a coffin, Lisa with white satin beneath, beside, and finally above her, Lisa as primped and painted shot, tamped into a cartridge and wedged with the most elegant wads. She was afraid that when the time came, she would be shocked to see the coffin lowered into the grave—she would instead be expecting the wooden capsule to be upended and blasted headfirst into the ground.

She walked down the pavement to the *Inquisitor*'s door and swung it open. The taped paper over the broken pane was obviously doing its job. The interior of the newspaper building was stuffy after the brisk chill of the outside. Down the hall she could hear voices, but the reception area was inhabited only by the receptionist Deb, seated at the desk and stabbing at a ladder in her stockings with red nail polish. ·

"Well, chicken, I didn't expect to see you in today." Deb plunged the brush back into the bottle of polish and churned it up and down. "I thought the Right Reverend Brother Orrin would let you have a long weekend, considering."

Jill smiled, but she felt a stab of confusion. "I just needed a break." She gave a small, nervous laugh. "The Right Reverend? I've never heard him called that before."

Deb pulled the brush from the bottle and attacked the ladder again. "Oh, you know. Father-Confessor-Comfort-to-the-Sick-and-Ailing-Editor-Judge-and-King Orrin Ivory." She wasn't looking at Jill, jabbering on at the rip in her stockings as if it were a sensible being. "Of course, we don't mean nothin' by it. Think the world of your father. It's just that he can be a little— you know . . ."

She left the sentence hanging, finally glancing up at Jill. "By the way, I haven't said anything to you about Lisa, but we all feel terrible. I didn't know her well, but she seemed nice."

Despite a sudden anxiety, Jill smiled. "Thanks. That Sergeant Ramsden is going to meet me here in a few

minutes. Would you mind telling her that I'm in my
father's office?"

"The police? What happened to the old times when
you had time to keen in peace?"

"I think that's for old grannies dying in bed," Jill
said ruefully. "Just goes to show true friends shouldn't
go around getting themselves murdered."

She ran up the stairs before Deb could reply. She
expected to see some of the production staff readying
ads for Wednesday's press run, but instead the room
was empty except for Bobby Grissom, clicking away on
a word processor. He glanced up as she walked in.

"Why, hullo." He pushed several keys, and from
where she was standing Jill saw the screen go blank.
"Don't tell me your dad's having you work today."

Jill felt herself colour. "No, the Father Confessor
was not pleased with me at all when I said I was coming here."

She removed her coat and hung it on a rack near
the door. Claiming the chair from the nearest desk, she
turned it around to face Grissom.

"God." She pressed both hands against the top of
her head and swirled around in the chair. "I had to get
out of that house. I mean, Mummy's all tears and
Daddy walks about giving out hugs like Father Christmas. I always knew that losing someone would be
agonising, but I had no idea how suffocating it could
be."

"Bit of a paradox, that," Grissom said. "You'd think
that when someone dies, they'd leave a hole. Instead,
it's like they wrap you in the shroud with them."

Jill looked at him, surprised. "That's exactly what
it's like. Only the hole is there, too. It's odd, isn't it?"

Across the room, a large framed print hung on an
otherwise bare yellow wall. Amid a border of gold and
green laurels, it depicted a printing press, a quill, and
a sheaf of paper. The title plate nailed to the bottom of
the frame read, "The Bricks of Utopia." When she was
a child, it had hung over the sofa in the living room;

now it had been moved to an equally prominent place in the newsroom.

She cast her eyes down at her lap and began straightening her hair grips. "Bobby, what's it like to work for my father?"

Grissom inhaled and caught the air in puffed cheeks before letting it burst out in a sigh. Glancing at his computer screen, he pushed his chair away from his desk and wheeled it closer to her.

"Well, I'd say he's quite good. Very good, actually. He's what I'd call a journalist's editor—not one of those grub-in-the-garbage kind. He really believes in what he's doing." He shrugged. "I like working for him. Why?"

"Deb was making fun of him downstairs just now. Not badly, just a bit. I wondered if he was well liked."

"I'd say respected. And that's more important in this field than being liked." With the tip of his shoe, he playfully knocked her foot. "Not many journalists worry about being liked, you know."

Jill flinched. She moved her legs out of range.

"Bobby, I need to talk with someone. Would it be all right . . . ?"

"Of course, Jill. Please." He reached towards her, but she crossed her arms and hid her hands.

"I just want to talk. Okay?"

"Sure." He leaned back, frowning slightly. "Talking's fine."

Jill hiked her leg onto her knee and slipped her finger through the loop in her shoestring. She took several starting breaths before she finally spoke.

"He doesn't want me to go into journalism." Grissom watched her, noncommittal. She twisted the shoestring around her finger and continued. "It's so strange. All my life I've heard about how important journalism is, how it is the truth that makes democracies work and without it we're no better than beasts."

Grissom snorted. "Bedtime stories for the innocent."

"See? I don't understand that attitude. I think my

father is right. When I was small and we were living in Preston, he did a series of articles on a child porn ring in Manchester. He worked on it for months, went undercover, talked to everyone from the parents of the children to the photographers to the publisher. This was fifteen years ago—of course, I was too young to remember—but I found the articles in a scrapbook two years back and read them. They're wonderful, truly wonderful. He was able to find out things the police couldn't, and eventually the ring was shut down. Think of all the children saved because of him."

She felt her face flush, and she pressed her hands to her cheeks before continuing. "Imagine having that kind of influence. I admire him so much. I want to be like him. But now that I'm grown, he doesn't want me in journalism, he wants me off, teaching or selling stocks or ... I don't know. Sometimes I wonder if I failed him somewhere."

"I don't think it's that at all." Grissom bent towards her. "Jill, your dad thinks the world of you. He worships you. If he doesn't want you to be a journalist, it's because he wants to protect you. This business isn't as pure as he'd like it to be."

She levelled her eyes at him. "I've heard that from him. 'It's the last great hope of the earth, Jilly, but not a nice place for girls to play.' So you agree with him?"

"I think you have more to offer the world. This is a dirty business. You can't help but be dirty in it. And, Jill, you deserve more. You deserve *better*."

The lightness she had felt earlier in her dream returned, this time in anger. She took a deep breath, trying not to lose her temper, trying not to unleash on Grissom all the frustration of the past six days. It didn't work. What ultimately saved Grissom from a tirade was the appearance of Sergeant Ramsden and Chief Inspector Halford standing soberly in the doorway.

Five pumps, in. Five pumps, out. Gale paced her breathing to the whirr of the small spinning wheel. Beneath her bare foot the wooden treadle clicked easily. The roll of unspun ecru wool she held in her hand twisted itself into a pulsing thread, a captive cyclone in her palm. She was aware of her strength, aware of the leaden concentration needed to sustain the gentleness the craft demanded. So she breathed. Five pumps, in. Five pumps, out.

Halford had left an hour earlier almost as soon as Katie Pru awoke from her nap, his face grim, the newspaper and photograph—with Gale's permission—folded under his arm. He had managed to calm her down somewhat, enough so that, incredulous and angry, she was able to give him an explanation about the old newspaper that he may or may not have believed. His angular face had been inscrutable except for a hardness in the eyes that had replaced both the compassion and the pain she had glimpsed earlier. His questioning had been subdued but stern.

"Tell me about the newspaper first," he had said.

She had inhaled deeply to steady herself. "It was taken from the archives. I could tell something was missing, but I couldn't tell what."

"Out of all those papers, you're able to tell that this was the one missing?"

"Yes."

They had been sitting on the study's love seat with him sideways, crouching on the edge as if prepared to spring forward should she try to run away. She had been aware that she was literally wringing her hands.

"I pulled it." She turned to him, desperate that he believe her. "About a year ago. I had never read any of the coverage on Tom's . . ." here she faltered, " . . . death. I hadn't wanted to face it. But in talking with Ruth Barker one day, she mentioned that article—*Did the Widow Know?*—like I was a part of the whole thing, like I may have been guilty. It just pissed me off, the way she was so sly about it. So I talked to Orrin and he let me go through the archives looking for it. Of course, the article itself is so innocuous. Orrin said he had written it to stop the gossip." She pointed to the paper folded in Halford's hands. "It's really a defence of me. Just read it."

Halford didn't so much as glance at the paper. "So you pulled it out. But you didn't keep it?"

"No . . . I sat right there in the archives and read it. I actually got mad at Orrin because of it. He was so canny. Supposed to clear my name, but can't pass up a chance at a sensational headline. Anyway, I didn't even take it home. When I finished it, I tried to put it back in the same stack, in some sort of chronological order, but the stacks were so tall, the dust so bad that I ended up just sort of jamming it in place. So there was always a corner from that paper sticking out, the edge flapped over. And that's what I didn't see when I was looking at everything with Sergeant Ramsden. The room was still in a shambles, but that flap was gone."

He reached over and placed the photograph in her lap. "And your explanation for this?"

She held it up, trembling, in her hands. She kept shaking her head, astonished. "I don't know how it got here. I'd forgotten all about it. My God, it was ages . . . so long ago . . . It was just something I did at college. . . . It was nothing."

Halford waited, silent. Her hands were cold. She dropped the photo back into her lap and clasped and unclasped them nervously.

"Tom and I were in an antigun club, a protest group. No one was paying us much attention, so we wanted to generate a little publicity. We needed a picture for a poster. A pawnshop owner let us use his stock."

Halford's expression was dubious. "Why would a man selling guns help antigun advocates?"

Gale's throat went dry. Even before her words were out, she knew he wouldn't believe her. "We didn't tell him the truth. We told him we were doing a poster for the NRA."

She predicted correctly. He continued to stare at her, skepticism making flint of his eyes.

"No problem," he said finally. "Just give me the name of the group, the names of the other members, the location of the pawnshop, and who the owner was."

She brought her clasped hands to her chin. "I can't," she whispered. "I don't remember. It was so long ago."

His mouth twisted wryly. "Well, I can tell you, Mrs. Grayson. We tried to investigate that group three years ago when we were looking into your husband's past. No one at your college had heard of it. We were never able to verify that it existed."

He had let the words hang in the air, waiting for her to respond, until Katie Pru wandered sleepily into the room. Halford stood up quickly. He gave the child a smile and then continued to stand there, perhaps expecting Gale to find the child something to occupy her in another room. She didn't, and he finally looked her in the eye and asked very slowly:

"If you expect me to believe that you know nothing of how these items got into your house, then you must tell me: Who's visited you here since the morning Lisa was murdered?"

Gale had hesitated, then shook her head. Halford had left, frustrated and furious.

Now, an hour later, Katie Pru sat at her mother's feet in the living room, chattering over a Winnie-the-Pooh picture book, while Gale slowed the rate of her breathing and forced the spinning wheel to calm its panicked circles.

"Can we have tea now?" Katie Pru looked up from her book. "You said we could have tea now."

Gale laid her hand atop the rushing wheel and gently eased it to a stop. "So I did, ladybug. I forgot. I'll go get it now. You wait here."

Carefully, she stepped over the child and headed towards the kitchen. At the study door she paused, then went in. The phone was packed against the com-

puter on her desk. Studiously avoiding her stacks of
notes, she lifted the receiver and punched in the Ivorys'
number.

Anise answered on the first ring.

"Anise," Gale said with a forced breeziness, "I was
wondering if Orrin was home. I need to talk to him."

Anise sounded clogged. "Sorry, Gale. He left a
while ago. The police wanted to talk to him down at
the newspaper office. About the break-in, I gathered.
They already have Jill there." She sniffed loudly into
the receiver. "I asked to go, but Orrin said no."

Gale wrapped the telephone cord around her wrist.
"Did they say why they wanted to discuss the break-
in?"

"I don't know. I think they must have found what
was stolen. Orrin wouldn't tell me." Her tone intensi-
fied. "I hate not knowing what's going on."

"You know it's nothing." Gale tried to mimic sympathy, but a iron knot had formed in her gut. "I mean,
we've been through this all before. The police have to
ask their questions."

On the other end of the line, Anise's voice sounded
equally strained.

"I realise that. It's not the police I'm losing patience
with. It's Orrin. I can handle a lot more than he credits
me with. I sometimes think he doesn't see how strong
I am."

Gale clinched the receiver tightly. She didn't want
a conversation. She frankly wasn't in the mood for Anise's coddled insecurities. Unwrapping the cord from
her arm, she stretched it as far as it would go and
picked up a striped pillow from the love seat.

"Of course you're strong," she placated, clutching
the pillow to her chest. "My grandmother used to say
that the man may bring home most of the bacon, but
it's the woman who determines the family's flavor. And
just look at your family, Anise. You have a lot to be
proud of. It takes strength to create a good family."

Instead of soothing, Gale's words seemed to fire something in Anise. Her voice mounted.

"But sometimes I think Orrin believes he's done it on his own, that Jill and I are the product of his hard work. He thinks I'm just a doll, Gale, and I'm fed up with it."

It was a statement surely meant to elicit support, but instead, Gale fell silent, unable to respond or console.

"You're depressed," she finally managed. "It's been a hard week for everyone. We all need rest."

Gale's words must have sounded condescending, for Anise's response was clipped.

"You're right," she said. "I have a wonderful family. This is just a bad time."

From the living room, Katie Pru started singing about teacups. "I'm sorry, Anise," Gale said. "I didn't mean to . . . I just have a lot on my mind. I really need to talk to Orrin."

It was a logical point for Anise to say good-bye, but instead Gale heard her take a deep breath.

"You missed the service," she said, a bit brighter. "It was quite nice. Jeremy always does a good job at these sorts of things. He's very compassionate. You could tell he truly cared for Lisa."

"Yes." Gale bit her lip nervously. "I considered going. But in the end I just couldn't."

"Oh, I didn't mean that you should have gone," Anise said hurriedly. "I just thought you might want to know that it was a good service. You loved Lisa, as we all did. She was such a charming child."

Katie Pru's singing changed to stomping. Immature, possessive, manipulative—those were the words Halford had used to describe Lisa. Gale, in the end, had added some of her own. If there was a betrayal, she had already committed it.

She grew bold. "Did you think so, Anise? Did you really think Lisa was charming?"

Anise gave a short laugh. "Oh, you mean her youth.

Well, of course, she could be tiresome sometimes. But what was that phrase Tom wrote in one of his poems? Something about 'bothered blessings'?"

Gale felt light-headed.

" 'In bothered blessings our new love thrives.' Is that the one you mean?"

"Yes, that was it. I know the poem is about love, but it suits youth as well. All young people are bothered blessings, don't you think. I loved the poem, Gale. Orrin put a copy of it on our bed just last month. He really can be romantic." She chuckled. "Listen to me. A few minutes ago I was acting like Sylvia Plath, ready to stick my head in the oven. And now look. I'm blushing. I really don't know what I'd do without the man."

Katie Pru appeared in the doorway, swinging back and forth from the jamb. "Mama . . ."

From the other line, Gale heard Anise gasp. "Oh, dear, Gale, I didn't mean to be insensitive. I hope you didn't take that wrong."

"Mama. I've waited real good. Can I have some tea now?"

Gale fought to focus her thoughts. "No, Anise. It's all right. I've got to go now. Katie Pru's hungry."

"Shall I tell Orrin you rang?"

"No, that's all right. I'll get in touch with him later."

She hung up the phone and stared vacantly out the window until Katie Pru plopped down on the floor and began whistling like a kettle.

Seated in the minuscule cubicle that passed as an editor's office, Halford carefully placed the photograph of Gale Grayson—dubbed 'Guns 'n' Poses' by Maura—on the desk in front of Ivory. Outside in the main room, Maura talked with Jill. Jill's calm voice drifted through the cubicle's open door. Halford tilted back in his chair and gently pushed the door closed. The modular walls, bland and inoffensive, were at least acoustically correct. The women's voices instantly disappeared.

Despite its safety in a clear plastic sleeve, Ivory

didn't touch the photo. He looked down at it briefly and then over at Halford.

"This is what was stolen from the archives? My God, how in the hell did anyone find it?"

"You're sure you recognise it then? You can pick it up to examine it closely if you wish."

Gingerly, as if he were reluctant to tarnish his fingers, Ivory lifted the photo by the sleeve and turned it over.

"Yes, I recognise it. This is my handwriting on the back. Eighty-three-percent. That's the size I wanted it shot for the paper. Here, on the front, you can see my crop marks."

"How did you come by it?"

Ivory carefully placed the photo back on the desk and settled into his chair. "Tom gave it to me," he said simply.

Halford let a moment pass. "Whatever in God's name for?"

Ivory ran his hands over his face. "In light of everything that's happened, this is going to sound absurd." He brought his hands down, leaving his face a bright pink. "About four, five years ago, I was planning an article on the stupidity of American gun laws. You know the type of thing—they may have five hundred and thirty-two television channels but they can't keep guns out of the hands of teenagers. One night I was over at the Graysons', just chitchatting with Tom about it, and he left the room and came back with this. Asked if it would make good artwork. Well, I took one look at it and said, hell yes."

"Did he tell you where the photo came from?"

"Of course I asked. It's quite an unnerving picture, after all. I mean, there must be what, twenty, thirty guns in that photo? Nasty-looking, too. He told me that he and Gale had taken it during their college days, for a poster in support of gun laws."

"And that seemed reasonable to you?"

Ivory crossed his arms. "Well, yes, at the time. What

other reason could there be? Understand, Chief Inspector, that this was probably a year or more before any of us knew of Tom's terrorist actions. In fact, considering he gave me the photo, I'd say it was probably before he even became involved with that group."

Halford slid the picture around and studied it. It was actually quite well executed—an outdoor shot of balanced black-and-white, no amateur fuzziness, the subject expertly framed. Mrs. Grayson looked like a dark-haired Bonnie Parker in her cotton print dress and white sandals. A slight wind caught at her hair and she smiled into the camera shyly, a pretty young woman pleased to be picnicking with her chosen beau. Only it wasn't cold chicken this wholesome American beauty offered on her checked tablecloth. Halford had to hand it to the two college students. If the story was true, their sense of irony was masterful.

He returned his attention to Ivory. "When did the article run?"

The editor shook his head. "It never did. An IRA attack wiped the story off the page. I finally just rewrote it as an editorial, some time later. I never used the photo."

"So what did you do with the photo?"

"Well, that's the damnedest thing. I would have thought I had given it back to Tom. I really don't remember. I suppose I could have filed it away in the archives somewhere. I simply can't recall."

"Who, besides yourself, would have known about it?"

Ivory shrugged and widened his eyes in dismay. "I don't know. It was so long ago. I suppose anyone at the paper could have known . . . of course, none of the reporters are here anymore, that's the nature of this beast. I really can't help you on that one, Chief Inspector."

"And the newspaper?"

Ivory looked at the old newspaper angled across the corner of his desk. "Well, I can't say positively that it came from the archives. It could have. Gale might know. Have you asked her?"

"Yes," Halford said shortly. "She thinks it's from the archives."

"She would know better than anyone. So, are you going to tell me where you found these?"

Halford picked up a manila envelope he had left reclining against his chair and carefully slid the photo inside it. "At Mrs. Grayson's," he said. "Among some of her papers."

This time Ivory's face reddened on its own accord. "Christ. Well, maybe these aren't from the archives then. Perhaps I gave Tom the photo after all. They could actually belong to Gale. It could be very innocent."

Halford stood and placed the envelope and newspaper under his arm.

"If that's the case, she did a lousy job of defending herself. No, Mr. Ivory, either Mrs. Grayson was stunned to find these two items in her house, or she is a consummate liar."

Halford opened the door to the cubicle. Once more Jill Ivory's confident voice flowed into the cramped space. "Of course," he said, "I'm convinced almost anyone can become a consummate liar if the stakes are high enough."

21

It was well past closing time and the streets dark before Maura located the peeled-paint offices of Keith Peter Duncan, Solicitor, situated on a busy narrow curve near Winchester's historic West Gate. Conveniently, the workaday stream of Winchester drivers had departed to their homes in the hinterlands, taking with them their horns and impatient expletives. So Maura puttered beside the pavement freely, squinting at the numbers over the doors, straining to read the names in the windows.

Finally she spied it, a skinny aperture between two huge "To Let" boards. A modest white sign, barely readable in the gloom, didn't so much announce as suggest that through the entrance and up the stairs, Mr.

Keith Peter Duncan was available for business. Maura glanced around, irritated. Despite her ingrained British belief that the only good tarmac is a blocked tarmac, the road was too curved for her to conscientiously stop the car. Grumbling, she settled for a vacant drive several hundred yards away. Her faith in the impending interview was little enough without the risk of returning Halford's car to him victimised and quaking.

As soon as Keith Peter Duncan answered the door, it was evident to Maura that he himself never parked a car—his exuberance drove him. He was a youngish man, in his early thirties, with broad shoulders and a crop of straw hair that seemed more suitable for a Mediterranean beach than a curtainless and cramped first-floor office. His teeth were big, which made his smile infectious, but in his more sombre moments his lips covered them clumsily so that he looked like a snarling horse.

He clapped his hands enthusiastically as he motioned Maura to a seat.

"Scotland Yard. I say." He beamed as he perched on the side of his desk. "Fabian, Whicher, the Brides in the Bath. I grew up on those stories, you know. My dad—he wanted to be a copper. Of course, he had bunions, couldn't have made it, I'm sure. Still, he loved the stories." He clapped his hands again and rubbed his knees excitedly. "So you're on the trail of a murderer. Damned good story I'll have at Christmas dinner."

"Yes, well, I have a few questions." Maura sat down in a rather stiff, rather tasteless gold faux-leather chair, and tried to ignore the squadron of model fighter jets suspended from the solicitor's ceiling. "You told our constable over the phone that a Miss Lisa Stillwell visited you around three months ago. Can you tell me about that?"

Duncan grinned and drummed his fingers beside him on the edge of the desk. "Hmmmm. Not much to tell. Pretty thing, young girl. Wanted an initial consultation. Sat right where you're sitting now."

"Right." Maura looked around her, noting that some of the planes had parachutists dangling from them. "Not many other places for her to sit, are there?"

Duncan laughed, obviously delighted with the Bill's wry display of humour. "It's not much, but it's money," he said happily. "So . . . Lisa Stillwell. What do you want to know?"

Maura tugged her notebook from her bag and clicked open her pen. "Well, for starters, why did she seek your professional help? It was for professional help, wasn't it?"

"Oh, yes, oh, yes," he assured her. "I remember her quite well. I'd never had anyone approach me for a child custody suit before, at least not under these circumstances."

Maura examined his cheery expression, wondering how anyone with his job could maintain such youth and enthusiasm. Above her head, several of the planes had teeth. On the whole of it, perhaps she preferred journalists after all.

"What circumstances?" she asked.

"A friend wanting a friend's child. Leastways, that's how she explained it. Said that she had a friend with a drug problem—heroin, prostituting for it, afraid of AIDS, the whole bit—and she wanted to know how she could get custody of this friend's child. Well, I said what about the friend's family, that if there were competent family members about, they would more than likely receive custody in the end if the courts had anything to say about it. This wasn't much to her liking— I could tell, because in the course of our conversation she shredded a tissue into bits all over my floor—but there you are. It was sound advice. She left. That's my tale."

Maura glanced up from her notes. "That's it? Did you refer her to anyone? Another solicitor, a social worker, a drug rehab center—anyone?"

Duncan's eyes, twinkling, widened as he shrugged. "Ummmm, no. She didn't ask. I told her to come back if she had any more questions or after she had decided what to do. I never heard from her again." He slid from his desk and landed with a little hop. "Frankly, I didn't believe the bit about the drugs. It was all that shredded tissue. A sure sign someone's lying."

Maura rolled her eyes and stood. "Thank you for your time, Mr. Duncan. By the way, you could have given us all this information over the phone. It would have saved me a trip."

The solicitor clapped his hands one last time and reached for the door to let Maura out. "But this is so much more thrilling, Sergeant. I can't wait to tell dear old Dad about my day at the office."

It was just past nine. The only light in Gale's bedroom was a soft glow in the hallway from Katie Pru's night-light, but she didn't need to see to slip a disk into her CD player and push the button. The guitars of the Notting Hillbillies nudged into the room playing "Railroad Worksong"—or "Take This Hammer," as she had always called it. The first time she had heard the album, it had mesmerised her: such a compelling fit, this coupling of Anglo soulfulness with the country songs of her childhood. She had loved this music growing up, associating it with the heavy heat of summer and the smell of a hot iron on clean clothes. As a teenager it had felt sweet to revel in the pretension of adult angst. Now the angst was no pretense, and her relationship with the music had changed. She no longer listened to it for effect: She listened to the music for peace, and it gave it to her, night after night, going on year after year.

Tonight, even as the music filled the room, she knew there would be neither peace nor sleep. Her mind was too busy raving for answers.

The poem Orrin left for Anise on their bed had been unpublished. It had been one of thirty-seven the police had confiscated among the piles of papers they deemed necessary for their investigation. When they had finally returned the poems a good seventeen months after Tom's death, satisfied that they neither held codes nor contained names, she had counted them carefully, to ensure that they were all there. They had been.

Yet today, when she finished her phone conversation with Anise and settled Katie Pru at the kitchen table with a cup of lukewarm tea and a piece of cake, she had re-counted the set of unpublished poems and found it one short. The "bothered blessings" poem was missing. She had no idea how long it had been gone.

Now she tossed in her bed, the sheets hot and the music more an irritant than a salve. She couldn't sleep and she couldn't explain.

The first time the phone rang, she hugged the covers around her head and lay still. After several rings it stopped, then started again, continuing on and on until, cursing, she struggled from the bed and ran downstairs.

It was Halford. "I want to come over and talk to you."

"You can't. I'm going to bed. I'm tired."

"I know. So am I." She believed him; his voice sounded utterly weary. "Listen, Mrs. Grayson, I have questions you must answer. I don't know how to tell you this any other way—you're quickly reaching the point where you don't have a choice anymore. I'll be there in about ten minutes."

The back of Gale's throat swelled, and her eyelids turned hot. "Okay. Ten minutes is fine."

"Thank you. If you feel you want someone there . . ."

"I don't."

She put the phone back in the cradle and crept into the study. The light from the desk lamp scarcely made a dent in the darkness. The pile of notes next to her computer looked alien to her—strange how another person's attempt at tidying could look so different from her own.

At one end of the study was an old cabinet where

she kept unfinished pieces of weaving and a few odd clothes. She opened it and removed a wrinkled cotton housecoat. Without bothering to brush off the loose bits of wool, she slipped it on.

Halford arrived in less than ten minutes. Gale met him at the door. Without a word, she led him into the study.

They sat where they had that afternoon, she on the love seat, he in the chair across from her. Between them was the trunk, bare this time, the niceties of hospitality not quite suitable to the occasion. Halford carefully laid a small tape recorder on the trunk. The light from the desk lamp barely reached them, and Gale thought how the two of them, seated on either side of the recorder, looked like parents peering through the dark at an ill-conceived child that would bring them both to grief.

Halford cleared his throat. "The tape recorder is for me only. It simply saves me the effort of taking notes. It cannot be used in evidence against you. If you prefer I not use it, fine."

He waited for her to reply, and when she didn't, he continued. "This is the way things stand. Someone broke into the newspaper offices but no one will say that anything has gone. The only place that looks as if it may have been disturbed is the archives. But you are the only person who has actually mentioned something was wrong with the archives, and it turns out that the paper you say is missing has ended up in your house." She nodded and he resumed. "At the same time, I have the murder of a young woman close to you. Now the two incidents may not have anything to do with one another, but the truth is there is at least one connection—you." He stopped. "Or rather Katie Pru."

She looked at him, startled. "What do you mean?"

Halford watched her for a second in the shadows and then rose to turn on another light. The tone of the room changed to a warm yellow.

"You say you wanted to read that particular article because someone in the village—Mrs. Barker—insinu-

ated that you might have known more about your husband's terrorist activities than you had let on."

"Yes, she did seem to insinuate that."

"Were you afraid of there being something in the
paper that would connect you to your husband's illegal
actions?"

"No. Of course not. I didn't know anything about
what Tom was doing. You know that. You certainly
investigated me well enough to know that I had no
idea."

"That's true enough. But your neighbours here
weren't privy to my information. Were you afraid of
something in the paper that would lead the village to
think that you were connected?"

In front of her the bank of black windows stared.
She had blinds for them, but she rarely pulled them
down, and now the night seemed to be ramming up
against the mullioned glass.

"I don't understand."

Halford sat motionless in the chair, his face unreadable. "When did you last see that photograph?"

"I don't know. It's been years. Probably not since I
left college."

"Did you know that Tom had given it to Orrin Ivory
to use as an illustration for an article Mr. Ivory was
writing?"

"No . . . I'm surprised it even still exists."

"So you didn't know that it might have been in the
newspaper archives for the past several years."

"No."

Halford fingered the buttons on the tape recorder,
but didn't switch it on. "Mr. Ivory confirms your story
about the picture, but it's based only on what Tom told
him. At this point, we actually have just your word as
to its origins."

"I'm telling the truth. It was all a joke, really. At the
time it just seemed like something fun and outrageous
to do."

Halford dropped his hand from the tape recorder.

"I can believe that," he said. "We all sometimes do stupid things without thinking of the long-term repercussions. And certainly, if what you say is true, you didn't know then what your husband's future would be. You couldn't have known then how damning that photo would look a decade later."

She peered at him, her nerves on edge. "Where is all this leading? What has this got to do with Katie Pru?"

"Mrs. Grayson, who could have put that photo and newspaper on your desk?"

"I don't know."

"When was the last time you looked through that stack of papers?"

"I don't remember."

"Who has visited you in this cottage since Saturday when Lisa was killed?"

She raised her eyes to his. "You ought to know better than to ask me, of all people, to do your detecting for you."

Halford's face erupted with fury as he abruptly swung himself out of the chair, slapping it sideways with such force that it tipped over.

"Oh, for God's sakes, Gale. What in the bloody hell do I have to say to get through to you? Either you took the goddamn newspaper and photo from the archives, or someone is doing a tidy little job of setting you up. Let me spell it out for you: Today we talked to a solicitor in Winchester who acknowledges that Lisa contacted him. The subject: child custody. We also have at least one person in Fetherbridge who confirms that shortly before she was murdered, Lisa said that she was trying to get Katie Pru away from you. Do I have to make it any plainer? Suddenly you have a dandy motive for murder, your alibi's been shit from the start, and you won't do a thing in God's bloody hell to help yourself."

Gale dragged her gaze from him to the chair. She heard it hit the floor again and again, each time louder until it sounded as one continuous roar in her ears. She blinked and stared up at him.

"Lisa said what?"

Halford set the chair upright and grasped its back. "She told people she wanted custody of Katie Pru. She discussed the matter with a solicitor. Now, what can you tell me?"

Gale closed her eyes. Behind her lids, the darkness broke into tiny specks. "Jeremy. Orrin. Helen." God, she was tired. "Anise. Editha Forrester. And Mrs. Simpson. They've all been here since Lisa's death."

She heard the click of the tape recorder. "Mrs. Simpson?" Halford asked.

"Jeremy's housekeeper. I left my watch at the vicarage. She returned it."

"When was this?"

"Yesterday. After I got back from the newspaper office with your sergeant."

"Did she come into the study?"

"I don't think so. I don't know. I went into the kitchen to get some of the dishes Jeremy brought over Wednesday night. I suppose she could have gone in then."

"And Editha Forrester?"

"She came over yesterday while Anise was here. Just to visit, she said, to see how I was getting along."

"Odd."

Gale breathed deeply. "Yes, it was. Anyway, I don't know if she came here into the study or not."

"Mrs. Ivory?"

"She was here about an hour. Said she would watch Katie Pru while I got some rest."

"And Mr. Ivory and Mr. Cart. Were they here any other time besides the meal?"

Gale shook her head. "Orrin drove Anise over, but he never got out of the car. Jeremy picked me up to go to the inquest, but I think he just waited in the foyer."

"You're not sure."

"No. Katie Pru left her coat upstairs. I went to get it. But I was only gone for a few seconds."

"Anyone else?"

"Not that I remember."

Halford sighed. "Gale, who is Mr. E.?"

For a full minute she sat still, fingering a snap on the crumpled cotton housecoat. In the silence, the tape recorder whirred. She should have been torn, crying in agony, but instead she felt a calm certainty. She stood and walked to the bookshelf. Standing on her toes, she reached up to the top shelf and pulled a book from a matching set. She placed it on the trunk beside the tape recorder.

"Page two hundred ten."

Halford flipped through the copy of Jane Austen's *Emma*, stopping about halfway through to bend it open. His eyes wandered down the page; his grip on the book tightened.

He read aloud. " 'A little upstart, vulgar being, with her Mr. E., and her *caro sposo*, and her resources, and all her airs of pert pretention and under-bred finery.' "

"It refers to the character of Mrs. Elton," Gale said tonelessly. " 'Mr. E.' was the term of endearment she used for her husband—the village vicar."

22

Angels in white sheets, angels in jeans, angels in grotty little pullovers with breakfast jam on their faces and nasal mucous creeping towards their mouths. Halford sat in the back pew and counted twelve of them, rather fewer than could fit on the head of a pin, but definitely more than Jeremy Cart and Helen Pane could effectively control. From what he gathered, the children were supposed to form a semicircle in front of the chancel. Instead, they cavorted across the nave like Brue-gelian revellers in training, pint-sized peasants who didn't care so much what they were celebrating, as long as they didn't have to leave the Saturday morning festival to toil amid the predictable terrain of their homes.

"All right, children. Look at me." Cart waved his

hands over his head and snapped his fingers. The celebrants danced on. "Mrs. Adams wishes to go over 'O, Come All Ye Faithful' one more time. Pay attention, please."

He might as well have been asking them to explain Dirac's theory of wave mechanics in Swahili for all they paid attention, Halford thought. Next to Cart, a small woman of about sixty, presumably Mrs. Adams, twittered and clapped her hands. "Now, children. Now, children," she chirruped. Miss Pane wrestled with a protocherub, trying to keep the child's leaping body pinned to the earth long enough to fit her with a pair of white wings.

Maura tapped Halford on the shoulder.

"Does he know you're here?" she whispered, sliding next to him.

"No. He's been busy. I thought I'd give him a minute or two. Did you see Roan?"

"Uh-huh. Gave him both Jill's and the solicitor's statements on Lisa's custody claim, such as they were. He's put a team on it to see if Lisa went any further with it, although he wasn't horribly optimistic."

"Neither am I. Any more on alibis?"

"An employee at the petrol station in Eastleigh confirms that both Orrin and Jill Ivory stopped there sometime around 9:50 Saturday morning. And they've got the receipt to prove it. Their story seems to check out."

One of the angels, a boy of about seven dressed in what looked like a gold-spackled pillowcase, took revenge on his tormentors by ascending the pulpit and flapping his arms. Cart reacted ecclesiastically: The vicar hiked up after the miscreant and yanked him to the netherworld by his skirt.

"What about Timbrook?"

"Nothing," Maura answered. "No one has said they saw or talked to him until Miss Pane's call at around 11:45."

"And Miss Pane?"

"Ben Hossett, the bookseller, saw her go into her shop at approximately nine."

"But can anyone testify that she remained there?"

The boy in the pillowcase broke into a dead run for the south door, but stopped short when he saw the detectives. All the children, prepared to cheer him on, promptly fell silent. Soon the entire space rang with spent noise.

Halford rose to his feet. "Ah, Mr. Cart. We were waiting for you to take a breather. When you're ready, we need to have a word with you."

Cart glanced at the children, now openly gawking, and trudged up the aisle.

"Now's a good time," he muttered, passing through the south door. "If you were Caiaphas's bleedin' multitude with swords and staves, now would be a good time."

The pace to the vicarage was brisk; the crisp morning air echoed in the crunch of grass beneath their feet. A book slapped against Halford's coat pocket. In his hand, its weight was insubstantial; hitting him as it was, it seemed to tease him with the possibility of being everything or nothing.

When they reached the vicarage gates, Cart turned to walk through them crablike. "What you witnessed in there isn't typical," he said, trying to focus his eyes on both detectives and, Halford noted with satisfaction, looking inept. "I think the children, like everyone else, have been impacted by Lisa's murder."

"Of course they would be," Halford said. "I'm a little surprised that under the circumstances they're expected to participate in a pageant."

Cart stopped and motioned Maura in front of him.

"At times I think you're quite right, Chief Inspector, and then I tell myself the quicker we return to normality the better off we'll be. After all, we can't just cancel Christmas. Besides, the idea was to use the pageant as a rite of passage—to put Tom Grayson's spectre behind us. That seems rather foolish now, I suppose."

Halford didn't comment. As they approached the vicarage door, Cart slapped him on the back. "Well, Mr. Halford. Hopefully you'll wrap this up quickly and the pageant can serve a double purpose."

Inside the study, Halford was careful to select the sturdier of the two chairs situated in front of the desk, allowing Maura the more fragile one. Cart fussed about the room, adjusting the blinds and offering the detectives water before finally settling down behind his desk.

"So," he said with a wide smile, "how can I help you?"

Halford pulled a copy of *Emma* from his coat. He slid it across the desk to Cart.

"Recognise it?" he asked.

Cart stared at the book for a few seconds but didn't touch it. "Austen. I've never read her."

"This came from Lisa's room," Halford said. "We found it last night. There is a character named Elton, the village vicar. His wife calls him 'Mr. E.' " The priest continued to gaze at the unopened book. "Lisa did us a great favour by mooning over you in the margins. Of course, to your credit she protests that in many ways you're not at all like Miss Austen's Mr. E.—he, evidently, was a bit of a prig. Whereas you, in Lisa's estimation, embody all the better qualities of genteel manhood."

Cart continued to stare at the book's cover. Finally he shook his head and spoke.

"I'm Mr. E. Imagine that."

From somewhere deep in the house a telephone rang, but the study desk phone was silent. Slowly, as if the ring had given permission, Cart opened the volume and turned the first few pages. Then he started flipping rapidly, stopping now and again to read and frown at the circular handwriting.

"It's so childish," he murmured. "It's like reading a schoolgirl's letters."

Halford let several pages pass beneath Cart's fingertips. "Was it childish when you were together?"

At first it wasn't apparent that Cart heard. Then he gently closed the book and steepled his hands in front of his nose. After a long pause he sighed.

"I can't describe it, really." His voice sounded hoarse. "Rather like being with Alice, I suppose, except Lisa didn't go running off in search of the White Rabbit. Or perhaps she did." He looked at Maura, but her face was sphinxlike. Cart passed his hand over the book. "That's why I find this so surprising. It's so adolescent. I've always thought of her as different—young and wise. I suppose I felt we were soul mates in a way. Young in years, wise in spirit."

Halford crossed his legs and gave his trouser cuff a sharp tug. "So what went wrong?"

"Nothing." Cart focused intently on Halford. "I didn't kill her. Maybe I loved her—I really don't know." He gave a weak smile. "Surely that exonerates me. No one kills because they don't know if they're in love or not."

"Depends on how deeply a person is committed to equivocalness."

"I know you're joking, Mr. Halford. You know I am not a violent man. I'm a minister of God."

"Ah."

Halford stood and walked to the window. Four swallows, startled from a tree in the vicarage garden, flittered from the branches and rolled through the cold sky like muscled puffs of smoke.

He kept his back to Cart. "Be a little more specific about your relationship with Lisa."

"Well, I guess it was rather nebulous. We enjoyed each other's company, I suppose. We talked a lot."

Maura asked: "Were you physically involved?"

Cart's voice unmistakably pitched higher. "We never had intercourse, if that's what you mean. That was obvious from the inquest."

"We didn't ask if you had engaged in sexual intercourse," said Halford. "We want to know if you were physically involved."

"Well, to a degree, I suppose—yes, there was some physical involvement."

"What about financial?"

Halford turned around. Cart picked up a pencil and began rolling it between his palms.

"Gale couldn't pay much. I helped out."

"As a favour to Mrs. Grayson or as a favour to Lisa? Did Mrs. Grayson know you supplemented her payments?"

"No, I don't think so. Not unless Lisa told her."

Halford returned to the desk. A deep blue bowl sat near its edge. Idly, he reached in and sifted its contents through his fingers.

"Were your payments to her regular?"

Cart twisted sideways in his seat. "Well, no. Just when I thought she needed something. Sometimes I gave her money and sometimes gifts and things."

"Such as?"

"Oh, well, a few pieces of furniture—a wardrobe, her bed. And then just other things—clothes and the like."

"Rather philanthropic of you. Considering your position, I would have thought buying a young woman a bed and clothes a somewhat dubious pastime. The good people of Fetherbridge must be a particularly affluent bunch for you to consider someone like Lisa a suitable charity."

"It wasn't church money, it was money that my father left me. I was careful to make sure it didn't even come from my stipend here. But you're right, it didn't look proper. And I told Lisa many times that we had to keep quiet about it. She agreed."

"It was worth her while," Maura said mildly.

"Now, wait." He rapped the pencil on the book. "I want the two of you to understand this. When I arrived at Fetherbridge, Lisa was one of the first people I met. She struck me as such a waif—no mother, father depressed, brother immature and not much of a companion. I thought she was such a child. But the more I got to know her, the more I realised I was wrong. And things just developed."

"So why not be open about it? A little more prudence with your gifts and why should the village have objected?"

Cart frowned. "You don't know very much about villages, Chief Inspector. I'm twelve years Lisa's senior and an outsider, for all my family's ties to Fetherbridge. As the bachelor clergy, I could have taken up with any one of the unmarried women around and probably gotten a lot of happy clucks from my parishioners. But not with Lisa."

Halford raised an eyebrow. "Being everyone's child, the village orphan was off limits."

"If you like. And there was another thing. My relationship to Gale. People here try to hide their feelings about her, but they can't always do it. She's an outsider and she brought death. My parishioners are willing to overlook my connection to her because it was Tom's folly, not mine, but their tolerance is limited. I can't afford to tweak their noses too often."

From the bottom of the blue bowl, Halford's rummaging brought a ring—battered and green and big enough only for a child. He slipped the tip of his little finger into it and lifted it out. "So how many of the unmarried women around have you taken up with?"

"Is it important?"

"I won't know until you tell me."

"I'm not a celibate. I don't consider myself promiscuous, but yes, there are women."

"Lisa was different."

"Well, yes, of course. I've tried to explain it to you—I realise I'm not doing a very good job, but she was someone special. She was . . . I don't know . . . Listen. I'm just a parish priest. I'm a helluva lot better at sorting out other people's feelings than my own. I can't be any more explicit with you than I have been. I liked Lisa. I cared about her. I didn't kill her."

"How much did you know about her plans to get custody of Katie Pru?"

"None. If she had such plans, she never discussed them with me."

"This is not the first time you've heard of them."

"No. The first time I heard of them was yesterday. You angered the wrong person when you went after Editha, Mr. Halford. She was at the Stillwells' yesterday telling everyone what she knew and how you reacted when she tried to pass it on." With the pencil eraser, Cart traced over the word "Jane" on the book's dust jacket. "So I'm Lisa's secret paramour. Am I in trouble?"

Halford palmed the ring and slipped the copy of *Emma* into his inside breast pocket.

"We'll let you know, Mr. Cart." He opened his hand. "By the way, do you know whose ring this is?"

Cart shrugged. "I always figured it was Katie Pru's. She's the only little girl who spends any amount of time around here."

Halford considered Cart for a moment. The ring made a delicate *ping* as he dropped it back into the bowl.

"Doubtful," he said. "Her mother would probably consider it a choking hazard. But let's assume you're right. What kind of a man, Mr. Cart, would find something that belongs to a child and not return it? For that matter, what kind of a priest takes on a pet parishioner and feeds it through the bars?"

"Mama, where my crayons?"

Katie Pru dropped to her hands and knees and poked her head under the child-sized table in the corner of the living room where she usually played. The basket of crayons was always there—it didn't matter where she left them, they always magically appeared on the table the next time she needed them. With her elbow, she pushed aside the chair and peered into the shadows on the floor. Dust, a scrap of paper, part of a doll's bottle—no basket, no crayons.

"Mama." She was getting angry. "Where my crayons?"

"You must have put them somewhere, sweetheart."

Her mother crouched in front of the spinning wheel, feeding it the hairy rolls that Katie Pru batted around the room like balloons. Usually, she enjoyed watching her mother spin. Now, however, she was getting mad. She wanted to draw a picture for Mrs. Barker, a picture of cookies, and her crayons were gone. She pushed herself up from the floor and stomped over to her mother.

"Mama! My crayons!"

Her mother put her hand on the wheel and looked at Katie Pru with an unhappy face.

"I don't know where they are, honey. Where did you have them last?"

Katie Pru stomped. "There. On my table."

"Well, I surely haven't touched them. Sit quietly on the floor there and think about where you put them. The spinning wheel will help you think. It helps me. And when you think about it, I'll bet you'll find them."

Her foot began pumping again, and the hairy rolls turned to nothing in her mother's hand. Katie Pru plopped down on the floor by her mother's feet and crossed her arms.

"The table," she said. Her throat grew hot and her nose tingled. "My crayons were on the table."

"Well," said her mother. "Go look. Real good this time. You'll find them."

Katie Pru stayed where she was. She wasn't going near the table again.

Ivory opened the door slowly and walked into Jill's room. She had wrapped herself head to foot in a blue thermal blanket so that she looked like a swaddled baby, a blond curl damp on her forehead and the fair

skin over her eyelids nearly transparent. Ivory studied
her. It was hard to tell in that blanket, and the midmorning light was dim . . . but there, he could see now
the movement of her chest as she breathed. He bent
over and unhooked a corner of blanket that had folded
against her cheek. To his relief, she sighed and clasped
the blanket tighter without waking.

He knew it was an obsession with him, but even
after eighteen years he was afraid his daughter would
die in her sleep. A few months before he and Anise
had married, the body of a nine-month-old had been
found in a car park in Preston. He covered the case for
the paper, followed the police down a dingy hall where
ancient watermarks stained the plaster, and stood by
the kitchen wall while a weeping mother said that she
found the baby dead in its pram and hadn't known
what to do. It was the first time he had heard of Sudden
Infant Death Syndrome. Thinking back, he supposed
his fear was as much a reaction to the words' grotesque
poetry as to the overwhelming clutch of fatherhood,
but over the years his terror had neither left nor less-
ened. Even now, he tiptoed into his daughter's room
once a night to watch her breathe. He didn't know
whether or not she knew. Anise did, of course, but Anise never criticised. She only tightened her legs around
his when he returned to bed.

Outside, an engine idled to a stop. Flipping back a
curtain, Ivory saw Timbrook slide out of his battered
white Leyland minibus and start up the walk. Glancing
once more at Jill, Ivory hurried from the room, anxious
to reach the door before the bell rang.

He swung it open just as Timbrook lifted his hand.
"Hullo, Timbrook. Didn't mean to startle you, but I've
a sleeping daughter upstairs. Come in."

"No need. I've got the pane ready to fix the door at
the newspaper. Since I've agreed to play the handy-
man, I was wondering if I could get a key."

"I wasn't expecting you until next week."

"No time like the present." The bite of tea was fresh

on the artist's breath. "I picked up the glass yesterday from London—I told you it would be damned hard to find that colour, but there was a shop over on the East End that stocked something very close to it—anyway, I cut it last night to get it out of the way. I've got that Christ-forsaken church window to get installed and I don't want any distractions."

"Well, yes, I'm sure, but couldn't we make it tomorrow night? Anise went to the Stillwells' and I hate to leave Jill. . . ."

"For God's sakes, Orrin, Jill's all grown up now, remember? I really am on a tight schedule."

With resignation, Ivory locked the door to his house and climbed into the Leyland's passenger seat. Within a few minutes, Timbrook pulled into the newspaper's rear car park. The minibus was assaulted with white clouds of dirt and the clatter of gravel against hubcaps.

"You'd think with the amount of rain we get . . ." Timbrook's voice trailed off as he opened the door. "That reminds me. Damnedest thing happened this morning."

Several stones skittered under Ivory's feet as he trudged to the back of the vehicle. "What's that?"

Timbrook unhitched the rear door and threw back a beige tarpaulin, uncovering a cardboard box of tools. Dragging the box forward, he pointed to another length of canvas wadded into the far corner.

"That tarpaulin's been missing. I noticed it gone yesterday, but I decided I had left it delivering a panel in Bath last Thursday. Then it turns up this morning."

"Perhaps someone borrowed it."

Timbrook looked peevish. "They could have asked."

Ivory laughed as he walked to the building's back door and slid a key into the lock. "Come on, Timbrook. You're not exactly approachable. It's that artistic disdain of yours. You send small children cowering behind their mothers' skirts."

"Can't see what I do to deserve that."

Ivory pressed his body against the brick facade to let Timbrook enter. An imprint of dust bloomed on his sleeve. "You work at it, my friend," he said, following Timbrook into the building. "I'd say you work at it very hard."

23

The recreation centre looked like an old schoolhouse evacuated in the middle of lunch. Erasures and scribbled notes smeared the marker boards, a detailed map of Fetherbridge and its environs hung on the blue cinder wall directly over a desk littered with wads of grease-proof sandwich paper. Only one aspect of the room was disturbingly unschoollike—the photographs of Lisa's twisted body tacked on a long bulletin board in the far corner of the centre.

Turning his attention away from the gruesome photos, Halford noticed on one of the tables a framed photograph of a plump, blond-haired child. As he picked it up, Roan came up behind him.

"My daughter," he said.

"Pretty. How old is she?"

"Ten. She lives in Manchester with her mother."

Halford raised his eyebrows. "Do you see her often?"

Roan shrugged. "What do you think? How often do you see your family?" He glanced at Halford's left hand. "But then you're not married, are you?"

"Used to be. It didn't work out."

" 'It didn't work out.' Quaint phrase, that." Roan's jaw jutted out. "It'll soon be three years since we separated—but I guess you can figure that out." He inclined his head towards his daughter's picture. "Nasty business, divorce."

Halford looked again at the photograph. The girl had Roan's high forehead and his heavy eyes, but there was a vibrant joy, an innocuous sense of mischief in them that had either eluded or deserted the father. The picture focused on the child's face, but enough of the background was visible to make out the top of a carousel. A fair or carnival, Halford thought, the obligatory father-daughter visit that they both probably dreaded and yearned for in equal measure. Three years ago. Dear God. There was no end to victims in a murder case.

"I'm sorry, Richard," he said finally. "It's the job."

"Yeah, that's right. It's just the bloody job."

Roan took the picture from Halford and set it on the table, adjusting it to face the phone. "So, you didn't arrest the good vicar?"

"No," Halford said, glad to leave the mine field behind. "Don't have the evidence for it yet. What do you think?"

"No, we don't have the evidence. I was just looking at the girl's bank accounts. Forty-five pounds deposited every Friday like clockwork. Mrs. Grayson reportedly paid her sixty-five pounds a week, so that fits. Twenty, thirty pounds here and there—nothing particularly unusual. If she was blackmailing Cart, she wasn't depositing the lolly anywhere we've found so far."

Halford rested against the side of the desk. "But then I wouldn't say money was particularly important to Lisa, would you? She was evidently willing to accept gifts—the furniture, the clothes. And that, of course, can be just as threatening to the blackmail victim as actual cash."

"So what did she have on him? Sex? The vicar certainly isn't one to keep his cock in his cassock. Fondling minor parishioners on the side, you think?"

Halford frowned and scratched his neck. "I don't know. . . . "

"Maybe that's why she was still a virgin—Cart got his kicks in other ways."

Halford pushed himself further onto the desk, careful not to disturb the picture of Roan's daughter. "If there was blackmail, I think it was over something besides sex. Cart seems rather unconcerned about his carnal habits. Unless it was indeed pederasty, I doubt he'd give a damn what anyone knew."

Roan, Halford noted, remained standing beside the table, scowling, arms crossed. Christ, he thought, hauling himself to his feet, I'd forgotten. This is *his* area, *his* space. He's probably urinated on the damned thing.

Through the centre's less than adequate door, Halford could hear Maura muttering before she actually entered the room.

"—And not only that," she said, flailing her handbag through the air, "God save me from old ladies with nothing to do. The retirement age needs to be upped to ninety-five or death, whichever comes first, just to keep the old biddies involved in something productive rather than sitting around drinking tea and plotting ways to undermine the free world."

"Pleasant little natter with one of our local matrons?" Halford inquired.

Maura thumped her handbag onto a desk. "It seems that Mrs. Adams, that sweet frippery thing conducting choral lessons this morning, ran over to Miss Forrester's cottage to tell the old busybody how we hauled that nice young vicar *out of the church*, mind you, practically in handcuffs, right in front of all those dear children. And why were we pestering the vicar anyway, with that *Mrs. Grayson* still roaming the street, pinching the arms of all the young women in the village to test their meatiness? Damn!" Maura wrinkled her nose. "I smell coffee."

Halford patted her shoulder. "I'll get it. You rest."

He was aware of Roan's scrutiny as he handed Maura her coffee. Dragging out a chair, Halford sat down and returned the stare.

Roan didn't drop his eyes. "Mrs. Grayson. Now that's a promising suspect."

Halford nodded. "In some ways."

"Right. In some ways. Like motive, means, and opportunity."

Halford bit his bottom lip. "All right. Let's break it down. Motive—Lisa's custody claim on Katie Pru. Legally unsound, and with the exception of one rather oblique interview with a solicitor, not much more than hearsay."

"But who's to say Mrs. Grayson wasn't one to hear her say it? From what I understand, the lady isn't too stable. Someone threatens your child, what's a mother to do?"

Halford shook his head. "Without evidence, it's useless supposition. So let's look at the means. Maybe the murderer was riding a moped, maybe a bicycle, maybe even a motorbike. The stick? We don't know a damn thing about the stick. The murder weapon? The scarf was at hand. Opportunity? I'd damn well say half this village had opportunity. It's not as if they were all convened on the church grounds for the annual sheep sacrificing ceremony. We've no more on her than we do several other people, and a good deal less than on others."

No reply, no agreement. Even Maura trained her eyes on her flaking nail polish.

Finally Roan walked to a coat stand in the corner of the room and retrieved his jacket.

"You may be fighting the tide, Daniel," he said quietly. "You do have experience with tides, don't you? They're strong, they go the way they want, and they fucking well sweep you along whether you like it or not." He shrugged into his jacket. "And one more thing: We all have leftover traumas, Chief Inspector. I suggest, like the rest of us, you get the hell over yours."

The door slammed behind him. Halford stared at the closed door for several seconds.

"What this investigation lacks is hard evidence," he said, turning to Maura.

She drained her coffee cup and crumpled it, the Styrofoam splitting into angles. "Well," she sighed, "we'll get hard evidence. You can count on it."

The phone rang and Maura reached across the table for the nearest receiver.

"Sergeant Ramsden," she said.

She listened a second, nodding, a smirk tugging at her mouth. "Just a moment, please, Mr. Cart. Chief Inspector Halford is here."

Halford grimaced as he took the phone. "Yes, Mr. Cart."

"Listen, Mr. Halford. Ever since you left this morning, I've been thinking about Lisa, wracking my brain to come up with something that could help."

I bet you have, Halford thought. *Honestly, Inspector, before you send me to the gallows, I seem to remember my dear late wife mentioning . . .*

"A letter," Cart said. "There was this letter . . ."

Halford rolled his eyes and, dragging a notepad across the table, flipped it open to a clean page. "There's always a letter, Mr. Cart."

"No, honestly. About three weeks ago. Lisa was at the vicarage. She had come for some guidance. She wanted to discuss ethics."

"Go on."

"She wanted to know if I thought people of posi-

tion—no, that's wrong, I think she said people of reputation—if people of reputation ought to be held to
higher standards than the rest of us. I said that God
holds us all to the same standards, it's up to us to strive
to achieve them. That answer wasn't to her liking. She
said she wanted my actual opinion, not a church position paper."

"Nice response."

"Yes, see, I said she was wise. Anyway, in the
course of the conversation, she said she felt such people
should have to constantly justify their positions of authority. A free society could not exist otherwise. She
said she had a letter she wanted explained to her."

"Did she have the letter with her? Did you see it?"

"No, she just wanted to discuss the basic issue."

"Did she say what the letter concerned?"

"Well, I figure it was about someone behaving in
less than acceptable ways. Otherwise, why the question?"

"She didn't say who it was about?"

"No."

"Where did she get it?"

"I don't know."

"Did she say where she kept it?"

"No."

"Did she say if she had talked to anyone else about
it?"

"No."

"Anything else you can tell me?"

"No. I think that's about it. Does it help any?"

You git, Halford thought. "It's not much, Mr. Cart,
but thank you for the effort."

He hung up the phone and rubbed his eyes with
his fingertips.

"When this case is finished," he said, "I may bloody
well become a Baptist."

For several seconds, he stared at the floor, breathing
deeply. "I guess, when it comes down to it, we're for-
tunate we're not all murdered before we reach thirty."

He forced a smile. "Get Roan back here. The Stillwell house needs going over again."

It wasn't until he was four feet from it that Grissom registered the oddity of a group of villagers spending a Saturday evening milling around the front of a bookshop. He politely wove his way past shoulders and elbows, looking for a sale table or a queue for an autographing author, but there was neither, just a posse of men and women in coats and hats, hands jammed into their pockets, expressions of anger and discontent on their faces.

Jacob Barker, huge, hulking, stood by the bookshop entrance. Grissom nodded his head in greeting and tried to gently push past him. Barker brought his hand from his pocket and prodded the reporter lightly on the chest.

"Bobby!" He grabbed Grissom by the arm and swung him around to face the bulk of the group. "Hey, it's Bobby Grissom here. He works at the *Inquisitor*. Maybe he's the one we should be talkin' with."

A few unintelligible sounds broke from the crowd, but for the most part the men simply looked at Grissom, sizing him up as they would a prospective son-in-law—or, Grissom thought wryly, a horse they suspected was going to cost them a perfectly good bullet.

"Well, mates," Grissom said brightly, burying his hands in his pockets in an attempt to match the milieu, "what's going on?"

Clive Kingston stood a head taller than the rest of the men, and his wife June nearly reached his jaw. In the dispersed light from the shop, both their faces looked honed. Kingston's voice held a sharp edge.

"It's this bloody murder, Bobby," he said. "Nothin's being done about it. The police come and ask questions, they leave. No arrests, not even a sign of an arrest. I can't let my daughter out alone. She's scared. My wife here doesn't sleep at night. It's not acceptable, Bobby."

"You're absolutely right. I agree." Grissom raised his hands in a sign of supplication. "It's unfortunate. But the police are working on it."

"That's what we want to know," Kingston continued. "Jacob says he ran into Nate Baylor last night. Baylor wouldn't say a thing about the murder—only that the police were 'workin' on it.' Well, dammit, Bobby, what's that to tell a man with a family? It's been a week, and they can't even say if it's a drifter or someone we know. Hell, man, am I going to reach the point where I tell my wife and daughter not to open the door, no matter who it is? We need something more."

The crowd became more vocal now, and Grissom, realising that he ought to be considering the story possibilities in the encounter, instead grew aware of a dampness on the back of his neck. He drew his hand across his upper lip.

"I can't argue with any of what you've said. Why don't you try going to the police, tell them your concerns?"

"You're missing the point!" June Kingston stepped slightly forward, her angled face livid in the light. "The police won't tell us anything. What we want to know is, what the hell have they told you?"

Someone pressed against Grissom's arm, and he glanced over to see Ben Hossett standing beside him. Grissom didn't know many people in Fetherbridge well, but he knew Hossett better than most. He was, after all, a man of letters, a bookseller. Grissom, who hadn't been aware of how tense he had grown, felt his shoulders sag and a deep breath involuntarily leave his lungs. He had support. Thank God.

"Well," Grissom started. "They keep us informed . . ."

"What in the hell have they told you?"

"They've told us what there is to tell," Grissom said. "The inquiries are continuing. They're eliminating suspects. Nothing definite yet, but it'll come together. I mean, they've got Scotland Yard on it, for God's sakes."

"Scotland Yard." Someone in the back of the crowd, a woman hidden by the press of bodies, fairly spit out the words. "Bloody lot of good they've done before."

"Yeah, Bobby," Jacob Barker said. "We want to know specifics."

"Look, lads, I'm not in the position—"

Laying one hand on Grissom's shoulder, Ben Hossett raised his arm. "I think I know what Bobby here is trying to tell us."

Grissom was grateful to hand the reins over to a native. Stepping back, he leaned against the shop window and gave Hossett centre stage.

"If you'll listen to him, you'll see that Bobby is telling us what we already know." Something in Hossett's tone sounded alien, and Grissom felt his belly contract in alarm. "The cops aren't talking, and the local newspaper is cooperating with them. Listen, mates. Lisa was one of ours. We—not the police, not the *Inquisitor*—we have lost her."

Next to Grissom, Jacob Barker nodded wildly. "She was like a daughter, she was. She was like my own."

"She was our own," Hossett continued. "When it's your own that's taken, when it's your own that's hurt, you can't always sit back and let others do the job. Maybe the police are trying their best. Maybe Bobby here is working his hardest—I know the man and if he says he is, then I believe him. But something's not right about this investigation, and I think it's time we looked into it."

He paused. A wave of nausea passed over Grissom.

Hossett continued. "Let me tell you gentlemen something. I read the national papers every day. Not a word on Lisa's murder. Gale Grayson's childminder is found strangled and not a goddamned word. How likely do you honestly think that is? We all remember Tom, don't we? Remember the press camped out in the fields, caravans of them, television crews, even bloody CNN. Beamed all over the fuckin' world, but now, three years later, *nothing*. I say something's wrong. I say there's been a cover-up."

The emotional pitch had soared and the crowd was clapping now, a few stomping their feet. Grissom felt dizzy, his face slick with sweat.

"And I'll tell you what else." Jacob Barker's fleshy face wobbled with conviction. "There's the little girl to consider. She's innocent of all this. She needs to be in a home that's decent."

The mass broke into a swell of assent. Barker's head bobbed as he began shouting, "That's right! That's right!"

"Wait!" Grissom yelled. "Wait!"

But his words were lost in the din. Hossett raised his voice. "I say we organise, right now. For starters, I say we call the national papers and tell them to get their bloody reporters down here to find out what the hell is going on. I say we demand that the police take *action*."

Fists in the air. Towers of them. Even Clive Kingston's angry face was blocked by arms pounding the night sky. Grissom sagged against the shop window. *Shit*.

Katie Pru was scared. She stared down at the construction of chairs and blankets she had built earlier in the day, a house for her and Space Lucy the Dinosaur to hide in and read books. She had made Space Lucy a bed from towels and the striped pillow from the love seat in her mother's study. Space Lucy had fallen asleep during *Where the Wild Things Are*, and Katie Pru had tucked him in gently, pulling the towel up around his neck so that he wouldn't get cold napping on the floor.

She looked at the towel tossed aside on the stack of books and at the empty striped pillow. It was her bedtime, and she had come to get Space Lucy so that he could sleep with her, safe and snug in her bed beside the Mickey Mouse night-light. She always slept with Space Lucy; she liked to watch his face in the yellow of the night-light until the bright spots of his eyes danced in front of her and she grew too tired to hold him anymore. She would fall asleep knowing that in the morning he would be there, along with her mother's good-morning kiss and a tight, warm hug.

She could hear her mother in the back of the house, out in the little room behind the kitchen where she washed clothes. Tugging a blanket from the roof of her house, Katie Pru wrapped it around her waist and ran to find her.

Her mother was putting the clothes into the washer, shaking each one out before she threw it into the big, dark hole. Katie Pru pulled the blanket tightly around herself.

"Mama," she said. "Did you wash Space Lucy?"

"No, sweetie. Is he dirty?"

"You got him?"

Her mother took Katie Pru's favourite nightgown, a white soft one with tiny pink flowers, shook it, and threw it into the hole.

"No, baby."

Katie Pru's eyes filled with tears and her chest hurt. "I can't find him."

Her mother stopped reaching for clothes and knelt down beside her.

"Come on, now, honey. I know it's been a busy day. It's been a busy couple of days. But there's no reason to cry. Space Lucy is somewhere. We'll just have to look for him, that's all. Wait until I finish with the clothes, then we'll look together. Okay?"

Katie Pru nodded.

"And if for some reason we can't find him, don't worry, he'll turn up. You've lost him before and he's always turned up. You can sleep with your bunny tonight."

Katie Pru wept. They weren't going to find him. He wasn't lost.

24

Helen was wretched, suffering under a bone-jangling cold that left her bitchy. She flailed her legs beneath the milky white duvet in an attempt to find a warm spot, but all her permutations met with shivers. She hunched as close as she could to Timbrook, flattening her belly against his back and wedging her leg between his, but he proved too somnolent to do anything but grunt and retreat. Exasperated, Helen threw the covers off him, picked up a glass of water from the upended crate next to the bed, and doused him with it.

Timbrook awoke sputtering. "What in the bloody hell was that for?" He yanked the duvet across his chest and rubbed his wet skin furiously. "What in the hell has gotten into you?"

Helen crawled to the bottom of the bed, opened a cardboard box, and removed two pairs of Timbrook's socks.

"It's one thing to invite women to spend the night with you, Timbrook," she said, pulling on a thick woolly sock. "It's another thing entirely to leave them to freeze their tits off in this sodding little treehouse you call a loft."

Timbrook yawned and, flipping away the wet covers, rolled onto his side. "It's the windows, luv. They let the light in—they do damn all to keep out the cold."

"Lovely." Helen jammed a second sock on over the first. "From now on, we do this at my place."

"How presumptuous of you." He reacted to her kick by reaching over and pinching her toes. "Joking, my love." He sat up, his upper body bare to the cold. "What time is it, anyway?"

A strand of moonlight trailed through the room, and Helen gingerly felt her way through a bramble of jewellery on the floor for her watch. Angling it toward the window, she rotated the face several times before she could discern the small flecks that passed for hands.

"Half five," she said. "I suppose it's time I got up anyway. I have a busy day. After church I'm having dinner with Gale. I told her I'd bring the salad, and I haven't put it together yet."

Timbrook dropped onto his back and drummed his fingers on his chest. "I thought we might pack a basket and motor down to the coast for lunch."

Helen laughed. "Have you gone nuts? It might, just possibly, reach forty degrees today. I'm not packing a basket to go anywhere."

"All right then. Why don't we go to London, do some museum hopping?"

Helen intentionally let her jaw drop. "To turn the question around, what the hell's gotten into you?"

Timbrook surveyed the ceiling. "I dunno. Too much of this village the past few days, I guess. I want to get away." He turned onto his side again and grasped her leg. "Let's do it, Helen. Put a sign on your shop door and let's go somewhere for a week. The continent, or Dublin. You've been wanting to go to Dublin to look for some of those old rags of yours. It could be a busman's holiday."

"You've gone barmy." Yanking her leg free, Helen curled onto her back, releasing the tension. "It's the Christmas season, remember? Parties, celebrations, big Christmas dinners with very wealthy people wearing extremely original 'rags,' as you call them, from a quaint little shop in Fetherbridge. And then comes New Year's. I'll make a whopping lot of money in the next few weeks."

"Fine." Timbrook sat up and whipped the blankets around his shoulders. "You stay and work. I'm going on holiday."

He scooted awkwardly across the bed and grabbed the ladder that led to the cottage floor. Before he could start his descent, Helen slid her arm around his thigh and pulled him back onto the mattress.

"You're not going anywhere, not down that ladder, and not on holiday. You have a church window to install, or did you forget?" She looked at him sternly, then reached up and tousled his hair. "Honestly, Timbrook, would you please tell me what's going on?"

"Don't go to Gale's."

"What? Of course I'm going to Gale's."

"Really, Helen, don't."

"Get out of it."

In the darkness, his movements were unanticipated and swift. Before she could register his action, his hands slammed against her collarbone, knocking her into the pillows and pinning her down by the shoulders.

"I don't think you heard me, Helen. Don't go to Gale's."

She stared at him, fighting for control. The thin moonlight didn't fully reach the loft, but she could see the curve of his cheek and hear his shallow breathing. She reached up and grasped one finger on his left hand.

"I don't know what you're talking about," she said evenly, "but you're hurting me. Get off me, please."

Instantly his grip loosened, and he moved away. In the dark she saw his hands slide up his face and his fists grab at his hair.

"I'm sorry. I'm sorry." He crossed his legs and bunched a corner of the duvet in his lap. "I don't think you know what you're doing, Helen. I don't think you realise what's going on."

She switched on a lamp and flooded the small loft space with a harsh light. Both of them winced at the brightness. Timbrook hauled the duvet once more to his shoulders and turned his head. Helen waited for the momentary flash in her eyes to subside before rummaging through the sheets for her street clothes.

"I think," she said slowly, "that what's going on is a great deal of stress and not a little amount of fear and sorrow. We're both a bit too wound up to be engaged in much of anything right now. It's time I left."

Timbrook handed her a shoe. "I mean you don't know what's going on about Gale."

"I know what you mean."

"Really?" His voice grew slightly louder. "You're damned cool about it."

"Look. Gale has been a good friend to me, more patient than I ever deserved, listening to me drivel on about everything from money to you. I'm not going to turn my back on her because some frigid old woman in a girdle latches onto a ridiculous idea."

"Maybe it's not a ridiculous idea."

"Oh, come on, Timbrook! Gale killed Lisa over Katie Pru? It's absurd." She glared at him. He looked so idiotic with the duvet wrapped around him, his hands gripping the corners to his too-white chest like a spinster conjuring up marauders in the night. She pounded the shoe on the mattress. "You know what this is about as well as I do. This gossip about Gale has damn all to do with Lisa. It's about Tom. And some bizarre notion of communal shame that I can't begin to comprehend."

"That's what Gale would have you believe."

"I don't understand." She shook her head at him, incredulous. "You *hate* this place. You hate the people in it. You were the one who taught me what they're like. 'Small-minded little hypocrites with provincial brains and provincial lives'—remember? So now Gale's the enemy and all these good honest folk are the salt of the earth? God, Timbrook, alert me when you've made up your mind."

She ripped his socks off her feet and threw them against the wall. Timbrook watched her without moving.

"Why are you so angry?"

"Why?" She practically yelled the word. "You are accusing my friend of murder, and you don't know why I'm so angry."

"I didn't say a word about Lisa's murder."

"You did."

"No, luv, I didn't." He tossed her stockings to her. "I would say that you've been taking the gossip a bit more seriously than you'd like to admit."

A small ache started in the back of her head. "I'm going home. I don't want to talk about it anymore."

"Seems to be a common reaction for you these days, doesn't it. 'Don't talk to me, I don't want to think about it.' Generally, when I feel that way, it's because thinking about it is exactly what I need to do."

She stopped threading her foot into the toe of her stocking. "What are you getting at?"

He examined the wall above her head, as if his socks had left splatters on the plaster. Sighing, he closed his eyes.

"Did you know that Gale and I had an affair?"

She returned her attention to her stockings. "Of course. Everybody did."

"Did you know why it ended?"

"Given your actions tonight, I can damn well guess."

"You'd be wrong. It ended because Lisa told Gale that she and I were involved. She was exaggerating, of course, but nonetheless Gale was furious. She came over here in a fit, saying that she was damned if she was going to indulge in an occasional screw with a man who felt it his right to 'canoodle' everything in sight. I got angry, I'll admit it—after all, I was wrongly accused. But when I tried to correct her, she went on the rampage about Lisa, about how infuriating she was and how livid it made her to have to leave Katie Pru with Lisa. I tried to pin her down to specifics, to calm the atmosphere if nothing else, but she was in a rage." He stopped and appeared to study her foot, still half in the stocking toe. "If someone had come to me an hour later and told me Lisa had been strangled, I wouldn't have been surprised."

Helen swallowed, aware that she was trembling. "Lovers' spat. People lose control all the time where sex is involved."

"How much more so, darling, when a child is involved."

Helen focused on the black shine of the nylon as it slid up her leg.

"You're fucked, Timbrook." Her voice was thick. "You're fucked to hell."

She hastily pulled on what clothes she could find and stumbled down the ladder. Grabbing her coat from the sofa, she slipped on her shoes and ran from the cottage.

Katie Pru was a rigid, wound muscle in her mother's bed, taut even in sleep. Gently, Gale touched the child's jaw, feeling the teeth grind beneath her fingers. The night before had been ungodly. Katie Pru had been wide-eyed with panic as they searched room after room for the stuffed dinosaur, finding nothing. The hunt eventually turned into a screaming fit, with Katie Pru refusing to go to bed alone and Gale cuddling her in a rocking chair. Finally she had drifted into this restless state. She had remained that way through the night with her mother fighting to cradle and calm her.

Gale cupped her daughter's chin, hoping to stop the grinding that had continued intermittently since midnight. The small mouth relaxed and Gale pulled the covers around the child's neck, tucking them under her small shoulders. She studied the delicate face, so perfect in the pearled morning light. Her chest constricted. The old joke about children looking like angels when they slept seemed painfully sadistic. She realised how much of her image of Katie Pru derived from the life in her black, vibrant eyes. With them closed . . . It wasn't a thought she was going to explore. It wasn't an emotion she was going to let in.

She straightened the blankets over Katie Pru and, replacing her presence with a pillow against the sleeping child's back, carefully slid from the bed. The bedside clock read 9:45 A.M. Given the trauma of the night before, there was no telling what time Katie Pru would awake, so Gale put on her slippers, pulled a woolen shirt over her nightgown, and padded downstairs.

The cottage was in less than perfect shape, the hunt for Space Lucy having taken its toll. Gale took the ground coffee from the fridge and piled three scoops into the filter. They had turned the cottage upside down looking for the damn toy—beneath furniture, under cushions, even behind the grate of the fireplace. The truth was, with Katie Pru's love of hideaways, it could be anywhere. Gale filled the pot with enough water for eight cups. If she couldn't find that dinosaur, it promised to be another long day.

With the coffee brewing, she tromped to the laundry room, a rickety addition that at one time had served as a buttery. The construction was so flimsy she had no doubt that within the decade it would have to be demolished, but for now it served as an adequate enough base for the rumble and perambulations of her washer/dryer.

Despite the cold morning air, the old buttery held the aroma of clean clothes. Gale retrieved a splint basket from the corner and, grabbing a handful of hangers, hoisted it to the top of the machine.

Her first thought was that she was back home in the States, and instead of the dryer, she had mistakenly popped open the door to the washing machine. Then, with dawning comprehension, she realised that this was the U.K., that her washing and drying were done in the same machine, and that the drum before her was black, dry, and totally empty.

Stupidly, she jerked the basket from the top of the machine and stared into it, willing the clothes to appear. Then she slammed and reopened the washer door, stooping to peer into the cooled metal interior. Gone. Their clothes were gone.

With her hand on her chest, she backed into the kitchen.

The coffee brewed on the counter; its rich, warm smell filled the room. Upstairs, a thin voice called out.

"Mama! Mama!"

Gale bolted up the stairs. Katie Pru sat straight up in bed, her eyes wide with fear.

"Space Lucy, Mama. You didn't find Space Lucy."

Gale darted to her dresser and pulled out the first clothes to touch her fingers. Then, scooping up her daughter and the blankets as one, she ran with her into the other bedroom.

"I know, baby. I know. Hurry, now, we got to get dressed."

Gale's hands were shaking as she pulled on her clothes. Taking deep breaths, she tried to calm herself as she guided Katie Pru's arms into a sweater.

It was too much. Katie Pru broke into a wail.

"Mama! Mama!"

There was no time to put on the child's pants.

Bundling her daughter into the blanket, Gale picked her up and raced to the car.

It was a little amazing to Halford that overnight the Fetherbridge High Street had gone from a quaint yet narrowly dictated stretch of county propriety to this lovely, winsome Christmas lane. Wreaths had appeared on shop doors, ribboned garlands were draped around windows and beneath the occasional eaves. He walked down the street feeling almost chipper.

The distance from the police station to the church-yard was meagre, and Halford was standing at the lych-gate in about four minutes. Sunday morning matins at St. Martin's Church was due to start in five, and the congregation, like a strange centipede of the faithful, bumped one by one through the south portal to receive their benedictive cheerios from Jeremy Cart.

With small churches throughout England having to go on circuits with reduced services and part-time parsons, Halford had to credit Cart with one thing: St. Martin's was evidently alive and thriving. Perhaps it was the spiritual aftermath of the Stillwell murder, or maybe just the imprinted call of the Christmas season, but as far as he could tell the whole of Fetherbridge and probably a respectable portion of the county was here.

A spartan door on the south transept creaked open. Cart, dressed in his Sunday vestments, carefully avoided his parishioners filing through the main entrance and flapped over to Halford.

"All right," he said, looking at his watch. "The service starts in three minutes. What can I do for you?"

"I appreciate your time constraints, Mr. Cart. This should take only a moment." Halford intentionally let several seconds tick by. "We searched the Stillwell house thoroughly yesterday. No letter, no note, nothing that seemed even tangentially along the lines you described. On the basis of your admission, and from the looks of her effects, Lisa was an uncomplicated young woman who had apparently captured the fancy of a man who in turn liked to lavish her with gifts."

"Oh, for God's sake! We've been over this, Halford. It was all very innocuous. I don't know what to tell you about the letter. I never saw it—she just told me about it."

"Did she? You didn't mention it during either of our interviews. Yet you say that this was one time when she came to you as a parishioner, not as a girlfriend." Halford knew Cart would wince at the word, and he did. "You knew she was dissatisfied with your answer. Given the weight of such a meeting, wouldn't you have thought seriously about her dilemma and tried to aid her more substantively after you had put more thought into it? Or, Mr. Cart, did you dismiss it as one of Lisa's childish little bouts, you of all people who thought her so wise?"

Cart was clearly flustered. He whipped around to face the church, and then turned back to Halford. A fine sweat beaded his upper lip.

"People come to me with problems all the time. I can't do much. I do what I can—console them, read them the Scripture, call a colleague if the problem is truly serious. Most of the time, they're just piddling little things that people need to talk out. You wouldn't believe what I have to listen to sometimes. I put Lisa's question in that category—no, it wasn't even that. It was an academic postulate. It was a sixth-form debate topic. I forgot about it as soon as she walked out the door."

The door of the church clanged shut, leaving the churchyard empty. Cart stared at Halford, sweat glistening on his brow and cheeks.

"Go to your parishioners, Mr. Cart," Halford said quietly. "And God help them."

Cart's mouth opened as if he meant to respond. Instead he spun around and ran back through the transept door.

The return trek to the police station wasn't nearly

as enjoyable as the earlier walk. The sun had made a rare appearance. It wasn't enough to quell the cold, but then he had begun to think that Fetherbridge's particular frigidity wasn't entirely generated by nature. In the brighter light, it was easy to see that the wreaths on the doors were fake, the ribbons creased and wrinkled from previous years' use. Ah, well, Halford thought, I ought to be the last person surprised to find things aren't always as they seem.

As soon as he entered the police station he smelled porridge. In the back of the room, huddled around Baylor's desk, sat the constable, Maura, and Gale Grayson. On top of the desk perched a clump of moving sweaters.

"Hullo," Maura said. "Glad you're back. We've got a wrinkle."

She set a bowl of porridge on the desk. A pudgy hand fumbled through the mound of clothes and reached for the spoon.

"Now be careful, darling," Maura warned. "I'm sure it cooled off some during the trip from The Proper Pale, but it might be a little hot all the same." She lifted Katie Pru's arm and slipped a droopy sleeve up to the elbow. Then she held the spoon out. The child grabbed it awkwardly and slapped it into the bowl.

Maura looked up at Halford. "They've had a bit of a scare, and they left the house before the child could eat. Or dress, for that matter. Baylor and I rummaged around and found these old things. Not a fashion statement, but it takes tops for warmth, right, K.P.?"

Katie Pru nodded, porridge dripping from the corners of her mouth. Halford turned to Gale.

"Perhaps we could talk over here and let Katie Pru finish her breakfast in peace." He dragged two chairs to the far side of the room, hoping it was at least out of the child's attention range if not actually out of earshot.

Gale glanced at her daughter. "It's all right, Gale," Halford said. "She's in good hands. Baylor, I understand, used to be a child, and Maura there has had all kinds of experience raising a husband." His attempt at humour elicited no response. He patted the back of the chair. "Come on, now. It's all right. Sit here and tell me what happened."

Reluctantly, Gale Grayson crossed the room. It was evident she had dressed hurriedly—under a man's ragged shirt her short nightgown bloused over a pair of baggy, torn jeans. She wore no socks; her bare feet were swallowed by a pair of black high-heeled shoes. Mascara smudged brown circles beneath her eyes, and as she sat, he noticed slits of blood on her dried and cracked knuckles.

He moved his chair so that he was scarcely a foot away from her. "Tell me what happened."

She breathed deeply twice and buckled her hands together. "Yesterday afternoon, I don't know exactly when, sometime after lunch, Katie Pru couldn't find her crayons. I didn't think anything about it—we lose things around the cottage all the time and they always turn up sooner or later. Then last night, she couldn't find her favourite toy. We turned the place upside down and never found it. Katie Pru pitched a fit—it was actually more than a fit, it was very bad—but still, I just figured she had hidden it somewhere and forgotten."

She pressed her hands, still fisted in an inverted clasp, to her stomach. "You'd think by now I'd have learned to listen to that child. She's nearly always right. Then this morning I went to get the laundry from the dryer. No laundry. Every bit of it gone. I didn't wait to see if whoever took it was waiting around. I got Katie Pru and came here."

"When did you see the clothes last?"

"Last night, around ten or so. I checked to make sure the machine was working right. Sometimes it messes up, but everything was fine."

"And what time did you find them missing this morning?"

"A little before ten."

"But you say the crayons and toy were missing yesterday, well before the clothes."

She folded her arms across her chest, grasping her elbows. "That's right." She began shaking. "But he couldn't have been in the house the whole time. Katie Pru and I searched everywhere. He just couldn't have been there."

Halford stood, took off his coat, and draped it over her shoulders. She clutched it closed beneath her chin.

"Do you think he was there?" she asked. "Do you think he was there the whole night?" All signs of defiance, anger, sorrow were gone; now there was only terror.

"No. Whoever it was may have come back during the night, but they weren't there the entire time. And if you want my opinion, Gale, there was no intent to harm you physically. You're being harassed."

She shook her head. "Why?"

"Well, think about it. Who is the first person blamed when a village believes the spirits have turned on it? How about the person they understand the least?"

She paled, and for a second he was afraid she was going to either faint or be sick. He placed his hand on her head to push it between her knees, but she straightened and brushed him away.

"I'm okay." She glanced at Katie Pru who was gleefully whacking Baylor on the torso with her spoon. "I'll be fine."

"All right, then." He stood up. "I say we get a crew to your cottage and let's go over the place. I'd like you to come with us. Katie Pru can stay here with Maura, if you don't mind."

"I don't know." She regarded the scene at the other end of the room and then sighed, running a hand through her unkempt hair. "Okay." She turned to Maura. "I don't want you to let anyone else take care of her. If something happens and you have to leave, bring her to me at the cottage."

Maura nodded. "Of course. And don't worry. Katie Pru and I have become mates."

The drive to the cottage was short. With Baylor at the wheel of Gale's black Mini, they passed houses empty of churchgoers. Before they came to a complete stop in front of the Grayson cottage, however, Halford leaped from the vehicle and strode towards the garden gate.

The withered bushes and low shrubs in the garden were now uprooted and thrown in clotted mounds against the cottage wall. Black paint covered the mullioned windows that fronted the study. Papers blew across the grounds like leaves. Gale's computer, which had been on her desk bounded by columns of books and years of research, lay smashed in the corner of the garden. The cracked lip of a dark green crock protruded from its broken screen.

Halford heard a step behind him and then a wretched whisper. "Oh no, oh no, oh no."

The front door was partially opened, its face pointing away from the midmorning sun. Nevertheless, the writing was easy to read. Either someone's a bit shaky with American history, Halford thought bitterly, or he has a fucking grand sense of irony. Directly across the door's wooden middle, in thick red letters, were sprayed the words *Yankee Dixie Bitch*.

25

However tidy and quiet the Grayson cottage used to be, it now rang with chaos. Katie Pru's wildly coloured drawings, which had lined the hallway, lay smashed on the floor, the pictures ripped with glass fragments from their own frames. In their place, a huge, painted penis spewed scarlet semen across the foyer's white-washed wall. It served as an obscene directional sign pointing the way to where the full force of the attack was evident.

Halford stood in the middle of the front room, taking it in. The simple white curtains lay in tatters on the floor; the cushions and pillows from the chairs disgorged their stuffing in fluffy mounds against the hearth. The cityscape that had hung over the mantel dangled, punctured, from the knob of a ladder-back chair. Indications of a sharp object were everywhere. The pew—hard, austere, forgiving—was pocked with deep, sharp gouges. The quilts and rugs were savagely lacerated. Strips of red-and-brown fabric, the late remnants of Gale's ascetic folksiness, were strewn throughout the room. With the shredded plugs of cotton wadding adhering to his pants and the rough surface of the cottage walls, the scene reminded Halford of a slaughterhouse for rabbits.

On the other side of the room, Baylor lifted a wooden altar stand off the smashed pieces of a spinning wheel.

"God Almighty," he breathed. "Who in the name of . . . ?"

The acrid smell of burning coffee seeped into the room, and Halford rushed into the kitchen. The hot liquid was splattered across the walls, the glass carafe left to scald on the appliance itself. Quickly, he unplugged the unit from its socket. Splayed along the length of the counter were the dumped contents from the cupboard. Perishables—eggs, bananas, tomatoes—lay smashed in front of the open refrigerator, congealing into a unappetizing aspic on the floor. The bronze statuette of the child with the thorn in its foot, which had stood on the front room mantel, had been flung against the far wall, leaving a blackened pockmark in the plaster. Halford walked to the windows and gently tapped his knuckle on what remained of the seventeenth-century bottle glass quarrels. He wagered someone had used the child's metal head to bust nearly all of them.

He left the kitchen and hiked upstairs. Here nothing looked disturbed. Well, he thought, calculating quickly, if Gale was accurate with her story, the vandals had at most forty-five minutes. More than likely, they waited until the church service started at ten-thirty, betting that few people in the immediate vicinity would be at home. That would have given them no more than twenty minutes. Time enough to do a helluva lot of damage, but restrictive enough to force them to pick and choose.

That there was more than one vandal he had no doubt. The garden was too completely ravaged, the house too minutely destroyed. He descended the stairs, stopping at the bottom to examine the red writing that ran up six of the risers. The words were less legible than on the front door—the letters jumped from riser to riser and the paint dripped and spattered across the planks—but he thought they read "Killer Whore."

He made only a cursory check of the study, confirming no one still crouched beneath the furniture. The desk lay toppled on its side, the drawers flung to the four corners. Here, as outside, papers coated the floor, and the bookcases were almost empty, the books themselves tossed hither and yon.

He left the room and exited the house. Gale Grayson stood on the walk, her face pale and stricken. She still wore his suit coat. She had slipped her arms into the sleeves, and as she surveyed the garden, she repeatedly pumped her fists into the pockets.

"You can come in now," Halford said. "I ask that you not touch anything." He waited until she joined him at the door. "The good news is the upstairs is undisturbed. But you really need to prepare yourself for the rest."

She entered the house silently, giving the obscene artwork on the wall only a glance before moving on. Surveying the front room and kitchen quickly, she came to a stop in the savaged study, standing motionless by the love seat. Her eyes moved from one object to another.

"So tell me, Chief Inspector." Her voice sounded dead. "You still think no one else was in this house all night?"

"No, I really don't. Watching you from outside, waiting for you to leave, perhaps." He stooped and retrieved a piece of notebook paper from the floor. The pencil drawing on it appeared to be a map of the Channel, with dotted lines scurrying back and forth between the English and French coasts. An unlikely configuration for ferry routes, he thought. More likely a map of the final sea battles of that Confederate ship she was researching—the C.S.S. *Alabama*.

He placed the paper on the love seat. "I need to ask you something," he said. "Were there any papers here, anything that you were working on, that might have been a threat to someone, or perhaps something that someone might want?"

"Yeah. The Civil War is a hot button in these parts." She picked up a Biro from the floor and twirled it between her fingers. She eyed him defiantly. "And as far as anything incriminating I might have, I dare say your men took it away during your last scavenger hunt here. If there ever was anything. If any of it mattered."

Halford studied the narrow face, the planes along the cheeks deeper and darker than they had appeared a scant five days ago. Her voice no longer lilted as it had during the early stages of their last interview; nor did it tighten with defensiveness.

"You can't stay here tonight," he said. "Is there someone else you and Katie Pru can spend a few days with?"

She looked him full in the face. "What do you think, Mr. Halford? Can you suggest anyone?"

He didn't do her the dishonor of glancing away. "No. No, I can't. I'll have Maura fix you up a room at The Proper Pale."

From the front room, Baylor's cry broke into the study's intensity. "Sir! You need to see this!"

Halford turned away, leaving Gale alone among the debris, and hurried into the front room. At first Halford thought the constable was directing his attention to the massive loom whose mangled yarn and bent heddles now looked like the favorite plaything of an overly ornery, overly large cat. But as he picked his way through the litter, Halford saw that the constable was holding a bundle of ropes and sticks tangled with strings of pink wool.

"It's a back strap loom." Gale spoke from the hall-way. "I never use it. I made it more as a diversion for Katie Pru."

"Yes, but look, sir, look." Baylor held the loom out to Halford. "Look at the stick."

He loosened a foot-long stick from the bundle, its surface sanded smooth, the ends blunt.

Halford spun around to Gale, silently cursing Baylor for drawing attention to the loom in her presence. She stood directly behind him now, staring at the loom, her face quizzical.

"What about that loom, Gale?" Halford asked urgently. "You made it by hand. Did you make any others?"

"Others?" she echoed. "No. There aren't any others."

He stared at her with mounting anger. Damn Baylor for his indiscretions. And damn her for that even, circumspect face. He couldn't tell if she was lying or not.

Anise was still in her Sunday dress when she spied Editha Forrester through the parlour window huffing her way up the Ivorys' front steps. Jill and her father had wanted to stay at church a bit after the service to visit with some of the younger members still reeling from Lisa's death, but Anise was tired. She was in the process of unpinning her hair for an early nap when Editha, bound in her ubiquitous black wool coat, hammered at the door.

"I know it's a bad time, dear, but I really must talk to you." She stepped into the house despite Anise's reluctance to yield the terrain. "In other circumstances, I would be going to the vicar's wife with my concerns, but there you are. No vicar's wife. But you, the wife of our local editor, I'm sure you can advise me."

Editha was in the parlour and nestled into the cushions of one of the white upholstered chairs before Anise could answer. "Well, of course, Editha," she said deferentially as she took her seat on the sofa. "Anything I can do."

The elderly woman launched ahead. "It's Brian Stillwell. Several of us have been discussing it and we all agree. The boy needs help. It would be my preference that he be taken out of that house for a while, but short of that, he at least needs some counselling. Edgar won't cooperate. We think you should talk to him."

Anise raised her palms in a gesture of helplessness. "I can't do anything, Editha. What do you expect me to do? Edgar's his father. It should be his decision."

Editha's pulpy face grew harder. "You know that's not acceptable, Anise. You saw Brian at the memorial service. You've seen him at his house. That boy is not functioning at the moment—if the truth be known, he probably hasn't been functioning since his mother left, but nobody's taken the time to do anything about it. Well, that was wrong of us, but it's not too late." She inhaled to her bodice's full extent and peered at Anise sternly. "As a community we have a responsibility to each other. We have to take care of that child."

Unsure what to say, Anise gazed anxiously around the room. Her eyes settled on the photograph of Jill and Lisa on the bric-a-brac shelf.

"He's not a child," she said softly. "He's an adult. He can make his own decisions."

Editha crossed her arms. "He's not able to make decisions right now, Anise. Maybe in the future, but not right now. He can't even dress himself, or use the toilet properly, for that matter. Surely you can see that he needs help."

Anise continued to gaze at the photograph, the girls' features growing fuzzy. "It's been a hard time for everyone," she murmured. "Gale told me that and she's right. We should give Brian more time."

Editha snorted. "That woman. I could pinch with a pair of tweezers what that woman knows about families, about responsibilities. Not even a decent mother herself. Keeps that child practically under lock and key.

I want to know what she's hiding. I want to know why she doesn't trust anyone."

Anise blinked. The girls swirled back into focus. "I should think that would be easy enough to answer. Her husband betrayed her."

Editha stood and clasped her plump hands over her belly. "Well, be that as it may, sometimes a caring community has to take matters into its own hands. Sometimes a caring community has to act in some rather unpleasant ways if it's going to take care of its own."

A button on Editha's black coat had broken in half, the remainder seemingly clinging by memory to its place. Anise stared at it abstractedly as she answered.

"Yes, you're right, Editha," she said. "Very unpleasant. Sometimes we just have to."

Their two suitcases, still packed, rested where Baylor had dropped them on the single bed in The Proper Pale's meanest room. Cuddled next to them was Katie Pru, who had fallen asleep in her coat, the hood serving to pad the skimpy inn pillow doubled beneath her head.

Gale sat on the bed next to her daughter. Halford had said it plainly enough: She was quickly running out of options. The immediacy of that statement hit her when she returned from her demolished cottage to the police station to get Katie Pru. Baylor had stalked across the room and, with his back to Gale, whispered something to Sergeant Ramsden. The other woman's expression deepened into a frown. As Gale helped Katie Pru into the coat retrieved from the cottage, she overheard the sergeant talking with Halford at the station door.

"Why haven't you arrested her?"

Halford's voice was stern. "On what evidence, Maura?"

"The stick, for God's sake."

"Not enough."

A pause. When Ramsden spoke again, her words were edged with frustration.

"You are going to put her under surveillance, aren't you?"

Halford kept his voice low.

"I hardly think she's going to do a bunk with a three-year-old in tow, do you?"

"Well, God knows you're not doing anything to stop her."

"Sergeant." It had been a warning. Ramsden had shut up and stormed from the station.

In the curtained sobriety of the inn room, Gale tilted Katie Pru's feet and checked her shoelaces. They were tied so tightly over two pairs of socks that she had whined from the time Gale tugged the shoes on at the police station until she fell asleep on the bed. Gale gently squeezed the shoes and repositioned Katie Pru's feet so that she could rest comfortably. Well, she thought, it appeared Chief Inspector Halford could be right and wrong simultaneously. He was right to say she was running out of options. He was wrong to think she wouldn't do anything about it.

Her watch read twelve-thirty. She stretched across the bed for the phone.

Helen answered in one ring.

"My God, where are you? I went to your cottage for lunch and the police were everywhere. All they would tell me was that you and Katie Pru were fine. What the hell happened?"

"Someone had a field day hacking the place up with a butcher knife and spraying obscenities on the walls."

"Oh, my God. When? Where were you when it happened?"

"I can't go into it now, Helen, but listen—I need to talk to you. Could you meet me at your shop, in about five minutes?"

Helen hesitated. "Well, of course. What about?"

"Please. I'll tell you when I get there."

Gale rang off and sat for a second studying her sleeping child. There were no choices, not anymore. She pulled on her coat and, hoisting Katie Pru onto her shoulder, slipped from the room. The rear door exit was on her immediate left, and glancing down the deserted hallway, she undid the metal latch bolting the door shut.

The Transitional Woman was over the road and several shops up from The Proper Pale. Trying not to jostle Katie Pru, Gale dashed to the other side of the High Street and down an alley until she came to the rear of the line of shops. Gravel crunched under her feet as she made her way past one shop to another, finally finding the neatly painted green door that signalled Helen's business.

She rapped twice. Helen answered immediately.

"What is this, Gale?" Helen pulled her inside and shut the door behind her. "What's going on? Here. Lay Katie Pru on these clothes. They ought to be soft enough."

Gale lowered her daughter onto a large mound of heavy wool garments piled against the workroom wall and pulled a discarded skirt to drape over her. Rising, she turned to Helen.

"You have to help me. I can't explain now, but I need a plane ticket. I have to get Katie Pru out of here. I can send her to my grandmother's, but I need to get a ticket."

"I don't understand. Call the airlines. Why are you coming to me?"

"Helen." Gale grabbed the other woman's hands. "Listen to me. I have to get my daughter out of here. I don't want there to be any foul-ups, any last-minute problems that would prevent that."

"What she's trying to tell you, Helen, is that the police don't want her to leave the country and if she tries to buy a ticket in her own name, she's afraid she'll be stopped."

Timbrook stood at the entrance to the shop proper, casually holding in his hand the curtain dividing the two areas. "Furthermore, she has to realise that by helping her, you would become an accomplice. Great friend, I'd say."

Gale increased her grip on Helen's hands. "It's not for me, Helen. You saw my cottage. It's not safe here.

I've got to get my daughter to the States. Please. I need your help."

Helen looked dazed. Her head trembled. "You don't need my help. Go to the authorities. Go to Jeremy."

Gale fought the panic rising in her throat. "I can't go to the authorities. They might take her. And Jeremy . . . there are reasons I can't trust him now. Believe me, Helen. I've no one else to ask."

Timbrook didn't move from his position by the shop door entrance. "This isn't your problem, Helen. Don't get involved. Besides, she's not been arrested. She can leave the country if she wants to. Unless, of course, an arrest is imminent. Her lover."

Helen looked at her lover, then back to Gale. "He's right, Gale. As long as you haven't done anything wrong, you don't have to worry. . . ."

Katie Pru rustled in her sleep. Gale dropped Helen's hands. "If you believe that, you're an idiot."

They were standing about five feet from the back door, which was shut but not locked. Moving backwards to Katie Pru, Gale lifted her in her arms.

"I have one more question, Helen. The loom I made for Lisa. The one Lisa and Jill made belts on. Where is it?"

Helen wrinkled her forehead. "Why?"

"Just tell me where it is. The last time I saw it, it was here, in the workroom. Where is it now?"

"I don't know. Still here somewhere, I guess." She rubbed her chin and looked around the room. "Let me think. . . ."

In the far corner of the room was a table, all but its metal legs hidden under a bundle of light-coloured clothes. Helen approached it, her brow still furrowed. "I remember we worked on it here," she said. "I don't suppose I've been near this table since the summer."

"Helen." Timbrook straightened suddenly and strode towards her. "Helen, wait!"

As he spoke, Helen began tossing off the clothes. Layer after layer, yellow, lime green, pink fabric flew into the air and settled on the floor beside the table.

Cautiously, with her sleeping daughter in her arms, Gale crept towards Helen, trying to get a clear view of the table without blocking her access to the back door.

The last piece of clothing floated to the floor. Helen pointed at the table and shrugged.

"Well, there it is. As we left it, still strung with that unearthly lavender Lisa thought would be the hot fashion last year."

Gale stopped two feet from the table, staring at the back strap loom, now a tangled mess. A two-inch band of purple weave lay strung between two sticks the width of a finger. A bright yellow nylon scarf, used to secure the loom around the weaver's waist, was wound around the lower stick. A shuttle, still wrapped with lavender yarn, was jammed between the threads. Gale's mouth felt cottony. "It's not all there, Helen."

"What do you mean?"

"The heddle rod. The stick we tied the string heddles to in order to separate the threads. It's gone."

"Huh. How odd. I wonder where it could have gotten to."

"You say you haven't touched the loom since the summer?"

Helen lifted the loom from the table. The lavender weaving swayed awkwardly from the remaining sticks. "I forgot it was here. I never used it, you know. Just the girls."

"Just Lisa and Jill? Did anyone else know about it?"

Timbrook eyed Gale suspiciously. "What are you asking?"

Gale ignored him. "Who else knew about the loom, Helen? Who else could have known that it was here?"

Helen looked at her blankly. "I can't think of anyone else, Gale. Just you and me and the girls." She gave a strained laugh. "Unless someone went rummaging around when I wasn't looking . . ."

Gale whirled around and headed for the door, but before she could reach it, Timbrook darted past her. He put his shoulder against the door and looked at her, his hand on the knob.

His voice was low, threatening. "Where do you think you're going?"

Katie Pru's head fell off Gale's shoulder. Gale shifted and propped the child back into place.

"If neither of you will help me, then I'll find someone else. My daughter's not going to suffer because of this."

"Really." Timbrook's hand was on her arm. He squeezed, his fingers pinching her flesh. "So tell me, Gale, who are you choosing to suffer in her place?"

Gale's eyes met his. "What are you talking about?"

His features were twisted, the light in his eyes cruel. "Not your child, is that right, Gale? Not your sweet innocent child. Never mind about anyone else." His grip tightened. "Isn't that what terrorists believe? Sacrifice everyone else? Tom may not have included you in his glory, but he sure as hell indoctrinated you well. But let me clue you in. You can't shift the blame this time. Your daughter will have to suffer like all the other children of murderers and terrorists. It's called divine retribution, luv. It's called the sins of the mothers."

A sharp pain shot through Gale's arm. She wrenched herself free from Timbrook's grasp.

"Get out of my way," she said. "You're a pathetic son of a bitch, and I don't have time to fool with you."

Timbrook's laugh was pitiless. He gave the door a kick and stood aside.

"Fine. Go see if you can find anyone else to help you. But let me warn you, Gale. Everyone in the village knows that Lisa's murderer used a stick to wreck her bicycle. I'm assuming you think that loom has something to do with it. But it won't be here when the police come looking for it. I promise you that. So I suggest you take your little morsel of knowledge and use it very carefully."

He swung the door open wide. With Katie Pru stirring, Gale shuddered as he slammed it shut behind them.

26

The phone booth stood at the west end of Fether-bridge, at the start of a row of private houses that originally buffered the manorial grounds from the High Street shops. Gale stopped in front of the phone, with Katie Pru awake and grousing at her feet, and fed in a coin.

As the ring sounded, she realised she hadn't considered what to do if Orrin answered. She was about to hang up when Anise picked up the phone.

"Anise. This is Gale. Is Jill there? I need some help with Katie Pru, and I was hoping I could talk her into it."

Anise didn't disguise her worry. "Oh, Gale. Orrin just learned of your cottage—he left to go there. I'm so

sorry. Would you like to bring Katie Pru here for the
afternoon?"

"No, I'm staying in a room at The Proper Pale, and
I've already put her down for a nap." Gale hurried past
the lie. "I was hoping Jill could come here and watch
her. I have a few things to settle over at the police station."

"Oh, all right." Anise's usual chipper sympathy was
constrained. "Jill has been so down lately, and Katie
Pru is such joy. Maybe it would be good for her. Let
me see."

If Anise sounded anxious, her daughter sounded
bored.

"Yes, Gale?" Jill said.

"Listen to me, Jill. I told your mother I needed you
to look after Katie Pru for me, but that's not true. We
need to talk. I want you to meet me."

Wariness sprang into the girl's words. "What for?"

"I'll tell you when I see you. Please, it's important."

Gale held the phone in silence for several long seconds. Finally Jill answered.

"All right," she said. "I'll meet you in the church."

Gale caught her breath. "Under no circumstances."

"Sorry, Gale. If you want to talk to me, it will have
to be there. Services are over, no one will disturb us.
I'll see you in fifteen minutes."

The dial tone pealed in Gale's ear. Shaking, she
hung up the phone.

The church was at the other end of the High Street.
To reach it she would have to march through town,
past the village shops in hopes that they were all empty
and bolted against Sunday custom, past The Proper
Pale with its bivouacked police, past the shiny glass
door of the police station itself; or she could hurry Katie
Pru along the alleys and back roads, aiming for speed
and obscurity.

She briefly considered going to the police. For most
of her life she had trusted them, raised with the smiling
cutouts of community helpers taped on her classroom

walls. But she was a grown-up now. She had heard Baylor's whispers and seen Maura's fury. She recalled Halford's grim face, as stark as the dim clicking of her choices, like dominoes, falling one by one.

Tom, too, had run out of options. He, too, had scurried along the back lanes, making for the church and what he must have seen as a last cry for redemption. The difference between them was their child. The difference was she had no intention of self-sacrifice.

She took Katie Pru by the arm and hauled her to her feet. "All right, baby. Let's go. We've got a ways to walk." Crossing over the High Street, they kept to the lanes and began snaking their way east.

Katie Pru jabbered next to her, something about Sergeant Ramsden and a game, but Gale wasn't listening. She had to be precise.

"How long, Mama? I'm tired."

"Not much further. Be quiet, now."

"Let's sing. You start."

"No, baby. Mama's gotta think."

"Mama's gotta sing. You start."

"No, Katie Pru. Not now."

"Now! I'm tired."

Gale dropped to her knees and pulled Katie Pru to her. She cupped her daughter's chin in her hand. "Look. I can't right now. I want to, but I can't, and you need to understand that. You have to, *have to,* walk quietly. Sing to yourself, but don't talk to me until I say it's all right."

The black eyes widened, but the child quieted. Gale released her grip and stood. She had to stay in control.

They continued in silence. Gale cast glances at the fields and interconnecting tracks, concerned they pass through unnoticed. For a Sunday afternoon, the outer byways of the village seemed unusually inactive. They saw no one, heard no cars revving up in adjacent streets. Nevertheless, Gale worried. She quickened her pace.

The corner of the church wall was upon them all at

once. They skirted along the side, Gale keeping so close to the wall's scabrous bricks that streaks of blackened moss smeared the sleeve of her coat. Rounding to the back of the churchyard, they entered the cemetery through a rear gate.

Katie Pru coughed. Gale stopped and propped the child against an angled gravestone to rest. Her mother's hold relaxed, Katie Pru jerked free and slid into a bundle on the damp grass.

Gale looked anxiously around the cemetery. Clutching her own collar around her throat, Gale stooped to secure Katie Pru's hood.

"Listen, baby," she said. "We're going into the church now. I'm going to sit you down in a pew and I don't want you to move, understand? It's very important. You must be quiet. In the pew you'll find some books. You can play with them, turn all the pages if you want, but you must be quiet."

The child nodded solemnly. Gale looked into her daughter's face, the black eyes serious, the mouth drawn into a replica of adult sternness. Gale's heart pounded as she took Katie Pru's hand and headed for the church.

The huge wooden door was heavier than she remembered. She pushed against it with her shoulder. In her nervousness, she snagged her fingernail on a tip of the door's ornate ironwork. A rim of blood seeped from beneath her nail. Burying the injured finger in her palm, she pressed against the door until it slowly whined open.

She didn't remember the building being so bright—in her memory the church interior had grown dolorous and webbed with shadows. Now the stone floors and walls reflected the winter sun into a restful grey. It was almost inviting. At another time in her life, she might have slid into one of the benches that banked both sides of the aisle and revelled in the happy solace of creaking pews and the smell of aging hymnals.

As it was, however, all she could do was fight the

figment echoes of a man's running footsteps, the blast of the gun, the shatter of glass. A wave of nausea passed over her. She kept her eyes carefully trained on her daughter, and guided her to a seat in the pew closest to the door.

It wasn't until Katie Pru's face lit up and she started to push past her mother that Gale realised they hadn't reached the church first.

"Kathleen Prudence!" The strength of Gale's remand reverberated through the space. The child stopped immediately and sat down in the pew. "You must follow my instructions. There are no choices here."

Whether or not Katie Pru understood her mother's words, she couldn't have misinterpreted the tone. Chastised, she rested her head on the seat of the pew and scrunched her body into a ball.

"No point in traumatising the child, Gale." Jill stepped to the centre aisle. The beacon from the yellow window over her head slanted toward the north wall. "I'm a little surprised you brought her."

Gale walked slowly towards Jill, each step jostling the mounting pain in her chest. She stopped halfway up the aisle. "Who could I leave her with? Who's left that I can trust?"

The girl's laugh was ugly. "Well, if that's the case, you've brought it on yourself, wouldn't you say? Trust is a fairly rare commodity in this village, thanks to your husband. You've managed to squander what little had been offered you. That must be a sad place to be. I truly feel sorry for you."

Jill took a step forward. Defiance had made her even more striking than usual. The dusky grey eyes had taken on a calculating glint, and the pale skin, which Timbrook had once jested looked marinated in lemon juice, was now a polished pink. She had tied her hair back in a ponytail, but somehow it appeared more sophisticated than her mother's bowed and ribboned buns. She was dressed in a bulky brown parka and similarly coloured trousers. Her boots were heavy, her hands gloved. The whole effect was one of maturity and bravado.

Gale focused on the girl's face, on the sculpted line of her mouth, which looked both petulant and victorious. "Do you feel sorry for me, Jill? I find that hard to believe."

Jill tossed the words off lightly. "Of course I do. Daddy and I have discussed it. You've really screwed your life up, haven't you? No one quite knows why you chose to stay. The innocent assumption is that it had something to do with Katie Pru. But if that's the case, you're doing your damnedest to screw up your daughter's life as well." She shoved her gloved hands into the pockets of her parka. "Of course, that's the innocent assumption."

Gale could hear her own pulse rushing. "So you and Orrin discussed it. You decided that my life, by my own accord, was past saving. So which one of you made the final decision to frame me?"

In the freshening light of the church, Gale could see Jill's features grow stony. "Explain that to me, please."

"Get off it, Jill. You know what I'm talking about. Was it you or your father who came up with the idea of framing me for Lisa's murder?"

"You're pathetic," Jill answered curtly. "No one had to frame you. It's kindergarten physics—bad things happen to bad people. It was only a matter of time before the villagers lost their tolerance for you. There's not much room for terrorists in real life, you know."

Behind her, Gale could hear Katie Pru kicking the pew. The aged wood squeaked unpleasantly through the consecrated space. "I'm not a terrorist," she replied tersely.

"Oh, no?" Jill's face flushed with conviction. She swung around to the altar, her arms wide, and with exaggerated precision measured out three paces. She hopped onto the chancel's stone step. "There!" she announced. She turned slowly. "I figure it was about here, don't you?" She placed a cocked finger between her lips and pantomimed pulling the trigger. She gave a little apologetic shrug. "Out goes the window. Out goes Tom. But he leaves behind his cohort. Pregnant, of course. I've always wanted to know—did you two plan it that way? It certainly couldn't have worked better for you. Bought you some sympathy around the village, and it certainly swayed police suspicion away from you. But now it's time, Gale. We all know it."

The beam from the amber glass rolled dust motes over the pews. The dread Gale had felt entering the church was gone. Now she wiped from her forehead the perspiration of a cold anger.

"I'm not a terrorist," she repeated steadily. "And I'll be damned if I'm going to take the blame for your father's kill."

For the first time a flicker of anxiety swept over Jill's features. Her eyes narrowed. "You're sick."

Gale took a deep breath. "I can help you, Jill. I honestly can. Come with me now and we'll find Sergeant Ramsden. She's sympathetic—she'll understand. She'll know that you only did what any daughter would do. No one will blame you. Not even me."

Even in the grey light, Gale could see the girl's face pale. "What are you saying?"

"I'm saying," Gale said, trying to balance anger with calm, "that framing me may have seemed reasonable, but it wasn't. Oh, for God's sakes, Jill, I am a mother with a child. How in the world can you justify doing it? How in the world did you let your father talk you into it?"

"He didn't talk me into anything." Jill beat her gloved hands together. Their muffled punches sounded like a bell's swaddled clappers. "God, you're talking crazy."

"The police know about the stick, Jill. They know it's part of a loom, and they'll soon know it came from the loom in Helen's shop—the loom that only you, me, Helen, and Lisa worked on."

"So? That means nothing. Anyone could have taken the stick. You could have."

Gale crossed her arms and hugged herself, trying to stop her body from trembling. "And the gun photo? Who else but your father knew of the photo?"

"You killed her!" Jill's face was taut, her words pitching close to a scream. "Lisa knew you were a terrorist just like Tom and she was going to take Katie Pru away. You stole that photograph and that newspaper from the archives so that police wouldn't find them and know that it was all true."

"But the police *did* find it!" Gale's voice rose now as well. "They found it, Jill. Whoever put them there knew that sooner or later, if I was strongly enough suspected of Lisa's murder, the police would search my house. Orrin knew how thorough the police are—he had seen them search before. Your father killed Lisa and then—"

"Shut up! You don't know what you're talking about!"

"Don't I? Listen to me, Jill. I know about Lisa. She could hurt people—I think it gave her pleasure. And she was a vicious flirt attracted to older men. She went after Jeremy. She went after Timbrook. God, for all I know, she went after Tom. Your father wasn't the first!"

The gloved fists were now striking Jill's thighs. She hammered out each word as she spoke, the rising hysteria in her voice ringing across the stones.

"You are wrong! You are so wrong!"

"No, I'm not. Your father was kind to her—kindness could mean love to someone like her. The poem your mother said he left on her pillow—Lisa gave it to him. She stole it from a box of Tom's unpublished poetry and she gave it to your father. He had to make up a lie so that your mother would think he meant it for her."

Without being aware of it, Gale had advanced to within a few feet of Jill. A mute wildness suddenly came over the girl. Her body jerked. Saliva speckled the corner of her mouth.

"No!" she whispered hoarsely.

Gale rushed towards her and grasped Jill's shoulders. "Orrin killed Lisa. You got him the stick to do it. She was a dirty, conniving bitch and this is a shit-eating pious little village. If Lisa even hinted about a relationship with your father—the principled newspaper editor screwing around with his daughter's best friend . . . Jill, it's easy to see how he felt threatened. But killing her wasn't the answer. And framing me isn't, either. You can't cover for him anymore. We have to go to the police. Now."

Jill's face blanched a grotesque white. Her jaw dropped slowly in almost comical horror, until her throat was a gaping toothed tunnel.

The noise that rose from her mouth—guttural, viscid—filled the church like an ancient, haunting yowl. Lunging, Jill kneed Gale in the stomach and sent her sprawling down the cold stone aisle.

From the back of the church Katie Pru shrieked. Gale twisted around to reach for the child, but a sharp pain shot through her knee. When she tried to stand up, her left leg buckled beneath her.

"It's okay, baby," she whispered. "Come here."

Behind her, she heard Jill step closer.

"I'm sorry," Jill said raggedly. "I'm sorry Katie Pru has to see this."

Gale turned to see a gun levelled at her head. The finger around the trigger paled as it tightened. Gale tried to yell, to struggle to her feet, but she couldn't. She did the only thing her body would allow—she threw herself at the younger woman and wrenched her knees from under her.

Jill tumbled sideways, her arms flung over her head. Her chin hit the stone floor. A crimson gush of blood flooded from her mouth. Incredulous, she tried to catch the flow in her cupped hand. The sickening stream leaked through her fingers. Fury filled her face as she pointed the wavering gun at Gale and fired.

The blast of the bullet in the nave was deafening. Gale saw rather than felt her own arm fling away from her and the sudden warm blossom of blood through her coat sleeve. The bullet's echo swelled in her ears, her head, until she screamed.

Her screams were met with a higher, thinner wail. Katie Pru stood at the back of the church beside the pew, staring at her mother, her eyes wide with panic.

Gale glanced over at Jill. The younger woman had scrambled to the altar rail. She sat, breathing heavily, the gun still held tightly in her hand. The blood from her mouth stained the collar of her parka. Her chin was dashed in scarlet streaks.

"You bitch," Jill spat. "You sanctimonious bitch in your fucking little cottage with your fucking pitiful books. Too stupid to be an intellectual, too stupid to be a mother. And I'll be damned if your stupidity is going to hurt my family."

Jill raised the gun again. Gale tried to judge her own distance from Katie Pru. She had no idea if she could make it or not.

The first car braked in front of the church without its siren. Doors slammed shut.

Jill looked at the church entrance and wiped her bloody palm on her coat. "You think I haven't thought all this out," she said, "but I have. I'm good at thinking things out. You tricked me into coming here. I brought the gun because I was afraid of you. You killed my best friend. Now you tried to kill me."

Jill's eyes were enlarged and eerily white in her pale face. The vividness of the blood around her mouth seemed to drain all the colour from her irises. Behind her, the altar rail barricaded the holy table beyond. *This is my blood which was spilt for you. This is my body . . .*

Tom's blood, Tom's body. Spattered on the green velvet cushions along the rail, dripping from the reredos and the sacrament on the table. Bits of his brain had clung like berries to the branches of a rough yew cross hung above the altar. The villagers had talked about it for weeks. Lisa had told her.

"Let me get Katie Pru outside, Jill," Gale said calmly.

"No. I won't hurt her." Jill was whispering now. "But you . . . you tried to kill me. I had to defend myself."

"No one will believe that."

Despite the building's thick walls, the sound of cars stopping along Boundary Road was clear. Gale couldn't tell how many—maybe six or seven. With despair, she realised what was happening. The police weren't going to storm the building. They had made that mistake once. They were going to choose their time.

Jill held the gun out steadily in front of her. "Who'll tell them differently? Katie Pru? She's just a baby. She won't know what happened."

Hearing her name from that bloodied mouth must have terrified the child. She started wailing again.

"Mama!" she cried. "Why's Jill hurting you? Why's she making you cry?"

Gale's throat went dry. The child continued to cry. "You're bleeding! Jill hurt you! Mama!"

The hand holding the gun began to quiver. Gale, her leg useless beneath her, began to inch her way backward towards Katie Pru. Jill's eyes darted from mother to daughter. Her face flamed an unholy red. Gale knew what she was thinking. She would have to kill the child.

Gale continued to pull herself toward her weeping daughter. "Please," she whispered. "Don't hurt her, Jill. You don't want to do this. Whatever else has happened, you don't want to hurt this child."

Confusion filled Jill's face as her hands shook uncontrollably. She stared at Katie Pru, biting on her lip so hard that her chin puckered. Outside, a cloud swept over the sun. The diffused yellow light overhead disappeared. Jill stood. Her eyes were suddenly glassy, her features serene.

"My father is a good man. You know that, don't you?" She gazed up at the window, her hands, still clasping the gun, raised to her chin as if in prayer. "What did I say, Gale? Did I say Tom stood about here?" She took several well-placed steps to the centre of the railing.

Slowly, the girl lifted the gun. Gale pitched toward Katie Pru and buried the child in her arms. Somebody, maybe Gale herself, screamed.

The heavy wooden south door clanged open. Shouts filled the church. Halford was through the narthex first, followed by Maura and Baylor. Then the church was filled with swarming figures in blue.

Gale didn't wait to see what happened. She curled her daughter into her body and drew them both into the protection of the pews. She heard the gun's blast, the shattering of glass. Later she would recall the rustling sound of a swathed body slumping to the stones. But at that moment, all she could think of was Katie Pru, and how much the child, clutched safely in her mother's arms, so closely resembled her father.

27

The inn was located in a residential area on the northern outskirts of Winchester, a two-storey red brick house ensconced in its own white fence like all the other two-storey red brick houses on the street. Bumped up to the side of the house was a child-sized toy car, its door open and its white plastic petrol cap dangling loose as if the driver had just hiked off in search of a call box. At eight P.M., the inn wasn't yet locked against nonpaying intruders. Halford depressed the front door latch and directed Maura inside.

Gale was waiting for them in the lounge. She sat alone on the sofa, the television blank in one corner, an aluminium Christmas tree with lights blinking blue, green, and orange in another. When they entered, she rose and smiled ruefully before hesitantly returning to her seat. From a side table, a stubby pink lamp bounced light off her bandaged arm.

Halford sat down in the chair next to her. "So how's the warrior?" he asked. "I see the doctors wasted no time patching you up and sending you back out for duty."

Gale grimaced as she gave the damaged arm a slight waggle. "I'm all right. Flesh wound, as they say. The hospital offered me lodging for the night, but I declined." She glanced around at the cheery lounge with its pink light and blinking tree. "The police found us much nicer accommodations. Thank them for me, okay?"

Halford gestured towards her leg, hidden under a pair of baggy beige trousers. "I'm surprised to see you could stand on that knee. From the looks of it this afternoon, I expected you'd be in a cast for a while."

"Oh, that's nothing. I was hobbling up and down the hospital halls within a few hours. It's amazing what you can do to avoid spending another minute around a bunch of folks in white shoes."

Maura eased down beside her on the sofa. "How's Katie Pru?"

"Fine, I suppose. They say children snap back so easily." She tapped the bandages thoughtfully. "Anyway, she's asleep now. The innkeeper here has young children. She made a fuss over Katie Pru, fixed her supper, gave her a whole plate of Christmas cookies." Gale pointed to a blue audio monitor standing on the side table. "Thankfully, she let me borrow that so I can hear if Katie Pru wakes up. If I suddenly bolt, don't think it's because I'm leaving town."

As if on cue, a faint mew sounded over the monitor. Gale tensed as she listened to Katie Pru shift in her sleep. She waited a moment, straining to hear more, then relaxed as the child resumed her even breathing.

"We arrested Orrin Ivory," Halford said. "He confessed to Lisa's murder."

Gale closed her eyes and sank against the sofa back. "God. I can't fathom it. I thought I'd be able to—but it seems so impossible now. I mean, to actually kill somebody. And then to have your daughter..." She stopped, her fingers twisting the rings on her left hand. "What about Anise? Did she know?"

Maura shook her head. "We're not sure yet, but apparently she knew more than she understood. She came to the police station today, very scared." Maura pressed her hand into the cushion between them, measuring her words. "She said things hadn't quite been normal around her house—she couldn't put her finger on it. Orrin was acting unusually anxious, worried. And then she overheard Jill tell you to meet her at the church."

From the monitor Katie Pru's breathing—whispery, delicate—filled the room. Maura stopped talking and looked expectantly at Halford.

"She said that's when she knew something was off," he continued. "She knew you'd never consent to meet in the church—she knew Jill would never ask you to do it. But when you agreed . . . well, she became frightened. She came to the police station for help."

"And that's how you knew we were there."

"That's how we knew."

"And how is she doing now?"

"Not too well," Maura said heavily. "Well, who would? Miss Pane and Mrs. Simpson are staying with her for a few days."

"And after that?" Gale asked. "Good Lord, how do you come through something like this?"

Over the beige trousers she wore a plaid flannel shirt whose hem she alternately crumpled and smoothed. In a motherly gesture, Maura reached over and rested her hand on Gale's. To Halford's mild surprise, Gale turned her palm up and returned the clasp.

He cleared his throat. "We do need to talk to you about something," he said. "Basically, Ivory confirmed what you told us. Lisa was blackmailing him—not for money, but affection. Perhaps even a bit more, an un-

breachable place in a real family. Or at least what must
have seemed to her a perfect family."

In its corner the Christmas tree continued its man-
dated winks. It evoked a cheeriness close to melan-
choly. "According to Ivory's statement," Halford
continued, "they accepted her as another daughter, but
over time, she wanted a more 'adult' relationship with
him. At first he just shrugged it off. Then one day, Lisa
came to him with a letter she had found in your bedroom."

Gale's mouth dropped open slightly, then immediately closed. She shook her head.

"My bedroom. You know, except for Katie Pru, I
never let anyone in there. I made that quite clear to her.
Yet I found her there several times."

Halford thought of Timbrook and the nonchalance
which betrayed his anger at Gale's withdrawal from
him. He thought of Cart and his overly attentive concern for his cousin's wife. He thought of himself, alone
in his flat, staring up at the two Hopper prints above
his couch. No doubt her daughter was the only person
Gale Grayson admitted.

Gale brought his attention back. "What letter was
it?"

He pulled at his moustache. "We were hoping you
could help us. Ivory said he burned it, but Lisa threatened to go public anyway. The letter was one he wrote
to Tom. About his involvement with the terrorists your
husband worked for."

Gale frowned. "Orrin? Involved with In Gaia's
Name?"

Halford nodded. "Ivory said Tom recruited him. He
eventually decided he wanted out, but by that time he
was too far in. He asked Tom to convince the other
members to release him from the group. The letter Lisa
found was supposedly about that. According to Ivory,
it detailed his participation. He was terrified that if it
got out he would be arrested and lose his family. The
final straw came when Lisa told Jill about it. He hadn't

wanted his family to know. He wanted to protect them.
So Ivory decided to kill Lisa. And since you probably
knew the contents of the letter and were therefore a
threat, he convinced Jill to help him set you up as the
scapegoat."

Gale tugged at the edge of the bandage, her frown
deepening. "That doesn't make sense."

Halford watched her face closely. "Why not?"

She shifted and pulled her wounded arm out of the
lamp's direct glare. She drew her engagement ring
along the line of light on her trousers. By the time she
answered, the diamond had made a thin cleft in the
fabric.

"After Tom died," she began slowly, "your men
took every piece of writing I had of his—all his poems,
his letters, every little scrap with every little note. Eventually, I got some of them back, like the box of his unpublished poems, but not all. His writings became an
obsession with me. Typed, longhand, it didn't matter.
If they were his words, I wanted them. Every now and
then I would find something—a ripped corner of a gro-
cery list, a scribbled phone message. They'd pop up at
the oddest times. I collected them all and kept them in
a hosiery box in my dresser."

The threads beneath her ring spread open. One
more pass and she would rend them. Suddenly aware
of her actions, she impatiently brushed at the spot.

"Anyway, during the early part of my pregnancy,
when Tom was still alive, we were given a diaper bag
as a present. I had tossed it into a cupboard and forgotten about it. Then one day I decided to take Katie
Pru with me to do some work, and I needed something
large to carry books and notebooks and bottles and
whatnot. . . . "

Her eyes filled with tears. Several seconds passed
before she grasped the cuff of her sleeve in her palm
and wiped it across her face.

"It was that day in Southampton. I had never used
the diaper bag before. I remember taking the tissue

from it, cramming all my things into it. I was at the tea shop rummaging through, when I found the letter. The envelope had a few lines of poetry scribbled on it. I guess Tom had kept the letter, grabbed it to jot the poem down, and for some reason crammed it into the bag. It was the first time I had seen an entire sentence in Tom's handwriting since his death. I was so disappointed when I took the actual letter out and it was from Orrin. And then when I read it—oh, God, it made me so angry."

Her smile was bleak. "I had just finished reading it when I looked up and there you were. Believe it or not, over the years I had forgotten about you showing up. It's a talent I have, I suppose—blocking out painful memories."

She said it without irony. Halford pinched the skin of his knuckle. "Do you remember what the letter said?"

She nodded. "That's why none of this makes sense. If Orrin felt threatened because he and Lisa were having an affair, that I would understand. But the letter . . . the letter was nothing."

"How do you mean?"

"Just that. Orrin was never involved with any terrorists. I don't know all the details, but the letter was an apology to Tom. Evidently, Orrin was planning a series of articles on terrorism, dealing with it from the terrorists' viewpoint, for publication in an American newspaper. Somehow he found out about Tom's connection—I don't know how. Orrin had started doing some anonymous interviewing when he decided it was something he didn't want to get involved with. I couldn't tell from the letter if it was fear or not. He painted it in terms of journalistic integrity—his sympathies were close to the group's goals, if not methods, and he might not be able to maintain his objectivity. At the time, it struck me as so spineless. But I can't imagine that there was anything, *anything* in it that he would have found threatening. Hell, I can't imagine anyone as savvy as Orrin Ivory writing something compromising, period. It's just not in character."

"Where was the letter the last time you saw it?"

"I put it, with the envelope, in the hosiery box. In my upper right-hand dresser drawer."

"Do you mind if we take a look?"

"I don't mind if Sergeant Ramsden takes a look."

Halford smiled. "Fair enough." He stood. "Anything you need, call us at the police station in Fetherbridge. We'll probably be here a couple of more days."

He paused, looking down at the bandaged arm, pink under the light. "Thank you, Gale—and see if Katie Pru would save me one of those Christmas cookies."

Little green lines on the black computer screen, little green lines that should work together to form letters and words. Grissom pounded his forefinger into the keys—*chdkdfpwlsshk*. A pen lay beside him on the newsroom desk. He hurled it across the room. Goddamnit. Goddamnit to hell. He didn't know what to say. He didn't know what to write.

"I'm not a fucking obituary writer!" he yelled. At nine at night, the room was empty, and his words swam around him like sharks. He took a deep breath and yelled again. "It's not supposed to be this way!"

The male voice from the doorway was subdued. "You're absolutely right, Mr. Grissom."

Grissom slapped the computer off and whirled his chair around to face the two detectives.

"I suppose you want to search the place. Fine. Go ahead. I won't interfere in the least."

Sergeant Ramsden stood by the window overlooking the High Street. The blinds were partially closed; she opened them and peered out at the dead street. Halford pulled a chair from beneath a nearby desk. With a pang, Bobby noted that it was where Jill had sat the afternoon they discussed her father.

Halford wheeled the chair closer to Grissom. "I'm sorry," he said. "I truly am."

Grissom cracked his knuckles. "Yeah, I suppose you are." He swung his chair back and forth, catching his knee each time on a desk drawer left partially open. "I'm sitting here trying to write the story. What do you think of this headline: Young Woman Kills Self for Father's Cover-up Scheme? Or, Daughter Blows Brains Out in Defence of Darling Daddy. I think I'll go with the latter. The reading public responds to immediate images, as the great editor Ivory likes to say."

"You're going on with the next issue?"

Grissom sneered. "Of course. It's my sacred duty. The news at all costs. Besides, it's a fucking great story. It'll make my goddamned career."

Halford was silent. Maura pulled absentmindedly on the shade's cord. "So," Halford said at last, "Jill was a special friend of yours."

Grissom poked at the computer keys. "No. I wanted her to be, but she wasn't. She truly was a daddy's girl, and I say that without sarcasm."

Halford leaned back in his chair. "I know you've already given your statement to one of our detectives, but I want to go over the morning of the murder with you again." His voice was gentle. Grissom hated gentle-voiced men. "I want you to tell me one more time what happened."

"What the hell for? You've got your murderer. Or do you police types replay murder scenarios the way dirty old men replay pornographic videos?"

It was nasty, even for him. He banged the desk drawer shut. "I'm sorry. This is all too much. I mean, I honestly respected the man. I admired him. Get this: I even thought I might want to be like him someday— beautiful wife and daughter, nice little house in a nice little village, newspaper of my own. Not right away, but someday. I even went so far as to fantasise that Jill . . ."

He brought his elbow down on the keyboard hard enough that several of the keys popped off and rattled around the desk like teeth.

Halford saved him. "The morning when Lisa was murdered, you arrived at the newspaper at—what time was it?"

"Seven-thirty, thereabouts."

"And in your statement, you said that Mr. Ivory and Jill were already here."

"Right. They had just arrived, because they hadn't taken off their coats yet."

"It was Saturday, wasn't it? Tell me how the morning went."

Grissom rubbed his eyes. "Well, we were the only ones here. Rarely does anyone else come in on Saturdays. I had two stories that I hadn't finished the day before, and I didn't have anything better to do."

Halford's look was politely skeptical. "Unlike the majority of us, you would rather work at seven-thirty on a Saturday morning than sleep in?"

"All right. I knew Jill would be here. I hoped to be able to talk with her."

"Did the Ivorys frequently work on Saturday?"

"Sure. Orrin loved this grotty little place. And that morning Jill was doing some work in the darkroom. I talked a little with her early on." He paused. "Anyway, a clamp on the press had broken the day before, and I guess it was about nine o'clock when Ivory came into the newsroom to say that the repair shop in Southampton had a new one waiting for him. He called to Jill in the darkroom to get her coat and come with him. I finished my first story and since the second was a little filler piece that probably wouldn't make the cut anyway, I decided to put it off and go downstairs for some coffee."

Halford nodded. "And then?"

Grissom ran his hands harshly through his hair. "Well, someone had left part of a cake in the kitchen, so I cut myself a piece. I was fixing a cup of coffee when I heard Orrin and Jill come down the stairs and go out the front door."

"And that was what time?"

"A bit before nine-thirty, I'd say."

"What did Jill say when her father told her to come with him to Southampton?"

Grissom shrugged. "I dunno. She was in the darkroom. I couldn't hear her."

"But you heard her say something."

"Well, yeah, I'm sure I did. I mean, he told her to get her coat, and, sure, she said something."

Halford leaned forward. "Mr. Grissom, it's important that you be precise. Did you hear Jill say anything to Mr. Ivory when he told her to get her coat and come with him?"

"I could have sworn I did."

"Did you see Jill leave the darkroom at any time that morning?"

"Well, yeah, at about eight-fifteen or so, she came out for some water or something, but she went back in a few minutes later."

"And you never saw her leave again."

Grissom shook his head.

"Not even to get her coat and leave for Southampton?"

"No, I told you. I was downstairs by then, fixing my coffee."

"And did you actually see Jill leave with her father at nine-thirty?"

Grissom's mouth went dry.

"No," he said.

"But you heard her coming down the stairs with her father."

"Well, no. I . . . I just assumed—"

Halford pulled at his moustache, studying his trouser leg. Grissom drew his hand across his forehead. It was wet.

"Besides getting your cake and coffee, did you leave your desk at any other time that morning?"

"No."

"To the loo perhaps?"

"Well, yes. Once. To use the loo."

"About what time?"

"I dunno. Before nine, I suppose."

"And did you ever actually see or speak to or hear from Jill after you returned to your desk?"

Grissom stared at him. "You don't think . . ." His throat constricted, and he went into a coughing fit.

Sergeant Ramsden was beside him, extending a cup of water. Grissom took a swallow and then looked at them through tears.

"Good God," he said. "I don't believe it."

"You weren't supposed to, Bobby," Halford said sympathetically. "You were supposed to believe you were in love."

The man seated in the Winchester police station's interview room was both past grief and before it. Halford looked at the circled eyes, the skin that seemed, at different angles, pale then blotched, flaccid then drawn. His life is over and he knows it, Halford thought. He knew it a week ago, but he held on, patching, working the plot, staving off panic with stupid hope. Halford placed the double-tape recorder and a folder on the table and sagged into a chair. He wondered how the infinitely estimable Reverend Cart would ever be able to comprehend such a sorrow, much less minister to it.

Ivory spoke hoarsely. "Will I be allowed to attend my daughter's funeral?"

"I think we can work something out. They tell me you don't want your solicitor with you."

Ivory's hands trembled as he raised them to his forehead. He made no indication that he had heard Halford. "Who's going to plan the funeral? Anise can't. How does this sort of thing work? Anise will need help. She can't do it alone."

"It'll be taken care of. Anise won't have to go through it alone. You can, however, give your wife a great deal of help, Orrin. And solace, I would think."

Ivory looked at him, his eyes wet and ringed in red. "How?"

"Tell me what happened. The truth. You may think it more painful, but I truly believe that in the long run, you'll both live easier."

Ivory's mouth opened, the tongue inside parched. "Live easier. God, you're a bastard."

"I'm sorry," Halford said. "I didn't mean for that to sound callous, or unsympathetic. I can't imagine what you're going through. But I do know, Orrin, that if you don't tell us the true story, there'll be no peace for you."

Ivory rubbed his eyes, leaving the tender skin at their corners a blistered red. "The true story." He spoke without humour. "I've told you the true story."

Halford opened the file. "Mr. Grissom has revised his statement. He still confirms your alibi for the morning of the murder. He does not, however, confirm Jill's. Furthermore, I've been over to the logistics—the distance between here and Southampton, the times you left the newspaper office and then arrived at the petrol station and the press shop. It would have taken precise planning and every single stroke of luck God has ever allowed a man for you to have committed that murder. In addition, it would have meant knowing exactly what time Lisa would be on Boundary Road. The evidence suggests that Lisa was late that morning, Orrin. You couldn't have known when she was going to be there. The murderer would have to have been waiting for her. You simply left the newsroom too late."

"I killed her," he whispered.

"On your daughter's bicycle? And then what? Rode it back home and hopped into your van? Or stashed it somewhere and walked to where the van was hidden? Not enough time, Orrin. It's simply not possible."

"Jill was waiting with the van."

Halford leaned on his elbow and buried his chin in his palm.

"Why is that easier? Why do you think it would be easier on your wife to believe that your daughter acted as your accomplice and then killed herself to protect you, rather than acted on her own with you doing the best you could to protect her?"

"I didn't . . . Jill wanted to help me . . . I killed . . ."

Ivory's shoulders heaved. "My God. Anise. To have her think that she raised . . . that her beautiful daughter . . ."

He sobbed, great painful sobs that sucked in air and hacked it back out. Halford waited until the crying grew quiet, the breathing shallower.

"I'm not worried about how your daughter was raised," he said gently. "I'm concerned about how you and Anise are going to survive this. The next months, years, you both are going to have so many questions— what you did right, what you did wrong. Don't you think your wife will be better able to accept Jill's death if she's allowed to ask the correct questions? Shouldn't she at least be allowed to find solace in the truth, if nothing else?" He clasped his hands on the table and drew closer to the editor. "Orrin, I've been dealing with grieving parents for years. There's a very complex comfort in knowing what really happened. Is it fair for you to deny your wife that comfort?"

Ivory's hands were splayed against his face; tears collected on the skin at the V-shaped base of his fingers. The look in his eyes was of agony, and when he closed them, the lids were terraced with red veins.

Halford strained to hear the rough whispers as Ivory spoke. He switched on the tape recorder, murmuring quickly the required date and names.

Ivory's voice was wretched. "That morning, when I was ready to go to Southampton for the clamp, I couldn't find Jill. She wasn't in the darkroom, not in the building. She had told me earlier that she had to do some shopping, so I assumed . . . I left without her."

"You didn't think it odd that she didn't tell you she was leaving?"

"It made me angry. But she's eighteen, an adult. She'd started acting more and more independent lately. So I didn't worry. But as I turned down Boundary Road there she was, on her bicycle, pumping hard, swerving all over the road. I knew immediately something was wrong. She looked scared, horrified . . . She was breathing so hard she couldn't talk. I got her into the minivan and put her bicycle in the back. I was carrying so much junk for the paper—it barely fit. I was going to continue west and circle back to take her home, when she started stuttering, telling me no . . . go the other way. . . .

"But by that time I saw the bicycle in the middle of the road, and then I saw Lisa. Of course, I knew she was dead. I knew that's why Jill was upset. But when I stopped the car to make sure she wasn't still alive, Jill started screaming. Screaming that she killed her."

He stopped, and Halford pushed the glass of water an inch closer to him. Ivory studied it, perplexed.

"I don't know," he said. "Maybe I should have done something different. Maybe if I had . . . But it was strange. I understood at once. And I knew it was my fault. So I stepped on the pedal and left. I didn't know at that point what really happened, but I knew Jill's bicycle would be important. The front wheel fork had been bent. It would have to be fixed. I remembered Timbrook kept a tarpaulin in his minibus, so we swung by there and took it. It was a risk, but I couldn't drive all the way to Southampton, do the things we had to do, with a broken bicycle visible in the backseat.

"By the time we reached Southampton, Jill had told me everything. I had been having problems with Lisa for a few months, nothing I considered that difficult, just a girlish infatuation. I tried to be kind to her, to discourage it without being hurtful, but she turned rather nasty about it. One day she showed me the letter I had written Tom and said she was going to give it to the police. I laughed it off—there was nothing in it that could have hurt me. I didn't give it another thought. But then she showed it to Jill."

He faltered. Picking up the glass with an unsteady hand, he took a large swallow.

"Halford." His voice became pitiful, almost pleading. "I want you to understand Jill. She loved us—Anise and me. We all three believed so fervently in each other. That's the kind of family we wanted, that's the kind of family we were. But there was a particular bond between Jill and myself. Anise doesn't understand my work. She doesn't understand why I put so much faith in it. Jill does . . . did. Sometimes I wished she didn't, but in my heart I was so proud of her. She and I were special to each other because of it. And that's why she . . . God help me, that's why she did it."

The sobbing began again, and Halford switched off the tape. He reached over, picked up a phone from a small table in the corner, and summoned Maura into the room.

The sobs had subsided by the time Maura sat down. In her hand she held a box of tissue which she placed in front of Ivory. Halford glanced at her somberly and turned the tape back on.

"So why did Jill think it necessary to kill Lisa?" he asked.

Ivory took a tissue and wiped his face. "God, she was so inexperienced, so naive. She thought that letter would hurt me. She thought I had somehow compromised myself, that the letter proved a connection with those terrorists, that I would be ruined by it. Looking back, I can understand why she thought that. I mean, she was fifteen when the business with Tom Grayson happened. We were close to Tom, had been for years. She saw how torn up the town was, how personally grieved Anise and I were. And she felt that I had somehow betrayed her, and my family. It became her responsibility to protect us from the notoriety Lisa threatened to bring."

"Do you think that was the sum total of it, Orrin— the fear that you were a terrorist? Do you think that perhaps Jill thought you were in love with Lisa?"

The tape whirred in silence for several seconds before Ivory spoke. "I've thought about it. I don't know.

Maybe she did. Maybe she thought I had betrayed her and Anise both physically and intellectually. Maybe in the end there seemed to her to be more reasons to kill Lisa than not to."

When he raised his eyes to Halford's, his expression was of amazement and horror. "They were both so young. And see what they did to each other."

His head sank to the table. Halford glanced at Maura. She had pulled a tissue from the pack and was rolling it into a thin, tight scroll.

"And Mrs. Grayson?" Halford kept his voice low.

Ivory lifted his head and wiped his nose with the tissue. "That was Jill's idea. She decided on it before the murder. I was against framing Gale. So you used the stick from the loom, I said—just leave it at that. But she was afraid you would trace it to her. And then she broke into the newspaper office and took the paper and the photograph. I didn't know she had done it until after I reported it to you. After that, I had to go along. I put them in Gale's study."

"When?"

"I dropped Anise off at the cottage to mind Katie Pru while Gale rested. I gave them enough time to visit a bit and then circled back once I thought Gale had gone upstairs. Anise let me in. The papers were inside my coat. I told her I needed to borrow one of Gale's books."

"And Lisa's custody suit?"

"I think Lisa did want custody of Katie Pru. At least, she fantasised about it. Like everything else. Maybe that's what this village taught her—if you talk about something long enough, it comes true."

"And what about the vandalising of Mrs. Grayson's cottage?"

"I don't know about that."

"One more thing, Orrin. Tell me about the gun."

A sob lodged in Ivory's throat. His chest jerked convulsively. The sight of his soundless grief was unbearable. Halford looked away. Finally, Ivory clasped the glass of water in one hand and held it, pitifully, as if the trapped liquid were an amulet.

"It was Tom's," he said. "I'm certain he got it illegally. When I stopped writing the articles on the group, I panicked, got very scared. He assured me everything was fine, but I wanted some protection. I was worried about my girls." This time the sob was audible.

"Anything else you want to add?"

Ivory examined the tissue, now a small, compact ball in his hand. He continued looking at it when he spoke.

"I haven't lied to you, Halford," he said quietly. "I was responsible. I killed Lisa. I killed them both."

Epilogue

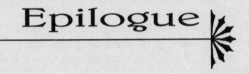

Three days before Christmas, the Fetherbridge High Street was postcard perfect: Wreaths and garlands decorated shop fronts, plump mauve ribbons stiffly encircled street lamps—and nary a soul was in sight. Halford slowed the car to a crawl. You could lift the whole damn place off the map, scribble on it, and stick it in the post, he thought.

He rounded the corner at Bracken Street and inched the car along. No one was visible, the houses lifeless. If he found buffalo bones bleaching in the gardens, he wouldn't be surprised. Families close down after death—the mother to one room, the father to another, each member escaping to writhe in his own privacy. This was the first time he had witnessed it in a community.

He eased the car to a stop in front of the Grayson cottage. The garden looked much as it had two weeks earlier when he and Maura came for the first interview. The ground was brown, the plants dead. Several moist holes now dotted the earth where shrubs had been uprooted, and black paint still covered the exterior of the study window; nevertheless, the place had generally been tidied up, the papers collected, the path swept.

At the front door he hesitated. The vandals' words were scoured away, but here and there in the grain of the wood he could still see remnants of red paint. It appeared that someone had taken a knife and tried to pry out the flecks; the task left the door brutalised, and the worker, quite rightfully, had opted for the reminders.

Gale was at the door before he knocked.

"I saw you from upstairs," she said. "Katie Pru is in her room grumbling herself into a nap, so if you could come in quietly . . ."

He stepped into the cottage. It, too, showed signs of repair—the hallway whitewashed, the stairs scrubbed. He brought a paper bag from behind his back and held it out to her.

"Here," he said. "We came across this yesterday. I pulled a few strings."

Taking the rumpled bag, she peered inside. "Oh, Lord, Daniel. Space Lucy. You have no idea . . . Thank you."

As he followed her into the kitchen, he glanced into the living room. All evidence of the attack had been removed—there was virtually no furniture. The Christmas tree, which had been crammed into the corner, stood in the middle of the floor, covered in ribbons and paper chains. The room was clean and, he noticed with a wrench in his stomach, stacked with packing crates.

"You're moving."

She took a jar of instant coffee from the cupboard. "You sound surprised. I would have thought you'd be more shocked to find me still here."

"I don't know. Believe it not, I always thought you fit this cottage rather well."

"Dreary, dark, unapproachable, sparse. Thanks."

She seemed definitely more relaxed—unburdened, almost—as she justifiably should. But as she turned sideways to retrieve two mugs from the cupboard, she winced, whether from the sudden movement of her injured arm or a more subjective pain, he couldn't tell.

He cleared his throat. "I don't know if you've heard. We've charged three people with the vandalism."

She looked at him, surprised. "Really? No one's told me. Somehow, I'd thought you'd never find out who they were."

"Well, they were more angry than adept when they went on their rampage." He paused, watching the fine planes of her face contract with tension. "Do you want to know who?"

She directed her attention to the jar of coffee, deliberately unscrewing the lid. "All right."

"Ben Hossett, Clive Kingston, and Jim Simpson. We found the toy and your missing clothes in the boot of Simpson's car."

She sagged against the counter and closed her eyes. "Mrs. Simpson. God. She seemed so sympathetic."

"It was her husband we arrested, Gale, not her. She may have known nothing about it. You can't hold her responsible for her husband's actions."

The words were out before he realised it. She studied him for a second before turning back to the counter and dumping a spoonful of coffee into the mugs.

"I'm sorry. I wasn't thinking."

"It's okay. Really. You're the last person I would criticise. After all, you believed me."

A column of cookery books towered from the center of the table and, removing the top one, Halford flipped through the pages. He didn't need to read the print to recognise it as foreign. The black-and-white pictures depicted salted hams curing in barns; long, food-laden picnic tables spread with checked cloths; genteel elderly ladies in wide-rimmed hats taking luncheon under chandeliers. Familiar, and yet just alien enough to make him feel edgy. It was when he came to the picture of Jimmy Carter holding a pig that he pushed the book away.

"So, I take it you're heading back to the States."

She turned on the tap, filled a battered metal pot with water, and set it on the cooker. Droplets ran down the sides of the pot and hissed into the blue flame.

"Yes. There doesn't seem to be much point in staying anymore. I called my grandmother yesterday. She seems . . . cooperative."

Halford opened the fridge and found a small carton of milk for the coffee. On the shelf below it was a glass dish of partially consumed fried chicken and a bowl of what he took to be green bean casserole. Funeral food, he thought, closing the refrigerator door. God, what rituals we cling to.

" 'Cooperative,' " he said. "Not a very enthusiastic word. It sounds as if she's agreed to sit down at the bargaining table. Your grandmother must be a tough lady."

"It won't be easy, going back. I don't know if it'll work."

"Surely you're not really worried. I mean, there's Katie Pru. What woman worth her salt wouldn't want a great-grandchild like her?"

She turned away sharply.

"That's the problem in my family. No lack of women worth their salt."

He knocked out a quiet rhythm on the tabletop. "You know I've got to ask it," he said. "I've got to ask why you never returned home."

She held her hand over the pot of water. Steam speckled her skin with moisture.

"It's because I had a daughter," she said finally. "I'd always said that if I had a daughter, I would leave the South. But I think I was wrong."

She grasped the handle of the pot and poured water

into the mugs. "So," she said, "what happens in your life now?"

"I don't know. More of the same. Or maybe not. I can't decide if I'm ready for a change."

To his right, the cracked bottle glass panes screened most of the light and he had trouble reading her face. She extended her arm to hand him a mug, and as he clasped his palms around it, he caught her wrist between his fingers.

He felt her shiver.

"Gale . . ." he started.

"Do you know what I think?" Her voice was rough. "I think Tom would have killed himself anyway, eventually. I think dying was important to him, the way Katie Pru is to me. Does that make sense?"

"Yes," he said. "Yes, it does."

"So don't think you're responsible. Don't think it's because of you."

His throat grew hot. "You've thought about this thoroughly, have you? This going back to the States? Katie Pru's quite the little Brit, you know. Very stiff-upper-lippish."

Tears hovered at her lashes. "Yes, I know. She's tough. It's not going to be easy to leave, even given what's happened. But we can't stay in Fetherbridge, and other than maintaining Katie Pru's accent, I can't find a good reason for staying in England."

Halford studied the black liquid swaying in his mug. "Perhaps there could be one," he said. "Perhaps I could give you one in time."

He didn't want to look up, to read in her face an answer. For a long time she was silent, and it wasn't until she sniffed that he knew she was crying. And, he was certain, going away from him as well.

"I'm sorry, Daniel. Maybe a while from now . . . I don't know. I have so much cleaning up to do. Katie Pru deserves a childhood, not her mother's pain. And my family, I suppose they deserve an answer." Her laugh was caught in a sob. "I'm tarnished enough now, you know. I can limp towards the South to be reborn. Hell, I can return home the conquered hero. I'll get flowers and parades and everything."

Her hands, so improbably tiny, trembled as they clutched her mug. Gently, he reached out and traced the outline of her fingers.

"I'd hardly call you conquered," he said. "Damned stubborn, but definitely not conquered."

The light was stronger when he later climbed back into his car. This time he didn't inch down the street; he rushed away from the cottage, bitterly aware of his release and his bondage.

He turned onto Boundary Road. Before him, the broad wall of St. Martin's Church blocked the cemetery from view. At the lych-gate, he slowed and peered into the churchyard. A blanket of flowers covered Madge Stillwell's grave. Beside them the ashen remnants of shoveled chalk gave testimony to the recent burial. Lisa Stillwell had been laid to rest, safe in the bosom of the village, forever coupled with her mother in sleep.

No such comfort for Fetherbridge's other daughter. Halford had seen Jill Ivory's grave the day before, a sullen chalk slash in a cemetery on the outskirts of Winchester. A grounds crew, not a sexton, would tend the gravestones there. Visitors, the few that came, wouldn't meander through the ancient markers and twining greenery to seek solace among the dead. Rather, they would park on the paved tarmac and walk up the steep, groomed hill to where she lay, a scant ten yards from Tom Grayson.

As he pressed the accelerator, Halford noticed a beat-up Leyland and a small, enclosed lorry parked by the south door. Christian Timbrook and Jeremy Cart stood talking, while behind them four men carried scaffolding to the east end of the church. The rear door to the lorry was open, and inside Halford could see a large round parcel.

Looking over, Jeremy Cart caught sight of the detective's car, but his only acknowledgement was a quick glance in the direction of the new grave.

Bloody good for them, Halford thought, easing his car towards the outskirts of the village. Let the installation begin.

ABOUT THE AUTHOR

TERI HOLBROOK can trace her southern roots to 1636 and her English roots to long before that. She is a former journalist and is currently working on her second Gale Grayson and Katie Pru novel. A Georgia native, she lives in Atlanta with her husband and two daughters.

If you enjoyed Teri Holbrook's
A FAR AND DEADLY CRY,
you will want to read her next mystery,
THE GRASS WIDOW,
which also features Gale Grayson and Katie Pru.

Here is a special preview of *The Grass Widow,*
coming in November 1996 from Bantam Books

Miss Linnie used to visit me at night, gliding down the hallway, hair glowing like a lamppost. I was just a blur of a girl, no more than six or seven, and it was years later that I learned she was dark-headed. To me, her hair was a light, drawn up in a puff around her face and shining as if there was a bulb down in there. Of course, that was before we had electricity here, but when I think of it, that's how I remember her, like she had turned on a lamp in her hair, so that all the strands gleamed and her face was left in shadow.

She reminded me of Guinevere. I saw pictures in my sister's book about King Arthur, and Miss Linnie looked to me like Guinevere with her hair all piled up. I could see her through a crack in my bedroom door, sliding down the hall, pausing in front of my parents' room, then my sister's, then finally stopping to peer into mine. She'd twist her head from side to side, like she was trying to direct some of that light from her hair onto my bed. But no light ever shone in—it just stayed balled around her head as if she wore a hood that had turned to embers. She'd keep at it a while, the light bobbing in the black hall, until she finally stilled herself, and disappeared into the back of the house. One time, I got up and followed her, but her feet, not having to touch the ground, were faster than mine.

I told my daddy about her once, and he just shook his head and told me to leave her alone. I said that she was kind, and a little sad, and he said, no, ghosts were evil. I said, but she wanted to check on me, she twisted her head back and forth so that the light would shine into my room, and he just said, no, Zilah, she wasn't twisting her head to see you better. She was braying like an angry mule, trying to get that cursed rope from around her neck.